HIDE AND GO SEEK

GOING TO ST. IVES

HIDE AND GO SEEK

-⋘◆⋙-

GOING TO ST. IVES

Colver Harris

COACHWHIP PUBLICATIONS
Greenville, Ohio

Hide and Go Seek / Going to St. Ives
© 2020 Coachwhip Publications

Hide and Go Seek first published 1933
Going to St. Ives first published 1934

Polly Anne Colver (Harris) Graff (1908-1991)
No claims made on public domain material.
Cover image: Miguna Studio

CoachwhipBooks.com

ISBN 1-61646-496-8
ISBN-13 978-1-61646-496-7

POLLY ANNE COLVER (HARRIS) GRAFF
(1908-1991)

Anne Colver was born to William and Pauline Colver in Cleveland, Ohio. (William Byron Colver was chairman of the Federal Trade Commission, 1918-1919, and one of the founders of the Scripps-Howard newspaper chain.) Growing up in Cleveland, St. Paul, and Washington, D.C., she earned her bachelor's degree at Whitman College (Walla Walla, WA). She married, and moved to the northeast, where her husband, Mark Harris, taught English at Williams College (MA). She published her first mystery novel, *Hide and Go Seek,* in 1933. Several more mysteries followed (using the pseudonym Colver Harris) during the 1930s, before she started writing popular historical and biographical fiction, particularly for children, as Anne Colver. Her well-received *Mr. Lincoln's Wife* was the Literary Guild Selection for June 1943. Later titles were co-authored (usually as Polly Anne Graff) with her second husband, Stewart Graff.

HIDE AND GO SEEK

(1933)

1
ALARM

In the first place I admit that it was largely through my own fault that I became involved in the investigation of the murder of Lina Castle. I often wonder now why I ever got myself into it. Perhaps it was because of a certain suppressed craving for excitement (the result, no doubt, of reading too much detective fiction), perhaps it was simply a reaction of nervous hysteria, or perhaps it was a plain case of not minding my own business. This last explanation, while hardly flattering, is, I confess, rather the more likely one—for if my vices were to be catalogued (which heaven forbid!) it would be impossible to overlook an embarrassing, and apparently incurable, tendency on my part to meddle in other people's affairs. But whatever may have been my motives, the fact remains that when the moment of choice came, I made my decision without hesitation.

The affair took place at the small, old-fashioned Almeda Hotel in downtown New York, whither I had come for a weekend from my home in Washington. A more unlikely place for excitement of any kind than the Almeda would be difficult to imagine. The whole atmosphere of the place is that of the quietly conservative family hotel, and, as such, it provides a comforting refuge for elderly couples and

lone women, like myself, who welcome a modest retreat
from the bright efficiency and scandalous prices of larger
hotels. Even the roar of downtown traffic seems somehow
remote from the genteel quiet of the Almeda's red plush
lounge, and haste is forgotten in the leisurely progress
of the antiquated elevator which bears one upward to a
region of wide corridors and high-ceilinged bedrooms,
furnished in the heavy, walnut elegance of a bygone day.

Trips to New York are still in the nature of big events
to me, for my government job in Washington, which I
have held for the eight years since leaving school, provides
me with neither the leisure nor the money for frequent
traveling. I must confess, therefore, that on the occasion
of my eventful visit at the Almeda I had all the thrilling expectancies of adventure which accompany naive pil-
grims to the "Big City." After all, eight years of typing and
filing stupid routine reports in a government office provides little nourishment for a romantic imagination, and I
was ready for excitement of any kind.

Small wonder then, that I deliberately chose to offer
myself as a witness in the murder which took place,
dramatically enough, in a room on the eleventh floor of
the hotel, directly over my bedroom on the tenth floor.
Even in my wildest imaginings I had never dreamed that I
should have any such adventure as this within the discreet
walls of the Almeda—yet I found myself, on the first evening of my visit, possessed of almost certain information
that someone, in the room above mine, had been shot, and
perhaps killed. Had I chosen to mind my own business, it
is hardly likely that, in the investigation which followed,
I should have been questioned at all. For such was the
nature of my evidence that none save myself would ever
have discovered that I knew anything of the unfortunate

affair. But I have already explained that I was in no mood for discretion, and I lost little time in reporting my alarming message to the hotel authorities.

It must have been about ten minutes past eight when I hurried from my room. In the haste of the moment I failed to notice the exact time, but later I recalled distinctly that the big gilt clock, which faced the elevator in the lobby downstairs, pointed to about twelve minutes past the hour when I stepped out of the car to approach the front desk with my message.

I found a young, rather stupid-looking clerk on duty at the desk. He looked up pleasantly at my approach, apparently unaware of my breathless state, and inquired if there were anything that he could do.

"You can," I said, as calmly as I could, "let me speak to whoever is in charge of this hotel."

He gave me the regular formula in reply.

"If you will tell me what it is you wish . . . ?"

Again I made an effort to keep my voice quiet.

"I wish," I said firmly, "to see the Manager of the hotel. At once."

Still the clerk smiled blandly.

"I think I can attend to the matter," he insisted, "if you will tell me—"

"Look here," I interrupted sharply, "I have a message to deliver—a message of the greatest importance. I must see the Manager at once. Is he here?"

"Mr. Evans is in his office," the young man admitted doubtfully, "but he left strict orders not to be disturbed."

"Is Mr. Evans the Manager?"

"Yes, but—"

"But nothing," I snapped, "you show me where his office is, and I'll take the responsibility for disturbing him."

"Well—" at last the clerk showed signs of weakening.

"I tell you," I went on desperately, "I've *got* to see him—and every minute counts."

For the first time the young man appeared to grasp the fact that my message was really urgent.

"This way," he directed briefly, and led me away from the desk and down a small corridor to a door marked Manager. "There you are," he turned away with a shrug which seemed to indicate that my fate, however doubtful, was no longer any concern of his.

I knocked.

"Come in."

The voice which came from within the office sounded neither surprised nor annoyed, and a moment later I was facing a small, pleasant-looking man who looked up from his desk with an expression of mild inquiry. In spite of Mr. Evans' strict orders "not to be disturbed" he gave not the slightest evidence of being busy. Indeed, I got the impression that he had simply been sitting idly at his desk, and he greeted my approach with a vaguely preoccupied courtesy.

"I'm sorry to disturb you, Mr. Evans," I began at once, "but something has happened—something alarming. I felt that I should report it directly to you."

"Yes?" said Mr. Evans politely. He seemed to receive my remark with no particular concern, although he went on to express a sort of automatic inquiry as to the nature of my alarm.

"This was no ordinary disturbance," I continued firmly, determined to impress Evans with the importance of my message. "I just heard a most terrifying scream in the room above mine—and immediately afterward there was a shot."

I observed that Evans appeared hardly to hear what I was saying, although he continued to look at me fixedly.

"You say you heard a scream?" he repeated blankly.

"Yes," I said, "a—well, a horrible scream—and then a shot."

"Where was it that this happened?"

"In the room just over mine," I repeated impatiently, "which must be number 1117—" I paused to watch Evans hopefully. At last he appeared to be paying attention. It was, in fact, at the moment when I mentioned the number 1117 that he became suddenly alert, and seemed for the first time to grasp what I had been trying to tell him.

"Oh," said Mr. Evans in a tone of dismay, "you—you don't mean that someone in that room has been—shot?"

"Of course that's what I mean," I insisted breathlessly.

"But when did it happen?" Evans demanded.

"Just now—or rather," I corrected myself, "some minutes ago."

"Why didn't you report it at once?" Evans' question was sharp.

By this time I had lost every scrap of patience.

"That's just what I *tried* to do," I snapped, "but first your stupid clerk delayed me by not letting me into your office—and now you stand there and ask me questions. Please," I hurried on desperately, "please won't you go and find out *what* has happened upstairs. I—I'm not just hysterical about this—" I stopped abruptly as Evans jumped to his feet. My insistence seemed finally to have shattered his curious air of indecision.

"Good heavens," I heard him murmur, "this is—this is *most* unfortunate."

And even in the midst of my agitation I remember thinking, in a momentary flash of amusement, how typical of the Almeda's genteel atmosphere was Mr. Evans' exclamation of distress. I imagined that never before had the quiet, dignified Manager been called upon to face any such emergency as this which I had reported. Yet, as Evans hurried toward the door, without another word for me, I thought I saw something more than natural anxiety in the look of unmistakable alarm which widened his mild blue eyes.

I followed Mr. Evans as he hurried down the small cor-ridor and through the lobby toward the front desk, but it was plain that he had completely forgotten my presence. A moment later I saw him speak briefly to his clerk and then disappear into the elevator, leaving me to wait, under the curious stare of the young man at the desk, for further developments. For an uncertain minute I hesitated, not being quite sure what I should do next. It was more than likely, I reflected, that my part in the affair was already finished, yet I resolved at least to be on hand in case any-thing further should happen.

Carefully I selected a place, as far from the front desk as possible, yet in plain sight of the elevator, and settled myself on one of the massive, red plush sofas to wait for the reappearance of Evans. Minutes passed, however, and still he failed to emerge from the elevator. My excitement over the whole matter began gradually to subside—and I thought, not without a trace of disappointment, that what-ever had or had not occurred in room 1117 was not going to involve me any further. I was, therefore, considerably startled when a voice at my elbow inquired suddenly,

"Are you the lady that gave Mr. Evans a message a few minutes ago?"

I turned sharply, only to see the absurdly freckled and reassuring face of one of the bellboys.

"Yes," I admitted, "I'm the lady."

"Well," he continued cheerfully, "Mr. Evans says will you come upstairs please. He's in room 1117."

There was, after all, nothing for me to do but to answer the summons, but I was conscious for the first time of a chill of nervous apprehension as I started for the elevator. And my state of mind was hardly improved by the boy's second announcement.

"Mr. Evans is awfully scared," he said, still cheerfully, "because the lady in that room is shot in the stommick—and it looks like she's dead!"

Even had I not been so thoughtfully forewarned by the bellboy's messenger speech, one look at Mr. Evans' face would have been sufficient to tell me the worst. He stood outside the door of 1117 as I approached, and I remember noticing that he seemed actually to be leaning against the wall to steady himself. For a moment after I appeared, he said nothing, then he repeated, in a low voice, what the boy had told me downstairs.

"Mr. Greeley's in there now," he motioned toward the closed door, "he's our house detective. I told him that it was you who gave the alarm and he said I'd better send for you. He says you don't need to worry—there will probably just be a few questions after the—the police get here."

It seemed such an effort for Evans to speak these last words that I glanced at him curiously.

"I'm very sorry indeed," he added after a moment, "that all this—this trouble should have disturbed you. I—I can assure you, however, that there is no reason whatever for you to feel the slightest alarm—" He paused to glance at me with an air half of apology, half of dignity—and somehow oddly touching.

It seemed, after all, rather ironic that Evans, who gave every sign of being badly frightened by what had happened, should be attempting to reassure me—when I had gone into the whole thing largely for the curiosity and excitement of it. Indeed, the sight of Evans' pale, anxious face, his constant gestures of nervousness as he fingered the diamond crescent stickpin in his tie, made me feel suddenly very confident and certain of myself. I hastened to protest that I was quite all right.

"Don't worry about me, Mr. Evans," I said grandly, "I'm ready to answer any questions about what I heard."

Evans made no answer to this, except to nod absently. I saw that he glanced continually at the closed door of 1117, and I imagined that he was listening, as was I, to the sounds from within the room where the house detective was moving about. For several minutes we simply stood there and waited in silence—a silence during which I, for all my recent confidence, felt myself becoming more and more nervous and unsettled. Then, just as I had begun to wish, once and for all, that I were out of the whole affair, the door of 1117 opened and Detective Greeley emerged to give us our brief instructions.

"Are you the one that gave this alarm?" he asked of me. His tone, and the suspicious glance with which he eyed me, were ponderously official.

"Yes."

"What's your name, please?"

"Miss Pell," I answered, "Joan Pell."

"H'mm—" Greeley appeared to find my answer unexpectedly significant. "Are you—ah—a guest in this hotel, may I ask?"

"Yes, I'm in room 1017 on the floor below."

"I understand you know something about this?" he jerked his thumb toward the half-open door behind him.

"Only what I happened to overhear—" I began, but Greeley cut me off abruptly.

"Never mind repeating the story now," he said. "Did you see anyone come in or out of this lady's room?"

"No."

"Were you near the room at the time she was shot?"

"No,—I was down in my own room. It just happened that I heard—"

"I see," again he broke in gruffly. "Well—I'll have to ask you to wait and give your evidence when the men get here from Headquarters."

After a brief consultation with Evans, Greeley decided that I was to wait in room 1116, fortunately vacant. It appeared that Evans had not brought his pass-key with him, and it was during the few minutes that the two men were occupied in finding a key to unlock the vacant room, that I—almost in spite of myself—glanced through the half-open door of 1117. Naturally I could see but a part of the room; a sofa, a corner of the bed, a row of suit-cases—apparently packed ready to be taken downstairs. All this seemed orderly enough, but as I stepped forward for a better view of the room, I started violently. Both Evans and Greeley noticed my gesture, and the detective stepped forward quickly to close the door. He was not, however, quick enough—for I had already seen the body of the murdered woman, sprawled face downward on the floor.

→ 2 ←
A ROSE BY ANY OTHER NAME—?

When I entered the room where I was to wait I was somewhat surprised to see that Evans followed me.

"Perhaps you wouldn't mind if I—stayed a few minutes?" he spoke with hesitation.

"Not at all," I said pleasantly. "After all, I'm glad to have company."

My words seemed to put Evans somewhat more at his ease, and we managed, for the next few minutes, to keep up a fairly normal conversation. I was willing enough to talk, but he pointedly avoided any mention of what had happened next door, with the result that our remarks remained strictly impersonal. As the time passed Evans became increasingly restless and it was plainly evident that he was giving scant attention to my efforts at small talk. It was natural, of course, that as Manager of the Almeda he should be distressed by what had occurred. Murders are, after all, extremely bad for the hotel business and Evans had every right to be troubled on that score—but the very fact that puzzled me was that I could no longer detect in his manner the slightest trace of professional concern. It is true that when I mentioned the fact that this was my first visit to the Almeda, Evans did express a purely perfunctory regret at this unfortunate introduction to the hotel. But it seemed obvious, to me at least, that his real nervousness over the matter rose from a fear of something more than bad business.

Under these circumstances—with Evans preoccupied by his own thoughts, and me absorbed in wondering what the cause of his preoccupation might be—it was not strange that our desultory conversation should die. It lapsed, in fact, right in the middle of some inconsequential remark which Evans was making. He was looking, strangely enough, up at the ceiling at the moment when his voice faded unexpectedly into silence. For an anxious moment he continued to look overhead and he seemed quite plainly to be listening for something. Naturally I listened also, but I heard no sound. Whether Evans heard anything or not, I could not know—but, at any rate, he never returned to his unfinished remark. He remained, instead, in a curious attitude of waiting, and more than once I saw that he glanced upward again, always with an expression of half-fearful expectancy in his pale, wide-set, blue eyes.

For my own part, I was none too comfortable. Something of Evans' unspoken apprehension had conveyed itself to me—and I caught myself listening intently to the occasional sounds of voices and footsteps which penetrated vaguely from the hall outside. It seemed to me that a long time passed while we waited thus, but actually not more than a quarter of an hour had elapsed before Greeley threw open the door to announce that the men had arrived from Headquarters.

The entrance of the police was followed by a series of rapid questions, most of which were answered by Greeley. Several times, however, he turned to Evans for assistance, and I observed that, for the time at least, the Manager seemed to have regained sufficient composure to speak with convincing assurance. He gave the name of the dead woman as Miss Rose Lovett, and stated that she had registered as a guest at the Almeda three days before.

"Who was the first one in room 1117 after the shooting?" The question was addressed to Greeley by the Police Inspector who appeared to be in charge of the investigation.

"Not me, sir," the house detective admitted regretfully. "I wasn't called until Mr. Evans had already seen what had happened."

"Well—?" the questioner turned to Evans. "Were you the first one in the room?"

"As far as I know, yes," the Manager nodded.

"Exactly what did you find?"

"Everything seemed to be in good order, except, of course, for the—the body."

"There was no sign of any intruder?"

"No."

"Did you search the room?"

"Why, no," Evans admitted, "I only took a quick look around, and saw that there was no one hiding in the closet or in the bathroom, and then I went out immediately to send for Mr. Greeley."

"And thus providing," the Inspector commented dryly, "an excellent opportunity for the murderer to escape unnoticed."

Evans flushed uncomfortably at the Inspector's words, but he made no effort to defend his behavior.

"Tell me this, Mr. Evans," the questioner continued unpleasantly, "was Miss Lovett dead when you entered her room?"

"I'm afraid I couldn't answer that positively," said Evans, "but I assumed that she was dead when I—"

"You *assumed* that she was dead?" the Inspector repeated scornfully.

"Why, yes. I—it never occurred to me that she might
still be living."

"Did you look at the body?"

"Not closely, no."

"Did you touch it?"

"Oh, no," Evans was quick to protest this, "I disturbed
nothing in the room."

"How did you find the windows and the door when
you entered Miss Lovett's room?" the Inspector shifted the
subject abruptly. "Were they open or shut?"

"The windows," said Evans promptly, "were closed. The
door was closed, but not locked."

The Inspector's eyebrows were raised sharply.

"Not bad," he drawled, "for 'a quick look around.'"
Then, with a final glance of something very near contempt
for Evans, the Inspector turned to Greeley. "Go on with
the story," he directed. "What did *you* do when you got to
Miss Lovett's room."

"First," Greeley began importantly, "I took a look at
the body. When I saw that it couldn't have been suicide,
on account of there being no weapon in sight, I knew right
away it was a plain case of murder I was looking at. So I
went straight to the telephone and sent for you, sir. And
in the meantime—"

"You sent for a doctor?" the Inspector suggested.

"No, sir, that I did not."

"And why didn't you?"

"Because, sir," Greeley explained in a tone of lugubri-
ous pleasure, "one look at that poor lady showed me she
was past a doctor's help."

"Oh," said the Inspector sadly, and for just a moment I thought I saw a glimmer of a twinkle in his eye.

Up to that time, the Inspector, who had introduced himself as Fowler of the Homicide Squad, had proceeded with his questioning in a strictly business-like and none too pleasant manner. I was not, in fact, very favorably impressed by his method, which seemed to me needlessly abrupt, and I definitely disliked his curiously insulting way of brushing aside the information which Evans and Greeley supplied in answer to his questions. As for my testimony, the Inspector did not even trouble to ask for it— although Greeley had mentioned at the outset that I was the one who had heard the actual shooting, and had given the alarm. Fowler had simply glanced at me when this fact was brought out, and then continued his questioning of the two men.

And during the routine quizzing, I had ample opportunity to study the Inspector, and to ponder on just why I felt such a definite antagonism toward him. I observed that his manner toward the three policemen, who were his assistants, was not unpleasant, and that they seemed on friendly enough terms with him. But for Greeley, Evans and myself, the Inspector adopted the attitude of veiled insolence which I have already described. I supposed, from the way in which Fowler was proceeding, that he was to be in full charge of the case—and I was none too happy in that thought.

Perhaps a part of my instinctive distrust of Inspector Fowler arose from the fact that he looked not in the least as I imagined a police detective should look. (My notions on this point were again, no doubt, the result of too extensive reading among the mystery novels.) In outward appearance, Fowler was distinctly an individual—strikingly tall, spare, and loosely hung together with enormous feet which seemed to draw him about, the remainder of his body following almost reluctantly. A deep furrow in his prominent forehead gave his long face a severely hard-boiled expression. Yet I had to admit that for all the Inspector's brusque manner, there was more than a hint of a reassuringly intelligent irony in his sharp brown eyes.

It was not until Fowler had returned from a brief investigation of the room next door, that he finally turned to me with a question.

"So you're the one who discovered this shooting?" he drawled.

"Why not exactly," I began, "I merely—"

"Name?" he broke in curtly.

"Joan Pell."

"Miss or Mrs.?"

"Miss."

"Just what did you hear?"

I described, as briefly and clearly as I could, the scream and the shot which I had earlier reported to Evans. The Inspector listened in the same oddly skeptical manner with which he had received the statements of the two men, but he did make one or two notes in a small book which he carried.

"You were in your room when you heard this?"

"Yes."

"Where is your room?"

"On the floor beneath this," I answered, "number 1017."

"H'mm," Fowler seemed to consider this for a moment, then he asked, "Are you familiar with the sound of a pistol shot?"

I paused in surprise.

"No, I'm not," I answered truthfully.

"Then are you quite sure that it was a shot which you heard?"

Again I hesitated.

"I mean," Fowler continued, "that the sound you heard might have been some part of the traffic noise outside, or even the sharp banging of a door near your room—am I right?" he was watching me closely with those annoying brown eyes.

"I suppose that *might* be the case," I admitted, "but as it happened I—"

Again the Inspector interrupted me with an abrupt question.

"How long have you been a guest in this hotel?" he inquired.

"Since five o'clock this afternoon."

"Where did you come from?"

I explained that my home was in Washington, and that I had come up for a weekend. In answer to a further question I stated the nature of my government job.

"Do you usually have weekends long enough to arrive in New York at five o'clock of a Friday afternoon?" Fowler put the question in an elaborately sarcastic drawl.

I more than half suspected that the Inspector hoped, by adopting this insolent tone, to throw me off my guard—so, although he was certainly succeeding in being highly irritating, I was determined to remain civil. What any of these questions had to do with the shooting of Rose Lovett I had no idea, but I answered quietly and truthfully.

"When you have worked in an office eight years," I said, "and have never asked for any time off, it is not, I think, too much to request one extra day on a weekend."

"I see." Fowler chose, for some reason, to make a note of this point.

"Were you in your room for any length of time preceding the—er—scream which you heard?" he inquired after a moment.

"Probably not more than ten minutes."

"And during that time did you hear any commotion in the room above you?"

"Not that I recall."

"Then since you noticed no disturbance—and since you admit that you wouldn't know the sound of a shot if you heard it—just *what* made you so certain that you had overheard anything so very alarming?" the Inspector put the question very pointedly.

I determined that on this matter at least I would be firm.

"I may not be a judge of shots," I said levelly, "but it happens that I *do* know a scream when I hear one—and I had just enough sense to realize that a woman who screams as Miss Lovett did, was not screaming over nothing."

Inspector Fowler gave no indication of what he thought of my answer, but, at any rate, he stopped picking on me for the moment, and switched to Evans suddenly.

"How well was this Miss Lovett known here?" he asked.

"Not at all," Evans admitted, "she had never stopped here before."

"Did she have friends in the hotel?"

"I would hardly know about that," Evans objected, "but I don't recall that she mentioned any when she arrived. I happened to be on duty at the desk when she registered."

We were interrupted by a knock at the door. It was one of the two policemen who had arrived with Fowler, and he evidently had some message for the Inspector. The two men stepped out into the hall, and through the closed door we could hear the murmur of their voices as they conferred. Greeley, Evans and I waited in silence until Fowler returned. He began speaking at once.

"My men report," the Inspector announced, "that they have searched Miss Lovett's room and find no trace of a gun. There are no signs of any struggle or violence, aside from the shooting of course, and no evidence that robbery was involved. In other words," Fowler looked away from us with a curious expression, "we have exactly nothing to go on except one odd fact—" he broke off abruptly and turned to me. "What do you know about *rigor mortis,* Miss Pell?" he demanded.

"I—I know what it means," I managed to answer.

"Ever observed it at close quarters?" he drawled.

"No." I succeeded in keeping a matter-of-fact tone, but the Inspector's next suggestion almost floored me.

"Would you—ah—care to have a look?" he asked, and his manner was elaborately polite. "It's rather interesting, you know."

From the corner of my eye I saw that Greeley and Evans exchanged a quick look. For a moment I hesitated, half expecting one of them to protest against this notion, but when neither spoke I gathered myself for the effort.

"You mean," I began, and I think I must have gulped a bit as I spoke, "that you want me to look at—at Miss Lovett's body?"

"Yes," said Fowler agreeably, "unless it will—upset you too much?" Again his tone was insolently polite.

I would have been, I believe, quite within my rights in refusing to enter Miss Lovett's room. I realized that a word of protest on my part would bring Evans and Greeley to my defense—that a symptom or two of hysterics or fainting would probably excuse me from any further part in the affair. But I was too boiling mad to resort to faint- ing-fits or hysterics. I happen to resent particularly the type of man who attributes everything a woman does or says to some sort of an emotional upset—and of course it was evident that Fowler was doing exactly that. For some reason best known to himself, he was choosing to doubt my testimony, but I was determined to show him that I could bear up under his heckling.

"I will do," I said, "exactly as you think best."

Without further discussion the Inspector led the way into Miss Lovett's room, and the three of us followed him in silence.

"After all, Miss Pell," Fowler smiled cryptically as he opened the door for me, "you *are* our only witness."

I remember thinking that it would be more to the point if the Inspector were to look about for more witnesses, rather than wasting time in picking on me. But I said nothing whatever.

A moment later I had ample opportunity to observe the dead woman, of whom I had caught only a glimpse earlier. More of an opportunity, in fact, than I had any desire for, but I forced myself to look directly at the sprawled body. I knew that Fowler was watching me, and I made up my mind, once and for all, that he was *not* going to have the satisfaction of seeing me falter. Resolutely, I concen- trated on observing the external details of Miss Lovett's body, trying not to remember the gruesome implication of the bellboy's words "shot in the stommick." At least I was thankful that there were no tangible evidences of violence. The woman lay face downward, so that all traces of the bullet wound were concealed, and I saw with relief that her beautiful, wavy red hair had fallen forward to cover the dead face. It was evident that Miss Rose Lovett had been a young woman, and a decidedly attractive one. She was dressed very smartly in a cream-colored, woolen street-suit, and everything about her indicated a degree of chic and dash which seemed oddly out of place in the gloomy, old-fashioned Almeda bedroom.

I glanced quickly at three men who stood, in a silent circle, staring at that still figure. Their faces were as expressionless as I hoped mine was, but I wondered whether they were thinking, as I was, that the circumstances which had connected such a woman as Miss Lovett with the quiet, unworldly life of the old Almeda Hotel, must have been mysterious indeed.

Moments passed as we stood thus, and still the Inspector made no move to carry on his cryptic intention of demonstrating to me the effects of *rigor mortis*. What, if anything, he had meant by that absurd threat, I hadn't the vaguest idea, but in the meantime I was beginning to breathe a bit more easily, and I occupied myself by looking slowly and attentively about the room. I had already heard Fowler say that no gun had been found near the body. But surely, I thought, in a room where, less than an hour ago, a woman had been shot and killed, there must be some sign of disturbance, some trace of the murderer.

Yet once more I was impressed with the fact that everything was in perfect order. It was evident that Miss Lovett had been on the very point of leaving the hotel when the shooting had occurred. Her baggage, which I had seen earlier through the half-open door, stood in a neat row. Miss Lovett herself was, of course, dressed for the street, and her hat, gloves and purse lay together on the dressing-table. There was just one thing in that room which caught my attention as being of possible interest. It was a large,

square florist's box which lay on a corner of the big walnut bed. I saw that the lid of the box was half off, and,
after a tentative glance at the Inspector, I stepped over to
peer curiously inside. There was a card, lying on the usual
green waxed paper, and I was able to see quite plainly the
message on it. Very neatly typed was a single phrase:

```
A rose by any other name --?
```

3
ROSE LOVETT INTO LINA CASTLE

"My God!"

The exclamation, spoken just at my elbow and with a suddenness which made me jump, came from the Inspector. I looked up to find him peering over my shoulder into the box of flowers. Just why the package, or the odd message which it contained, should have moved Fowler to exclaim quite so violently, I was not to know for some time. But it was more than evident that he had come upon something which he regarded as of considerable importance. For the first time since his arrival he showed signs of really having an idea as he turned quickly and opened the door into the hall.

"Hey, Morty," he called.

"Yes, sir," the police officer who had made the earlier report appeared at once.

"Where did *that* come from?" Fowler pointed to the florist's box.

"Joe found it in there," the policeman indicated the clothes-closet, "when we were going through the room. It was on the floor, Joe said, shoved back in a corner."

"Uh-huh," the Inspector squinted one eye thoughtfully as he considered, then abruptly he put out his hand. "Let's have those papers," he directed.

Morty began to fish obediently in various pockets.

"Those that was in the lady's hand-bag?" he inquired.

"Yes and hurry up," Fowler snapped his fingers impatiently.

"Here they are, sir," Morty produced a small package, and Fowler began at once to examine the contents eagerly. Presently he came upon a small card, and paused as if satisfied. From where I stood, it appeared to be an ordinary visiting card, but undoubtedly it held some special significance for the detective.

After a moment Fowler looked up and addressed a question to Evans.

"Did you ever hear of a woman named Lina Castle?" he demanded.

I glanced quickly at Evans and saw the look of surprise which crossed his face. But before the Manager could speak, Greeley startled us with an exclamation.

"*Lina Castle!*" he exploded, "why she's the one we're ordered not to let into this hotel." As he said this, Greeley turned to Evans, and the Manager nodded in somewhat reluctant agreement.

Instantly, the Inspector snapped at the information.

"What do you mean by that?" he demanded.

"Why, we had orders, sir," Greeley explained, "not to let a woman named Lina Castle register here. Not," he added importantly, "under any circumstances."

"Why not?"

"I couldn't say that, sir. All I know about it is the orders that came to me."

"And who gave those orders?"

"I couldn't say that either, sir." Greeley sounded disappointed. "It was Mr. Evans that passed the information on to me, when I first started to work here."

"Well," the Inspector shifted impatiently to Evans, "where did the order come from?"

That Evans was upset by the turn which the questioning had taken, was evident—but he was ready with an answer.

"Mr. Deal gave the order," he said quietly.

"Deal—?" the Inspector repeated. "Who's he?"

"Mr. Deal is my employer," said Evans.

"Meaning that he owns the hotel?" Fowler inquired.

"Not exactly, sir." It was Greeley who spoke. "It's Mr. Harvey Deal's mother who owns the place, and he runs it for her, owing to Madam Deal being quite old and not able to manage the hotel herself."

"What reason did Mr. Deal give," the Inspector addressed Evans, "when he told you to keep this Lina Castle from coming here?"

"None," again Evans' voice was quiet. Almost, in fact, inaudible.

"Did either of you," Fowler indicated the two men, "know this woman by sight?"

Both signified that they did not.

"And you were given no description of her?"

Again they shook their heads.

"Then," Fowler spoke excitedly, "it would have been possible, wouldn't it, for Lina Castle to get into the hotel merely by registering under another name?"

"I should think, sir," Greeley admitted, "that such a thing might have happened, even though I made every effort to carry out Mr. Deal's orders. Of course," he added thoughtfully, "she couldn't have gotten in if Mr. Deal had happened to see her himself."

"You mean," the Inspector demanded eagerly, "that Deal *did* know the woman?"

"I couldn't exactly say that for certain, sir," Greeley ventured with admirable caution, "but I should think he must have known Mrs. Castle or he wouldn't have been so anxious to keep her away."

Evans said nothing.

It was evident that the Inspector was disappointed by Greeley's tentative answer, but he proceeded with his theory concerning the identity of Lina Castle.

"It looks," Fowler said slowly, "as if that were exactly what Lina Castle did. She got into the hotel by the simple means of registering under another name. And the name she happened to choose was—Miss Rose Lovett!"

Evans, Greeley and I received the announcement in silence, but after a moment Evans spoke.

"What—what makes you so sure," he began rather uncertainly, "that this woman is—Lina Castle?"

The Inspector eyed him.

"Plenty," he answered briefly. But he apparently had no intention of explaining.

"Well, if you're right, sir," Greeley observed admiringly, "and I haven't a doubt that you *are* right;—you're certainly making progress."

Fowler laughed shortly, and then he sighed with an air of genuine discouragement.

"Oh, yes, we're progressing, Greeley," he remarked dryly, "in fact, we've progressed right to the point where most cases begin. We actually know now who was murdered."

But a moment later Fowler was proceeding more briskly. Indeed, he seemed for the first time to be really snapping into action as he began issuing abrupt directions to us all. Officer Morty was summoned, and told to fetch the Medical Examiner, then Greeley, Evans and I were ordered to return to the vacant room next door.

For my own part I was only too glad to leave Miss Lovett's room, and the sight of that still figure on the floor, and of course I was not a little relieved that the Inspector should have apparently forgotten his promise to demonstrate the effects of *rigor mortis*. What his intention in that direction had been, I still had no idea, but I was certainly content to let the matter drop.

When we had been returned to room 1116, Fowler left us for perhaps ten minutes, and when he came back he plunged immediately into further plans for investigation.

"First," he said to Greeley, "I want you to get this man Deal and bring him here. Next," he addressed Evans, "I want to know who has rooms 1118 and 1119 directly across the hall?"

"A Mr. and Mrs. Clark," Evans informed him, "have the suite consisting of the two rooms you mention."

"I see." Fowler was once more jotting things down in his notebook. "Now we already know," he continued, "that Miss Pell has the room below 1117—how about the one just above?"

Instinctively I looked at Evans. He was looking down as he answered.

"My own apartment," Evans said, "is number 1217."

Fowler glanced up quickly in evident surprise at this reply, but he made no comment on the curious circumstance. He summoned his second policeman from the hall and directed him to get hold of the Mr. and Mrs. Clark whom Evans had mentioned, and also to find the maid who had taken care of Mrs. Castle's room.

I observed with interest the fact that the Inspector had abruptly dropped the name of Rose Lovett, and from this time on referred to the murdered woman as Lina Castle. Evidently his reasons, whatever they were, for believing

that Miss Lovett was actually Mrs. Castle, were fairly con-
clusive.

It happened that room 1117 was at the end of the corridor, which meant that, excepting 1116, which had been
vacant, the Inspector had accounted for all the rooms
whose occupants might have been within earshot of the
disturbance in Lina Castle's room.

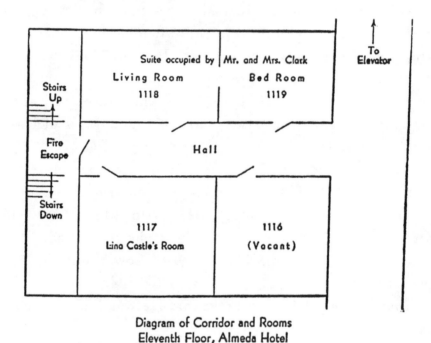

Diagram of Corridor and Rooms
Eleventh Floor, Almeda Hotel

An enclosed fire-escape staircase at the end of the hall
supplied an easy and inconspicuous access to the door of
Mrs. Castle's room. That Fowler had observed this fact
was evident when he directed Morty to search the steps of
the fire-escape carefully for possible clues.

While we waited for the summoned witnesses to arrive,
the Inspector moved restlessly about the room—fetching a
cigarette, opening the window, idly rearranging the writing materials on the desk. Suddenly he paused before me
with a question.

"Look here, Miss Pell," he said, "did you by any chance forget anything in your statement of what you heard from the room above yours?"

Once more Fowler had adopted that irritatingly skeptical manner of his, and once more I gritted my teeth and answered him civilly.

"I didn't," I said, "omit anything intentionally—if that's what you mean."

"Well, I was only wondering," the Inspector's tone was more mild, "if you happened to have heard any sounds which might have been made by the murderer approaching Lina Castle's room?"

"And the answer is," I said firmly, "that I did not."

"Nor, I suppose, did you hear any sound which might have been interpreted as the murderer escaping after the shooting."

Again I indicated positively that I had not heard any such thing.

"Then I take it, Miss Pell," said Fowler, "that there was complete silence in Mrs. Castle's room tonight until suddenly, with no warning preliminaries of any sort, the poor woman screamed with horror, and a moment later was shot dead by this extraordinarily silent intruder—who then proceeded to leave the scene of his crime without making any sound whatever. No footsteps—no closing of a door—nothing. Am I right?"

"You may be right or wrong, Inspector, but that hasn't anything to do with what I've told you." I spoke sharply. "I've told you exactly what I heard—which was a scream and a shot, nothing more. And considering the fact that the walls and floors of this hotel happen to be unusually solid, and also considering that murderers are not, I believe, in the habit of stamping in and out and banging doors, I think it is not too strange that I heard neither the approach nor the escape of the person who fired the shot!"

In spite of all my resolves to keep my temper in hand, I found myself getting pretty much heated over the Inspector's insinuations, and it was fortunate for me that our conversation was ended abruptly by the arrival of the first witnesses.

It was the police officer who announced that Mr. and Mrs. Clark, the occupants of the suite directly opposite 1117, were outside, and Fowler ordered them to come in immediately. It developed that this elderly and amiable couple knew nothing whatever of what had happened in 1117. When they were informed of the tragedy they seemed genuinely shocked, and were willing to answer Fowler's questions as fully as they could, but their testimony shed very little light. They had gone down to dinner a little after six o'clock, and had not returned to their apartment since then, having remained in the lobby downstairs. In answer to the Inspector's query concerning Mrs. Castle, they agreed that they had observed her only as an unusually attractive young woman. Mrs. Clark finally recalled that late in the afternoon she had overheard angry voices, which seemed to come across the hall, but she had failed to hear any actual words of the quarrel.

"Could you tell," Fowler inquired, "whether the voices were those of men or women?"

"Why, I couldn't be *sure*—but I *think* I heard a man's voice," Mrs. Clark's answer was almost painfully conscientious.

"And had either you or Mr. Clark at any time observed any visitors to Mrs. Castle's room?"

This question brought a prompt negative from both the Clarks, and ended the interview. The couple departed with

many protestations of their willingness to help further in
the investigation at any time, but when they had gone
Fowler shrugged his shoulders impatiently.

"Just so much time wasted," he commented as he
glanced at his watch. It was by this time about quarter of
ten, and certainly very little had been accomplished since
the police had arrived, nearly an hour before. Progress was
further delayed when a message was brought concerning
Hulda, the maid in charge of room 1117. It developed that
she had left the hotel to go home at about seven o'clock—
thus there was no possibility that she had been near the
room at the time of the shooting.

In spite of his skeptical altitude toward me, Fowler had
evidently decided to accept my statement that Mrs. Castle had been murdered at approximately ten minutes past
eight. He seemed, at any rate, to be going on this assump-
tion when he turned to Evans with his next questions.

"You say that you occupy the room just over 1117?" he
inquired.

"Yes," Evans' answer was steady, "1217 is the living
room of my suite, and 1216 the bedroom."

"And you were on duty downstairs at ten minutes after
eight?"

"Yes, I went down to my office at six-thirty this evening."

"There was no one in your apartment, then, at the time
of the trouble?"

"I believe that—my wife was there at the time," Evans'
tone was even, but the hesitation in his answer was quite
apparent.

The Inspector's eyebrows were raised sharply.

"Just what," he queried unpleasantly, "was your idea in
holding out on that fact?"

Evans flushed uncomfortably, but it struck me that his answer was more an expression of embarrassment than guilt.

"I—I certainly didn't mean to be holding out anything, but you didn't ask me about it and—" the explanation faltered lamely.

Fowler stared for a moment in silence, then he dismissed the matter with a curt gesture.

"Your answer is quite beside the point," he informed Evans, "but that fact is also beside the point. I shall have to question your wife, of course. Will you get her on the telephone and ask her to come down here?"

Looking quite thoroughly abashed, Evans went to the phone without a word, and Fowler began a murmured conference with Greeley, who had been sent to fetch Deal. It appeared that Harvey Deal was nowhere to be found. The detective brought word from the Deal apartment upstairs that Harvey Deal had gone out about four o'clock that afternoon, and had not returned since. He had left word that he would not be in until late in the evening, but had given no indication of where he could be found. His two clubs had been telephoned, but without success. All this added to the Inspector's growing impatience, for he seemed to be hampered on every side by the most aggravating delays.

A few minutes later Morty reported that the fire-escape stairs had yielded no clues, and he was ordered to continue by searching the roof, to which there was easy access by means of the same fire-escape stairs.

In answer to an inquiry, Fowler was informed that none of the employees on duty downstairs recalled the entrance or exit of any strange persons during the evening, nor had the elevator operator observed anything unusual. The fact that the Almeda is essentially a residential hotel, made it likely that these reports of the staff were correct. All of the hotel employees would undoubtedly recognize the guests of the house, most of whom had patronized the Almeda for many years.

All in all, it was a discouraging series of reports, and when Evans turned back from the telephone with the news that his wife failed to answer the call, Fowler lost all patience. He accused us all of being in his way and told us without further ado, to get the hell out.

We, after all, were only too glad to go. Personally, I was getting pretty sick of the Inspector's changeable moods, and it was plain that, for the time at least, the case was at a standstill. I rose at once, and Fowler managed, with evident difficulty, to thank me curtly for my help.

"Too bad to have kept you, Miss Pell," he added casually; "you'd better just forget this thing."

"You mean you won't want me for any more questions?" I asked in surprise.

"I hardly think so," the Inspector's sarcastic drawl indicated all too clearly that he regarded any evidence I might give as worse than useless.

For the last time I bit my tongue to keep from answering back, and with a short good-night I was gone—glad to be rid of Fowler's insolence, and out of the whole mess.

4
THE TRICK

Once back in my own room I sat down with a cigarette to think things out a bit. A reaction to the excitement of the early evening left me with an unpleasant feeling of anti-climax, and the manner in which Inspector Fowler had dismissed me seemed definitely to have ended my part in the affair upstairs. It was not difficult, at this point, to convince myself that I was well out of it—and perhaps I was right. But right or wrong I was not allowed to remain aloof very long. For within the next few minutes I was to discover, *on my own desk,* the most astounding and confusing bit of evidence which had so far come to light.

I came upon it quite by chance. It just happened that I went to the desk to hunt for a fresh package of cigarettes, and that as I rummaged for the carton I scattered a small pile of letters and papers. In picking them up, quite absent-mindedly, I chanced to notice a small card. Still idly, I turned it over—and the effect of what I saw was like an electric shock. There were the neatly typed letters which spelled the cryptic message which I had seen before:

```
┌─────────────────────────────────────────┐
│                                         │
│                                         │
│        A rose by any other name --?     │
│                                         │
│                                         │
└─────────────────────────────────────────┘
```

Unquestionably it was the same card which had lain in the box of flowers on Lina Castle's bed upstairs! But *how* or *why* it should now be among *my* papers in *my* room—indeed I could not possibly imagine. In blank amazement I stared at the strange message for several moments, but no hint of explanation occurred to me.

How could anyone have entered my room to place it with my things? Why should anyone wish to put it there? What, in short, could it possibly mean? The questions whirled through my mind in a meaningless circle.

Out of all my confusion came only one persistent possibility; someone was trying to plant something on me. Fantastic as this idea appeared to be, it was certainly the only explanation which I could summon, and in the event that it might be true, I saw quite plainly that there was but one thing for me to do. I must go straight to Inspector Fowler with the card! Little as I liked his attitude, I felt that my one chance lay in an immediate statement to him. After all, someone *knew* that I had that card—and to have the information come out later would, indeed, place me in an even more difficult situation.

Once I had taken my resolve, I started upstairs immediately, bearing the card in my hand, and hoping fervently that Fowler would choose to believe my story. One of the policemen was stationed outside the door of 1116, and when he had taken my message to Fowler, I was allowed to enter at once.

I found that Evans and Greeley had gone, and apparently Mr. Deal had not yet been located, for the Inspector was alone. He rose as I came in, and spoke in an exaggeratedly sarcastic drawl.

"Come in, Miss Pell," he said. "I'm told that you have important light to shed on this case. So?"

This was just the attitude I had foreseen, but since there was nothing else for me to do, I told as briefly as I could of finding the card on my desk.

I carefully refrained, of course, from saying that I suspected that it had been planted.

As I had feared, Fowler received my report with a skeptical smile, and when I handed him the card he barely glanced at it.

"Thanks so much, Miss Pell," he said, "this may be useful later." His effort to treat me casually was quite obvious—but what his motive might be, I most certainly did not know. At any rate I had cleared myself as best I could, and I had no other course than to accept his attitude.

I waited in silence for his next move, and for several moments he said nothing. Then, very deliberately he spoke.

"Oh, by the way, Miss Pell, since you are interested in those flowers—you might like to know who sent them to Mrs. Castle?"

Naturally I made no answer to this bait, and he went on.

"The florist shop reports that they were ordered by a lady, about six o'clock this evening, who took them out of the store herself. The clerk fortunately remembers that she was young, had dark hair, and wore," he spoke with careful emphasis, "a green coat trimmed with black fur."

I had to wait a moment before I could compose myself sufficiently to answer Fowler, then I rose and faced him.

"Now you look here," I said in the most level tone I could manage, "I understand perfectly what you mean. You are saying that *I* ordered the flowers for Mrs. Castle. You are *trying* to say that either I shot her or I know who did. You have treated me insolently since the first moment you got here and you've decided, heaven knows why, that I'm implicated in this murder. Well, I suppose it's your job to suspect everybody—but I *won't* stand for your stupid methods of trying to trap me!

"It just happened," I went on angrily, "that I *did* know something about this case—I offered what information I could in the first place, and I'm still willing to help if I can—but if you don't change your tone and change it fast— I'll . . . well, I'll go straight to Headquarters about it."

My furious speech ended rather lamely—for in my rage I could think of nothing but that foolish threat. The Inspector had listened to my outburst in silence—and now I looked at him to see how he was taking it. He stared a moment, and then, with a suddenness which very nearly startled me out of my anger, Fowler threw back his head and laughed!

"So *you*," he exclaimed, "are going to report *me* to Headquarters? And what will the charge be? Bad manners?" Plainly he regarded all this as highly amusing.

At least, I thought, I had gotten some reaction from him. Even to be laughed at was better than being alternately ignored and baited. But my next words were still peevish.

"You know just as well as I do," I said, "that I didn't buy those flowers nor send them to Lina Castle. If you've checked up on me enough to know that I wear a green coat with black fur—and heaven knows how you found that out—you ought also to know that at six o'clock this evening I was up on the roof of this hotel watching the sunset. And you needn't take my bare word for it either, because I've got two witnesses to prove it. A little boy, who told me his name was Wally, was up on the roof with his nurse—and both of them will tell you that I was there until after six o'clock."

Fowler was watching me closely. His laughter had subsided into a pleased grin which, even in my irritation I couldn't help liking. And when he spoke again, it was in an entirely new tone.

"I hardly think, Miss Pell," he began amiably, "that it will be necessary to call in the estimable Wally and his nurse to check on your alibi—because I'm very much inclined to believe your story. And what's more," he added gallantly, "I like your spirit."

It was my turn to eye the Inspector suspiciously. That he could possibly have altered his opinion of me quite so quickly, I found it difficult to believe—and I found myself wondering whether this latest speech were not simply another of his traps. Yet when he spoke again, I felt my lingering doubts weakening beneath that unexpectedly disarming smile.

"I'll make a deal with you, Miss Pell," Fowler was saying, "that from this minute on I won't annoy you with any more suspicions or threats or harsh words. Now will you make up?"

Well, I am not, after all, a very difficult person to mollify, and I suppose it was the smile that did the trick. It was only a moment until I had a grin to match his own—and there we stood, suddenly, but firmly, the best of friends. On an impulse I put out my hand, and the Inspector gripped it cordially.

"Friends?" he asked, still smiling.

"Friends!" I echoed.

"Everything's jake?"

"Everything's jake," I said happily.

In the immense relief I felt at this sudden change in the Inspector's manner, I was, for the first time during that strange evening, at ease. When he motioned me to a comfortable seat and drew up a small chair for himself, I was more than ready to talk.

"In the first place," he began, "I apologize for the way I hounded you earlier this evening."

"Just what," I asked mildly, "*was* the big idea?"

For a moment the Inspector stared at me without speaking. Something about his expression made me fear that he was going to return to his previous tactics, but his surprising answer relieved my mind on that score once and for all.

"I suppose I might just as well be frank with you, Miss Pell," he said, "and admit that I treated you badly for a very good reason of my own. I didn't care, you see, to have Evans and that remarkable house detective catch on to the fact that I was very much interested in your ideas on this case."

"*My* ideas . . ." certainly this was unexpected.

"Exactly," Fowler nodded. "When I got here this evening and looked around a bit—well, this has all the earmarks of a pretty tough case, and I saw just one ray of light."

"And that was?" I asked eagerly.

"You."

"Me!"

"Exactly," said Fowler once more.

"But why . . . ?"

"Because, in the first place, you're a woman."

"Yes."

"And in the second place you knew something about what had happened."

"A little," I admitted.

"And in the third place," Fowler finished triumphantly, "you're smart."

I made no answer to this, but the Inspector persisted.

"You *are* smart, aren't you?" he asked.

"Well, I . . ."

"Precisely," said Fowler. "I was right. And this is just the kind of case in which I'm going to need the help of some feminine gumption, a need, however, which I should hardly care to divulge to the quivering Evans and our hotel sleuth. It's the sort of thing that—" he hesitated—"well, you could scarcely call it a professional attitude."

"Hence," I said, "the snooty way you treated me before the two men?"

"Right the first time. I intended all along to talk to you after school—like this."

"I suppose," I ventured, "that you were going to send for me if I hadn't happened to come back.

The Inspector regarded me with an air of reproach.

"But I did send for you, Miss Pell," he protested, "and you got my message."

"Your message—?" I was thoroughly puzzled.

"Why, yes," the Inspector continued innocently, "the little white card, you know."

Quite suddenly the surprising light dawned on me.

"You don't mean," I exclaimed, "that *you* put that card in my room?"

"Yep," said Fowler proudly, "I did it. I meant it to fetch you down here—and it worked."

"But when did you do it?" I asked in amazement.

"Just after you and Greeley and Evans were ushered back in here from the conference in Mrs. Castle's room. You see, I knew that you had looked at the card in the box of flowers—so I simply hiked downstairs and put the little message among some papers that I found on your desk."

"And just what," I asked, "did you expect would happen?"

"Exactly what did happen," said the Inspector triumphantly. "I knew that if you were the type I was looking for, you would bring that card straight to me the moment you found it."

"But at least," I observed, "you took a chance on my finding it so promptly."

The Inspector shrugged.

"Even detectives," he admitted, "have to take chances. But I made as sure of succeeding as possible by taking all the cigarettes but one out of the package on your table—and hiding the carton under the papers on the desk."

The man was smart—I had to admit it. But still I persisted with another question.

"How," I demanded, "did you know that I was going to smoke more than the one cigarette you left in the pack on my table?"

"Well, I didn't exactly know," Fowler said modestly, "but two things led me to think that you smoke a good deal. First the fact that you buy your cigarettes by the carton, and secondly these—" he pointed to the telltale nicotine stains on the fingers of my right hand.

"Oh, and by the way, Miss Pell," he added suddenly, "here are the cigarettes I swiped from your pack." I was presented with a loose handful of Old Golds which Fowler had extracted from his pocket.

"Have one," I said weakly, "you deserve it."

Then I tried one final question.

"Why," I inquired, "did you greet me so casually when I did appear with the card—and what was the point of that absurd accusation about me buying the box of flowers for Lina Castle?"

"That," said the Inspector calmly, "was simply one last test to see whether you were as smart as I hoped. And," he concluded gallantly, "you were. As matter of fact, of course, I can't get any report from the florist until morning, and I haven't much hope in that direction anyway, because the shop where the bouquet was bought is a pretty big one—and the flowers are so thoroughly wilted that I think surely they were sent to Lina Castle a couple of days ago. In which case there is very little chance of a clerk recalling the individual purchaser."

"I hope you'll pardon my being personal," I said after a moment, "but in heaven's name who are you? I thought Police Inspectors were—well anyhow not *whirlwinds!*"

"Now there, Miss Pell, is a sad thing," Fowler spoke solemnly. "I was not, as you have guessed, born to be a Police Inspector. Nor was I even raised to be one. Indeed, I was marked for a very different sort of success— and I got it. But sometimes, Miss Pell, success can be a very precarious thing—and there came a time, Miss Pell, when I knew that the Indian sign was on me." He sighed. "Well, there seemed to be only one safe thing for me to do then, and that was to join the Force. So I did, and you see I've been promoted rather well. I often tell myself that there are successes and successes—but that's a pretty long story. And now if you will excuse me a moment, Miss Pell, I shall have to go and consult with the Medical Examiner."

With a cordial bow, Fowler departed, leaving me, by this time, quite speechless. And to this day I have never found out enough about the Inspector to know whether any part of his absurd recital was true or not.

5
I FIND A JOB

When Inspector Fowler returned from his brief conference in the next room he again seated himself with me and began to outline the case (what there was of it, at that point) in a businesslike manner.

"Now here we are," he said, "with the death of Lina Castle on our hands. Item One: what do we know about her?" He looked up.

"If you don't mind," I remarked, "I'd like to put in a question and find out just what evidence it was that suddenly made you so certain that the woman is Lina Castle?"

"Well that," Fowler squinted thoughtfully, "was fairly easy. You see, when my men went through her room they couldn't find a damn thing to show that the woman was Rose Lovett. No letters, no papers, bills, messages, initials—in fact nothing to suggest that name. On the other hand there were certain things which pointed to the name of Lina Castle—but not quite enough to be sure about it. So it wasn't until I saw that card in the box of flowers that I began to catch on—do you see?" he paused and looked at me with the question.

"I think I do," I nodded, "if you mean that the message, 'A rose by any other name' might refer to the fact that Lina Castle was trying to change her name. 'Rose' Lovett ties in nicely, of course."

"Good girl," the Inspector gave me an approving smile. "That's exactly what I mean—and when I sprang the name of Lina Castle on Greeley and Evans and got the reaction I did—well, I was pretty sure my hunch was right. Of course, I can't be positive yet because there isn't any real proof—and so far we haven't located anyone who can or will identify the body."

"How about Lina Castle's family," I suggested, "or her friends?"

"As for family," Fowler shrugged, "I'm afraid we're going to find ourselves up a tree. You see, when she registered here she gave an address in Paris as her home. Well— she gave the wrong name but I have a feeling that's the right address, and in that case it's going to be pretty hard to locate any family. Besides," he added reflectively, "just to look at her, Lina Castle doesn't strike me as the sort of woman who would have any family to speak of."

"Oh, but surely," I protested, "anyone is likely to have *some* relatives—and of course they'll show up when this all comes out in the papers."

The Inspector shook his head.

"Not her kind," he repeated stubbornly, "you watch."

"But what is 'her kind'?" I was equally persistent.

Fowler looked at me sharply, then he glanced away.

"Too damn good looking, that's all," he said shortly, "and the wrong kind of good looks. Now to get on with what we know about Lina Castle. She was planning to sail for Europe, sometime this evening on the S.S. —, the passage we found in her purse proves that. And she was on the point of leaving the hotel when she was shot."

I nodded my agreement with this, recalling the neatly packed luggage and the fact that she had been dressed in street clothes.

"We'll have the steamship office check on the sale of her ticket in the morning," Fowler continued, "and of course that information will be important."

He was scribbling in his note-book constantly during this conversation. "I like," he explained, "to make a picture of the case as I go along. Now for Item Two: who probably killed Lina Castle?"

"That seems a little previous," I objected doubtfully, but I was promptly overruled.

"I'm not asking," the Inspector informed me, "who *did* kill Mrs. Castle, but only who *probably* did, which is quite different. Once we have a fair notion of what the murderer might be like—it is a little bit easier to hunt around among the available suspects to find one who fits the picture. In this case we have two possibilities to begin with—either that the murderer came from outside the hotel or that it was an inside job. Well, the arguments for the probability of an outsider seem rather slim. No one was seen coming in or going out who seemed in any way to key in to the time of the murder; it's hardly likely that anyone would walk up eleven floors and then down again—yet the elevator boy is positive that no one came up to the eleventh floor except guests known to him; and lastly the fact that Lina Castle was shot just as she was on the point of leaving would indicate a murderer who was in a position to follow her plans very closely.

"On the other hand the evidence of an inside job is rather plentiful. First, the fact that there must have been people in the hotel who knew her (since the management

had barred her), and also there must have been someone
here *she* wanted very much to see (since she took the trouble to come here under an assumed name). Second, it looks
to me as if the murderer knew his way around this hotel
mighty well.

"Now—if we say that someone on the inside probably
did the shooting—we've got two possibilities again: either it was one of the help, or one of the guests. I figure
it probably wasn't help, because there wasn't any robbery,
and she hadn't been here long enough to get in any sort of
a row. That leaves us the guests to work with, and it means
we've got to know who, in this hotel, knew Lina Castle.
Once we get that list we can narrow it down again—because there are some other things we already know about
the murderer."

Very slowly the Inspector said all this, writing as he
talked, and when he listed the next items he emphasized
each with a jab of his pencil.

"We know," he mused, "that the murderer was on the
eleventh floor of the Almeda Hotel at ten minutes past
eight this evening. We suppose that he was cold-blooded
enough to plan out this shooting, and that he didn't hesitate when the time came. We suspect that Lina Castle had
no fear of what might happen to her, since it seems that
she had not even locked her door."

"How do you know that?" I interrupted.

"Evans told me," he explained, "that he found the door
unlocked, so I think we have a pretty safe bet that Lina
Castle was *not* expecting what she got. Now—back to our
probable murderer. We must add one more point about
him; he was careful. As far as I can see he left *no* traces of
himself, and that means real foresight and, incidentally,
brains."

"How about the box of flowers," I asked. "Wasn't that a clue?"

Fowler considered a moment.

"Of course it's true," he admitted, "that if we are right about the meaning of the message with the flowers, the person who sent them was indicating to Lina Castle that he or she knew that the name Rose Lovett was a fake. But somehow—" the Inspector paused and balanced his pencil thoughtfully—"somehow, Miss Pell, I haven't an idea in the world that the person who left the flowers killed Lina Castle."

"But why not?" I inquired.

"Oh, I don't know," he turned my question aside lightly, "only that murderers don't present bouquets as a rule."

"No, but seriously," I insisted, "why couldn't it have been the same person?"

"Because, Miss Pell," this time Fowler spoke soberly, "anyone who would leave a box of flowers with a cryptic message like that has a—well, what I'd call a fancy turn of mind. You know, the dramatic, roundabout kind who fly off the handle if anything really serious happens. And our murderer, on the other hand, is decidedly the clearheaded type. So clear headed that he removed his gun, his traces and himself very promptly and damned efficiently."

"In other words," I said thoughtfully, "you mean that if the person who sent Lina Castle the box of flowers had been the murderer, he would have left a very different sort of trail behind him. Is that right?"

"That's my idea exactly," the Inspector nodded emphatically; "it's only a hunch, I admit, but I think it's a pretty good one. He would have been the type of murderer who would stamp down the hall, probably manage to bump into a half a dozen witnesses, would barge into his victim's

room and be more than likely to lose his nerve and wind
up in a fist-fight or hysterics rather than a shooting. And
if by chance such a person *had* gotten to the point of actually committing the murder, he would have gone off leaving his gun in plain sight, fingerprints and footprints all
over the place, and probably a hat with his initials would
have been discovered beside the body."

"That sounds rather like the sort of trail," I suggested, "that Detective Greeley would follow up with crashing
success."

The Inspector smiled.

"But it's a very different kind of murderer," he sighed,
"that we're actually dealing with. So far, he hasn't left us a
single tangible clue."

"How about the possibility," I inquired presently, "that
your hypothetical murderer is not a 'he' at all—but rather
a 'she'?"

"A very likely point, Miss Pell," Fowler agreed, "and
particularly because the whole thing seems to have been
pretty well thought out beforehand. Women are, of course,
apt to be much better plotters than men. Another thing—
if we are right in thinking that Lina Castle did *not* expect
this attack, it suggests that the murder might have been
the pay-off for some past grudge—perhaps long past. And
I imagine you would agree that women are considerably
ahead of men in the matter of holding on to old grievances."

For a moment the Inspector studied his "picture" of the
case in silence, then he turned a page of his note-book and
began to scribble again.

"Next," he went on more briskly, "for a list of those in
the hotel who knew Lina Castle. It's a list which, for the
moment, must begin and end with this Harvey Deal."

"And you're not sure," I pointed out, "that Mr. Deal really belongs on the list."

"True," the Inspector admitted thoughtfully, "but if he doesn't, well, I'm wrong about a lot of things. However, we move on to those who might have known her—or at least something about her. So far we have only the jittery Evans . . ."

"By the way," I interrupted, "have you any idea what makes Evans jitter?"

Fowler shook his head.

"None whatever," he declared, "unless it's just his nature."

"That couldn't be," I said firmly, "or he'd never be a hotel manager. They're the coolest and most collected race in the world."

The Inspector smiled.

"In any case," he observed, "Evans must stay on our list until he explains himself off it—likewise Mrs. Evans who was so conveniently missing this evening. And that," Fowler concluded, "is about all we have for a picture of the case just now. Later, God and Harvey Deal willing, we'll have some more—but in the meanwhile, there's enough to start on right there," he tapped the little note-book. "The next thing, of course, will be to hunt down some more of these witnesses—and that, by the way, is where you come in, Miss Pell."

"Me?"

"Yes—if you will."

"But how?"

"You say," Fowler reminded me, "that you are a stenographer."

"Yes, but . . ."

"And you came to New York for a weekend vacation."

"Yes."

"Well," the Inspector grinned, "you know what post-men do with their holidays."

"I believe they *are* supposed to go walking," I admitted, "but in my case I really—"

"Now, Miss Pell," he interrupted me soothingly, "this is just a little extra work if you want it. If you'd rather not—O.K. But think it over."

"Just what is it," I was still puzzled, "that you want me to do?"

"Simply this," Fowler explained. "The case looks to me like the kind of thing that's got to be solved, if at all, pretty quickly—and right here on the scene of the crime, so to speak. Well, I'm asking the District Attorney's office for thirty-six hours' grace to go about this murder in my own way—because I think, and I only hope the D.A. will believe me, that I can settle the thing within that time. And during those thirty-six hours I'm going to be asking a lot of questions and getting a lot of answers. In other words, Miss Pell, I'm going to interview everybody I can get my hands on who looks as if he might have known anything about Lina Castle. Well—those interviews will be the most important evidence that will come out in this case, and I've got to have someone who will take down every word of them. For my own reasons, I prefer not to have a stenographer from Headquarters, and God knows I don't want one of those underlings from the D.A.'s office for an assistant. So you see, Miss Pell, I'm offering *you* the job—if you want it." Fowler paused for a moment and watched me closely.

I suppose it was plain that I was weakening, for he quickly added the final touch.

"Incidentally, Miss Pell," the Inspector confided, "I'd like your opinion on the evidence we gather."

Well—perhaps I should have refused—perhaps I ought to have pronounced the whole idea absurd—perhaps . . . But anyway I didn't. I was surprised by Fowler's unexpected offer, but I was flattered too, and it didn't take me long to say yes. This was not, I think, too strange on my part, considering my penchant for excitement which has already been admitted.

Once it was agreed that I was to assist Fowler, he gave me my directions briefly. Since it was by this time past midnight, I was not to begin work until morning. Meanwhile, the Inspector said that he would attend to the formal details of the case; make his report to Headquarters, interview the press, and in general get the routine things out of the way. And he would, he declared, wait for Deal and Mrs. Evans to turn up if he had to stay on the job all night!

"There's just one thing about this case that worries me," I observed, as I rose to bid the Inspector good-night.

"And what's that?"

"Simply that my vacation is a pretty short one. I have to be back at my regular job, you know, and I'd hate to have to leave this case just as things were beginning to get exciting."

"When must you be back?" Fowler inquired.

"Monday morning," I said ruefully, "at eight forty-five—sharp."

"Oh, that's all right," he assured me cheerfully, "this is only Friday night, and you remember I've only asked for thirty-six hours' grace. You'll still have Sunday left for your vacation."

"Do you mean," I asked curiously, "that you actually expect to solve this case in—"

The Inspector cut me off abruptly.

"I mean whatever you think I mean, Miss Pell." His smile was cryptic. Then he added rather sweetly, "Goodnight."

6
WE BREAKFAST

Next morning I was eager to begin my work as Inspector Fowler's stenographer—so eager, in fact, that I did not even stop for breakfast before dashing up to the eleventh floor. Whatever remorse I should have suffered, for having involved myself in so serious an affair, was, I confess, quite smothered beneath the excitement and curiosity of the moment. It was not difficult to rationalize myself into thinking that I had really been forced into the case—and, after all, my position as assistant to the Inspector seemed supremely secure.

I was admitted immediately to room 1116, which Fowler was evidently still using as headquarters, and when I entered I found the Inspector engrossed in nothing more professional than his breakfast. He greeted me cheerfully.

"Have a cup of coffee," he said. "This is turning out to be the *damnedest* case!"

I observed that for all his brisk manner, Fowler looked drawn and tired. His rumpled clothes and the many half-burned cigarettes which filled the ashtrays were proof that he had been at work nearly all night.

"What's the matter with the case?" I asked, "and are you sure you can spare the coffee?"

"Everything's wrong about this case," he remarked sweepingly, "and I can spare the coffee because I ordered a whole extra breakfast for you."

"What made you think," I inquired, "that I'd hurry up here this morning without stopping to eat?"

"Well," Fowler handed me a cup with a sweet smile, "I did hope you'd show *some* interest in your new job." As he spoke, the Inspector was uncovering various dishes to reveal the breakfast he had ordered for me.

"Smart man," I said approvingly, "you knew I liked orange juice and dry toast and fried eggs turned over. And I *am* hungry."

"I sort of thought, Miss Pell," Fowler went on, "that all the excitement last night might have kept you from sleeping, but I hope I wasn't right."

"Sorry," I shook my head, "you weren't right. I slept like a log. *You* look tired though," I added sympathetically.

"Well, I should think I would look tired." The Inspector's tone was grieved. "I put in one hell of a night trying to get started on this case."

"You haven't told me yet," I reminded him, "what ails the case."

"Well, the chief trouble," Fowler settled down seriously, "is the fact that I'm having a dickens of a time laying my hands on any of the witnesses."

"What seems to have happened to them?" I inquired.

"Various things." Fowler sighed. "For instance, Mrs. Evans has gone to Washington."

"To Washington?" I echoed in surprise. "I wonder what took her there."

"According to her husband," the Inspector explained, "she was called home because of a sick brother."

I watched Fowler curiously as he said this, wondering whether he were not a bit skeptical of so obvious an excuse as a sick brother, but he appeared to be fairly well convinced by it.

"Evans telephoned," he continued, "just after you had gone downstairs last night. He said that he had just returned to his apartment, and had found a note from his wife explaining that she had been called to her home in Washington."

"But what time was she supposed to have left?" I asked.

"According to Evans, at about seven o'clock yesterday evening."

"It seems very strange," I observed, "that she would have gone off with simply a note for her husband—when he was in the same building all the time."

"It seems darned strange," the Inspector agreed heartily, "but I couldn't get a thing out of Evans last night. He simply said that his wife had tried to get hold of him to say good-bye—and failed to reach him."

"But that's absurd," I protested. "You remember Evans admitted last night that he was on duty downstairs from seven o'clock on."

"I know it," Fowler shook his head, "but the dickens of it is that the telephone girl downstairs checks on his story. She claims that Mrs. Evans tried to call her husband, and that Evans had left his office on some errand or other— and by the time he had returned, Mrs. Evans had already left the hotel."

"Did Evans say what the 'errand' was?" I inquired.

"No," said Fowler shortly.

I wondered why he had not made more of a point of the matter—but since he seemed inclined not to pursue it, I shifted to another question.

"What," I asked, "does it mean, when Evans says his wife left the hotel at seven o'clock? Is there a train leaving for Washington at that hour?"

"There's one at seven-twenty," Fowler informed me. "She could have taken that."

"Which would arrive in Washington," I added, "sometime after midnight. I should think anyone would have preferred to wait for a sleeper."

"I suppose," the Inspector said wearily, "she was in a hurry. The sick brother, you know."

"That's right," I agreed, "I was forgetting him."

"The trouble is," Fowler continued, "that Evans didn't notify me of his wife's departure until after midnight—so I had no chance to check on her arrival there. If I'd known it earlier it would have been simple enough to wire Washington and have a detective meet her train."

"But how about checking up now," I suggested. "You could send a detective to her Washington address and find out—"

The Inspector cut me off with a short laugh.

"The hell of it is," he explained surprisingly, "that I don't know her Washington address."

"Oh, but surely," I began, "Evans can be made to tell you—"

Again an exasperated laugh interrupted me.

"Strange as it may seem, Miss Pell," Fowler said, "Evans claims that he hasn't an idea what that address may be. That's his story—and believe me, he understands the technique of sticking to it!"

Once more I had occasion to wonder that the Inspector passed so lightly over Evans' strange reticence, but I was, after all, in no position to protest his methods.

"And for the moment," he was saying, "we'll have to admit that Mrs. Evans left the hotel at seven o'clock. The doorman, at least, checks on that point."

"Well," I said, "that makes one witness pretty thoroughly missing. What about the others?"

"Harvey Deal hasn't turned up yet," the Inspector informed me, "and I can't find where the devil *he* is."

"Has he been gone all night?" I asked in amazement.

"He has," Fowler sighed, "and his family claim he's at some golf club on Long Island—which might be very enlightening except for the fact that his mother says she can't remember the name of the club."

"Well, why pick on his mother," I protested, laughing, "couldn't someone else in the family give you more information?"

"There isn't any more family," the Inspector explained, "except Deal's little boy. The wife is dead."

"And I take it," I said, "that the old lady is in something of a fog."

"She certainly seems to be," Fowler admitted. "I couldn't even get her on the telephone myself, but she sent me a couple of vague messages by a secretary or something."

"Maybe," I suggested, "the fog is intentional."

"Oh, yes," the Inspector nodded, "she may be holding out on me, but I'm inclined to think not. You see, I found out that she hadn't been told about the murder yet—because whenever Deal goes away he leaves strict orders that no disturbing news shall be told to his mother. Of course, I *could* have insisted on seeing the old lady last night, but that would have meant breaking the news of the murder to her—and, as a matter of fact, I far preferred to have her know nothing about it for the time being."

"You mean," I ventured, "until you've had a chance to see Harvey Deal?"

"More or less." Fowler nodded. "At least I wanted a chance to find out definitely whether or not the Deal family have any real connection with Lina Castle."

"Well—" I asked, as Fowler paused, "have you come to any conclusion?"

"Not exactly," he admitted, "that is, I have no actual proof of the fact just yet—but I have some fairly good ideas on the subject."

The Inspector apparently did not wish to divulge anything further concerning his suspicions, but I naturally assumed from what he had already said, that he believed the Deal family *was* somehow concerned in the fate of Lina Castle. I was frankly curious to know what clues he had discovered which would lead him to this conclusion, so I inquired hopefully if he had found any further evidence in going through Mrs. Castle's possessions.

"I went through that room myself, Miss Pell," Fowler said, "and I have an idea I was just wasting my time. Not one thing turned up that's going to be really useful, unless—" he was consulting his notebook as he spoke—"unless a couple of notions I picked up might turn out to be worth something."

"And what were they?" I demanded eagerly.

"Well, the first thing," Fowler began slowly, "which might or might not mean something, was the fact that practically every darn thing that belonged to Lina Castle was new. Clothes, baggage, everything—and I mean," he explained earnestly, "so *blamed* new that even a masculine eye couldn't miss it. And what's more, I found just one suitcase that looked good and shabby—both outside and in. Now, unless I'm wrong, that means that Lina Castle came to this hotel four days ago with one suitcase full of worn-out clothes—and she was leaving last night with a regular Gloria Swanson trousseau. And the question is, how did she do it?"

"It's not so difficult," I reminded him, "in New York."

"But darned difficult, Miss Pell, unless you have either cash or credit—in New York or any other place. And there's no very good reason for thinking that anyone whose

worldly goods had dwindled down to that one suitcase had
much cash or credit. And I ask you, Miss Pell, how do you
tie that up with all the money Lina Castle must have spent
on those clothes?"

"I don't know," I shook my head as I puzzled over it,
"but I think I *do* see one thing—and that is that somehow,
when Lina Castle came to New York, she must have known
she was going to get some money. Because after all, a girl
who was broke would hardly come to the Almeda."

"That's sense," Fowler agreed. "There are certainly
plenty of cheaper places to stay. She might even," he suggested, "have gotten hold of the money before she landed
in New York."

"Not so likely," I objected, "if she really came from
Paris. After all—no one is going to pass up Paris clothes if
she can help it—and it's plain that Lina Castle was definitely style-minded."

"Sensible again," said the Inspector, "but in either case
the fact remains that Lina Castle suddenly acquired some
money. How in the dickens did she get it?" He squinted
thoughtfully. "She might have inherited it, won it, earned
it, stolen it, found it, forged it or extorted it! Well," he
concluded cheerfully, "what's your guess?"

"None just yet," I admitted, "but give me time."

"The other fact I picked up," Fowler continued, "may
shed some light on the matter of the missing passport. You
remember I mentioned that we couldn't locate the usual
letters and papers among Lina Castle's things. Well—that
fact puzzled me from the beginning, but when I went
through her baggage myself, it gave me an idea. You see,
her things were all very carefully packed—you know what
I mean—things fitted into the suitcases closely," he waved
his hands in an effort to express himself.

"I understand," I nodded.

"Well, here's the funny thing, Miss Pell," he went on. "Right across the end of one of the suitcases there was a big space, as if something had been lifted out *after* the bag was packed—do you see what I mean?"

Again I nodded. "And you think," I suggested, "that perhaps it was a package or box of papers that was so neatly lifted out?"

"Might have been, mightn't it?"

"Certainly," I agreed, "and if that *is* the case, then I suppose we assume that the murderer shot Mrs. Castle—rummaged till he found the papers, then made his getaway."

"I'm afraid it's not *quite* so simple," the Inspector was frowning thoughtfully, "because there's one other fact to be considered, and that is that I found the suitcase locked, and standing, with the other bags, ready to be carried downstairs. Now the keys for all of Mrs. Castle's luggage were put away neatly in her purse—and it hardly seems likely to me that the murderer would have lingered long enough to look for those keys, search through the bags, replace everything and relock the suitcases, then return the keys to Mrs. Castle's purse."

"Then how on earth—?" I began, but Fowler cut me short.

"There isn't a bit of use, Miss Pell," he said wearily, "in asking 'how' anything, at this point. You go on and finish your breakfast, because I'm going to put you to work very soon."

There was an interval of silence while I obediently concentrated on eating, and the Inspector—having finished his own enormous plate of toast—obligingly helped to consume my order.

"By the way," I said presently, "how's the hotel taking all this?"

"The hotel?" Fowler looked blank.

"I mean," I explained, "that the Almeda is such a staid, stuffy place—I should think the sort of people who stay here would be utterly horrified to hear that a murder took place practically under their noses. In fact," I went on, "I can't yet quite realize that there *was* a murder at the Almeda. Violence seems so hopelessly out of place in this Victorian atmosphere."

The Inspector helped himself to another piece of toast.

"Don't let this place fool you, Miss Pell," he was munching reflectively, "just because the lobby is red plush and Manager Evans wears an old-fashioned collar. *I* think the Almeda is sort of a likely place for a murder. Particularly," he added cryptically, "the murder of a woman like Lina Castle."

7
WE BEGIN

Before I had had a chance to ask for an explanation of the Inspector's surprising opinion, the telephone rang.

"That's probably Deal calling," Fowler spoke excitedly, "because his mother promised he'd be in by nine o'clock—and it's just about that time now."

Harvey Deal proved to be as good as his mother's word, for it was he calling, and from the Inspector's remarks I judged that they were arranging for an immediate interview. When Fowler turned away from the telephone he started for the door at once, and motioned abruptly for me to follow him.

"Here's where we begin, Miss Pell," he said. "Are you ready?"

"All ready."

I had seized my notebook and pencil and was hurrying after him. On the way up the fire-escape stairs to the twelfth floor, the Inspector reminded me once more of what I was expected to do.

"Take down," he said hastily, "everything that's said—important or not—and put in your comments as you go along. I mean, if you think anything sounds fishy—make a note of it. Do you get me?"

I nodded, for at the moment I was too breathless with nervousness and running upstairs to speak, and before I had had a chance to recover, we were being admitted to the Deal apartment.

Harvey Deal himself opened the door for us. He greeted the Inspector briefly and eyed me rather uncertainly.

"This is my assistant, Miss Pell," Fowler explained, and motioned for me to enter the room.

Harvey Deal continued, however, to regard me rather curiously as I opened my notebook. He was evidently startled at the idea of having anyone take notes of his statements, but he made no protest to the Inspector. The longer I was to know Deal the more firmly was it to be impressed on me that he was the sort of person who disapproves of a good many things—but who prefers usually to take the line of least resistance rather than to make any disturbance. He was a strikingly handsome man, quite youngish looking in spite of the gray hair at his temples, and I found his quiet, reserved manner decidedly attractive. I observed, however, that although Harvey Deal seemed a rather more sophisticated person than Mr. Evans, the two men had in common a certain air of unmodern reserve. To be sure, there was nothing in Deal's outward appearance to warrant such a view; he seemed simply a well-groomed and polished gentleman. Yet I wondered if perhaps his somewhat formidable manner might not conceal the confusion and uncertainty of a man who never quite faces the realities of the world about him.

My rather elaborate speculations were cut short when I recalled myself to the business of taking notes. Harvey Deal had been listening attentively while the Inspector related briefly the events of the preceding evening, and when the account was finished, Deal made the perfectly conventional response. He expressed dismay that such a dreadful thing as a murder should have happened at the Almeda, declared himself willing to cooperate with the police in every way, etc., etc.

The Inspector, however, appeared to view this attitude with some distrust. Rather brusquely, he waved aside Harvey Deal's expressions of professional concern.

"It will be necessary," Fowler said shortly, "to question a number of people in the hotel."

"Oh, but surely," Deal protested, "you don't think that—" he paused with a deprecating gesture.

"Surely I don't think what?" Fowler's tone was sharp.

"I meant merely that—I trust you are not suspecting any one of our guests," Mr. Deal's manner was as smooth as ever.

"I'm not suspecting any particular persons at the moment, either inside the hotel or out of it—but it's my business to investigate, and naturally I begin with the people who are nearest the scene of the crime."

"Of course, of course," Deal said soothingly, "but you can surely understand that I must protect my patrons from any embarrassment."

"You can probably spare them a good deal of embarrassment," said Fowler, none too pleasantly, "if you choose to answer a few questions yourself."

"But of course, my dear fellow—I'm only too willing."

"Good. You can start by giving me the exact layout of the rooms on this floor."

"Gladly, but I hardly see how that applies."

"Would you see any more clearly, Mr. Deal, if I were to remind you that the murder was committed in room 1117?"

"Oh, quite. I see you want to question the people who would be likely to have heard some commotion at the time of the—ah—trouble. Is that it?"

"Well," the Inspector answered dryly, "it's—something like that. Now I already know, Mr. Deal, that the rooms directly over 1117 are occupied by Mr. and Mrs. Evans, but I want to find out about 1218, next to the fire-escape."

"Room 1218," said Harvey Deal, "is my bedroom. It adjoins this, 1219, which you see is my living-room."

"And—is that all there is of your apartment, Mr. Deal?"

"No, but I fail to see how the arrangements of my family concern you?"

"Sorry, Mr. Deal, but they do concern me—for the moment."

I was wondering, during this conversation, whether the insolent manner of Fowler's questioning was angering Harvey Deal as much as it had me, the evening before. But if he were irritated, Deal kept his patience remarkably well. After only a moment's hesitation he answered Fowler quite civilly.

"My mother, Inspector, occupies the bedroom adjoining the opposite side of this room, and beyond her is another bedroom for my son and his nurse."

"Thank you," said Fowler. He glanced at me and I nodded, signaling that I had taken down this information by hastily sketching the floor-plan of the entire wing above Mrs. Castle's room.

There was a moment of silence before Fowler turned to Deal again and asked, quite casually, another question.

"Will you tell me, please, why you gave orders that Lina Castle was not to be admitted to this hotel?"

"Certainly, Inspector." Harvey Deal gave not the slightest sign of being disconcerted. "I gave the order simply because the woman had been here before, and had caused a great deal of unpleasantness and trouble."

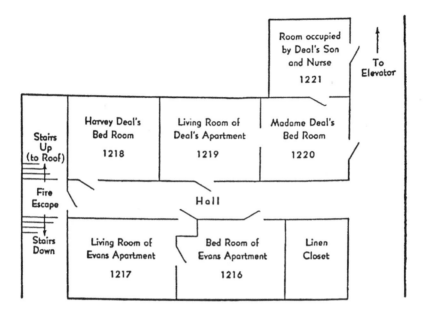

Diagram of Corridor and Rooms
Twelfth Floor, Almeda Hotel

"What sort of trouble?" I recognized the skeptical note in the Inspector's voice.

"Rather a long story, Inspector, but it concerned a small theft, and in the process of investigating the matter it developed that this Mrs. Castle had some highly undesirable—followers. Naturally, it's my business to see that such people are not admitted to the hotel, otherwise one runs the risk of just such things as happened last night."

"I see, Mr. Deal. Then you didn't know that Mrs. Castle had managed to get into the hotel by registering as Miss Rose Lovett?"

"As it happens I did know it, Inspector. Yesterday afternoon I saw her in the lobby. I have an unusually good memory for faces, and I was quite positive that I recognized her. I went to Evans immediately and he told me that he had admitted the woman under this other name. I went straight to her room and asked her, quite plainly, to leave."

Fowler's eyebrows were raised sharply.

"Weren't you, Mr. Deal, rather—overzealous about keeping Mrs. Castle away?" he inquired.

"Perhaps I was," Deal admitted, "but I—well, I might as well be frank about it—it is because of my mother that I am forced to be very strict about who comes here. You see, she owns this hotel, and of course I respect her orders. She is particularly anxious *not* to have persons of Mrs. Castle's type as guests here."

"I see," said Fowler slowly, and from his tone I felt quite certain that he saw more than either Deal or I realized.

"What," the Inspector inquired presently, "can you tell me about Mr. Evans?"

"I can tell a great deal." The answer was prompt. "Evans has been at the Almeda for years—first, I believe as a desk clerk, then as head clerk. And when my mother and I came here to take over the hotel, he was promoted to Manager. He's a thoroughly capable and trustworthy person—quiet, and inclined to mind his own business," this with an emphasis which appeared to be directed at Fowler, "but at the same time he's very keen and alert."

I remember my feeling of surprise at Deal's unexpectedly profuse defense of Mr. Evans. It was the first time that Deal had altered his rather aloof manner to speak of anything or anybody with enthusiasm—and it struck me also that his remarks were somewhat inaccurate. I had difficulty in imagining Evans as either keen or alert. Curiously, I glanced at the Inspector to see how he had taken the surprising speech, and I saw that he was regarding Deal with a disconcerting intensity.

For some moments there was silence, during which Fowler continued to stare fixedly at Harvey Deal. It was evidently his intention simply to wait for Deal's next remark, and it was not long before his method had its effect. I saw that Deal was shifting uncomfortably before that penetrating look, and finally he spoke again—this time a bit defensively.

"Wh-why should you ask me, Inspector," there was more than a hint of uncertainty in Harvey Deal's voice, "about Mr. Evans?"

"Oh, no special reason, Mr. Deal," Fowler's tone was indifferent, "except that Evans happened to be the first person who entered Mrs. Castle's room after the shooting. And," he added thoughtfully, "he entered alone."

It was evident that Deal had not missed the implication.

"Look here, Inspector," he began indignantly, "you can't mean that you suspect Evans of any any—"

"Any what?" Fowler inquired with an air of innocent surprise.

Deal ignored the question.

"If you are any sort of a judge of character, Inspector," he said pompously, "you must have seen from Evans' face that he is a man of unquestionably upright character. His duty as Manager of the Almeda made it necessary for him to take charge of this unfortunate affair before the arrival of the police—but as for casting any suspicion on his actions or his motives, you must see that the idea is absurd."

"I can see this much at least, Mr. Deal," the Inspector's tone was level, "that to clear any man of suspicion because he has an honest face and an unquestionably upright character is simple stupidity. You forget that murders have been committed by some of our best people—and for amazingly high-minded motives."

Apparently Deal could summon no retort to this last observation, for he remained stubbornly silent, and the

subject of Mr. Evans and his character was, for the moment, closed.

Of Mrs. Evans, Harvey Deal had very little to say—although his attitude on this subject was decidedly more
natural and far less aggressive. He admitted, in answer
to the Inspector's questions, that Mrs. Evans had been at
the Almeda for about two years. She had, in fact, been
employed at the hotel as telephone operator until her marriage to Evans a year ago.

"Are Mr. and Mrs. Evans quite—happy?" the Inspector
asked unexpectedly.

"Why, really," Harvey Deal shrugged, "I could hardly
know about that."

"Um-hum," Fowler nodded thoughtfully for a moment—then he produced a second surprise. "Is Mrs. Evans
good looking?" he inquired.

"Yes, she is rather," Deal's answer was convincingly
casual.

The Inspector was evidently satisfied, for when he
spoke again, it was on an entirely different tack.

"If you don't mind, Mr. Deal," he said, "I'll have to
ask you one or two things about last evening. You see,"
he explained rather more pleasantly, "we are having some
trouble establishing the exact time of the shooting, and
it would help me very much if you could clear up a few
points. Now—I don't like to bring your family into this,
but if you could simply tell me who was in the apartment
here at about eight o'clock last night?"

"Well, I couldn't say positively, Inspector. You see I
wasn't in the building at all yesterday after about five in
the afternoon."

"But it would be likely, wouldn't it, that at that hour
your son, and perhaps your mother also, would be in the
apartment?"

"Very likely," Deal admitted. "The boy is put to bed at about that time, and his nurse, of course, would be up here with him. As for my mother—she usually dines in her room when I'm not here."

"In that case, Mr. Deal," said the Inspector, "I'll want to speak to this nurse—and to Madame Deal also. Naturally, I want to get any information I can on what either of them might have heard."

"Certainly, Inspector, I'm sure both of them will be quite willing to tell you anything they can." Deal gave no evidence of being displeased with this idea, but after a moment he added a request. "I *would* like," he said, "to speak to them first myself, if that's all right."

To my surprise, Fowler consented to this.

"You see," Harvey Deal went on to explain, I shouldn't like to have my mother upset by this thing, and I have no idea how much she knows about what happened last night. I was away overnight, you see, and when I came in this morning I had only a word with her before this interview with you."

"I quite understand, Mr. Deal. I'll be downstairs in room 1116 and you can call me whenever it would be convenient for me to see them. Meanwhile, thank you for your information." Fowler rose and held the door for me.

"You're welcome, of course, Inspector, and if I can help further—I'm more than anxious to see this thing straightened out." Deal spoke very sincerely.

I was already out in the hall when, to my surprise I looked around to see Harvey Deal motioning Fowler back into his room. I started to follow, but I heard Deal say something about a word alone, and a nod from the Inspector sent me on my way downstairs by myself.

Whatever it was that Harvey Deal had chosen to tell the Inspector in confidence was not a lengthy matter, for I had scarcely sorted out my notes of the interview upstairs, when Fowler appeared.

"Well," he drew a long breath and reached for a cigarette, "what reactions, Miss Pell?"

"Several," I admitted, "but I don't know whether they're of any use."

"Good! Let's have them. I'll admit I had some ideas myself—"

I consulted my notes.

"First of all," I said, "it struck me that Deal started out by hedging—conventional chagrin and all that sort of thing."

"Undoubtedly," Fowler nodded.

"And then I thought the little story about Mrs. Castle causing trouble here three years ago was—well, a bit too pat."

The Inspector looked doubtful.

"On the contrary, Miss Pell," he objected, "I would have said that the trouble with Deal's story was that it was not nearly pat enough!"

"Well, at least," I observed, "we agree that his statement was *not* convincing. Particularly the part about Deal's going to Mrs. Castle yesterday afternoon and asking her to leave the hotel."

"I grant that all right," Fowler nodded.

"After all," I added, "it would have been a ridiculous time for Mr. Deal to make a scene and order her out, when she was sailing for Europe within a few hours."

"A point, by the way," the Inspector murmured thoughtfully, "which Deal failed to mention."

"I expect there were plenty of points," I said, "that Deal omitted for one reason or another."

"What special reason," Fowler inquired, "would you think prompted him to say that he *did* go to Lina Castle's room yesterday? It might have been simpler—and safer—for Deal to deny that he knew anything about Mrs. Castle's presence in the hotel."

"I can't see," I confessed, "any particular reason for that statement, unless—" I hesitated doubtfully.

"Unless what?"

"Well, unless Deal were trying to clear himself ahead of time. Just in case, you see, that someone were to tell you that he was in Lina Castle's room at five o'clock yesterday afternoon."

"Then you think he was there?"

"Yes, I do."

"And we both think, of course, that Deal had some other reason than the one he gave, for keeping Lina Castle out of the hotel—or trying to."

Again I nodded, but when Fowler asked me what I suspected the real reason might be, I hesitated.

"I have no definite idea," I said, "except for the fact that it seems more likely to have been a personal matter, rather than one of hotel policy."

"Well," the Inspector heaved himself out of his chair with a sigh, "there may be a way of checking on that impression right now."

He went to the telephone, and I heard him ask to speak with the room clerk. A moment later he was inquiring whether Mrs. Lina Castle had ever registered at the Almeda. There was a long pause, then Fowler thanked his informant, and turned back to me.

"The room clerk reports," he announced, "that no Mrs. Castle has ever registered as a guest at this hotel."

8
TWO PASSAGES FOR EUROPE

"Well," I said, when I had heard the Inspector's announcement, "what does that make Harvey Deal?"

"Something of a liar, I guess," Fowler shrugged, "but the more important question is—what does it make us?"

"It makes us," he answered himself soberly, "a couple of pretty good detectives. Our hunch about Deal's story was right—but the trouble is that this new evidence leaves us right back where we started from. We don't really know a thing about Lina Castle yet—and this means that the interview with Deal was a flop."

"Oh, surely," I protested, "we got *something* out of talking to Mr. Deal, even if he did lie about his reason for keeping Mrs. Castle out of the hotel. At least we know now that he had some reason for lying about it."

But Fowler only shook his head gloomily.

"I knew that much before we saw Deal," was his discouraging answer.

"Anyway," I persisted, "we got an impression of Deal himself, which certainly helps some."

This time the Inspector nodded his agreement.

"You're right about that, Miss Pell," he admitted. "Deal's a pretty peculiar person, and the better we gauge his personality, the better we're going to get along on this case."

"You haven't told me," I reminded him, "just what you thought of him."

"I thought a good many things, Miss Pell," the Inspector said slowly, "and probably most of them are wrong. But one thing in particular struck me—and that was the way Harvey Deal brought his mother into the conversation. You remember, he said that *she* was the one who was particular about the type of guests here. Well, after all, it's sort of strange that Deal should be worrying about his mother's opinion of the guests' morals."

"But don't forget," I pointed out, "that Madam Deal is the one who owns the hotel."

"I don't forget it," Fowler said, "but it still looks funny to me that Deal should have mentioned his mother in the way he did."

"You mean that you think there might have been some trouble between the old lady and Lina Castle?" I asked.

"I don't know what I think yet," said the Inspector abruptly, "except that I have one hunch—that Deal was, for some reason, afraid to have Mrs. Castle in this hotel, and that the reason had *something* to do with his mother!"

There was a silence as I meditated on this last statement, and the Inspector puffed on his cigarette. Finally he spoke again.

"Anyhow," he said, "two things were certainly clear about Deal. First that he was damn queer about Evans, and second he was mighty anxious to get it over to me that he was *not in the hotel* last night at eight o'clock!"

"Yes," I agreed, "he certainly emphasized his alibi—and you didn't pick him up on it either. I thought you were going to question the fact that he went to his golf club on such a rainy day."

"No use," said Fowler gloomily, "not now, anyway."

And once more we lapsed into silence.

"Was it," I asked presently, with some hesitation, "something important Mr. Deal spoke to you about—after I left?"

"Oh, no, Deal simply called me back to speak about you."

"Me!"

"Why, yes. What's the idea of jumping half out of your chair?" Fowler looked at me with amusement.

"Well, I—I just wondered what he could possibly have told you about me."

"But he didn't tell me anything—he simply asked me something, and that was that you shouldn't be admitted when I talk to the old lady—you know the line—your taking notes would make her nervous and so on. That's all." Fowler smiled again at my expression of relief.

"Well, what did you say about it?" I inquired.

"Oh, I said it would be all right, I'll just put you in the next room, and you can take your notes there—" Fowler's words were interrupted at this point by an impatient knocking at the door.

In answer to the Inspector's "come in," a very young, very enthusiastic lad burst into the room and began at once to address the Inspector. It was evident that the boy was fairly bursting with excitement, and it was with difficulty that Fowler interrupted long enough to introduce him to me as his assistant, Tommy. The youngster paused only for a hasty nod in my direction, then proceeded with his eager account.

"Boy, oh boy, Chief," he exploded, "listen to this! I've got some real dope—"

"Where from?" the Inspector inquired, "the Steamship Office?"

"Yes, *sir*," Tommy nodded violently, "I got the report you sent me for, and—"

"Let's see it," Fowler's tone was dampeningly unenthusiastic.

"Here it is, Chief, but you won't find out much from *that*—only that Mrs. Castle's ticket was bought three days ago and paid for in cash—but, gosh, I've got some other dope!"

Fowler scanned the report rapidly, and almost immediately he tossed it aside.

"No good," he said briefly, then turned back to the boy, who waited breathlessly to tell his story.

"All right, spill it," he said abruptly.

"Well, when I got this report and saw it wasn't any good, I remembered what you told me about getting more news than I was sent for, and I thought maybe I could get some kind of story out of whoever sold the ticket to Mrs. Castle. You know—did she look worried, or something like that. So I went out to the office and asked questions for awhile, and finally a man says yes, he remembers selling that ticket a few days ago. And the reason he remembers is because the lady didn't buy it herself—a man came in and got it for her. Didn't give his name, just said reserve it for Mrs. Lina Castle.

"Well, of course I asked what was this man like—and the clerk says he was good looking, tall and he remembers he was carrying a new looking pigskin billfold. He said he can't exactly describe the man's face but thinks he'd know him again for sure."

This enthusiastic recital was halted for a moment as the young sleuth paused for breath and to look hopefully for some sign of approval. Fowler, evidently not much interested in the developments so far, merely nodded his encouragement.

"When I saw the clerk couldn't tell me any more, I got to thinking maybe this Mrs. Castle was going to travel *with* somebody, and then I thought well, if she was—then probably the other party wouldn't have sailed last night if they found out at the last minute that Mrs. Castle had been shot. So I asked a lot more questions, and finally I got to see the list of canceled reservations for last night's sailing. Well, there was only *one* name—"

The young man paused dramatically as he saw a look of interest dawn on the Inspector's face. It must have been a moment of triumph for him when his hard-boiled chief urged him on.

"What name was it?" the Inspector's voice was eager.

"It was Harvey Deal!"

A low whistle from Fowler indicated his amazement.

"So that's what he was up to," he said slowly, "well, I'll be . . ." Then abruptly he turned back to the young man.

"Wait a minute," Fowler said, "how could Deal have canceled his sailing last night if—"

"But he didn't, Chief, I was just getting to that. He canceled it yesterday afternoon. You see, I talked to the guy that took the order—and he said Deal phoned about three o'clock."

Three o'clock! Fowler and I looked at each other, remembering that Harvey Deal had told us that it was not until five o'clock that he had discovered Lina Castle's presence in the hotel.

"What reason did he give for canceling the trip?" the Inspector asked.

"Well, the funny part is that Deal didn't buy his own ticket either, and he said on the phone that his secretary had ordered it for him, and that she'd gotten the wrong date. So he wanted it canceled."

"His secretary?" Fowler asked sharply, "what about that? Did you find out about that order?"

"No, sir. I tried, but none of the clerks who were there today remembered making the sale. But they said one of the men was home sick—and they thought he was probably the one. So I got his address, and I can go around there, if you say so, and quiz him about the 'secretary.'"

"Good boy, Tommy," Fowler rewarded his young assistant with an approving nod, "make for that address as quick as you can and get your story."

"Yes, *sir*," the Inspector's praise was received with an almost jaw-breaking grin from Tommy as the boy hurried on his way again.

When he had gone, we remained in silence for some moments. I could see that the Inspector was puzzled and excited by this latest development, and I waited eagerly for his comments on the situation. Personally, I had been completely taken by surprise by the obvious implication of Tommy's report. Through Fowler's suspicions and my own, I had been prepared for the fact that Harvey Deal had had some part in the fortunes of Lina Castle—but I certainly had *not* expected to find him involved to any such degree as this. Indeed, I found it utterly impossible to imagine the dignified Mr. Deal planning a runaway trip to Europe with a red-headed woman. Or any other woman, for that matter.

"So," the Inspector said at last, "that was the way it was. It looks as if our friend Deal had been planning himself a holiday with Lina Castle, doesn't it?"

"It does," I admitted.

"But somehow," Fowler proceeded thoughtfully, "it *doesn't* seem quite likely, does it?"

"It does not." This time I agreed more heartily. "Mr. Deal certainly doesn't look like the type who—"

"Now, Miss Pell," the Inspector interrupted me reprovingly, "you're making the same old mistake again. I've warned you not to be taken in by the respectable atmosphere around this place. Just because Deal looks like a back-number in morals doesn't mean that he isn't perfectly capable of going off on a bat. It means, if anything, that he's just the type who *would* do it."

"Well," I said meekly, "what's *your* reason for thinking that the story doesn't sound likely?"

"My reason," he said earnestly, "is simply that the details of the story don't make sense. Why, for instance, should Deal have given that order to keep Lina Castle out, and why should he have given up his reservation on the boat at three o'clock yesterday afternoon?"

"And how," I added, "did all that mix-up about his secretary making the reservation for him come about?"

"How indeed, Miss Pell?" Fowler sighed as he spoke, but I noticed that the weary discouragement, which he had shown before Tommy's visit, had vanished.

"By the way," I asked presently, "what do you make of the mysterious man who bought Lina Castle's passage to Europe three days ago?"

"I make just this much," Fowler said, "I'm going to take the first chance I get to see whether Harvey Deal carries a new pigskin billfold! And," he added, as the telephone rang, "it looks as if I were going to have that chance right now."

It was Harvey Deal calling, but this time it was to inform the Inspector that Madam Deal was in her apartment and ready for an interview. And once more I gathered up my notebook and pencil to hurry after Fowler to the twelfth floor.

Again it was Deal himself who admitted us to the apartment, but this time we did not enter the living-room. Instead, we went around the corner of the hall to the door of 1221.

"This, you may recall," Deal explained as we entered, "is the room shared by my son and his nurse."

As he spoke, I was conscious that a subtle change seemed to have come over Harvey Deal since our earlier interview. His manner was still smoothly reserved—but there was a new expression which somehow conveyed itself through a certain added alertness in his eyes. The calm poise, which had seemed so natural to him a few minutes ago, appeared now to be maintained by a deliberate effort of suppression. I wondered what had happened, in that brief interval, to bring that faint suggestion of fear to Harvey Deal's face.

"This," Deal gestured toward a closed door, "leads into my mother's bedroom." At this he glanced expectantly towards me, and I quickly took my place by one of the windows, so that I should be well out of Madam Deal's sight when her door was opened.

Without another word, Deal led the Inspector into the adjoining bedroom, and a moment later I heard him say quietly, "Mother, here is Mr. Fowler whom I spoke to you about. He wants to ask you one or two things about last evening, you know."

The Inspector had followed Deal into the room, and I barely heard his murmured acknowledgment of the introduction. From Madam Deal I heard nothing at all, and in the long moment of silence which followed, I found myself eagerly leaning forward to catch her first words. I could imagine her, haughtily looking over this intruder, deciding how she would treat him. Out of the long quiet her voice finally came, so clear and firm that I had no difficulty in hearing each word—slowly and elegantly pronounced.

"Yes, Harvey," she said, "I remember quite well about Mr. Fowler. I believe you told me he wished to know what I might have heard last evening?"

"That's what I would like very much to know, Madam Deal." Fowler spoke more courteously than I had heard him before. "It's very good of you to see me this morning—and I'll try to be quite brief."

"I shall be glad to talk to you, Mr. Fowler, and I think perhaps it would be best if we were alone— Please, Harvey, would you mind?

I was surprised indeed to hear Mr. Deal so ordered out of the room, and I was even more amazed when the sound of the door closing indicated that he had gone, quite like an obedient child, who leaves his elders to talk of serious matters. But I had only a moment to reflect on this, for the Inspector had begun his questioning, and I was kept busy with my notes.

Scarcely had Fowler spoken, however, when that cool, firm voice interrupted him.

"Please, Mr. Fowler, will you tell me first just what happened last night downstairs? You see, my son is quite determined to treat me as a very old lady—which is, by the way, precisely what I am—and as a result of this I am seldom informed accurately of anything—unpleasant. And in this case I am anxious to know exactly what occurred."

It took Fowler only a few minutes to sketch the circumstances of the murder, and again I pictured the expression of the old lady, as she must be listening to the gruesome story. It was perfectly evident that she was following him closely, for several times she interrupted with a question about some detail. When he had finished his account Madam Deal said nothing for a moment, then quite plainly I heard her sigh.

"So you wish me to tell you what I know about this, Mr. Fowler?" she asked quietly.

"If you will be so good."

"I am so sorry, Mr. Fowler," she said gently, "that I know nothing whatever about it."

"But Mr. Deal has told me," the Inspector answered, "that you were here in your apartment last night between seven o'clock and nine, and it would be a great help to me if you could recall whether, in those hours, you heard anything at all unusual."

"At the moment I recall nothing special—no commotion of any sort—but perhaps you mean voices or footsteps—something of that sort?"

"Exactly," Fowler's voice sounded eager; "if you don't mind, Madam Deal, I'd like to know where, in the apartment, you were during that time."

"I had my dinner here in my room at about seven o'clock," she replied slowly, "and, let me see, I stayed here quite steadily from then on, although I recall going once or twice into the nursery to speak to my grandson."

"Then you didn't go into the living-room or into Mr. Deal's bedroom at any time?"

"No, I'm quite sure of that. You see, my son was not here, and when I am alone I always stay in my own room, to be near Wally if he should need anything."

"Wally is Mr. Deal's son?" Fowler inquired.

"Yes."

"But I thought his nurse was with him."

"So she is, Mr. Fowler, but Wally is put to bed about half-past seven, and after he is asleep Miss Ellen, the nurse, likes to go out for a bit of air, and then I must be here to stay with the boy."

"I see. Then Miss Ellen went out last night?"

"Yes, after Wally was in bed she asked if she might take a short walk, and I sent her along."

"That must have been sometime after seven-thirty then?"

"Yes, shortly after, I should say."

"And do you happen to remember how long Miss Ellen was gone?"

"Perhaps half an hour or more. You see, she likes to go up to the roof—it's more pleasant than walking in the crowded streets."

"And are you quite certain that she went to the roof last night?"

"No, as a matter of fact I merely assume that she did. Miss Ellen did not speak to me after she returned—except to call 'good-night' from her room."

There was a pause before the Inspector's next question.

"How long has Miss Ellen been with you?" he inquired casually.

"More than six years," came the prompt reply. "We are quite devoted to Miss Ellen, and she adores Wally." Madam Deal's emphasis implied pointedly that Fowler was wasting his time on such a question.

Evidently Fowler was willing to take the hint, for he switched the subject quickly.

"Do you happen to remember," he asked, "hearing any unusual sounds from the Evans' apartment across the hall?"

"As a matter of fact, I do," the old lady's voice was deliberate, "although what I heard is probably of no concern to you—as it happened not in the evening but in the late afternoon—between five-thirty and six, I should say. Someone came to the door of the Evans' apartment and knocked—several times."

"Was that all you heard?" the Inspector's voice sounded somewhat disappointed.

"That was all," Madam Deal admitted, "but I mentioned it because the person seemed unusually persistent. When there was no answer from the apartment, the caller—whoever it was—went off down the hall, but in a very few minutes returned to knock again—and again. I noticed all this particularly because I was resting at the time, and the continual knocking disturbed me."

"I wonder," this time Fowler's tone indicated that he was beginning to be interested, "whether this person ever succeeded in getting into the apartment?"

"I can tell you that they did." The old lady's answer was surprisingly positive. "After the third and last series of knocks, I distinctly heard the apartment door open and close."

"Then someone finally let the person in?" the Inspector inquired.

"Possibly—but I should be inclined to say not. It seemed to me that the caller simply walked in. There was no sound of voices, you see."

"M'mm, I do see," Fowler observed, "and I wonder how long the visit lasted."

"That," said Madam Deal, "I cannot say. The opening and closing of the door was the last thing I remember noticing before I dozed off—and when I wakened it was my dinner time."

"Do you recall the exact time when you wakened?" the Inspector asked.

"As it happens, yes. I woke with a start—and it seemed to me that I had slept very soundly. For a moment I thought I might have overslept my dinner hour, but when I looked at my watch I saw that it was only quarter of seven."

"By the way, Madam Deal," Fowler's tone was casual, "where was Miss Ellen at the time you heard the knocking at the Evans' door?"

"She was not here." For the first time the old lady spoke sharply. "Why?"

"No particular reason," the Inspector said quickly, "only that I wondered if she heard the knocking also."

"She couldn't have heard it," Madam Deal explained more amiably, "because she was up on the roof at the time. Wally has an early supper, you see, and then he goes up with Miss Ellen to play until his bedtime. And it is during that time, while the apartment is quiet, that I have my nap."

"One more question," Fowler said. "Were you here all during the evening?"

"In this room," the old lady answered firmly.

"And you heard nothing more after you woke up?"

"Nothing that I noticed as being in any way unusual. Miss Ellen and I had our dinner brought up at seven— then she went for her walk, as I have told you, after Wally was in bed. I read until about ten o'clock, when someone telephoned from downstairs to ask if my son were here."

"Quite so. That was one of my men who called, and we were very anxious to locate Mr. Deal—in regard, of course, to the—er, accident."

"Naturally," Madam Deal agreed, "it was unfortunate that he wasn't here to help you last night. As a matter of fact, I was quite surprised when he telephoned from his club, just after dinner, that he would not be back until morning. Harvey seldom stays away from the hotel overnight. I could have sent for him, had I known how important the matter was, but your—messenger failed to inform me of what had happened."

"Then you knew nothing of the murder until this morning?" Fowler asked.

"The first I heard of it, Mr. Fowler, was when Harvey himself spoke to me—after your talk with him. You remember I told you that my son regards me as a fragile old lady, and he always leaves instructions that I am not to be told anything disturbing in his absence."

I observed with amusement the resigned note in Madam Deal's voice, but I felt quite sure that though she might pose as being in sheltered innocence, nothing much actually escaped her sharp notice.

"So you see, Mr. Fowler," the old lady's voice continued placidly, "I can't give you very much help in this case. I should like to tell you more if I could. Naturally I am distressed that such a thing as this murder should have happened in the hotel—but I fear that I have no very definite light to shed."

I wondered whether Fowler were going to accept this dismissal and end the conversation, but apparently he had no intention of doing so.

"On the contrary," he said quite briskly, "you have told me some things I very much wanted to know—and with your permission I should like to ask one or two more questions."

There was a brief pause, and again I plainly heard a long sigh from Madam Deal.

"Certainly, Mr. Fowler," she spoke more quietly than before, "ask whatever you like."

"First," the Inspector said, "I wonder if you could tell me why Mrs. Castle was not allowed in this hotel?"

"That, Mr. Fowler, is my son's business, not mine nor yours!" Madam Deal's voice was suddenly angry.

"Forgive me, but I shall have to insist that it *is,* at the moment, very decidedly my business. You forget that it is necessary for me to find out all I can about Mrs. Castle— and it's a matter of great importance to know why she was excluded from the Almeda, and why, knowing that she was not to be admitted, she took the pains to force her way in under an assumed name!"

The Inspector's tone was every bit as firm as the old lady's had been, and I was not surprised when, after a moment of silence, she spoke in more gentle, persuasive tone.

"Well, after all, Mr. Fowler, there is no reason why I shouldn't tell you why we thought it best not to have her here. You see, my son and I are Washington people, and when we acquired this hotel, a few years ago, we naturally brought with us a rather large clientele of our friends. This Mrs. Castle was involved in a most unpleasant affair two or three years ago, and was perfectly well known to all these Washington people. Obviously it was unwise to offend our guests by allowing her to come here to the hotel. That's all—it's quite simple, after all, isn't it?" she spoke, pleasantly and clearly.

"Again forgive me, Madam Deal," Fowler's voice was equally pleasant, "but I'm afraid it's not quite as simple as that. For one thing—Mr. Deal told me quite a different version this morning."

I would have given much, at that moment, to see the old lady's expression as the Inspector made this calm statement, but if she was upset by it, her voice gave no sign of the fact.

"I'm sorry, Mr. Fowler," her tone was as smooth as ever, "if my son and I were guilty of mentioning different details of the story. There happen to have been a good many things about Mrs. Castle which made her undesirable."

"Including the fact," Fowler persisted, "that she was here as a guest several years ago—and became involved in some theft or other?"

"Quite possibly, Mr. Fowler. Such a thing could readily have happened—and I not know a thing about it. I have mentioned twice to you that my son insists on keeping from me . . ."

"I quite understand," the Inspector's manner was becoming noticeably impatient. Evidently he had tired of exchanging elaborately polite remarks with the old lady, for his next question was snapped out with a suddenness which almost made me jump.

"Did you happen to know," he demanded, "that your son was planning to sail for Europe last night on the same boat with Lina Castle—or was that one of the details that he chose to keep from you?"

It was evident, even to me in the next room, that this thrust was too much for Madam Deal. In the silence which followed Fowler's abrupt question the only sound from the old lady was a single, low exclamation of despair.

"I thought so," the Inspector observed after a moment, "I thought you wouldn't like to hear that." Then his tone softened a little as he continued, "Well, I'm sorry—but I had to ask you. I won't trouble you any longer now, and thank you."

Quickly Fowler passed through the room where I sat, motioning for me to follow him, and as we both went out into the hall we heard once more, from Madam Deal, that low-breathed exclamation of dismay.

9
EVANS TELLS A STORY—
AND STICKS TO IT

"Well," I demanded eagerly, when we had returned to the floor below, "what was the old lady like?"

The Inspector tapped a cigarette and frowned thoughtfully.

"Like nothing I've seen for a long time, Miss Pell." He shook his head.

"She sounded," I ventured, "very much in the 'grand manner.'"

"And she looked it, too," Fowler said. "She's a regular old-time dowager. Piles of white hair, black silk dress, plenty of jewelry—and an eye like a hawk!"

"No wonder," I observed, "that Harvey Deal worries about what 'mother' will think."

"You're right," the Inspector nodded emphatically, "the old girl is about six times as smart as son Harvey—and as cagy as they make 'em."

"It's too had," I smiled, "that Mr. Deal can't absorb more of his mother's technique. It might make him a more convincing liar."

"Then I take it, Miss Pell, that you thought the old lady was giving us the run-around?"

"Why, yes," I looked up in surprise, "didn't you?"

"Undoubtedly," the Inspector shrugged, "she was lying part of the time. But, at that, I'd trust her a whole lot further than I would her son."

"On what grounds?" I asked curiously.

"Well, chiefly," Fowler explained, "because she's so much more clear-headed. She certainly doesn't stick to the truth altogether—but when she makes up her mind to fib, you can be pretty sure it's for a good reason. And, of course, a well-motivated lie—provided you can detect it—is by way of being a swell clue."

I was beginning to see the Inspector's point.

"And I suppose," I added, "that Harvey Deal gives just the opposite impression."

"Exactly," he agreed. "Deal struck me as very much the sort of witness who begins to lie the minute he gets scared, or cornered—or just plain muddled."

"All of which," I commented, "he seemed to be a good part of the time."

I was exceedingly anxious to hear Fowler's reactions to Madam Deal's actual testimony, but our discussion was interrupted by two policemen who arrived simultaneously with reports for the Inspector.

One of the men had brought a bundle of the morning newspapers, and Fowler scanned these hastily while the rest of us waited.

"Good," he murmured presently, "they put this story way back with the small-time items. That means the District Attorney's office'll leave it alone for a while. They never get further than the first page for news."

"Sorry, Chief," it was Officer Morty who stepped forward with a grin, "but the D.A.'s after you already."

"What do you mean?"

"They sent word from Headquarters," Morty explained, "to give you this." He produced an envelope and handed it over. "It's from the D.A.'s office," he added apologetically.

"Oh, Lord," the Inspector groaned, "I suppose they want to 'confer.' Well—I've still got half of my thirty-six hours of grace left—and believe me I'm going to use them."

"Yes, sir," Morty's grin widened, "but what am I going to tell 'em? They want an answer at Headquarters."

"Have them telephone the office," Fowler directed, "and say that I've got the situation here well in hand. That I'm not ready to make any arrests yet—but I've got my eye on the right people. And you can say that if I don't get the answers by tomorrow morning, the D.A. can send all his bloodhounds up here—and that means they'll have handcuffs on every guest in the damn hotel. And now," the Inspector took a long breath and looked somewhat more pleasant, "have you two got any more cheerful news?"

"Mine ain't so very good, Chief," the other officer announced, "but you said there'd be another statement for the press this morning, and the boys are waiting downstairs now."

"O.K.," the Inspector nodded, "I'll be down in fifteen minutes."

"And I've got a report," the officer continued, "from the flower store about that box that was found in the lady's room."

"Good," Fowler looked interested. "How did you make out?"

"Not so bad. I talked to the clerk that made the sale—and he says he remembers it because a good-looking young lady bought the flowers, and she wanted some kind of special roses."

"Young lady, eh?" the Inspector's eyebrows went up. "Did you get any details?"

"Not much, only that she was kinda small, and wearing some sort of a green coat. That's about all the clerk remembered."

"H'mm," Fowler considered a moment, "I wonder if by any chance that woman might have been Lina Castle herself?"

The officer shook his head positively.

"I know it couldn't, Chief," he said, "because I remember now that the clerk said she had dark hair."

"Well," Fowler shrugged indifferently, "that's out then."

He did not even glance in my direction, but I wondered if he recalled that when, the evening before, he had accused me of buying those flowers, his description which was supposed to incriminate me tallied exactly with the true report which the officer had just given. It was certainly an odd coincidence. Even, I felt, a bit uncomfortably odd. But Fowler's next question and the answer which followed, put me rather more at ease.

"When," he inquired of the officer, "were the flowers bought?"

"Day before yesterday, in the afternoon."

"All right, Joe," Fowler dismissed him, "you go and tell the press boys I'll be there in a minute—and then I want you to get up to the twelfth floor and get hold of the nursemaid who takes care of Deal's kid. You'll find her in room 1221, and if she's not there, wait in the hall until she comes back. Then bring her to me."

"O.K., Chief." Joe started for the door.

"And wait a minute," the Inspector added, "don't bother the old lady upstairs—just hang around until you get a glimpse of the nurse. And *don't* give the girl a chance to talk to anyone before you bring her here."

When Joe was once more on his way, Fowler turned back to Officer Morty who was evidently waiting with more news.

"What have you got, Morty?" he inquired. "Not any more letters from the D.A. I hope."

"No, sir, I only wanted to ask what I ought to do about that Hulda you sent me after."

"Hulda?" Fowler looked blank.

"She was the maid," Morty explained, "that took care of Mrs. Castle's room. And you told me to find her."

"Oh, yes," the Inspector appeared to be enlightened, "where is she?"

"That's just the trouble, Chief," Morty announced in a grieved tone. "I can't find out where the *hell* she is. One of the other maids says Hulda was fired last night—but the housekeeper says she doesn't know anything about it. In fact," Morty added philosophically, "it looks to me like nobody around this hotel knows anything about anything!"

Fowler smiled sympathetically.

"It's beginning to look that way to me too, Morty," he agreed, "but let's get on with this business about Hulda. What makes the other maid think she's been fired?"

"Well, the girl says Hulda told her last night she'd lost her job."

"Did she say why?"

"Nope. She just came down to the lockers and took all her things and beat it. Said she'd worked in this place for twelve years, and now she'd got the sack. And that," Morty concluded, "is all *I* can find out from the Swedes except that Hulda hasn't showed up for work this morning—and she hasn't sent word about being sick or anything. The housekeeper says she don't know what to make of the whole thing."

"Did you get Hulda's home address?" the Inspector inquired hopefully.

"Yep."

"Then there's no use wasting any more time here. Beat it around to where she lives and find out what it's all about. If the girl seems to know anything, bring her here," Fowler directed, "and on your way, stop at Headquarters and tell them to wire the Washington Detective Bureau to find out whether they have any record of Mrs. Lina Castle in that city."

"Was she from Washington?" Morty looked surprised. "I thought we found out she lived in Paris, France?"

"Unless somebody's a liar," the Inspector explained briefly, "she was in Washington a couple of years ago—and while she was there she got mixed up in some kind of a scandal. And listen, Morty, while you're about it, get the Detective Bureau to check on the Deal family. It seems they used to live in Washington too."

"What I mean, Chief," Morty grinned, "this case is a regular Washington Merry-go-Round, ain't it?"

"You haven't been reading books, have you, Morty?" Fowler asked reproachfully.

"Uh-uh," Morty shook his head cheerfully as he started toward the door, "I saw the movie."

A moment later Fowler turned to me with the newspapers.

"Take a look at the stories, Miss Pell," he said, "while I go down and feed the boys some more pap for the afternoon editions. And by the way," he added, over his shoulder, "I'm sending Evans up—and if either he or Miss Ellen get here tell them to wait. I'll be right back."

The brief newspaper accounts of the murder stories proved to be nothing more than a collection of the more usual phrases, "No motive for the shooting has as yet been discovered, but the police are investigating every possible angle of evidence obtained from hotel employees," etc. To my relief, and somewhat to my surprise, I observed that Fowler had kept from the press all the names so far involved in the story. There was no mention of Mrs. Castle's assumed name of Rose Lovett, nor was anything said about my name or Evans' or Deal's.

I was, of course, thankful not to be mentioned in connection with the matter, but I confess I wondered why Fowler had chosen to be quite so secretive on all the details of the case. The Medical Examiner was quoted as stating that Mrs. Castle had been shot at close range with a .32 revolver; that her assailant had been facing her; that the bullet had penetrated the heart, and that death had evidently been instantaneous. The account closed with the fact that no weapon had as yet been found.

Scarcely had I finished glancing through the articles when Fowler returned, and almost immediately after him came Evans, who seemed somewhat more composed than he had been the evening before.

For a few minutes the two men discussed the case in general, Evans expressing the usual hope that something definite would develop soon,—then Fowler broke in quite casually with the question I knew he had been waiting to ask.

"I understand, Evans," he said, "that you didn't know before you telephoned me last night, that your wife had gone to Washington?"

"No, I didn't."

There was a brief pause, but Evans offered no further comment.

"Just when was it you discovered that she had gone?" Fowler inquired.

"About an hour after I left you here. You remember I tried to reach her by telephone at your direction, and got no answer—but I supposed that she had gone out on some errand or other—or else that she was downstairs in the lobby. So when I left you I returned to my office to finish up one or two things, and then I went up to our apartment, fully expecting to find my wife there."

"And instead you found that she had left for Washington?"

"Yes, there was a note on my desk from Mrs. Evans saying that she was going unexpectedly—that she had tried to reach me downstairs and had been told that I was not in my office at the time, and that she had therefore had to go without saying good-bye to me."

Evans spoke in a matter of fact tone—but Fowler appeared to find his statement rather surprising.

"Wasn't it unusual," he asked, "for Mrs. Evans to go off quite so suddenly?"

"Why, no," Evans still spoke calmly, "I believe I mentioned to you, Inspector, that my wife's family lives in Washington—and that her young brother is seriously ill. The note which Mrs. Evans left for me explained that she had received a telegram saying that the boy was worse. Under the circumstances, I should say that it was quite natural for her to leave suddenly."

"You say," Fowler repeated slowly, "that the telegram informed Mrs. Evans that her brother was *worse?*"

"Yes."

"Then I take it that the boy has been ill for some time?"

"Yes."

"And you, of course, knew this?"

"Why—yes, of course I did," there was a barely perceptible hesitation in Evans' answer.

"What," the Inspector's tone indicated casual interest, "is the matter with Mrs. Evans' brother?"

If Fowler had hoped to catch his witness off his guard by this question, he was doomed to disappointment, for Evans' answer was delivered promptly and naturally.

"Infantile paralysis," he said, "and the infection has settled in the brain."

But still the Inspector was not through with experimenting.

"In other words," he spoke deliberately, "your wife's sudden departure last night had nothing whatever to do with the murder?"

"Why, no—nothing whatever."

Again Evans' answer was given so simply and convincingly, that I felt certain Fowler must be impressed by it. And perhaps he was—for with his next question he resumed a less precarious topic.

"I think I recall," he observed, "that you told me that you were on duty downstairs last night from six-thirty until eight-fifteen, when Miss Pell informed you of the disturbance up here. That's so, isn't it?"

"Yes, I did say that, Inspector—I was there."

"And yet you just tell me," Fowler interrupted, "that your wife was unable to reach you a few minutes before seven o'clock—and that when she went through the lobby, on her way to the station, you failed to see her!"

"I told you," Evans' tone was patient and unperturbed, "that my wife could not get in touch with me because I was not in my office at the moment when she called— and later when she came downstairs I had not yet returned."

"Not yet returned from where?" Fowler's question was put sharply.

"From attending to a matter for Mr. Deal. I hardly think it concerns us now."

"I think it does concern us," the Inspector snapped. "Mr. Evans, where were you when you left your office between six-forty-five and seven-thirty?"

"I've made my statement, Inspector, and I shall not say anything further. If you choose to doubt me . . ." Evans shrugged.

"Where were you between six-forty-five and seven-fifteen?" impatiently Fowler repeated his question. "Are you going to answer me or not?"

"I—I'm sorry, Inspector, but I am not."

For a moment the two men faced each other, the Inspector glaring angrily, Evans coolly returning the stare. Then Evans spoke again.

"If you will excuse me now, Inspector, I have some things to attend to—"

"I will *not*," it was Fowler's turn to be defiant, "You'll stay right where you are until we get this thing settled. Either answer my question—or I'll put you under arrest. *Do you hear?*"

"Perfectly," said Evans gently:

To say that this stubbornness on the part of Evans astonished me would be putting it mildly. Remembering his nervous timidity of the evening before, I could scarcely believe that this was the same man who now faced the Inspector so calmly. And I was more than ever confused by the fact that Evans, even in the midst of his sudden aggressiveness, seemed somehow to remain a meek, conscientious, worried little man. I had to admit that he was putting on a good show—yet it seemed to me that there was something a little pathetic in his defiance of the Inspector. While I wondered whether Fowler was sharing this impression, Evans suddenly confused me with an un-expected question.

"You seem to be quite thoroughly involved in this business, Miss Pell," he observed with a smile. "Is it the Inspector's custom to make use of witnesses as stenographers?"

Not having the vaguest notion what to reply, I looked to Fowler for a cue—but he had apparently failed to notice the question. Instead he had gone to the telephone, and a moment later he was speaking to the switchboard operator downstairs.

"This is Inspector Fowler talking," he said. "Can you tell me who was on duty as operator last night between six o'clock and eight?"

A pause, then Fowler continued.

"You were? Good. Now listen—I want you to get some-one to take your place for a few minutes, and hurry up here to room 1116. It's important!"

As the Inspector delivered his order, I looked quickly at Evans. Perhaps I imagined it, but I was quite certain that for just one instant I caught a look of fear in his pale blue eyes. But when Fowler turned from the telephone, Evans was regarding him as coolly as ever.

"If you won't talk," the Inspector said angrily, "we'll get someone up here who will. Now sit down and wait!"

"Thank you, Inspector," Evans seated himself in the only comfortable chair, "I *was* rather tired of standing."

We had only a short wait before a very timid knock at the door told us that the telephone operator had arrived. It was evident when the girl entered that she was more than a little frightened by this interview, but Fowler treated her to his most reassuring smile before he began to question her.

"I feel sure that you can help us," he said pleasantly, "if you will just answer one or two little questions, Miss—"

"Donaldson," she supplied, "Myra Donaldson. I—I'll try to help if I can, sir." The girl seemed willing enough, but it was plain that the presence of Evans troubled her, for she kept glancing uneasily in his direction.

Fowler noticed this, of course, and I observed with interest that he twisted his questions about, so that Miss Donaldson could scarcely realize that his actual purpose was to check on the whereabouts of Evans.

"You came on duty at what time last night?" Fowler asked.

"At six o'clock, sir—to stay on until ten."

"Then you were at your switchboard continually between six and a quarter past eight?"

"Yes, sir."

"H'mm," Fowler looked very grave and thoughtful for a moment, "Miss Donaldson—I don't mean to doubt what you say—but you understand that in a case like this it is most important to check the statement of each witness. Now you, for instance, might have forgotten that you left your post for a few moments during that time."

"Oh, no, sir," the girl protested anxiously, "I'm perfectly sure I didn't."

"I see," Fowler's tone was judicious, "but I shall still have to ask whether there is some second person who will check on that statement."

Miss Donaldson made no answer to this, but simply regarded the Inspector, wide-eyed. She certainly presented a picture of absolute honesty as she stood there, and I marveled that Fowler could keep a straight face as he pretended gravely to doubt her testimony.

"I mean, Miss Donaldson," he continued, "that you can prove that you are telling the truth by naming someone who saw you at the switchboard during that time. For instance, did Mr. Evans see you at any time?"

The trick worked like a charm. In relief the girl turned to Evans, who remained silent and apparently unconcerned.

"Why, yes," she exclaimed, "Mr. Evans *was* there. He came down at half-past six, and he knows that I stayed at my place—well, at least until he left to go upstairs."

"And what time was it when he left?" Fowler inquired.

"Well—" the girl looked troubled, "it was before seven o'clock—"

"How much before?" the Inspector asked sternly.

"I don't remember exactly," Miss Donaldson admitted, "but it must have been nearly seven."

"And did Mr. Evans say where he was going when he went upstairs?"

"No, sir."

"You're quite sure about that?" the Inspector frowned.

"Yes, sir, I'm perfectly sure. You see," she went on eagerly, "Mrs. Evans telephoned after he had gone, and I had to tell her I didn't know where he was."

"Did you make any effort to find him when Mrs. Evans called?"

"Oh, yes. You see, she told me it was very important—and she said she was in a hurry, so I had one of the bellboys look for Mr. Evans—but we couldn't find him anywhere."

"Can you tell me what time this was?"

"Only that she called just after Mr. Evans had left."

"I see. Did she, by any chance, say why it was that she wanted to get in touch with Mr. Evans?"

"Well, no, she didn't but," the girl paused uncertainly and looked at Evans.

"But what?" Fowler prompted her.

"I was only going to say that I thought her call might have had something to do with her going away."

"Going away?" Fowler pretended surprise.

"Yes, sir. You see, it was just a few minutes after she called that Mrs. Evans came downstairs with a suitcase, and she told the doorman then that she was going out of town."

For the first time during this interview Evans' expression changed. At Miss Donaldson's last statement he turned to Fowler with a triumphant smile which, needless to say, the Inspector completely ignored.

"Did you mention the telegram and his wife's call to Mr. Evans when he returned from his errand?" Fowler asked.

"I didn't have a chance, sir, because Mr. Evans had just come back to his office when he was called to Miss Lovett's room—I mean Mrs. Castle," she corrected herself, "and then he went upstairs and didn't come down again for more than an hour."

"All right, that will be enough, Miss Donaldson, and thank you," the Inspector said.

The girl looked very much relieved as she was dismissed, and when Evans gallantly opened the door for her, she gave him a beaming smile.

In the silence which followed Miss Donaldson's departure, I found myself wondering what tack the Inspector would try next. Obviously the girl's testimony had not upset Evans' story in any way—it had, in fact, merely emphasized the facts as he had presented them. True—his whereabouts between quarter of seven and quarter past had not yet come to light, but it seemed (to me at any rate), that it was useless to try to force the information from him at this point. If Evans had seemed to waver for a moment when Miss Donaldson had been sent for—he was certainly not wavering now. I felt certain that the renewed confidence with which he now faced the Inspector would make any further questioning futile, particularly in view of the fact that Fowler was plainly becoming too thoroughly exasperated and impatient for real effectiveness.

It was Evans who broke the silence.

"May I go now, Inspector?" he asked quietly.

"H'mph."

Fowler's answer was a sort of a snort, as he turned abruptly away from us to stare out of a window. But a moment later he swung back to address Evans in a level tone.

"You can go—yes," he said, "but you've put yourself in a very dangerous position by refusing to answer my question, and I warn you not to leave the hotel; my men will stop you if you try. That's all." Once more he turned to the window.

The look of triumph on Evans' face had deepened as the Inspector spoke, and he started, without a word, to leave the room. Before he reached the door, however, Fowler halted him with one parting shot.

"By the way, Evans," the detective drawled the question over his shoulder, "I don't suppose you kept that note from your wife that told you she was leaving for Washington?"

It was no use. Evans was ready with *his* parting shot.

"I kept the letter," he said quietly, "and I have it with me now, and, if you like, I will leave it with you." As he spoke, Evans drew from his pocket a large square envelope which he laid, with a gesture that was almost a flourish, on the desk. Then he started once more for the door—and this time there was no further question to halt him.

10
MISS ELLEN KEEPS THE FAITH

A gloomy pause followed Evans' departure. I concentrated discreetly on my notes, meanwhile keeping half an eye on the Inspector as he moved restlessly about the room. Once he went to the desk and glanced at the letter which Evans had left, but it was evidently of no interest, for he replaced it almost at once.

"Oh, hell," I heard him murmur thoughtfully. A moment later he turned to me. "I made a mess of that job, Miss Pell," he said slowly, "and the funny part of it is—I don't quite know what was wrong. It seemed to me that Evans' story was as full of holes as a sieve—but I—I don't know," he shook his head doubtfully.

I was saved from the necessity of venturing an opinion in this direction by the explosive arrival of young Tommy, who had returned, evidently triumphant, from his second quest. Even an impatient frown from his Chief failed to check the youngster's enthusiasm, and after a moment the Inspector relented somewhat.

"All right, Kid," he spoke rather wearily, "let's have your story."

Tommy was more than ready to begin.

"I got hold of that clerk," he said eagerly, "and sure enough he was the one that booked the reservation for Deal's passage. At first he was sort of leery—and said he didn't remember what kind of a person bought the ticket, but I bluffed him along for a while and told him we knew from Deal himself that it was someone claiming to be his secretary—and finally the clerk warms up a little and says yes, he remembers the customer was a young lady.

"Right away I tried to get a description of her—but he began to stall again, saying he didn't want to make any misleading statement—so I tried to think what he'd be most likely to notice about Mrs. Castle,—and I remembered you said she had red hair. Well—I asked the fellow was the lady tall or short—and he couldn't say. Then I tried him on the color of her eyes—and he said he hadn't noticed. Finally I said, 'Well, then I don't suppose you remember what kind of hair she had,'—and sure enough, Chief, his face lights up right away. 'Yes, I do recall that,' he says, 'because it was an unusual color—a very dark red.'

"Well—at that I was pretty sure that the so-called secretary was Mrs. Castle herself—but I went on with some more questions—and when it came to what the lady had been wearing, he said he remembered that she had some kind of a light coat—he called it pale yellow—*and,*" Tommy concluded magnificently, "I figured that just about cinched the fact that my hunch was right!"

Fowler and I exchanged glances. I fancy that he was remembering, as was I, the woolen suit, of a deep cream color, which Lina Castle had been wearing when she was found the night before.

"How about it, Miss Pell," the Inspector asked, "could that coat have been called 'pale yellow'?"

"It undoubtedly could," I admitted.

"Well—" Fowler ruffled his hair reflectively, "I'll be damned! We know that Deal and Lina Castle were both planning to sail on the same boat last night—and now it looks as if Deal went down and bought *her* ticket—and the very next day she made *his* reservation! I just don't get it, that's all."

"And," I reminded him, "don't forget that on the third day Harvey Deal telephoned to cancel his passage!"

"And I'm not forgetting either," the Inspector added, "that Deal's mother took it hard when she heard about that trip to Europe! She may have been lying all the rest of the time—but there's no doubt about the fact that she was thrown off her guard by the news that Deal was planning a vacation with the red-head. Oh, well—" Fowler broke off wearily, "there isn't a bit of use in trying to patch up any theory yet—when we haven't a single key piece." He turned to Tommy again, "Did you get any more information, son?"

"Not much, sir, only that the lady paid cash for the ticket—and that she took the money off a big roll of bills."

"New money?" Fowler inquired sharply.

"Oh, gee! I forgot to ask that," Tommy was obviously crestfallen at having overlooked this point.

"Never mind," the Inspector said, not unkindly, "only remember another time. Now look here, you've been working well—and I want you to do one more thing for me. Go to the Western Union office and trace a wire from Washington, D. C., delivered here last night, a little before seven o'clock, addressed to Mrs. Donald Evans. Find out from what Washington office it was sent—and get me a copy of the message."

"OK, Chief," Tommy bounded off on this latest errand with bis usual eagerness, and nearly collided with a young woman just outside the door.

"Who's there?" Fowler called, as he heard her exclamation and Tommy's apologies.

"It's I, Miss Royce," the girl explained, as she stepped into the room. "I—I was about to knock at the door when the young gentleman came out rather suddenly."

Immediately I recognized her as the woman who had been with young Wally Deal on the roof the afternoon before.

"I believe you sent for me," she said, as Fowler looked perplexed. "I'm Master Wally Deal's nurse."

"Oh—then you're Miss Ellen!" the Inspector exclaimed.

"Yes, sir,—Ellen Royce."

"Good—I've been waiting for a talk with you, Miss Ellen—sit down."

She seated herself primly in the armchair and waited for Fowler to begin. I remember thinking, as I looked at her neat gray dress and demurely folded hands, that Miss Ellen was a perfect picture of the traditionally discreet Victorian "governess." But little did I know . . .

"I understand," Fowler began, "that you have been in Mr. Deal's employ for some time?"

"It was six years in September."

"How old was the boy when you first took charge of him?"

"Wally was just a year old—he is seven now."

"And was Mr. Deal's wife living at the time?"

"No, sir, I think Mrs. Deal died about six months before I came into the family."

"Then I presume that Madam Deal was living with her son?"

"Oh, yes, sir, I believe that she has always made her home with Mr. Deal—even when his wife was alive."

"Hm'm," the Inspector considered a moment, "was the family in Washington, Miss Ellen?"

"Yes, we only moved to New York three years ago when Madam Deal took over this hotel."

"And what was Mr. Deal's business in Washington, Miss Ellen,—was it something concerned with hotels?"

"Well—I don't know that I ought to say this—" she hesitated and looked appealingly at Fowler, "but I suppose our talk is quite confidential?"

"Oh, quite," the Inspector assured her.

"Well—I was going to say that at the time I came to the family, Mr. Deal was not in any business at all—and that fact troubled his mother very much—so when this hotel failed (Madam Deal's husband once owned it, and she had kept part interest in it), she said to me, 'Ellen, there's the very thing for us. I'm going to take over the Almeda and make that boy (meaning Mr. Deal) run it. It will give him something to do—and get him away from Washington'—"

"Get him *away* from Washington?" Fowler repeated sharply.

"Oh, dear," Miss Ellen's expression was wide-eyed dismay, "I shouldn't have said that."

"Why not?" the Inspector succeeded in keeping his tone casual.

"Because Madam Deal always hates to have anything said about the—trouble in Washington."

"Trouble?" Fowler inquired innocently.

"Yes, sir, you see Mr. Deal got mixed up with a woman —and so naturally his mother doesn't like to have the matter talked about."

"Naturally not," the Inspector agreed sympathetically, "especially as I suppose the woman was—rather an unfortunate type?"

"Oh, *most* unfortunate," Miss Ellen exclaimed virtuously, "in fact the whole affair was the talk of Washington!"

"Tch, tch," Fowler shook his head solemnly, "that must have been very trying for Madam Deal."

I wondered how on earth Miss Ellen could be convinced by the Inspector's absurdly "shocked" attitude—for it was all I could do to keep from laughing at his sudden piety—but apparently she saw nothing amiss, for she continued her confidences eagerly.

"No one knows better than *I* do," she proceeded dramatically, "what poor Madam Deal suffered during that scandal! Of course she never really blamed Mr. Deal for it, nor do I, for that type of woman simply *pursues* a man—and often he's quite helpless—but it did seem especially terrible in this case because of poor little Wally!"

"Of course," Fowler echoed sadly, "but still—it was fortunate that Madam Deal succeeded in stopping the affair while the child was still young—that is, I assume that it *was* broken off when Mr. Deal came to New York?"

"Oh, yes, sir, Madam Deal said to me when we first came here, she said, 'Ellen, this whole matter is closed. I have told my son that he must return any letters from this woman unopened—and I've given strict orders that she is *not* to be even admitted to the hotel.' And since then," Miss Ellen concluded, apparently unaware of the stunned glances which Fowler and I exchanged, "Madam Deal doesn't allow anyone to so much as mention the affair—and so you see I'm not at liberty to tell you anything about it—not even the lady's name."

It was difficult for me to keep from exploding with laughter at the sight of Miss Ellen's prim and satisfied expression, when she had just given away the secret she obviously prided herself on having guarded. Even the Inspector's composure seemed to be threatened for a moment, but fortunately he recovered himself to ask another question.

"Am I to understand from that," he began, "that Mr. Deal and this lady were—er—" he paused and coughed delicately, evidently at a loss as to how to express himself without offending the virtuous Miss Ellen.

She saved him the necessity of going further.

"The woman was a mistress," Miss Ellen declared solemnly, "of the worst sort."

Just what a mistress "of the worst sort" might be, I had no idea, and I noticed that the Inspector seemed also to have been startled by Miss Ellen's curious qualification. Indeed, he found it necessary to cough again—this time quite suddenly into his handkerchief. I was relieved when his next question returned the interview to safer ground.

"I am told, Miss Ellen," he said, "that last night at about half-past seven you left the Deal apartment to go for a short walk. Is that correct?"

"Yes, sir. It was just after I had put Wally to bed."

"And you went to the roof?"

"Yes. Madam Deal thought the air would do me good."

"Madam Deal thought so?" Fowler inquired.

"Oh, yes, she suggested that I should go. You see, I have my time off in the afternoons, so I never expect to go out in the evening, except Saturdays, but last night Madam Deal said I looked tired, and I *did* have a little headache, so she really *insisted* that I ought to get a bit of air. She's always *so* kind and thoughtful about things like that," Miss Ellen concluded with enthusiasm.

"She does seem to be a remarkably thoughtful woman," Fowler murmured. "Do you happen to remember how long you stayed away from the apartment, Miss Ellen?"

"Well—it happens that I do remember exactly, because when I came in I found little Wally very much upset—in fact he was in tears. Of course that surprised me—as he always goes right off to sleep—and I said to him, 'Now, Wally, aren't you ashamed—here it is quarter past eight o'clock (and I showed him the time), and you not asleep yet!' So that's how I happen to remember what time it was."

"What was the trouble with the boy?" Fowler inquired sympathetically. "Had something disturbed him?"

"Well, no, sir, it was really nothing at all—only Wally just got some silly idea that his Grandmother had gone out and left him alone—and he simply got frightened, the way children will, you know."

"What made him think that his Grandmother had left?"

"Why, he said that he had called her several times and she didn't answer him—but of course that was just Wally's imagination, because I'm sure Madam Deal wouldn't *dream* of going off and leaving him alone," Miss Ellen spoke with placid conviction.

"No doubt you found Madam Deal in her room when you returned?" Fowler asked.

"Why, I didn't actually *see* her," Miss Ellen admitted, "because the door between her room and the nursery was closed, but I'm sure she was there—because a few minutes later I called 'good-night' to her, and she answered just as usual."

"By the way, Miss Ellen," Fowler's tone was casual, "did you happen to meet anyone in the halls on your way to or from the roof?"

"Yes, sir, I did," the reply was prompt. "As I was starting for the roof I ran into Mr. Evans in the hall, and I said, 'Good evening, Mr. Evans,' but he didn't answer— which was strange because he's usually so pleasant."

"Didn't he say anything at all?" the Inspector asked.

"Nothing at all—but I really don't think he heard me speak. He seemed very much upset."

"What makes you think that, Miss Ellen?"

"Why, the way he was frowning—and the fact that he was in such a hurry."

"Where was he hurrying from?" the Inspector demanded. "His own apartment?"

"Oh, no," Miss Ellen spoke positively, "he was coming from further down the hall—probably from the fire-escape stairs, I should say."

"And he was headed down the hall?"

"Yes, he hurried right past me and around the corner to where the elevator is."

"I see," Fowler nodded thoughtfully. "And did you see anyone else, Miss Ellen?"

"No, sir. When I came down the hall was empty."

"You didn't see Mrs. Evans at any time?"

"Well—I didn't see her just *then*." Miss Ellen's emphasis was unmistakable.

"You mean you did meet her earlier?" Fowler asked quickly.

"Yes, sir. Late yesterday afternoon I met Mrs. Evans in the hall outside our apartment."

"Was she coming out of her rooms, or going in?" the Inspector interrupted.

"She wasn't doing either, sir, I was just coming to that. As a matter of fact," Miss Ellen drew herself up primly, "she was knocking at the door of Mr. Deal's bedroom!"

"Well!" Fowler managed to look properly shocked, "that was surprising, wasn't it?"

"I couldn't say that it was exactly surprising to me," Miss Ellen continued, "it was just about what I would have expected from *her,*—the way she's been acting about Mr. Deal."

"Oh, but surely, Miss Ellen, you must be mistaken," the Inspector spoke solemnly. "Mr. and Mrs. Evans are undoubtedly a devoted couple."

"That's just the very worst part about it," the young woman exclaimed. "Mr. Evans *is* devoted—and Madam Deal says it's absolutely disgraceful the way Mrs. Evans tries to flirt all the time with Mr. Deal! Why, she even makes a fuss over little Wally just to get Mr. Deal to look at her."

"Then Madam Deal has noticed it, too?"

"Indeed she has, and often she's said to me—"

"But you were telling me," Fowler broke into her indignant reminiscence, "about yesterday afternoon, when you saw Mrs. Evans."

"Oh, yes—well, I saw her knock several times—and she got no answer—then she turned around and saw me, and what should she do but ask *me* to take a message to Mr. Deal for her. . . ." Miss Ellen paused dramatically.

"What sort of message?"

I knew it must be difficult for Fowler to conceal his interest in these developments, but he played up admirably to Miss Ellen's naive manner—evidently sensing that any indication of official curiosity on his part might frighten away her confidence.

"Well—Mrs. Evans turned to me," Miss Ellen continued, "and she said, 'Please, tell me where I can find Mr. Deal!' I was surprised to have her even speak to me—as she usually doesn't bother to—but I just told her I had no idea where he was."

"How did Mrs. Evans seem," Fowler asked, "was she at all nervous or excited?"

"Yes, sir, she certainly *was* nervous—and the next thing she said was, 'Miss Ellen—you've *got* to help me find him—there's something I must tell him.' I didn't know what to say to that—so I just answered, 'Well, Mrs. Evans, I'm afraid I can't help you at all—my duty is to take care of Master Wally, and I can't be disturbing Mr. Deal,' and with that I started to walk away, but she caught hold of my arm. 'Please, Miss Ellen,' she said, 'can't you realize how important this is? I've got to warn Mr. Deal about something.'"

"Are you sure she said 'warn'?" the Inspector demanded.

"I'm positive, sir,—that was just her way of making her silly message seem important—and for a minute I almost believed her—then she said, 'You mustn't believe the lies that old woman tells about me—I'm trying to help him, Miss Ellen!'

"Well—that just finished the thing with me, because I won't even *listen* to anyone who speaks that way of a wonderful woman like Madam Deal—so I just said nothing at all and I went on down the hall and left her standing there." Miss Ellen concluded her story with an emphatic nod.

"Did you mention this matter to Madam Deal?" the Inspector asked.

"No, sir," she replied promptly, "I never bother her about unpleasant matters like that—as I'm under strict orders from Mr. Deal not to tell his mother anything which might upset her."

"And did you report the conversation to Mr. Deal?"

"I didn't have a chance last evening, sir, because he wasn't in for dinner, and later Madam Deal told me that he would be away overnight."

"Then you don't know whether Mrs. Evans succeeded in getting her message to him or not?"

"No, sir, I don't." Her manner indicated that she regarded this "message" as a matter of indifference.

"Miss Ellen," Fowler inquired, "do you happen to know the name of the golf club to which Mr. Deal belongs?"

She hesitated a moment, then asked doubtfully, "Do you mean the Green Tree Club on Long Island?"

"Perhaps that's the one," the Inspector answered. "I wondered if Mr. Deal had driven there yesterday afternoon."

"Oh, no, I'm sure he didn't—because that Club closes on the first of November—I've often heard Mr. Deal say that he wished they would keep the course open as long as good weather lasts."

"I see!" Fowler did not quite succeed in concealing his surprise at this last statement, and at his startled exclamation Miss Ellen suddenly looked uneasy.

"I—I think I ought to be going, sir," she said, "I really don't think there's any information I could give—"

"Oh, but you've been very helpful, Miss Ellen,—and now if you could just tell me one or two things. . . ."

In spite of Fowler's soothing tone the young woman looked more troubled than ever.

"Well—" she hesitated doubtfully.

"Just one or two little things," Fowler repeated persuasively, "you see, you may be able to help us find out what happened last night—and you know both Mr. Deal and his mother are very anxious to have this mystery cleared up—"

The Inspector stopped, for it was evident that he had said the wrong thing. Miss Ellen's confidential manner vanished, as she answered him firmly.

"I'm very sorry, sir, but I can't tell you anything at all about *that*," she evidently referred to the murder, "because

Madam Deal warned me particularly this morning not to answer any questions at all on the subject."

"But, Miss Ellen," Fowler protested, "Madam Deal must know that under these circumstances it's your duty to give any information you have."

"I'm very sorry," she repeated stubbornly, "but Madam Deal said to me just this morning, 'Now, look here, Ellen, you don't know *anything* about this affair, and I don't want you to answer any questions at all—because the first thing you know you'll have told something you shouldn't.'"

Even the Inspector seemed to be silenced by this astonishing statement. Miss Ellen calmly rose.

"I'm not sure," she added earnestly, "that I've made it quite clear to you what a wonderful woman Madam Deal is—"

Fowler cleared his throat with some violence.

"On the contrary, Miss Ellen," he said gallantly, "I think you've made it perfectly clear."

The young woman gave him a gratified smile.

"Then I'm sure you understand," she concluded sweetly, as she opened the door, "that I *really* can't answer any questions about what happened last night—because I'm so *absolutely* devoted to Madam Deal, and to Mr. Deal, that I wouldn't betray their confidence for *anything* in the world."

11
THE TELEGRAM

For several moments after Miss Ellen's remarkable exit, Fowler remained, evidently stunned into silence, staring at the door which had closed behind her. Then he turned to me—and simultaneously we burst into laughter.

"Whew—" the Inspector gave a long whistle as he dropped into a chair and mopped his forehead, "*that,* Miss Pell, is what is known as keeping the faith!" Then after a pause he added, "But seriously—we must check over what we learned from Miss Ellen. To begin with—was she telling the truth?"

"Well—" I considered a moment, "I hardly think anyone could *lie* quite as naively as that. Yes, I should undoubtedly say that Miss Ellen, although possibly misguided on one or two points, is essentially a truthful woman."

"That was my impression exactly," Fowler agreed, "now then—what was the first item of her information?—I'll admit," he grinned, "that I was so dazzled by her personality, that I'm afraid I almost lost track of some of her statements."

"Let me see," I consulted my notes, "the first significant thing was her remark that Harvey Deal had no job in Washington, and that 'Mamma' took over this hotel in order to put him to work running it. Then," I continued, "came the reference to the affair with the unscrupulous woman whose name Miss Ellen so loyally refused to divulge. I suppose we take it that the lady was Lina Castle?"

"I think," the Inspector grinned, "that we are quite safe in assuming that the 'mistress of the worst sort' was none other than Lina. And what have we next?"

"Next," I said, "comes the fact that it was Madam Deal herself who gave orders that Lina Castle should not be admitted to the hotel—but you remember that the old lady stated this morning that she knew nothing about the order."

"That's not surprising," Fowler shrugged, "I was pretty sure she was stalling on that point—but I haven't decided yet just how much of a motive the old girl had for that lie."

"Well," I ventured, "from the rest of Miss Ellen's remarks I don't think that any of Madam Deal's motives look exactly *innocent*."

"True, Miss Pell, true," the Inspector sighed, "but when you've investigated a few more murder cases you may discover that there are generally at least a half-a-dozen persons who don't look 'exactly innocent.'"

"You certainly ought to know," I admitted, "and therefore will probably consider the next remarks of Miss Ellen to be of little significance. One was that Madam Deal *urged* Miss Ellen to take that bit of fresh air on the roof—at the very time that the murder was committed,—and the second was that young Wally Deal claimed his Grandmother had gone off and left him alone in Miss Ellen's absence."

"Oh, I'm perfectly willing to admit, Miss Pell, that we have some pretty damning information against Madam Deal—" Fowler's tone was patient, "but I was merely pointing out to you that at present we really know very little, and personally— well, I have very little love for circumstantial evidence. . . . As far as Madam Deal is concerned I'm certainly anxious for another talk with her."

"And what," I asked, "is your reaction to Miss Ellen's remarks about Mrs. Evans?"

"That's pretty hard to say," Fowler answered slowly. "Her connection with the whole affair has been just about the most puzzling element so far—and Miss Ellen's statement didn't help matters much. Personally, I'm completely in the dark as to whether Mrs. Evans has any connection with the case or not."

"We must remember, of course," the Inspector added presently, "Mrs. Evans' effort to reach Harvey Deal yesterday afternoon. By the way—what did you think of Miss Ellen's theory of a flirtation between those two?"

"Well—?" I said doubtfully, "of course it would depend on Mrs. Evans—but I rather suspect that Miss Ellen is the type who hopes to find something to disapprove of in every woman more—" I hesitated, "well, more attractive than herself!"

"A good point, Miss Pell,—and probably right," Fowler nodded, "and furthermore, you remember that Miss Ellen clearly stated that Madam Deal was also alarmed about Mrs. Evans' advances. I imagine both those women spend a large portion of their time brooding over the safety of Harvey Deal!"

"No doubt they do," I laughed. "Miss Ellen herself would certainly give the impression of being a self-appointed guardian of *all* men against the wiles of designing women."

"Exactly," said Fowler, "and in her case I think it's safe to say that she probably would *not* carry her guarding to the point of violence—but . . ." he paused.

"But what?" I asked.

"Well—only that Madam Deal *may* not be so gentle," the Inspector said lightly. "Anyway we are forced to assume that *someone* was planning violence yesterday afternoon."

"I wonder," I remarked, "if that may have prompted the 'warning' that Mrs. Evans was trying to get to Deal."

"It may," Fowler murmured, "if the message had anything at all to do with the case."

"But I should think," I said, "that it would be sensible to assume, for the present at least, that it probably was significant—after all, unless Miss Ellen exaggerated her story, it seems fairly obvious that Mrs. Evans had some really important news for Deal, and the fact that this occurred only a few hours before the murder—well, if her message had nothing to do with Mrs. Castle then it was a pretty strange coincidence."

"That's logical enough, Miss Pell," the Inspector conceded, "but you see, since I am no believer of circumstantial evidence, it goes without saying that I *am* rather inclined to grant the existence of frequent and amazing coincidences. However—by all means go on with your theory—have you any notion what sort of warning Mrs. Evans may have been trying to convey?"

"Unfortunately not," I admitted ruefully. "I'm afraid my efforts at explanation stop short of the useful mark."

The Inspector smiled at my perplexed expression.

"Don't let that bother you," he said, "theories are seldom of any use—but, in the absence of facts, they are often comforting. In this case, for instance, we might work up rather a neat little explanation by assuming that Lina Castle, wishing to resume a profitable affair with Deal, forced her way into the hotel under another name—intending to lure him away from his protective, and possibly oppressive, mother. Apparently she had succeeded in persuading him to cut loose to the extent of a European holiday—and in so doing she ran head on into the plans of two other designing ladies, thus supplying one possible motive for two possible murderers."

"You mean Madam Deal and Mrs. Evans?" I asked.

"Exactly," Fowler nodded, "either an outraged mother or a jealous rival might well have fired that shot. The only serious flaw in my theory," he added after a moment, "is that, up to the present at least, we have no very good reason for believing that there *was* either a vengeful mother or a desperate rival. You see, the bits of evidence which lead us to suspect Madam Deal might just as logically point to a *worried* mother—and that would explain her strange conduct quite innocently—even to the fact that she warned Miss Ellen not to answer questions. And as for Mrs. Evans—we're probably way off the track about her."

Our discussion was cut short at this point by the entrance of Tommy, whose comparatively dejected attitude indicated that his last mission had not been as successful as the first two.

"I couldn't find out a thing about that wire to Mrs. Evans, Chief," he announced sadly. "The two nearest offices don't know anything about it, and finally one of 'em said they'd telegraph Washington and see if the message was ever sent to Mrs. Evans. But it didn't do any good. I told 'em all there *must* be a record of that telegram somewheres—but they just kept saying there wasn't. I don't know—" Tommy paused to heave a sigh and ruffle his hair, "I don't know whether the telegraph records are all wet—or whether I did something wrong. . . ."

"I—I wouldn't worry, Tommy," the Inspector spoke absently, "I think you did all right." Fowler was staring straight ahead of him with eyes thoughtfully narrowed. It was plain that something in Tommy's report had given him an idea—but just what it was that he was planning, we were not to know for some minutes.

Suddenly the Inspector turned to Tommy and addressed him briskly.

"Listen, son," he said, "you get yourself down to the front desk and keep an eye on Evans. If he starts to come upstairs—go to the telephone and warn me—I'll be in the Evans apartment upstairs." Then, to my astonishment, Fowler directed me to follow him.

"Come on, Miss Pell," he said abruptly, "here's where we turn to and do a little snooping."

I knew, of course, that he planned to enter the Evans apartment, probably with a pass-key. What it was that he hoped or expected to find there I did not know—but I had not the faintest desire to help with the "snooping."

"I don't think I'll go, Inspector," I said.

He stopped short and faced me curiously.

"Why not?" He seemed surprised.

"Well, I simply feel that I haven't any business prowling in Mr. Evans' apartment, that's all. I'm not a professional detective, you know." I think my tone was rather nasty, and a moment later I was regretting it.

The Inspector continued to watch me with those uncomfortably shrewd eyes of his. It was the first time since our original interview on the preceding evening that Fowler had seemed anything but friendly—and I found myself braced for an unpleasant retort. I was wrong, however, for when he finally spoke, the Inspector's tone was quite noncommittal.

"I think you'd better come along, Miss Pell," he said quietly, and turned to the door.

Without a word I followed him.

We entered the Evans apartment, as I had supposed we would, by means of a pass-key which Fowler carried. No doubt he had obtained it from the house detective. Once inside the apartment I felt more at ease, for I saw that Fowler was not intending to make what I should call a "snooping" search. Of the living room he made only the most casual examination, and even when we had proceeded to the bedroom he showed no tendency to pry into the Evans' possessions. Rather, he appeared to be searching for some particular clue which he had already in mind, as he stood looking about him with that thoughtful squinting expression which I had come to recognize. It was the desk which finally attracted him. For several minutes his hands moved, apparently aimlessly, over the papers and letters, pencils and pens, which lay on the flat-top writing table. Presently, however, I saw that he held a sheet of note-paper and an envelope at which he was looking closely. He was, of course, comparing it with the stationery on which the letter from Mrs. Evans to her husband had been written. From where I stood it certainly looked exactly like the large, square white paper I had seen downstairs. Evidently Fowler also was satisfied on that point, for after a moment he replaced the paper and turned away from the desk.

"It just cancels out," he murmured impatiently, "with the business about the telegram." He paused, as his eye lit on the waste-basket beneath the desk. "Unless—" he continued eagerly, "unless— By holy cats *there it is!*" This last as he extracted some scraps of paper from the basket. They were yellow scraps.

I jumped forward quickly.

"What is it?" This was the first time I had spoken since we had entered the apartment.

"I—think—it's—" Fowler answered me slowly as he fished about among the scraps, "Yes—it is!" he exclaimed suddenly.

"Is what?"

"The telegram," Fowler informed me, "which summoned Mrs. Evans to Washington last night. "Look—" he pointed to four of the larger scraps. They were easily pieced together to form a message.

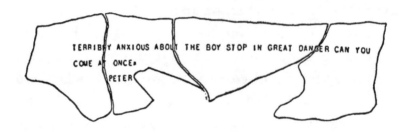

"Well," I began slowly, "it does look as if Mrs. Evans really had a sick brother, doesn't it?"

There was no answer from the Inspector. I turned to see that he was thoughtfully fingering the remaining scraps of the telegraph blank. Evidently he was not content with the amount he had already fitted together, for he was carefully gathering all the bits from the basket and placing them in a pile on the desk.

"I want these," he remarked finally, "all of 'em."

I handed him one of the large envelopes.

"Shall I put the scraps in this?" I suggested.

"I'll do it," he reached for the envelope.

"Oh, damn," Fowler exclaimed suddenly. With a quick gesture he had half upset the ink-well which stood at his elbow. He caught at it in time to prevent a complete spill— but some of the ink had splattered on his fingers and on the desk-top.

"Hell's bells, where's a blotter?" he looked about help-lessly.

I extracted one quickly from beneath a pile of letters.

"Here," I said.

"Oh, thanks."

Carefully, the Inspector blotted up the little pools of ink from the desk and from his hand. Fortunately no papers had been stained, so that when he had cleaned things up no tell-tale spots were left to give us away.

"Here," Fowler returned the blotter to me, "stick this back where you found it, Miss Pell." Then he placed the few remaining scraps of the telegram in the envelope and straightened up. "I guess that's all we need," he said slowly. Then, after a final glance about the room, "Come on, Miss Pell, let's beat it."

When we had once more reached our "headquarters" in room 1116, the Inspector turned to me with a half smile.

"Well, how about it, Miss Pell?" there was a hint of a drawl in his voice. "Was it as bad as you expected?"

"Oh, not quite," I answered lightly.

Fowler's smile widened a bit, but he made no further comment on the episode. He had gone to the telephone and presently I heard him asking Tommy to come up to the room. When the youth appeared, he was presented with the envelope which contained the fragments of Mrs. Evans' telegram.

"Do you like puzzles, Tommy?" the Inspector inquired.

"Yes, *sir*."

I observed that Tommy's enthusiasm had returned to normal.

"Then put this telegram together," Fowler directed. "I want it carefully done—the whole thing, letter head and all. Understand?"

"Yes, *sir*." Tommy was already seated at the desk as he spoke. "Are these all the scraps?" he asked after a moment.

"All we could find, Tommy. Now get to work while I go out and get me some lunch. . . . Gosh," Fowler yawned wearily, "I don't know whether I'm hungrier or sleepier—but anyway I've got to eat before I tackle old lady Deal and little Harvey again. You, Miss Pell," he turned to me, "get your lunch and then type out this morning's notes for me, if you will. I've got a couple of errands to do—but I'll probably need you again about four o'clock—so if you'll be ready. . . ?"

"I'll be in my room," I promised, "you can get me by telephone."

"Good," Fowler nodded, "and—by the way, Miss Pell,—keep your eyes open in the meanwhile."

I agreed to observe what I could, but, as a matter of fact, I hardly expected to have much occasion for sleuthing.

12
I PLAY HIDE AND GO SEEK

My hasty lunch, at a cafeteria near the hotel, was uneventful enough, and immediately afterward I returned to the Almeda and began work on my typing. It took me nearly two hours to transcribe the notes of the morning's interviews, and when I had finished I was badly in need of a little exercise and fresh air.

Accordingly, I hurried up to the roof, and I found the chilly November breeze very pleasant. It had been here that I had seen little Wally Deal and Miss Ellen the afternoon before—and I rather wondered if I should encounter them again. I feared that a meeting with Miss Ellen might be a bit awkward, after the morning interview—but I had no reason to worry, for presently Wally Deal appeared, quite alone. He approached me at once, evidently anxious to be friendly, and we exchanged grave greetings. After a very few minutes of conversation, he informed me that this was Miss Ellen's day out, and that he was very glad to find someone who would play with him.

I explained that I had only a half-hour for play myself, but agreed to enter into any game he might suggest for that time. A solemn consultation ensued, during which football and wrestling were hopefully proposed—only to be rejected by me on grounds of insufficient equipment. Eventually we compromised on hide and go seek.

"Who," Wally demanded, "will hide first?"

Eeny—meeny—miny—mo settled the fact that I was to be IT, and accordingly Wally instructed me to shut my eyes and count "as high as I could."

"You stay right there," he ordered, "until you get through counting."

I promised faithfully not to peek, and Wally trotted off to find his hiding-place.

As our game progressed, I found Wally Deal an extraordinarily engaging playmate—and I proceeded to enjoy myself thoroughly at the thrilling business of hide and go seek, particularly the final dashes when the seeker has discovered the hider, and both race for the "home base."

It was while I hid behind one of the large chimneys in a far corner of the roof that Wally abruptly ended our game by a startlingly sudden exclamation.

"Oh, *look*," I heard the child scream excitedly, *"look* what I've found!"

Instantly I abandoned my hiding place, and a moment later I discovered Wally on his hands and knees, peering beneath a sort of ledge at the edge of the roof.

"What is it, Wally?" I called anxiously.

"Oh, *look*," he exclaimed again as I approached, "it's a *gun!*"

Stooping down beside him, I looked. And there, surely enough, lay a revolver—obviously no toy. Before I could stop him, Wally had picked it up and began to flourish it in the most terrifying manner.

"Hand it to me, Wally," I forced myself to speak quietly, in spite of my rising alarm.

To my infinite relief, the child obeyed me at once, and with the gun safely in my own hand I breathed more easily.

As calmly as I could, I explained that it was not the sort of thing for us to play with, and I managed some feeble excuse to put off his immediate and persistent questions about how the revolver had come to be hidden beneath the ledge.

"Look here, Wally," I said presently, "you like secrets, don't you?"

He nodded emphatically.

"Well—" I tried to sound enthusiastic, "let's you and I keep this a secret about finding the gun. Shall we?"

Wally stood meditatively on one leg while he considered this proposition.

"I won't tell Miss Ellen or Granny," he conceded at last, "but I *might* tell Daddy."

"Oh, but it wouldn't be a secret," I protested, "if you tell anyone at all. *Do* promise me you won't tell—anyway until to-morrow afternoon."

It took all the tact I possessed to extract the promise from Wally—but finally we swore a solemn vow of silence—and I felt that my duty was done. Naturally, I could not know what Inspector Fowler would make of the matter of the strangely hidden weapon, but at least I wanted to make sure that Wally would not blurt out the news to the wrong person.

Before long we were chatting as amiably as ever, and the boy seemed to have quite forgotten the odd incident. I was, needless to say, more than eager to show this new evidence to the Inspector, but I realized that he had probably not yet returned to the hotel. So we passed the remaining minutes until four o'clock with playing "Simon says thumbs up."

Presently an idea struck me.

"This is a nice roof, isn't it, Wally?" I began conversationally.

"Um-huh," Wally's answer was hardly encouraging.

"I suppose," I continued brightly, "ever so many people come up here?"

"Um-huh."

"Well, who for instance?"

"Oh—" Wally regarded me vaguely, "most everybody comes here."

"But who is here the oftenest?" I persisted.

"Well, me mostly, and Miss Ellen and sometimes Granny, and people I don't know—like you, and . . ." He broke off suddenly and pointed. "Oh, look," he exclaimed, "there's Daddy! Now we can all play some more."

Wally was obviously delighted at this interruption which would end our conversation, but I felt no small misgivings as I saw Harvey Deal approach us. What, I thought anxiously, would he say when he found me playing with his son. And what a dreadful situation if Wally should tell about the gun, or indicate to his father that I had been questioning him about what people were accustomed to visit the roof.

I had only a moment for a whispered reminder to Wally of his promise of secrecy—and when Mr. Deal joined us, I was still in terror for fear the boy would blurt out the news anyway. But to my great relief, Wally kept his word like a gentleman—at any rate, as long as I was there.

Rather to my surprise, Harvey Deal greeted me with a pleasantly noncommittal smile, and presently the three of us were chatting about the recent game of hide and go seek. Meanwhile I clung firmly to my purse, in which I had safely secreted the revolver. After a very few minutes I excused myself, and once out of sight of Wally and his father, I hurried as quickly as I could down to room 1116.

Inspector Fowler had not returned, but I found Morty waiting, and he informed me that Fowler had telephoned that he was on his way back to the hotel. Scarcely ten minutes had passed, during which time I never relaxed the nervous grip on my purse, when I heard the Inspector's voice outside the door. Another moment—and I breathed a great sigh of relief, for Fowler was safely in the room, and I could hand over my precious evidence to him.

"Why, hello, Miss Pell," the Inspector seemed surprised to find me awaiting him, "what's up?"

"I think I've got hold of something," I explained as calmly as I could, "something pretty important."

Evidently Fowler was impressed by my earnest expression, for he directed Morty to wait outside, and once the door was closed he asked quickly:

"What is it?"

In silence I opened my purse and held it toward him, so that he could see the revolver which lay inside.

"My God," Fowler exclaimed excitedly, "where did you get *that?*"

"From Wally Deal," I answered calmly.

"My God!" said the Inspector again, even more piously.

Very gingerly, with his handkerchief protecting possible fingerprints, Fowler lifted the gun from my purse and examined it eagerly. Meanwhile I was recounting the strange circumstance which had brought the evidence into my possession.

"It was a breathless moment," I admitted, "when I looked down and saw the boy pick up the gun—but I kept my voice calm, and he handed it to me without a murmur. I'm afraid I messed up the fingerprints somewhat—but you see I had to take it away from Wally."

The Inspector, still preoccupied, nodded his understanding, and I went on.

"I tried to get some information from Wally," I said,
"about who goes up to the roof most often—but I didn't
make much headway. He just named over his own family
and said sometimes strangers wander up. Guests from the
hotel, I suppose, like me."

"H'mm," Fowler was scarcely listening to me as he
turned the gun over to examine it completely. "It's a .32,
all right," he observed with satisfaction, "and just one
shell has been discharged. I guess it's the gun that did the
job—not much doubt about that. But how in thunder do
you suppose it got up onto that roof? Morty told me himself that he went over every inch of the roof last night—
and I'm damn sure he would have found it if it had been
tucked under the ledge then."

"And doesn't it strike you," I inquired, "that it was
rather a stupid place to hide the gun anyway? After all, if
Wally hadn't found it—someone else would have been sure
to."

"It was a dumb thing to do, all right," Fowler nodded,
"and the funny part of it is I *don't* think our murderer was
dumb. So there you are."

"I suppose," I suggested, "that whoever hid the gun
there might have been planning to return and get it later."

"Yes, Miss Pell," the Inspector agreed thoughtfully,
"that's just what they might have planned." He paused for
a moment and then added reflectively, "And didn't you tell
me, Miss Pell, that it was Harvey Deal who came up to the
roof just before you left it—a few minutes after Wally had
found the gun?"

Before I could answer, there was a knock at the door,
and Morty's anxious face appeared.

"I don't want to butt in, Chief," he began apologetically, "but I got this dumb Swede out here and I don't know how long I'm gonna be able to keep her."

Fowler looked up quickly.

"Who is it you've got, Morty?" he inquired. "Is it the missing Hulda?"

"Um-huh," Morty rolled his eyes comically as he nodded. "And did I have a time gettin' her here! She's scared stiff and says someone's gonna kill her if she stays in the hotel."

"All right, bring her in," Fowler directed.

While we waited for Hulda to appear, the Inspector asked me for the notes I had typed. Having left them in my room, I went down to fetch them, and when I returned I found the terrified Hulda already being questioned.

Naturally I began with my notes at once, but, somewhat to my amusement, I found that there were practically no notes to be taken. The interview up to that point had evidently consisted solely of various and strenuous efforts on the part of Fowler to get any response at all from his witness.

"Listen, Hulda," he was saying patiently, "we aren't going to hurt you, we aren't going to frighten you—you only need to answer a few little questions. You will do that, won't you?"

Silence—while Hulda regarded the Inspector with an expression of the most concentrated suspicion.

"Hulda—" this time Fowler's voice was even more persuasive, "Hulda, what is it that makes you frightened? Nothing can happen to you. After all," here he put in a coaxing smile, "after all—you've already lost your job, haven't you?"

A nod from Hulda.

Encouraged by even this rudimentary answer, the Inspector proceeded more briskly.

"Well, Hulda, you see the worst has already happened—now certainly you aren't going to be afraid to tell us a few things, are you?"

Another silence—but this time accompanied by a more hopeful expression.

"Now then," Fowler started off bravely, "you took care of the rooms on the eleventh floor, didn't you, Hulda?"

A nod.

"And on the twelfth floor too?"

A second nod.

"You knew the lady who was in room 1117, didn't you?"

There was a brief hesitation—then suddenly Hulda spoke for the first time.

"Mees Lovett," she declared positively, "have room 1117."

"That's right, Hulda," the Inspector encouraged her, "now when you took care of Miss Lovett's room, did you ever see her?"

"Yah, I see her two, t'ree times."

"Did she ever say anything, or do anything, that you thought was queer?"

"Qveer?" Hulda repeated, obviously baffled.

"Yes. I mean did she ever do funny things—you know," the Inspector was gesturing helplessly, "different from other people."

At this Hulda brightened.

"Yah," she nodded, "Mees Lovett have red hair. Dot vas different."

I think that at that moment the Inspector very nearly gave up in despair. Certainly it seemed that Hulda was either too dumb or too frightened, or both, to be of any use whatever. But by a stroke of good fortune, Fowler decided to try one more question—and it was the right one.

"Did you see anyone, Hulda," he asked, "go into Miss Lovett's room at any time?"

The effect was electric. Hulda shook her head violently.

"I t'ink I couldn't say dot," she declared firmly.

"Why not?"

"She tell me not to," Hulda explained.

"Look here now," for the first time the Inspector was speaking sharply to the girl. "You tell me exactly who you saw in that room, and hurry up about it!"

"Vell—" she hesitated miserably, "you von't let her get me?"

"Nobody can get you," the Inspector snapped impatiently, "now tell me who it was."

"Meester Deal," Hulda said meekly.

I saw Fowler's shoulders droop suddenly. Undoubtedly he was disappointed at hearing the identity of Lina Castle's visitor—for we could pretty well assume that Harvey Deal must have been in the room at some time or other, without going to all this trouble to extract the fact from Hulda.

"Well, Hulda," the Inspector sighed, "when was it that you saw Mr. Deal go into the room?"

"It vas yesterday afternoon—dot's vy I lose my job," Hulda nodded sadly.

"What do you mean by that?" This time Fowler's question displayed more interest. "Was it Mr. Deal who discharged you?"

"No-o-o," Hulda's denial was emphatic, "Meester vouldn't do dot. It vas the old lady who make me go—Meester Deal's mamma."

Even after this startling admission Fowler had a good deal of difficulty in extracting the rest of Hulda's incoherent testimony, but eventually we managed to piece together her story.

It appeared that Hulda had several times seen Deal enter Lina Castle's room, but had thought nothing of the matter until the afternoon before, when she (Hulda) had gone to the Deal apartment on some errand or other. While she was in Madam Deal's room, Hulda had overheard the old lady inquire on the telephone where she could reach her son. And, since no one downstairs seemed able to supply the information, Hulda had helpfully remarked that Mr. Deal was in room 1117. Madam Deal had immediately pounced upon that fact, and had questioned the maid at length in an effort to discover who her son was visiting. Whether or not the old lady had been able, from Hulda's answers, to determine that "Mees Lovett" was actually Lina Castle, it was impossible to judge. But at any rate she had warned Hulda severely to say nothing further to anyone concerning Harvey Deal's visits to 1117.

"And was it then, Hulda, that you lost your job?" the Inspector's tone indicated his surprise.

"No-o-o," Hulda shook her head.

"You did something else later that made Madam Deal angry?"

Again the maid shook her head violently.

"I didn't do nothing else," she declared, "but do my vork—the same as I done for tvelve years. But yust about eight o'clock last night, ven I get ready to go home, the old lady she send for me. And ven I get up to her room she vas terrible mad with me."

"But what about, Hulda?"

"I don't know," Hulda's wide eyes revealed her utter bewilderment. "Only she tell me to get out and never come back."

And in a terrified whisper, the maid went on to describe the details of her mysterious dismissal. It appeared that Madam Deal had informed her, in no uncertain terms, that if she ever returned to the Almeda, or answered any questions concerning Mr. Deal's whereabouts that afternoon, that she, Madam Deal, would personally see to it that Hulda was punished in some unnamed but dreadful manner. And the maid, naturally enough, had departed from the hotel in short order—not even pausing to inform the housekeeper of her dismissal.

"Dot's vy," Hulda concluded unhappily, "I didn't vant heem to bring me here," she indicated Morty, "and now, Meester, you got to let me go please—before dot old lady catches me." The poor girl glanced about fearfully, as if she expected to see Madam Deal emerge from some corner to carry out her dreadful threat.

It was evident that Hulda had contributed all the information she could, and Fowler excused her with further assurances that she was perfectly safe from any vengeance on the part of Madam Deal. Morty was appointed to escort the terrified maid back to her lodgings, and when they had gone, the Inspector mopped his forehead wearily.

"Gosh," he shook his head, "that old lady certainly spent some time warning people not to answer questions about this business."

I looked at him curiously. It was evident that in spite of all the testimony we had heard which definitely implicated Madam Deal in the crime—he was still inclined to take the possibility of her guilt lightly.

"You just naturally don't believe any of the evidence against Madam Deal, do you?" I asked.

"Oh, it's not as bad as all that, Miss Pell," Fowler smiled at the irritation in my tone, "but I'll admit I have a hard

time taking the old girl very seriously. You see," he added
more thoughtfully, "I get the impression that she's pretty
damned smart—and if she really had anything to cover
she wouldn't be making all these fool slips about warning
people not to talk."

"But if she *hasn't* anything to cover," I protested impatiently, "what's her big idea in messing around in the
case so much. For one thing—she told about six deliberate lies this morning—for another, it's perfectly plain
that she sent Miss Ellen to the roof last night so that she
could send for Hulda and give her the devil—and finally,
it looks to me as if she not only knew that Lina Castle
was in room 1117, but also knew about the murder! And
if she's as smart as you seem to think—she wouldn't be
concealing all that evidence and frightening witnesses into
silence for no reason at all."

"Oh, I've no doubt she has plenty of reasons," Fowler
agreed, "and she may, for all I know, be covering her own
tracks. But my point is that she didn't leave any of these
clues floating around by *accident*. That's all."

"Well, maybe so," I admitted grudgingly, "but after all,
I don't think we have much to go on in building theories about the Deal family. The interviews with them this
morning were hardly satisfactory."

"I grant you that, all right," the Inspector nodded,
"but give me another hour and I think we'll have some
more material. I've already sent for Harvey Deal—and
when I get through with him I'm going to tackle the old
lady again. And this time I've got some pretty little bits
of evidence to rub their noses in—and it might even make
'em tell the truth for a change. And by the way, Miss Pell,
I might as well tell you now that while I was out this
afternoon, I went to Deal's bank and found out that on the

very day that Lina Castle registered here—Deal drew out
five thousand dollars in cash. *And* I discovered that this
very morning—just after my talk with Madam Deal—the
old lady called up the bank in a hell of a temper and wanted to know if little Harvey had been drawing out large
sums of money!"

"All of which," I observed, "seems to settle the matter
of the sudden wealth which Lina Castle enjoyed during
the last three days of her life, and which tends, I should
say, to make Deal look like a—"

My sentence was cut short by the Inspector's signal for
silence. Someone was coming quickly down the hall—and
a moment later a brisk knock on the door indicated that
Harvey Deal was outside.

13
THE WARNING

"You sent for me, Inspector?" Deal inquired pleasantly.

"Yes, come in, Mr. Deal," the Inspector motioned him to a chair. I noticed that Fowler stood directly in front of the desk, so that Deal was not able to see the gun which still lay there.

"I hope, Inspector, this means that you have come to some conclusion about this unfortunate affair?" Deal spoke quietly as he seated himself, but it was not difficult to observe that he glanced about the room with a certain apprehension.

"Unfortunately," the Inspector replied shortly, "we have come to no conclusions whatever."

"I'm very sorry to hear that—naturally I had hoped to get the matter settled and out of the way as soon as possible." Harvey Deal seemed to speak almost mechanically, as his eyes darted about more and more nervously, as if in search of something.

"Are you looking for anything, Mr. Deal?"

At the Inspector's sharp question Deal's nervous glances stopped abruptly.

"Why—no, nothing at all," he managed a short laugh as he spoke. "After all, Inspector," he added more genially, "what should I be looking for?"

"Oh, I don't know," Fowler was watching him closely, "a gun, perhaps—?" he drawled the question.

"You must be joking, Inspector," again Deal laughed nervously, "I should hardly be looking for a—" he hesitated, "a *gun*."

"*This* gun, possibly?" As Fowler spoke he stepped quickly aside, revealing the revolver which lay behind him.

Instantly Harvey Deal was out of his chair—and before the Inspector could make a move to stop him, he had seized the gun in his two hands.

"*Put that down!*" Fowler shouted furiously.

Deal obeyed him at once, but not before he had quite certainly smeared away any remaining fingerprints.

"Oh—I'm sorry, Inspector," he apologized, "I didn't realize that I wasn't to touch it."

"Oh, you didn't, eh?" Fowler snapped. "I suppose you think I don't know what you picked it up for?"

"Why—to look at it, of course," Deal explained innocently, "I thought perhaps I might be able to identify it. But unfortunately, I never saw it before."

"Oh, yeah?" Fowler drawled unpleasantly, "don't you mean that you were afraid *I* might identify some fingerprints on that gun?"

As Deal failed to reply, the Inspector went on angrily.

"I suppose you never *heard* of fingerprints—is that it?" he inquired belligerently.

"Well—I admit I should have stopped to think, Inspector," Deal's tone was apologetic, "but in the excitement of the moment I confess I—"

"You *confess*, eh?" Fowler repeated angrily, "well, let me tell you it would be a big help to this case if you *did* do a little confessing. Yes, you and that whole family of yours," he added as Deal made a gesture of protest.

"If by 'that whole family' of mine you refer to my mother, Inspector, I must ask you to speak more carefully," Harvey Deal adopted a tone of quiet dignity, which failed, however, to silence Fowler.

"I refer to your mother, all right," he growled. "If you and she had managed to come somewhere near the truth in the statements you made this morning—we might have made some headway by this time—"

"Really, Inspector, if you cannot speak more respectfully—"

"Oh, cut out the injured innocence racket!" Fowler exclaimed, "and get down to business. You're too deep in this thing, Deal, and so is your mother, to start pulling that dignity stuff now."

Deal was silent for a moment, then he seated himself and spoke quietly.

"Very well, Inspector, I shall assume nothing whatever—and you can ask what questions you like. I told you this morning that I am most anxious to have this case settled—and that I will do whatever I can to help you. Believe it or not—I mean that."

"You can help me in the first place," Fowler suggested meaningly, "by telling me the truth when you answer a few of my questions."

"Certainly," Deal nodded his consent, without a trace of resentment.

"Which is more than you did this morning," the Inspector pointed out.

This time Deal made no answer.

"For instance," Fowler continued, "perhaps now that you have offered to tell the truth, you wouldn't mind explaining why you lied about the reason Lina Castle was denied entrance to this hotel?"

"Simply because," Harvey Deal shrugged, "if I had told you the real reason, you would have gone off on a tangent of suspicions involving my entire family—and you would probably have unearthed a great many past matters, which have nothing whatever to do with this present affair, but which would have caused publicity and embarrassment to my mother, my son and to me.—You see," he added pointedly, "I have a rather unfortunately accurate knowledge of police procedure in a case of this kind."

That Harvey Deal spoke with sufficient conviction and truth to make his point, was evident from the angry flush which flooded the Inspector's face.

"Whether you like the methods of the police or not, Mr. Deal," he replied angrily, "you are not justified in telling outright lies in a case of this importance. You will please tell me exactly why Mrs. Castle was barred from the Almeda Hotel."

"It is quite evident, Inspector, that you already know—or think you know—the reason. But if you want it in my own words, it was simply that Lina Castle had been trying, for a number of years, to blackmail me."

"On what grounds?"

"On grounds that are none of your business," Deal replied coolly.

The Inspector ignored the insolence of this answer.

"It was breach of promise, wasn't it?" he asked.

Deal made no reply whatever.

"At least," Fowler insisted, "you won't deny that there was some sort of a past affair between you and Lina Castle?"

"Naturally, Inspector, you don't expect me to answer that question."

"Very well, Mr. Deal," I could see that the Inspector was keeping his temper with the greatest difficulty, "perhaps you *will* find it convenient to explain your statement

of this morning concerning your action when you discovered that Lina Castle had entered the hotel under an
assumed name. You will recall that you said this information reached you late yesterday afternoon—yet I am
informed that you had already visited Mrs. Castle in her
room before yesterday."

"As a matter of fact, Inspector," Deal admitted reluctantly, "I was notified of Lina Castle's presence in the
hotel shortly after she registered."

"Who notified you?"

"She did—indirectly."

"Explain that, please."

"It was simple enough," Deal shrugged, "she slipped a
note under my bedroom door, on the morning of her arrival. It said, 'Come to room 1117 at once.' There was no
signature, but being unpleasantly familiar with both Mrs.
Castle's handwriting and her tactics—it was not a difficult
matter for me to guess who was summoning me. I went
down to the desk and questioned Evans immediately. He
informed me that one Rose Lovett had taken 1117. From
his description I was further assured that the woman was
Lina Castle—and I went to her room at once with the intention of asking her to leave."

"But after seeing her," Fowler suggested, "you changed
your mind about ordering her out?"

"I suppose," Deal spoke after an uncomfortable hesitation, "that it was something of the sort. When I had seen
Mrs. Castle she explained that her errand here was entirely
an innocent one, and she assured me that she had no further intentions of blackmailing me."

"And you—?"

"It must be apparent to you, Inspector," Harvey Deal
sighed, "that I am, unfortunately, something of a fool,—
otherwise Mrs. Castle would never have selected me as

possible blackmail material in the first place. And—to make a long story short—I believed her."

"And you agreed to let her stay in the hotel?"

"Yes—" again Deal sighed.

"But surely you were aware that if Madam Deal were to see her—there might be," Fowler paused, and then added insinuatingly, "there might be—serious trouble?"

Deal looked up angrily at this—but he checked what was evidently going to be an unpleasant retort.

"I happened to know," he answered shortly, "that Lina Castle was a woman of some discretion."

"Still—even a woman of discretion might accidentally have met Madam Deal—say, in the elevator—" Fowler paused, watching the other man closely.

There was unmistakably a growing nervousness in Harvey Deal's manner—but he managed a casual reply to the Inspector's menacing inference.

"It was foolish of me perhaps to allow Mrs. Castle to stay," he admitted, "but I took the chance. And, as a matter of fact I am quite sure my mother had no notion that Lina Castle was in the hotel—until I told her myself, this morning."

"And did you also admit to your mother that you had *known* she was here?"

There was a barely perceptible hesitation before Deal's quiet answer.

"I did not," he said.

"And why not?" Fowler persisted.

"Timidity," Harvey Deal answered laconically.

"Then you admit, Mr. Deal, that you are afraid of your mother?"

Deal shrugged.

"Let us rather put it," Fowler suggested pointedly, "that you are afraid of what your mother might do—under certain circumstances."

"I don't follow you," Deal answered coldly.

"I merely mean," the Inspector explained, "that when things displease Madam Deal—you are apt to look for—shall we say, tangible evidence of her displeasure?"

"Again I don't follow you," Deal repeated. "Will you please state quite clearly what you are trying to say."

"Certainly not," said the Inspector firmly, "the very fact that you are deliberately choosing to misunderstand me gives me the information I wanted."

I felt that the Inspector's menacing attitude was largely bluff—but it was quite certainly having the desired effect on Harvey Deal—for his composure was visibly shaken by these veiled hints.

"Now look here, Deal," Fowler continued briskly, "wasn't it because of your mother's disapproval that your affair with Lina Castle was originally broken off?"

"Really, Inspector," Deal exploded angrily, "that's getting too damn personal!"

"Oh, very well," Fowler proceeded calmly, "for the moment we'll overlook the reason for that break, between Mrs. Castle and you—but you won't deny that Mrs. Castle convinced you, the other day, that the breach should be patched up."

Harvey Deal was silent.

"Since you don't answer," the Inspector continued, "I assume that you do not disagree. Very well—you relented toward Lina Castle—you gave her proof of your forgiveness by a substantial present of five thousand dollars, which sum you drew from the — Bank, shortly after your interview with Mrs. Castle. This money was taken from the joint account shared by your mother and yourself, without the knowledge or consent of your mother—although you must surely have known that she would disapprove. . . . Am I right, Mr. Deal?"

Again Harvey Deal was silent. His expression had remained successfully noncommittal during this recital.

"Once more," Fowler spoke triumphantly, "your silence assures me that I am proceeding correctly. . . . Now then, having given Mrs. Castle the money, you urged her to buy herself a new wardrobe—which she did—and you further urged her to embark upon a trip. In order to make doubly sure about the trip, you yourself went to the Steamship Office and purchased a passage for Mrs. Castle—"

At this point Deal seemed about to interrupt with a protest, but the Inspector was too quick for him.

"You not only bought that passage, Deal," he said, "but you took the money to pay for it out of a pig-skin bill-fold, and I hardly think you will care to deny it!" Fowler thrust his face close to Deal and spoke with deliberate emphasis.

I thought the Inspector was running a rather long chance—since the identity of the man who had purchased Mrs. Castle's ticket had, after all, not been more than vaguely established. But the bluff appeared to be successful—for Harvey Deal sank back into his chair without attempting a reply.

"By the way, Mr. Deal," Fowler added, "would you care to show me your bill-fold?"

"All right, Inspector," Deal admitted wearily, "you win that point. I do happen to carry a pigskin wallet—and of course I am aware that no police inspector would ever admit that two men on the island of Manhattan might own bill-folds of the same general description."

Deal's attempt at nonchalant irony was not too successful, and I was not surprised to see a look of satisfaction on the Inspector's face.

"Fortunately, Mr. Deal," he remarked, "your opinion of police methods are of no importance whatever in this case, but I'll have to remind you that it is your own aversion to making any clear statement which forces me into this hide-and-seek procedure that you dislike so much. . . . If you don't approve of my version of the story—suppose you tell it your own way."

"It would be quite impossible, Inspector," Harvey Deal made an effort at a light tone, "for me to do half justice to the account. After all, you know so much more about it than I do—pray go on. What did I do next?"

If Fowler was nettled by this playful manner which Deal had chosen to adopt, he gave no sign of it. Fortunately, he was more than a match for his elusive witness.

"I'll take up the story," he proceeded calmly, "at the point where you had purchased Mrs. Castle's passage to Europe. You returned to the hotel to deliver it to her—and it was then that Lina Castle persuaded you to accompany her on the trip—"

"I tell you—I—" Deal's voice sounded almost choked as he tried to protest, but the Inspector gave him no chance to finish his objection.

"Don't try to deny it, Deal," he went on accusingly, "you may just as well admit that Mrs. Castle talked you into going with her—and you promised to do it, even though you knew it meant a break with your mother—that it meant giving up your son—that it meant losing your inheritance. . . . Even in the face of all that," Fowler was leaning toward Deal and speaking rapidly, "even when it meant such a sacrifice," he continued, "you promised to go away with Lina Castle—and the very next morning she went to the Steamship Office and bought, with your permission, a passage for you on the same boat—"

Without warning Harvey Deal leaped to his feet and faced the Inspector furiously.

"*By God that's a lie!*" he shouted, "I never promised Lina Castle I'd go away with her—I was sending her to Europe to get rid of her—I swear I never wanted to see her again—*you've got to believe that,* do you hear me?" desperately Deal emphasized his words.

The Inspector remained composed in the face of this sudden outburst.

"Don't forget, Deal," he said, "that you make your own case look bad if you insist that you were 'trying to get rid' of Lina Castle. . . . Don't forget," he continued, as Deal remained silent, "that Lina Castle was murdered by someone who wanted to get rid of her."

"I can't help how it looks," Harvey Deal insisted, "I'm telling you the truth now, I'll swear it! I didn't shoot Lina, you can believe that or not, but you've got to listen to me when I tell you that I never promised her I'd go away with her—*never.*"

"But you admit, don't you," Fowler inquired, "that she did go to the Steamship Office and—"

"Yes—yes, I know she did," Deal interrupted, "but I tell you I didn't send her. I didn't even know she had done it until—" he checked himself abruptly.

"Go on," Fowler urged him, "until—what?"

"Until yesterday afternoon," he admitted slowly, "when I was warned that Lina was planning to force me to go with her."

"What do you mean, 'force you'?"

"I mean just what I say, Inspector," Deal maintained. "You remember I told you that for some time Mrs. Castle had been threatening me with blackmail. Well, this was simply another of her schemes."

"But you also told me," Fowler reminded him, "that she had promised to stop all that business."

Deal laughed shortly.

"A promise," he said, "meant exactly nothing to Lina Castle."

Unexpectedly, Fowler shifted the subject of his questioning.

"Was it when you lived in Washington, Mr. Deal," he asked, "that you knew Mrs. Castle?"

"It was."

"How long ago was that?"

"Nearly nine years."

"And how long were you on friendly terms with her?"

"Two years."

"During that time, Mr. Deal, did you give Mrs. Castle money?"

Harvey Deal looked up with a curiously startled expression, then quickly he lowered his eyes.

"During that time," he said shortly, "I supported her entirely."

"I see. And after you ceased being—friends, did you continue to supply her with funds?"

"For a short time I made her a reasonable allowance."

"Was this with your mother's knowledge?"

"No."

"Why did you keep it a secret, Mr. Deal?"

"Because my business is my own."

"Yet, in spite of your precautions, your mother discovered the fact, didn't she?"

"Yes."

"How did that happen?"

"Lina Castle went to my mother," Deal said slowly, "and told her the state of affairs."

"Did she go with your consent?"

"Certainly not—she did it behind my back—in the hope of getting more money from my mother than she had been getting from me."

"Did she succeed?"

"No. She found it quite impossible to frighten my mother with her stupid threats. When I found out what she had done—I cut off the allowance I had been giving her—and shortly after that she began annoying me with these threats of blackmail—to which I paid as little attention as possible."

"It was about that time, I believe, that you came to New York?"

"Yes—naturally the trouble that Mrs. Castle was making for my mother and me made us glad to get away from Washington."

"Did you see Lina Castle again after you left Washington?" Fowler inquired.

"Never," said Harvey Deal positively, "until four days ago when she put in an appearance here at the hotel."

"And had you, in the meantime, received any letters or messages from her?"

"Once or twice," Deal admitted, "she wrote to me—but I returned the letters unopened."

"Then when Mrs. Castle came to the Almeda you had heard nothing from her for nearly three years," Fowler concluded, reflectively.

"Nothing whatever," Deal repeated firmly.

"And yet," the Inspector observed, "she took the trouble to enter the hotel under an assumed name expressly to see you. She must have had some very important message for you, Mr. Deal,—what was it?"

"She wanted money," said Harvey Deal.

"Not blackmail?"

"No. This time," he spoke bitterly, "she simply pulled a hard luck story on me."

"Do you mean to tell me," the Inspector asked incredulously, "that you gave Lina Castle five thousand dollars—on the strength of a story?"

Deal laughed unpleasantly.

"That makes me a bigger fool than you thought, doesn't it, Inspector? Well—I'm afraid it's true," he sighed, "but I think it's only fair to say, in my own defense, that Lina Castle was a pretty clever girl. She put on a damned good show, and at the end of an hour she had convinced me that she was honestly trying to turn over a new leaf. Said she was out of money—trying to make a fresh start—promised that if I would make her a loan she'd get a job and pay me back. Oh, well—" he broke off with a gesture of impatience, "what's the use of going over it all? The only important thing is that I was crazy enough to believe her."

"Then the five thousand dollars," Fowler observed, "was the loan which she asked for?"

"Not exactly." Again Deal laughed shortly. "You see, I even went so far as to make the final *beau geste*—I offered to *give* her the money and to send her to Europe, all on the single condition that she would never try to see me or any of my family again."

"And she accepted the condition?"

"She gave me," said Harvey Deal ironically, "what she called her word of honor, and—as I have pointed out before—I believed her. You already know that I bought her a passage on a boat sailing last night, and when I saw her yesterday afternoon, it was with the intention of bidding her good-bye—for the last time."

"At that time, Mr. Deal, did Mrs. Castle try to persuade you to change your mind about not seeing her again?"

Deal colored uncomfortably.

"I have told you, Inspector," he said, "that I will not go into my personal affairs when they are of no importance as evidence. Whatever Mrs. Castle may have said, I left her with the definite understanding that she would never try to see me again."

"And yet," Fowler protested, "Lina Castle had purchased the second passage—on the same boat as her own—and made the reservation in your name."

"God knows, I don't know why you should believe me," Deal exclaimed suddenly, "but I swear I knew nothing about that until late yesterday afternoon. I tell you I wasn't warned until—"

"Ah, yes," Fowler interrupted quickly, "you mentioned that warning earlier. Who gave it?"

"I don't know," Deal answered simply.

"What do you mean?"

"The information came to me anonymously," Deal explained, "through a typewritten note which was left in my office. I—I think I have it with me—" he was opening his bill-fold as he spoke (the pigskin one, I observed). "Yes, here it is," he concluded, handing a small slip of paper to the Inspector.

Fowler examined the message intently for a moment, then he handed it over to me.

"Put that in with your notes, Miss Pell," he directed.

It was my turn to read the mysterious warning, neatly typed on a plain strip of white paper.

Lina Castle is planning
something worse than you
think. She has bought a
ticket and wants to make you
go with her tonight. For
God's sake keep her away from
your mother.

That was all. Not, one must admit, too enlightening.

14
AN ALIBI ABANDONED

I was still engaged in studying the mysterious message, when Inspector Fowler's next question recalled me to the business of taking notes.

"Did you, Mr. Deal," he was asking, "see Mrs. Evans at any time yesterday?"

I realized, of course, the train of thought which had led the Inspector to this question. He was remembering Miss Ellen's remark about Mrs. Evans' strange effort to reach Deal with a "warning."

"Why, no," Harvey Deal looked up in surprise, "I'm quite sure I didn't see her at all."

"And you received no message of any kind from her?" the Inspector insisted.

Again Deal appeared to be genuinely puzzled.

"Is it possible," he asked, "that you think she was the one who warned me?"

"Would *you* think it possible?" the Inspector countered.

"Why—really, I would certainly think it unlikely," Deal replied earnestly.

"You told me this morning," Fowler observed, after a pause, "that you know Mrs. Evans only slightly. Is that true?"

"Yes—it's perfectly true," Deal looked straight at the Inspector as he spoke, and his words had every indication of sincerity.

"You had never met her in Washington?"

"Never."

"Had you any reason to think," Fowler inquired, "that Mrs. Evans was mixed up in any way with Mrs. Castle?"

"None whatever." Deal's reply was prompt. "But then," he added, "knowing nothing whatever of Mrs. Evans' personal affairs—I would hardly have been aware of such a matter, one way or the other."

"Perhaps," Fowler persisted, "Lina Castle might have made some mention of Mrs. Evans?"

"Never in my presence," said Deal firmly. "On that point I can be quite sure."

"Tell me," the Inspector directed, "exactly what you did after receiving this warning message."

"For probably ten minutes or more," Deal began, "I just stayed there in my office, wondering what the warning meant and what I ought to do. My impulse was to go straight to Lina Castle and confront her with the information, and yet I hesitated for fear—" Deal paused uncertainly.

"For fear of what?" Fowler prompted him.

"To be quite frank, Inspector," Deal admitted, "I couldn't help thinking that in some way this might be a trick, and I was afraid to do anything that might be—well—walking into the trap."

"What sort of a trap?" Fowler inquired curiously.

"I didn't know, Inspector," Deal sighed ruefully, "but I had every reason to distrust Lina Castle—and I naturally feared that this might be more of her plotting."

"You mean," Fowler asked with some surprise, "that you suspected Mrs. Castle herself of having sent the warning?"

"I tell you I didn't know what to think," Deal repeated wearily, "but finally I realized that I must discover for myself what was going on. I went to Lina's room—and had it out with her."

"You accused her of buying the ticket in your name?"

"Yes."

"What was her answer."

"She denied it."

"Denied it, eh?"

"Flatly, furiously—and almost convincingly."

"Well, what then?"

"Then—" Deal shrugged, "there was a prolonged and futile scene. . . . And in the end I telephoned the Steamship Office and asked about the reservation."

"Yes?" the Inspector was listening intently.

"The Office confirmed the fact that there had been a passage booked, in my name, by a young woman claiming to be my secretary—and, as far as I was concerned, that ended the argument for me. Of course I canceled the reservation—and then I simply walked out."

"How did you leave Mrs. Castle," Fowler asked, "was she still angry?"

"Furious."

"And yet she made no attempt to force you to fall in with her plans—as you were warned that she would?"

"Not directly. That is—" again Deal moved uneasily, "she said nothing to my face about it, but after I had left her room I did hear one threat. . . . She was, you understand, thoroughly hysterical by this time, and as I went off down the hall she went on abusing me. Her remarks were largely incoherent—but one thing she said I did remember, even to the exact words."

"Yes?"

"I heard her say," Deal continued soberly—almost fearfully, "'You think you can bully me for five thousand dollars—but before I leave this hotel tonight, by God, I'll have every cent you own—and on my terms!'" he paused and looked at the Inspector.

"What did she mean by that, Deal?" Fowler asked.

"I never knew," he answered simply. He had sunk back in his chair and his white face showed clearly the strain of worry and confusion which he was apparently suffering. "I—I was pretty much shot when I heard that," he went on slowly, "you see, the whole business was beginning to look bad for me—particularly because I didn't know what Lina Castle was up to."

The Inspector regarded him for a moment in silence.

"Well—what next?" he asked briskly, "when you left Mrs. Castle's room did you return to your office?"

"Yes. I didn't know where else to go, and I wanted to think for a few minutes."

"Think about what?" Fowler inquired.

"About what to do next," Deal answered shortly, "I've admitted, Inspector, that I was frightened,—perhaps foolishly—but I couldn't help suspecting that Lina Castle was planning something pretty rotten against me—and I think it was only natural that I tried to protect myself." He spoke rather defensively.

"Oh, quite, Mr. Deal," said Fowler dryly, "and what plan of—protection did you decide on?"

"It seemed to me that my safest move was not to move at all," Deal replied. "You see, I hardly cared to leave the hotel—because in that case there was no telling what Mrs.

Castle might attempt, but on the other hand, it seemed best to have her *think* that I had left, for in that way I could forestall any efforts on her part to try to see me again."

"So you decided," Fowler inquired, "to stay in your office?"

"Exactly," Deal nodded. "I sent for Evans and told him to give the word that I had gone out—not to return until late in the evening. I also instructed him, of course, to let no one into my office."

"And that, Mr. Deal," the Inspector commented ironically, "is what is known as playing safe."

"I don't blame you for laughing," Deal admitted quietly, "but I tell you I *was* nervous—not quite without cause, I think, in the light of what happened later. Lina Castle was no woman to trifle with. And," he added significantly, "last night she was hysterical. I was simply doing my best to avoid any such trouble as—as what happened in there." He motioned toward the room next door.

"How long did you stay in your office?"

"Until nearly seven o'clock."

"And at that time you left the hotel?"

"Yes."

"To be gone overnight?"

"Yes."

The Inspector looked skeptical.

"Look here, Deal," he said seriously, "you're telling me a damn queer story. First you received a message—warning you that Lina Castle was plotting some sort of monkey-business. Next you tell me that Lina Castle was a dangerous woman—and that you had reason to fear her threats. Fear them," Fowler added pointedly, "to the extent of hiding in your office. You admit that?"

"Yes," Deal's answer was almost inaudible, "I admit that."

"And you expect me to believe," the Inspector continued, "that you had no idea *what* it was that you feared? That you never discovered what Lina Castle's threat might be?"

Deal was staring down at his hands.

"That," he answered slowly, "is the truth."

"Very well," Fowler spoke with an air of indifference, "it's your own affair, of course. But I warn you—when you tell that story on the stand, there's not a man who will believe it." I saw that he was watching Deal closely as he continued. "You must remember, Mr. Deal," he said, "that the message of warning which you have turned over to me, specifically instructed you to keep Mrs. Castle from reaching your mother. This instruction you deliberately disregarded when you left the hotel at seven o'clock last night. It points, Mr. Deal," carefully the words were emphasized, "it points to just one thing. That after you left—Mrs. Castle did go to your mother. That the threat—whatever it was—frightened Madam Deal. Frightened her to the point of desperation . . ." he paused meaningly.

Unquestionably the veiled suggestion had had its effect. Deal faced the Inspector angrily—but this time there was no outburst from him. Rather, his tone had a certain dignity as he answered the accusation levelly.

"For my own story, Fowler," he said, "I have only my bare word—and God knows why you should believe me when I tell you that I didn't kill Lina Castle. *But I know that my mother didn't do it.* I *know* it, do you hear me—because I never left this hotel last night. I went from my office at seven o'clock to my own bedroom in my own apartment—and I stayed there from that time until you saw me at nine this morning. I did it for the very reason you just mentioned—to keep Lina Castle from reaching my mother. And all the time I waited there, I was listening and watching to be sure that Lina should not get in. And I can swear to you that only Miss Ellen left the apartment, and only a maid, Hulda, went in. *My mother never moved from her room!*"

The very desperateness with which Deal's words seemed to be wrung from him made it almost impossible not to believe that he was telling the truth. When he had finished speaking he sank limply back into his chair, and he appeared scarcely to hear the Inspector's next question.

"Are you saying," Fowler asked, "that your family was not aware of your presence in the apartment last night?"

After a dazed moment, Deal rallied himself to answer.

"No one," he said wearily, "knew that I was in the hotel except Evans. He was with me in my room for about three-quarters of an hour, and when he left to go downstairs at eight o'clock, I directed him to bring me word the moment Lina Castle was safely out of the hotel. But I heard nothing from him," Deal concluded bitterly, "until after the murder had been discovered and you had arrived."

"But the telephone call," Fowler objected, "when you informed your mother that you would be away for the night. Where does that come in?"

"I made that call, Inspector, from my own bedroom," Deal explained. "Well," he added with a sigh, "that spoils my alibi, but I've told you the truth."

"Mr. Deal," said the Inspector suddenly, "you were in your room last night at eight o'clock. To quote your own words, you were 'watching and listening.' You must have heard the shot which killed Lina Castle."

Harvey Deal looked up quickly, and I felt certain that his expression of surprise was genuine.

"Strange as it seems, Inspector," he said clearly, "I heard no shot."

To my surprise, Fowler did not press the point further.

"That will be all now, Mr. Deal," he remarked briefly. "But I shall ask you not to leave this room until I come back. I am going," Fowler added as he rose from the edge of the desk where he had been sitting, "to interview Madam Deal."

"Look here, Inspector," Deal protested sharply, "I won't have you bothering my mother again. Surely I've told you enough to make you see that she had absolutely nothing to do with what happened—"

"I prefer," the Inspector interrupted coldly, "to get that statement from Madam Deal herself." He turned to me. "Come along, Miss Pell," he said.

And, ignoring Harvey Deal's final gesture of protest, Fowler opened the door and followed me into the corridor.

15
THE OLD LADY SPEAKS

In the hall Fowler stopped to speak to Morty. I heard him
give orders that Deal was to remain in 1116, then he asked
where Tommy had disappeared to.

"I left him with a telegram to piece together," the
Inspector was saying, "and the kid's been missing ever
since I got back."

Morty grinned.

"I told him he shouldn't have gone, but he had the
thing all put together when I got back this afternoon—
and he went out to get some paste to stick it with. Said he
wanted it just right before he showed it to you."

"Where's the telegram?" Fowler demanded. "I can look
at it all right even if it isn't pasted together."

Still Morty grinned.

"*I* haven't got it, Chief," he shrugged.

"For Pete's sake," the Inspector exploded impatiently,
"the kid didn't take it with him, did he?"

"Yep," said Morty cheerfully. "Even after I told him he
hadn't ought to."

Fowler was frowning distractedly.

"Did you get a look at the telegram, Morty," he inquired.

179

"No, sir. Tommy said he didn't want anyone to see it until he had it just right to show to you."

"Oh, hell," the Inspector turned away abruptly, "I don't know what I bother with that kid for. Someday," he added unkindly, "he's going to be so damned anxious to please me that he's going to stub his toe and break his damned neck."

"Yeah," said Morty appreciatively, "that's what I've been thinking all along, Chief."

"If he comes back while I'm upstairs," Fowler directed, "get the telegram away from him, and hang on to it!"

I had time for only one remark as we hurried up the fire-escape stairs.

"Why," I asked curiously, "didn't you make more of the fact that Deal claims he didn't hear the shot last night?"

For a moment the Inspector stopped short, looked at me, then he hurried on ahead.

"Because," he spoke over his shoulder, "the answer is too easy. You ought to see that."

I made no further comment, for we were entering the nursery upstairs. Once more I took my place by the window, and Fowler knocked sharply at the old lady's door. Fortunately Wally was not in sight, and Miss Ellen, of course, was off duty for the evening.

A long silence followed the Inspector's knock. At last Madam Deal spoke.

"Who is it?"

"Inspector Fowler. I'll have to ask you to open the door."

Again there was a long pause.

"I am sorry I cannot see you now, Mr. Fowler," the old lady's words came to me clearly, but somehow her voice sounded very far away. "I am resting," she added calmly.

I could see from the Inspector's expression that he was not going to mince any words this time.

"Open the door," he said sharply, "or I'll come in."

There was no sound from Madam Deal's room. When it was evident that she had no intention of admitting him, Fowler simply opened the door and walked in. I listened, half expecting some protest from the old lady—but there was none. Presently the Inspector spoke.

"Madam Deal," he said sternly, "in the course of our talk this morning you told me several lies. In one way and another I have managed to check up on most of them—but there's one thing I still want to know."

"Well?"

"Why did your son fear Lina Castle?" Fowler put the question sharply.

I waited intently for the old lady's reaction, but I was certainly not prepared—nor, I imagine, was the Inspector—for the unexpected answer.

"Because," Madam Deal said distinctly, "my son is a coward."

"That's a clever reply," Fowler observed, "very clever. But I'm afraid it won't quite do. The mere fact that he is a coward will not explain why Mr. Deal should have given the woman five thousand dollars, nor why he was sufficiently frightened to hide from her for hours—first in his office, and then in his own apartment last night—nor why he loses his head at the mere mention of the name Lina Castle, nor why both you and he found it necessary to lie to me today about his relations with her. If you can answer all these questions, Madam Deal, I'm willing to listen to you."

"I have no wish, Mr. Fowler," the old lady's tone was like ice, "to be listened to by you. But the answer to all your insulting questions is that our family affairs are not, and never will be, the business of the police."

"That," the Inspector snapped, "is another answer that just won't do. Your affairs are very much my business when your son finds himself involved in the murder of his former—" Fowler hesitated briefly. He was evidently reluctant, angry as I knew he was, to offend the old lady. But he need not have worried.

"Say what you mean, Mr. Fowler," she said sharply, "my son's former *what?*"

"His mistress."

"Who told you that lie?"

"It's no use, Madam Deal," the Inspector drawled, "the information came from Miss Ellen, and Mr. Deal himself made no effort to deny it. I'm afraid you won't get very far by calling it a lie."

In the silence which followed Fowler's statement I found myself leaning forward in my anxiety to catch Madam Deal's next words. But when at last she spoke, I had no difficulty in hearing her crisp words.

"Ellen," she said, "is a fool. Even you must have seen that. And Harvey was probably afraid to tell you the truth. But I'm not afraid. Lina Castle," she announced, "was my son's wife, my daughter-in-law—now do you understand?"

"I—I think—I'm beginning to," the Inspector spoke slowly. It was the first time I had heard his voice sound really shaken—but, after all, it was an amazing thing which the old lady had revealed.

"Harvey married her," Madam Deal continued imperturbably, "nine years ago—without my consent. Two years later he divorced her for dragging our name through a vile scandal—but even after that he went on giving her money. Lina had a deadly hold on my son from the very first day he saw her, and she never missed a chance to take advantage of that infatuation. For three years after the divorce Harvey gave her an allowance—without my knowledge—but even that was not enough for Lina. She came to me one day, hoping to get more money by threatening to take my grandson from us. I sent her packing—" the old lady's voice was as hard as granite, "and her stupid threat with her. Giving us Wally was the only decent thing Lina Castle ever did—and she had long ago sacrificed every right as the boy's mother. Lina Castle wasn't fit to touch Wally." Madam Deal spoke with a strangely fierce tenderness. It was the first time that a hint of emotion had crept into her measured words.

"It was that threat of taking the boy away from us, I believe," she went on after a moment, "which finally brought my son to his senses—and from that day on Harvey hated Lina Castle as she deserved to be hated. We came to New York shortly after that, and later we heard that Lina had married Wayne Castle and that they were living in Paris. Naturally, I had given orders that Lina was never to be allowed inside this hotel—for I knew that if she ever came here it would be for one thing—*money*. Money," the old lady repeated bitterly, "was Lina Castle's only love."

There was a moment of silence before Madam Deal resumed her story, and when she spoke again, her voice was once more calm and controlled.

"When several years had passed," she said quietly, "I believed that we were at last safe from Lina Castle. I believed that, Mr. Fowler, until three days ago—" Again the old lady paused with a sigh.

Evidently the Inspector preferred to let Madam Deal proceed in her own way, for he offered neither question nor comment in the interval before she continued speaking.

"You see," she explained presently, "as far as anyone here knows, Wally's mother died when he was a baby. For the boy's sake, and for our own, Harvey and I have preferred to let everyone believe that. Even Miss Ellen was told that Wally's mother was dead when she came to take care of the child. It was at the time of the threatened trouble in Washington that Ellen happened, most unfortunately, to encounter Lina, and she came straight to me to ask who the woman was. I told Ellen that Lina was nothing more than the worst sort of a mistress, and I spoke the truth. But I should have known that it was a mistake to tell Ellen even that much. . . . And now," the old lady concluded, "I have told you all that I know. Who killed Lina Castle, or why, I cannot say—but if ever a woman deserved to be murdered—it was she." Madam Deal's final words were spoken with the impartial, unfeeling justice of a court's sentence.

There was a brief silence before the Inspector spoke.

"Thank you," he said finally, "I'm sorry you had to tell me."

And without another word, he left the old lady's room and passed quickly through the nursery, motioning for me to follow him into the outer corridor. As we closed the door behind us—I listened—but this time there was no sound from Madam Deal's room.

Neither Fowler nor I made any comment as we returned to the floor below. Outside the door of 1116, Morty met us and handed a telegram to the Inspector.

"Is this the one from Tommy?" Fowler asked.

"Nope. This one just come up from Headquarters—I reckon it's the information from Washington you sent for this morning."

When he had scanned the message quickly, the Inspector passed it on to me with a short laugh.

"That would have been a damn sight more useful," he said, "an hour ago. We don't need it now."

I saw that the telegram was, as Morty had suggested, from the Detective Bureau in Washington, and that it contained the report on the Deal family and on Lina Castle which Fowler had requested.

REGARDING MRS OSCAR DEAL AND SON HARVEY DEAL FOLLOWING FACTS AVAILABLE STOP FAMILY LIVED HERE UNTIL THREE YEARS AGO EVIDENTLY WEALTHY IN GOOD SOCIETY STOP DEAL MARRIED EVALINA DEBLOIS NINETEEN TWENTY STOP DIVORCED NINETEEN TWENTY TWO WITH BAD SCANDAL ABOUT MRS DEAL AND LOCAL MILLIONAIRE STOP DEAL FAMILY MOVED TO NEW YORK NOTHING KNOWN ABOUT THEM SINCE STOP EVALINA DEAL MARRIED WAYNE CASTLE BELIEVED LIVING ABROAD STOP PROBABLY SAME PERSON AS MRS LINA CASTLE REFERRED TO YOUR MESSAGE STOP CAN CHECK THIS FACT FURTHER IF YOU SEND DESCRIPTION OF MURDERED WOMAN.

There was, as Inspector Fowler had said, nothing new to us in the message. I put the telegram in my notebook together with the transcript of the second interview with Madam Deal. If Fowler had had any doubts about the old lady's story—this latest evidence certainly proved the truth of her surprising information.

When we entered the room we found Harvey Deal waiting quietly. He looked up, wondering, I imagine, how much or how little his mother had told the Inspector, but neither he nor Fowler spoke of it at the moment. It seemed to me that the Inspector was in some strange way discouraged by the sudden turn which the case had taken. He was frowning as he moved restlessly about the room—and when finally he addressed Deal, his tone was oddly impatient, as if he had suddenly lost interest in Harvey Deal as a witness.

As briefly as possible, Fowler repeated the facts which he had learned from the old lady. He hardly looked at Deal when he spoke, and it was evident that he had no intention of questioning him further.

I was, however, curious to see how Deal was taking the news. To my surprise, I saw that he looked almost relieved. For the first time it occurred to me that Deal might have hated lying to us—that he was, perhaps, glad that his mother had finally swept aside the pride and fear which had been choking back the truth. But no doubt I was imagining all this. One could not, after all, deduce anything much from the single comment which Harvey Deal made when the Inspector finished speaking.

"I suppose," he said simply, "that you understand now why I hated Lina Castle."

For just a moment Fowler halted his restless pacing to stare at Harvey Deal, then abruptly he turned away again.

"Why you hated her—yes," he murmured thoughtfully, "but we haven't got it yet—" he was ruffling his hair as he spoke, "we haven't quite got the secret—" A sharp knock at the door cut short his musing.

It was Morty who entered, hearing a long envelope.

"Here's that telegram Tommy pieced together, Chief," he announced. "I sent the kid home for his dinner."

Eagerly the Inspector ripped open the envelope and unfolded the sheet of paper on which Tommy had neatly assembled and pasted the yellow fragments which we had rescued from Mrs. Evans' waste-basket. Whatever it might he that the reconstructed telegram revealed—it was evident that Fowler was profoundly surprised. Surprised—and then baffled, for I saw that his frown deepened furiously as he continued to stare at the message in his hand. When finally he looked up, it was to gaze vacantly at me for a moment, apparently still perplexed. Then slowly light seemed to dawn on him.

"Holy cat, I wonder if that could be it," the Inspector said slowly, "I wonder if—" Suddenly he checked himself, and looked once more at the sheet of paper. Evidently the second examination confirmed his suspicion—for a moment later he had snatched his hat, and was preparing to leave us for some mysterious errand.

"I'll be back," he said hastily, "as quickly as I can. Deal, go get yourself some dinner and a drink of gin. You need it—but don't leave the hotel. And you, Miss Pell, wait right here until I get back. If I'm not mistaken," he added excitedly, "I'll be bringing home a nice, fat slice of bacon!"

And with that, Fowler was gone—leaving us without the vaguest notion of *what* bacon he hoped to capture. It was several minutes before Deal collected himself sufficiently to depart, with a murmured apology to me, for his dinner—and probably the gin too. The moment he was safely out of the way, I made straight for the telegram which Tommy had pieced together—for I was frankly curious to see what, in that message, had so mysteriously startled the Inspector into action. But I was doomed to temporary disappointment. The telegram, which Fowler had left upon the desk was pieced together exactly as I had seen it earlier, and there was not one single hit of new information on the reconstructed blank.

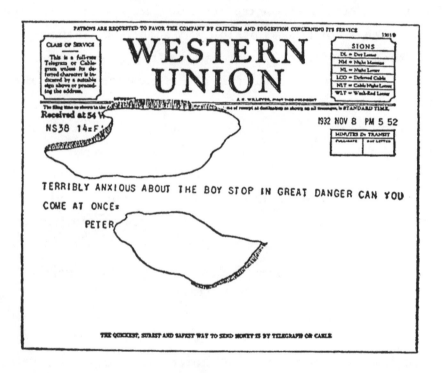

There was but one significant thing about the message and that was, of course, the fact that certain of the scraps had not been pasted in. It seemed to me that this omission pointed to one of two things. Either that Tommy had been unable to piece the missing hits together—or that we had failed to resurrect them from the waste-basket upstairs. And I confess that for the moment I failed to see in either possibility the hidden meaning which had sent the Inspector hurrying on his mysterious errand.

16
FALSE ALARM

When I had waited for perhaps fifteen minutes, I left 1116 temporarily to go to my own room on the floor below. I intended, of course, to be back at my post before the Inspector returned, but I had scarcely closed my door when a sharp knock startled me. It was Fowler.

"I didn't expect," I said lightly, "that you could capture the bacon quite so quickly. I just sneaked down here to find some cigarettes while you were gone."

To my surprise, he made no reply whatever, nor did he make a move to return to 1116. Instead, he entered my room and closed the door behind him.

"Well," I tried to make the best of his strange behavior, "do sit down—and have one of the cigarettes."

"No, thanks. I prefer to move around—and I don't smoke while I'm thinking." The curtness of Fowler's tone was unmistakable—but I made one more effort to start a natural conversation.

"By the way," I said, "how about that mysterious bacon? Did you manage to get it?"

"I did," he answered briefly.

For a moment I waited, still half expecting that Fowler would explain his errand, but he said nothing further. He was moving about the room with the same restlessness I had observed upstairs, but this time his mood seemed different. Instead of looking confused and discouraged, as he had earlier, there was an air of suppressed excitement in his manner. Suddenly he halted his pacing before my desk. I saw that he was looking at the typewriter which I had used to transcribe my notes. Presently he slipped a sheet of paper into the machine and began slowly to pick out some message.

"Lousy typewriter," he commented politely. "Is it yours?"

"Yes," I replied sweetly, "it is lousy. And no, it is not mine. I borrowed it from Mr. Evans this morning."

I was still utterly at a loss to account for the abrupt change in the Inspector's manner, but I was determined not to let it upset me.

"Did you discover anything important while you were gone?" I inquired. "I thought perhaps I should enter it in my notes, and—well," I added frankly, "I'm curious."

"Are you, Miss Pell?" Fowler spoke casually as he continued to peck at the typewriter keys. "As a matter of fact I did find out something important."

"About the telegram?"

"Yes."

A pause.

"Well—*what* about it?" I was getting really impatient.

"Why simply, Miss Pell," the Inspector did not look up as he answered me, "simply that the message was *not* received by Mrs. Evans, but sent by her instead."

"Do you mean," I asked after a moment, "that she sent the telegram to herself?"

"No, I don't. I mean she sent it to—" Suddenly Fowler broke off and leaned forward to examine the words he had typed.

"Hold everything!" he exclaimed excitedly. "Who did you say this machine belonged to?" For the first time since he had entered my room, the Inspector looked directly at me.

"To Mr. Evans," I repeated. "He loaned it to me this morning."

"Then," Fowler announced triumphantly, "we've got it!" He rose so abruptly from the desk that he very nearly upset his chair.

"Come on, Miss Pell," he directed, "and if we can make the damn fool talk we'll have the case settled in twenty minutes!"

And even as I hurried to follow the Inspector, I could not resist pausing to glance at the words which he had typed. But once more I was doomed to remain unenlightened. I had expected to see some message of mystic importance, and instead I beheld the most innocuous of all phrases, written over and over down the page.

```
"Now is the time for all good
men to come to the aid of the
party
"Now is the time for all good
men to come to the aid of the
party, etc.
```

When we reached room 1116, Fowler's first move was to send Morty for Mr. Evans. Evidently *he* was the one to whom the Inspector had referred as "the damn fool" who could clear up the case if he would only talk. I wondered about that—but I said nothing.

Evans' manner, when he arrived a few minutes later, was much as it had been that morning. He seated himself

calmly, and waited—apparently with perfect composure—
for the Inspector to begin.

"Tell me one thing, Evans," Fowler demanded sharply,
"does your wife wear a green coat trimmed with black fur?"

The effect was instantaneous. That one question was
sufficient to shatter Evans' attitude of cool indifference. I
saw the unmistakable look of alarm which crossed his face.

"Why, I—I—why yes—she does," he faltered miserably.

"I thought so," the Inspector nodded with an air of satisfaction, "and in that case, Mr. Evans—there is one more
question. Where did you keep the typewriter which you
loaned to Miss Pell this morning?"

"It was in my apartment upstairs. I always leave it there
so that—"

"Quite so," Fowler cut short the explanation with another nod of satisfaction. "Mr. Evans," he continued,
"there have been two typed messages which have come to
my attention as bits of evidence in this case. Both of them
were anonymous and both were typed on your machine."

"That's—that's quite impossible," Evans made a half-
hearted effort to protest. "How can you possibly know—"

"Easily," the Inspector interrupted. "Your machine has
an unfortunate defect which makes it quite simple to identify any message written on it. The letter 'o' happens to
stick, with the result that each time an 'o' appears on paper it is noticeably fainter than the other letters." From
his pocket Fowler drew a small white card which I recognized as the one that had lain in the box of flowers. He
handed it to Evans. "You can see what I mean from that,"
he explained.

Hastily I flipped back through my notebook to find the
typed warning which Harvey Deal had turned over to us—

and there, surely enough, I observed the faintness with which the "o" appeared.

Lina Castle is planning something worse than you think. She has bought, etc.

"That message," the Inspector was pointing to the card which Evans held, "was discovered in a box of flowers in Lina Castle's room. Furthermore, we have a statement from the florist who sold the flowers that a young woman purchased them on the day before Mrs. Castle was killed. A young woman," he continued slowly, "wearing a green coat with black fur. In other words, Mr. Evans, your wife bought the flowers and typed this message—in order to take them to Lina Castle!"

For a moment Evans seemed stunned into silence.

"It's not true," he said at last, but there was no ring of conviction in his tone. "It's not true, I tell you, because Catherine was gone from the hotel before any of this business happened. She didn't know anything about it, I tell you, she couldn't—"

"Do you mean," Fowler cut in sharply, "that your wife didn't know Lina Castle?"

"Oh, my God," with a gesture of despair Evans sank back into his chair and covered his face with his hands.

"*Well—?*" Fowler prompted him impatiently, "did your wife know Lina Castle, or didn't she?"

"I don't know," Evans' voice was muffled by his hands, "I don't know," he repeated stubbornly.

"What do you mean by that?"

"Just what I say," Evans looked up at the Inspector with an expression of wretched confusion. "I swear to you I have no idea whether Catherine knew that woman or not."

For a moment the Inspector regarded him in silence.

"Evans," he said suddenly, "why have you put up such a bluff in this case? Why did you deliberately choose to act mysterious and defiant this morning?"

"Because," said Evans slowly, "because I was frightened."

"I see. And you hoped, by making me suspect you—to distract my attention from Mrs. Evans. Is that right?"

Evans nodded miserably.

"Certain things," he explained, "worried me. I knew that Catherine had nothing to do with the—the murder, but I also knew that sometimes things can *look* queer."

"Suppose you tell me," Fowler suggested, "exactly what the incidents were which worried you."

"I will tell you," Evans was evidently making a desperate effort to keep his voice steady, "exactly what happened. I'm telling you the truth, Inspector, because I *know* that if Catherine were only here she could explain everything. You must believe that."

It seemed impossible, to me at least, to look into his pale, wide-set blue eyes and not be convinced of Evans' sincerity.

"Never mind," said Fowler, "about that. Just tell me what made you suspect that Mrs. Evans may have known Lina Castle."

"The first thing," Evans began, "happened nearly a year ago, when I mentioned to my wife the fact that Mr. Deal had given orders not to admit a Mrs. Castle to the hotel. At the time, the order meant nothing to me—and I was naturally surprised when Catherine took a great interest in the matter."

"What sort of an interest?" the Inspector demanded. "Did she seem upset?"

"No. She simply asked a number of questions about why Mr. Deal had given the order—and I was unable to answer, not knowing any reasons myself. Finally I asked if she knew the woman, but instead of telling me, she just laughed. Then I said, 'If you *don't* know her—why are you so curious about it?'"

"What did she say then?"

"She stopped laughing all of a sudden, and looked almost angry. Then she said, 'Oh, nothing, only it's interesting to see how good Mr. Deal thinks he is all of a sudden.' Well," he went on, "neither of us mentioned the matter again, and I had really forgotten about it until—until three days ago."

"Three days ago," Fowler repeated thoughtfully, "that would be just about the time Mrs. Castle registered here, wouldn't it?"

"Yes. Mrs. Castle had come in late the afternoon before, and it was at breakfast that Catherine asked me who had room 1117. I thought it rather odd, because Catherine never pays much attention to the business of the hotel—but I answered that a Miss Lovett had the room, and asked her why she wanted to know."

"What reason did she give?"

"She said she simply wondered because she had been disturbed until late the night before by the noise from downstairs. You see, 1117 is directly under the living-room of our apartment. That seemed odd too, because I had noticed no noise, and when I said so, Catherine answered, 'Maybe you didn't—but I imagine Mr. Deal was disturbed all right!'"

"Did Mrs. Evans explain what she meant?"

"No. She only told me to wait and see if she weren't right—and sure enough, when Mr. Deal came down to his office that morning he asked me the very first thing who had been put in room 1117!"

"Well," the Inspector prompted him, "what next?"

"That was all," Evans admitted, "except when I found the—" he checked himself suddenly, "except what you have just told me about the typed messages."

"What," Fowler snapped, "did you start to say then? Except when you found the—*what?*"

"Why—why I didn't mean—" Evans halted in confusion.

"You started to say," Fowler informed him, "that you noticed nothing odd until you discovered the note which told you that Mrs. Evans had gone to Washington. Am I right?"

As Evans failed to answer, the Inspector turned quickly to me.

"Get that note, Miss Pell," he directed.

When I had handed him the envelope, he held it before Evans' unwilling eyes.

"That's not your wife's handwriting, is it, Evans?" he demanded.

After a wretched moment, Evans shook his head.

"You knew from the beginning that it was not your wife who left that note, didn't you?"

Again Evans hesitated.

"I don't know," he said at last, "who wrote the letter. I—I found it on our desk upstairs."

"Mr. Evans—do you know where your wife is?"

"No. I wish to God I did. I tell you if only Catherine were here, she could explain all this. You can't believe that she had anything to do with the murder—when you *know* that she had left the hotel an hour before Mrs. Castle was shot. You *must* know that—"

"I'm sorry, Evans," the Inspector said calmly, "but that alibi won't last any longer. Lina Castle was not murdered at ten minutes past eight—but more than an hour earlier."

"But look here," Evans was making one last desperate effort, "Miss Pell gave the alarm—"

"Miss Pell," said Fowler clearly, "was lying."

As both men turned to stare at me—Evans with a look of blank amazement, and Fowler with his least pleasant expression—I did my very best to face them out.

"I'm afraid," I said coldly, "that I don't understand."

"Oh, yes, you do," the Inspector drawled. "You know quite well that you deliberately gave a false alarm at ten minutes past eight. If the shot had actually been fired at that time—Madam Deal would have been certain to hear it, and so would Mr. Deal. Yet they heard nothing. Instead, it was fired at about, I should say, twenty minutes of seven, at which time only two people appear to have been within earshot: Madam Deal, who remembers being wakened sharply from her nap at that time—and you, Miss Pell, who probably heard the sound from your room beneath 1117."

17
REVELATIONS

This time I saw that it was useless to go on with the lie. I said nothing at all when Inspector Fowler paused to regard me triumphantly. After a moment, Evans spoke.

"Why," he asked incredulously, "why did you do it, Miss Pell?"

The Inspector answered for me.

"She did it," he said briefly, "to give your wife an alibi." And before Evans could express his amazement, Fowler had turned quickly back to me.

"It's your turn to talk, Miss Pell," he said. "Tell me exactly what you did after you arrived at the Almeda yesterday afternoon."

I hesitated, for even then I was uncertain just how much the Inspector knew.

"Begin at the beginning, Miss Pell," he prompted me. "It was the message from Mrs. Evans which brought you to the hotel, wasn't it?"

I looked at him fearfully.

"It was simple enough," he explained, "to check that fact. A trip to the nearest Western Union office proved that my hunch was correct. The telegram which Tommy pieced together was actually a message sent from Mrs. Evans to you in Washington. The missing dateline and signature gave me the clue, of course, and I found that the rest of the signature was 'Evans.' Why Catherine Evans should have signed herself 'Peter Evans' I don't know—just yet. But she did send the message, didn't she?"

I nodded wearily.

"If you've discovered that much," I said, "I may as well tell you everything. It *was* the telegram from Catherine which brought me here, and she signed herself 'Peter' because that was an old nickname. We were friends at school, you see—inseparable friends—and we were often called 'Joan and Peter.'"

I looked up to see that Evans was watching me with growing amazement. "I realize," I explained quickly to him, "that you knew nothing about this friendship. When Catherine married—she had to break with several of her closest friends, and I was one of them. It was because," I spoke with difficulty, "we were those who knew about—something which Catherine was trying to forget."

I turned back to Fowler.

"When I reached the Almeda yesterday afternoon," I went on, "I went straight to Catherine's apartment, but to my great surprise she was not there. It was I who disturbed Madam Deal's nap by knocking repeatedly at the Evans' door. I simply couldn't believe that Catherine had gone away when she had telegraphed me to come to help her. Finally I tried the door, and, finding it unlocked, I went in. Surely, I thought, she must have left some message for me. Yet I found nothing. After that, I went back to my room and waited. I was anxious about Catherine—and when more than an hour passed and still I heard nothing from her, I decided to go up to her apartment once more.

This time I didn't knock, however, because I heard voices in the living-room, and I knew better than to burst in on Catherine when she was with someone who," I avoided Evans' eyes as I spoke, "who probably knew nothing about the—the trouble. Well—the fact that I had heard Catherine's voice relieved me somewhat, and I decided to go up to the roof for a little air. It was there that I encountered Wally Deal and Miss Ellen—as I told you earlier, Inspector. For ten or fifteen minutes I stayed on the roof, and it must have been about twenty minutes of seven when I started down. I had intended to go straight to my room, but as I came down the fire-escape stairs, I paused on the eleventh floor landing—"

The Inspector was leaning forward eagerly.

"What stopped you?" he asked sharply.

"The sound of a shot," I said.

"Then what?"

"I opened the door into the corridor," I explained, "and I saw that a woman was coming out of a room just ahead of me. When she turned around— Look here," I broke off abruptly, "I—I can't go on with this while—while Mr. Evans is here. Please," I appealed to the Inspector, "can't I tell the rest just to you?"

Fowler turned to Evans.

"That," he spoke not unkindly, "will be as Mr. Evans pleases."

"I'll stay," Evans' white face was set, but he managed to speak quietly. "Go on, Miss Pell," he said to me.

"Very well," I continued after a moment, "the woman turned, and I saw that it was Catherine Evans. By some miracle we kept from speaking, and Catherine simply took my hand. Together we hurried upstairs, and she led me into her apartment. Once we were there, with the door safely locked, she told me what she had done. She had murdered her sister, Lina Castle, in order," I spoke slowly, "to save her son." I could not bring myself to look at Evans—but I heard him draw a sharp breath.

Even the Inspector was silent for a moment.

"Her son," he said presently, "was 'the boy' referred to in her telegram, of course, but was it—Wally Deal?"

I nodded.

"Catherine was Wally's mother," I explained, "but the boy was adopted by Mr. Deal and Lina Deal on the day he was born. It all happened seven years ago in California where Mr. and Mrs. Deal were spending the winter. Catherine, you see, was not married—and her sister promised to take the baby. She and Mr. Deal claimed that it was their own child—because they hoped, in that way, to reconcile Madam Deal to Lina. The old lady hated Harvey's wife, of course, but they knew that she was fanatically anxious for Harvey to have an heir—and they believed that the baby would win her over to accepting Lina."

"Did Deal?" Fowler interrupted curiously, "know that Mrs. Evans was Wally's mother?"

I shook my head.

"No one," I said, "knew that—except Lina and myself. Mr. Deal was aware, of course, that the baby was adopted—but Lina never told him who the mother was. As a matter of fact, I don't believe he ever knew that Lina had a sister. Catherine and Lina had been almost strangers for years—neither approved of the other, and they were never together."

"How did it happen that they met in California?" the Inspector asked.

"It was," I explained, "purely an accident. Lina had gone there with her husband, of course, and Catherine—because of her trouble—had gone to the Coast in order to hide her misfortune from her family and friends in the East. Catherine told me once how she and her sister met. It was in a shop in Los Angeles, where the two sisters happened to come face to face in an elevator. They recognized each other, of course, and since poor Catherine's condition was evident, Lina soon had the whole story. Lina gave her sister some money, and she was kind enough to promise that she would say nothing to anyone about their unfortunate meeting."

"How did it happen," Fowler interrupted again, "that Lina came to her sister's rescue in adopting the baby?"

"Lina," I said, "did it for her own advantage. I've told you that she hoped, by pretending that the baby was really her child and Harvey's, to win over her mother-in-law—and her mother-in-law's fortune. It was easier, after all," I could not keep the bitterness out of my tone, "for Lina to take her sister's baby, than to bother about having one of her own."

"You told me," Fowler murmured, "that Harvey Deal knew that Wally was adopted?"

I nodded.

"It was easy enough," I explained, "for Lina to convince Harvey that they should adopt a baby and claim that it was their own—in an effort to please old Madam Deal. Poor Harvey was so infatuated with his wife, and so anxious to win his mother's approval, that he fell in readily with the plan. Particularly, since even he must have known Lina well enough to realize that she would never consent to having a child of her own."

The Inspector nodded slowly.

"I think," he said, "that I'm beginning to understand the whole complicated story. I suppose," he added, "that it was not difficult for Lina to keep Deal in the dark about who the baby's real mother was?"

"Not difficult at all," I shook my head, "because Deal was willing enough to let Lina handle the whole business of the adoption—and she simply went to her sister and offered to take the baby as soon as it was born. Catherine was desperate, of course, and she had no choice but to let her sister carry out the plan—although she was utterly wretched about it. She knew that Lina would care nothing for the child, and after the adoption Catherine was always miserable for fear Lina would somehow let the secret be known. When Lina and Harvey Deal were divorced, Catherine was more terrified than ever, lest Lina should tell the truth about Wally in order to spite the Deal family. But somehow, the crisis was passed—and when finally Lina married again and went to live in Europe—Catherine felt for the first time that she was safe. You know, of course, that shortly after the Deals took over the Almeda, Catherine came here as telephone operator. She did it in order to be near Wally, and to be able to see him occasionally."

"But, good heavens," the Inspector broke in, "wasn't she afraid of being recognized?"

"Not at all," I said, "because Lina was, it seemed, gone forever—and there was no one else, not even Harvey Deal, who could possibly recognize Catherine as Lina's sister, or as the boy's mother."

Again Fowler nodded thoughtfully.

"You remember," I reminded him, "that Catherine and Lina were comparative strangers, and that neither had ever wanted to claim the other as a sister. The family had been split up when Lina and Catherine were children, and the two girls grew up separately—and very differently. Catherine's friends were never Lina's friends—and *vice versa*."

"I understand," said the Inspector. "Go on, Miss Pell. What happened after Catherine came here to work?"

"It was then," I continued, "that Catherine began, for the first time, to be somewhat happier. She saw how devoted Mr. Deal and his mother were to Wally—and she really believed that they were all safe from any further disturbances on the part of Lina. Since Catherine's marriage," again I found myself carefully avoiding Evans' eyes, "she has been perfectly contented, and she never dreamed that her past troubles would return to ruin that happiness.

"I could not," I went on, "blame Catherine for what she did last night. Lina Castle's second husband had left her and taken his millions with him, and Lina came to this hotel four days ago with the deliberate intention of forcing Harvey Deal to go back to Paris with her. When he refused, she planned to reveal the secret of Wally's birth to Madam Deal. Catherine hadn't known this until yesterday—up to that time she had been half-amused by the trick which Lina had used to get into the hotel. It must have been during the first day or two that Catherine left the box of flowers in her sister's room—perhaps she intended the cryptic message half as a joke, half as a warning to Lina. At any rate, it was not until yesterday that Catherine discovered Lina's real intention—and from that time on she was desperate. She tried every method she knew, every bribe, every persuasion, to keep Lina from going to Madam Deal and carrying out her threat. It would have meant, of course, that Wally would lose his name, his home, security, inheritance—everything. And Catherine had no one to turn to for help—because she feared, more than anything else, that if her secret were known it would be the end of her own marriage.

"Perhaps you see, Inspector, why I deliberately chose to withhold evidence in this case. When Catherine told me that she had shot Lina—I had but one thought—to help her. And I knew that we must both work fast. I managed to persuade her that her one hope lay in running away—and while she tried to telephone her husband, I packed a suitcase for her, and reassured her as best I could. She managed to get away by seven o'clock, not more than twenty minutes after the shooting, and when she was gone, I fixed everything for her as carefully as I could. First of all I left the note for Mr. Evans, explaining his wife's departure. I simply invented the incident of the sick brother—and counted on him not to give the thing away. Then it occurred to me that to leave the fragments of Catherine's telegram to me, in the waste-basket would give her an even stronger alibi. Of course, I tore out the date-line and the tell-tale half of her signature—never dreaming that anyone would take the trouble to piece the whole message together again.

"The next thing I had to do," I said, "was the hardest of all. I went to Lina's room, as Catherine had asked me to do, and bit by bit, I searched her luggage. In one suitcase I found the precious packet of papers and letters which contained the information about Wally. It was in removing that package, I suppose, that I left the unaccountable space which you discovered later. I went through that room as carefully as I could, trying to remove every bit of evidence which might point to Catherine."

"And there," the Inspector put in dryly, "you certainly succeeded."

"But," I continued, "I missed one thing—the box of flowers, which I knew nothing about, and which Lina had pushed back into a corner of the closet. I rescued the gun which poor Catherine had left beside Lina's body, and I hid it in my room. The package of papers I managed to burn and then my job was nearly done.

"It was, however, evident by this time that by some miraculous good fortune no one had heard the shot—nor had been aware of any disturbance. And it was that fact which gave me the idea of giving the false alarm about having heard the shot and the scream. I hoped, in that way, to better establish Catherine's alibi—and if not that, at least to confuse the exact time of the shooting. Perhaps I was wrong—perhaps I was reckless— perhaps I gave myself away by that false move—but any way, I did it. And the rest," I sighed, "you know."

When I had finished speaking at last, I was utterly exhausted. I felt as if I could never care about anything again, as I leaned back in my chair and closed my eyes.

Presently I heard the Inspector ask,

"Where is Mrs. Evans?"

"In Washington," I answered, "in my apartment on Connecticut Avenue."

It was then that Evans spoke for the first time since he had heard my story.

"I must go," he said quietly, "to Catherine."

And I knew from the sound of his voice that, whatever else might happen to Catherine Evans—she had not lost her husband.

When Evans had gone, there was a long silence. I hardly dared to look at the Inspector—for I dreaded to know what he must think of me. Vaguely I imagined that he might arrest me—clap me into jail—sentence me for perjury. The phrase "accessory to the crime" whirled dismally about in my weary brain. But minutes passed, and still Fowler said nothing at all. At last I took courage and looked up at him. He was standing, in his most characteristic attitude, squinting thoughtfully at his pencil.

"Well," I asked humbly, "what shall I do now?"

"What shall you do?" the Inspector echoed, "Why really, Miss Pell, I haven't the vaguest idea—but if you want my suggestion, I advise you to get a good dinner and go to bed early."

It must have taken me a full minute to recover my breath.

"Do you mean," I finally managed to inquire, "that you aren't going to—to *do* anything to me?"

"Do anything?" Fowler repeated blankly, "What should I do?"

"I mean aren't you supposed to arrest me or something, for the way I lied to you?"

"Oh," the Inspector nodded, "that. . . . Well," he added generously, "I wouldn't worry about that, Miss Pell. After all, if I went around arresting all the lying witnesses in this town, I'd have my hands full."

"That's nice of you, Inspector," I said gratefully, "but I do feel badly about having held up the case—especially when you trusted me enough to let me be your assistant."

The Inspector gave me an odd look.

"Well, don't let *that* bother you too much, Miss Pell," he said gallantly. "But while we're on the subject, please tell me one thing—when did you put the gun on the roof?"

"Last night," I said, "after our second interview."

"And did you intend to have the kid find it?"

"Good heavens, no. I was really frightened when he got hold of it. You see, we were playing hide-and-go-seek—

and I hardly thought Wally would be looking for me under that low ledge."

"You're—very fond of playing hide-and-go-seek, aren't you, Miss Pell?" Fowler's tone was half indulgent, half critical.

I felt myself blushing uncomfortably.

"I used to think," I said, "that I was—but now I'm considering swearing off."

"Why?"

"Because," I said sharply, "some of my opponents are too smart. It's not fair." I saw the slow smile which spread over Fowler's face. "And while we're on *that* subject," I added, "there are a couple of things *I'd* like to know. First—how did you find out that I had written the note to Evans?"

"Not so difficult, Miss Pell. You see, I looked over that desk in the Evans' apartment pretty carefully—but I failed to see any blotter. Yet when I spilled the ink, you grabbed one right away from underneath a pile of letters. It—it rather suggested to me that you had used the things on that desk before."

"I see it now," I nodded ruefully, "but I certainly didn't then. Well, my second question is just this. When you mentioned *rigor mortis* last night—did you really mean anything, or were you just trying to frighten me?"

Again I saw that slow smile.

"A little of both, Miss Pell," said Fowler sweetly, "I had to wait for the Medical Examiner of course, but I had rather a hunch that Lina Castle had been dead more than half an hour when I got there. And then I thought a little spooky talk might loosen you up a bit on your testimony—but I was wrong there."

"You had me plenty worried," I admitted. "I'm glad I didn't show it too much."

"Well, you know, Miss Pell," the Inspector observed, as he turned to go, "there were times when you had me worried too. And now," he looked suddenly serious—and tired, "I suppose I've got to do my duty by having Catherine Evans arrested."

The case has not turned out too tragically after all. Poor Catherine Evans has suffered, of course, but she has had two blessed compensations; her husband's loyalty, and the fact that Wally has stayed on as before in the Deal family. It was due chiefly to the efforts of Inspector Fowler, and his apparently endless influence, that Catherine was given such a light sentence, and that the case was given so little publicity that Madam Deal has never been disillusioned about the identity of her adored grandson.

With me, the Inspector continued to be indulgent. I have taken weekend trips to New York somewhat more frequently since that fateful November visit, and several times I have seen Inspector Fowler. It was, in fact, his suggestion that I make a book out of this case. I objected at first, on the ground that it would be impossible to tell the story if I were to begin with my true part in the affair.

"And," I added, "if I *don't* tell what I knew about the murder, it makes it all too mysterious." I looked up earnestly, only to see that odd glint in the Inspector's eye which had puzzled me before.

"Look here," I said suddenly, "there's something that bothers me. Did you hire me as your assistant in that case because you really wanted me to help you—or because you suspected all along that I knew more than I had told?"

For a moment he simply looked at me—with his most irritating grin.

"You go ahead and write your story, Miss Pell," he said finally, "and let the readers answer that question."

The following images are selected from those accompanying the 1936 *Detroit Free Press* printing of *Hide and Go Seek*. Several larger newspapers during this period featured short novels in this fashion.

"*I understand perfectly what you mean. You are saying that I ordered the flowers for Mrs. Castle. You are trying to say that either I shot her or I know who did,*" *said Joan.*

"You'll stay right where you are until we get this thing settled. Either answer my question—or I'll put you under arrest."

Before I could stop him, Wally had picked up the gun and began to flourish it in the most terrifying manner. I forced myself to speak quietly: "Hand it to me, Wally."

"Why did your son fear Lina Castle?" Fowler asked the question sharply "Because," Madam Deal said distinctly, "my son is a coward!"

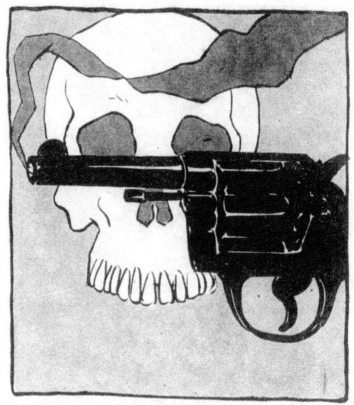

"What stopped you?" Fowler asked sharply. The answer came quickly: "The sound of a shot."

GOING TO ST. IVES

(1934, *periodical*; 1936, *novel*)

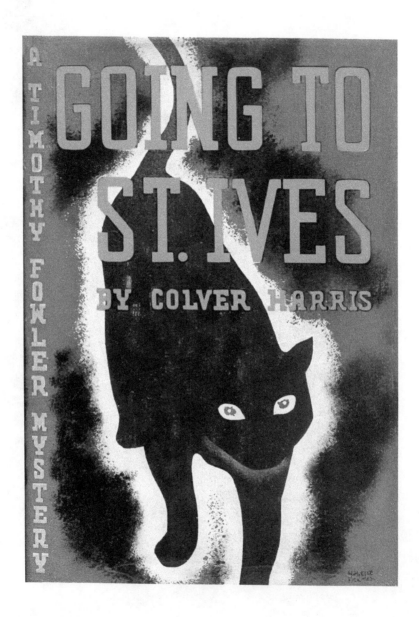

1
AS I WAS GOING TO ST. IVES

It was my foolish fondness for a cat named Emma that led me into trouble—a fact which, I am certain, must provide some of my friends with considerable secret satisfaction. Not that even the least cat-minded person could actually hold Emma morally responsible for what happened, but it might well be argued that had I not insisted on bringing my cherished cat to Baltimore with me, I would in all probability have taken a taxi directly from the railroad station to a hotel, and thus I would not have been in front of St. Ives Cathedral when the trouble started.

Not only was Emma responsible for my presence in the unfortunate vicinity of St. Ives at the very moment when murder was discovered within the gloomy stone Cathedral walls, but it was upon Emma, and Emma alone, that my alibi was later to rest. And as an alibi she proved anything but effective. I have been told that it was patently absurd of me to expect a police Inspector to believe that any woman in her right mind would have gotten off a train in a strange city, checked her luggage, removed her crated cat from the baggage car, and proceeded to search out the nearest park—with the sole intention of there uncrating, exercising and solacing the cat—all before seeking out any

219

hotel or proper lodgings for herself. Be that as it may, I was accused of inventing the entire alibi, of using Emma as a deliberate blind to excuse my presence at the Cathedral, and finally of seeking publicity by presenting what the press insisted on calling "sensational testimony."

That any of these three accusations was simply and obviously untrue might, it always seemed to me, have been fairly well established by the most superficial examination of my background, occupation, and general character. Belinda Stebbins, spinster, head of the English Department at conservative Maplewood College for conservative young ladies, was surely an unlikely person to suspect of being willfully involved in a brutal murder. And to those even remotely familiar with the chaste principles of academic life, it must have seemed even more preposterous to accuse a dowdyish, middle-aged professor of seeking newspaper publicity. Yet no evidence which I or my friends could present served to really convince either police or press of the complete respectability of my straight and narrow past, and the entire innocence of my part in the affair at St. Ives.

And again it was Emma who was to blame. For I was assured by many persons well versed in the mysterious ways of publicity that had it not been for what one reporter called the "cat angle" of my testimony, I should have been allowed to remain what I actually was—an innocent bystander. Instead of which I was to be grilled by a suspicious police Inspector and heralded by the newspapers as "the little gray-haired woman of mystery," and by one obnoxious journalist as "The Cat Woman," with sinister references to the "Pig Woman" of another famous murder trial.

I am compelled to admit here, in the interests of a New England conscience, that I am by no means wholly ungrateful to Emma. She is, indeed, still my cherished pet, and she lies upon her accustomed chintz pillow near my desk as I write out this chronicle. For even though nothing in my life previous to the twentieth of last June should have prepared me in any way to take part in a murder or the investigation thereof, and though there were moments when I had grave doubts of just how Dr. Prentiss, the President of Maplewood College, would react to the fact that a senior member of his faculty was spread all over the front pages of newspapers in connection with a sensational killing—(and I may add now that my doubts in this direction were extremely well founded)—there is no denying that doubts and qualms were more than once forgotten in a feeling of positive exhilaration as I considered the aplomb with which my hitherto sheltered spirit adapted itself to the eventful role I was called upon to play in connection with the murder at St. Ives. It was, moreover, with definite satisfaction that I pictured the horror and amazement with which my former pupils would learn from the daily papers that Miss Stebbins ("Imagine, my dear," they would say, "that *funny* old Miss *Stebbins!*") was entangled in the gory violence of a murderer's plot.

My purpose in travelling, on that fiendishly hot June afternoon, from Maplewood to Baltimore, could not, in all conscience, have been further removed from crime and bloodshed. I had come to the city for nothing more sinister than to accept an honorary degree of Litt. D. which the Trustees of Granger College had been generous enough to offer me. It had happened that our Commencement exercises at Maplewood preceded those of Granger College by nearly a week, and I had, therefore, journeyed to Baltimore several days in advance of the actual time when I was to receive the degree. Since I intended to rest and shop and generally amuse myself a bit during those days, I had notified no one at Granger of my early arrival. All of which was innocent enough—but it was a revelation to see what sinister meaning the whole plan took on when the "inside story of Miss Stebbins' secret journey to Baltimore" was later blazoned forth in the press.

Of the motive which led me, on the afternoon of my arrival, to check my luggage at the station and set out on foot toward St. Ives, I have already spoken. I was, and it still seems to be a case of *believe it or not,* carrying my poor crated and discomfited pet cat to the haven of the Cathedral close (which was actually a small public garden) where, a sympathetic station attendant had assured me, it would be both safe and proper to allow Emma a little outing.

So much for the explanation of my presence in front of St. Ives at the precise moment when things began to happen. My train reached Baltimore at five-thirty that afternoon, which gives me at least a starting point to calculate the time element. Allowing perhaps ten minutes at the station, during which I checked my luggage and rescued Emma from the baggage-room, I started to walk up Pearl Avenue toward Charles Street at approximately twenty minutes of six. I had only two short blocks to travel, so I must have reached the gate of the Cathedral close not later than twelve minutes of six. And at that very moment the first dreadful thing happened.

It was an accident.

It happened directly in front of the Cathedral steps, and before my horrified eyes. That particular corner is one of the busiest in Baltimore, and there must have been at least a score of persons who saw, as I did, the young man who ran down the Cathedral steps and out into the street—

directly in the path of a shiny black roadster. There must
have been others who, like myself, uttered an involuntary
and useless cry of warning—and no doubt those others
also heard the shrill screaming of brakes and the ghastly,
inhuman thud with which the young man's head struck
the curb. But at the moment I was aware of no one save
myself. I had no thought even for the victim—nor for the
fact that I was likely to be needed as a witness to the accident. I had just one idea, and that was to get off the street
before I fainted dead away.

I think I must have been aware of that faint coming on
at the very moment when I saw the unknown young man
struck, and yet I was somehow able to hold off the actual
waves of unconsciousness until I could attain a suitably
private retreat in which to collapse. It was a control which
arose, I imagine, from my deep-rooted aversion to persons
who give way to feelings in public places. (An aversion
which is probably shared by any who have experienced
life in a girls' school.) At any rate I do remember, all too
plainly, looking about me in that frantic moment for some
escape from the crowded street—and vividly I recall the
relief with which I realized that the great Cathedral door
loomed just in front of me.

I have an impression, vague to be sure, that at the moment when I entered the Cathedral, the vestibule was deserted. There was, however, at least one other person in
the building at the time, for I distinctly recall colliding
with a large woman who was hurrying out of the church
proper just as I hastened in. I need scarcely say that I did
not pause to observe the woman with any care, but I *was*
conscious of her bulk, and of the bright, mustard yellow
dress which she wore.

That unpleasant shade of yellow was, indeed, the last thing I saw, for once inside the dim Cathedral, I had barely time to grope my way into the nearest pew and plunk down poor Emma's crate, the handle of which I had somehow continued to clutch. Then the growing whirls of dizziness blackened everything, and, with infinite relief, I sank back upon the cushioned seat to faint in peace.

→ 2 ←
THE MAN WHO KNELT

The first sound which bore itself in upon my returning consciousness was the insistent clanging of a bell. For a foggy moment I struggled with an impression that I was hearing the familiar summons of my own alarm clock, but it was not long before I opened my eyes and stared upward into the great vaulted ceiling of St. Ives. Slowly the memory of the accident returned to me, and with it came the realization that the bell which had awakened me was the sound of an ambulance which must have been summoned to fetch the injured man outside.

My first thought was to wonder how long I had lain unconscious, and to hope—woman-like—that no one had passed by to observe my unconventional position stretched prone upon a pew in the great Cathedral. Surely not many minutes had elapsed between the time of the accident and the arrival of the clanging ambulance, and since there was no sound to indicate that anyone was near me, I concluded that my unceremonious fainting fit had gone unobserved. This comforting reflection seemed to restore my strength somewhat, and with the return of normal common sense and composure, I began to think of getting myself up from the pew and out of St. Ives as promptly as possible.

Rather gingerly, I sat up. Only a slight dizziness remained to remind me of the shock I had suffered. I sighed with relief as I reflected that no one need ever know of this unseemly collapse. Looking back on it now, my anxieties lest someone should have discovered my swoon seem laughable—for two days later I would have given a good deal for a single witness who could prove to a skeptical detective that I had actually been unconscious during the ten minutes which followed the accident outside!

At the moment, I certainly had not the slightest foreboding of danger. I was chiefly occupied by the business of straightening my hat, composing my rumpled dress, and peering anxiously into the small crate beside me in order to discover how Emma had survived her first trip to church. It was not until, having offered Emma what consolation I could, I was on the very point of taking my departure, that I suddenly became aware of the fact that I was not alone in the Cathedral.

Several pews in front of me, and over toward the side aisle, was a man who knelt, apparently in prayer. Why I had not seen him earlier I cannot say, unless it was because of my somewhat agitated condition, and the fact that it was very dim inside the great Cathedral. Heavy stained-glass windows shut out nearly all of the June sunlight, and the huge Gothic pillars cast a crisscross of deeper shadows. There was no artificial light save one small, flickering red lamp which glowed upon the altar.

I leaned forward to peer through the dimness. Something about the man's position seemed odd—almost uncanny. And the next moment I was repenting my curiosity. For in a startling flash I had received my second shock of the afternoon. Small wonder that the man's attitude seemed unnatural! He knelt, yes, *but not in prayer*.

He was slumped down and leaning upon the pew in front of him, apparently held in that position by his arms which hung over the pew-back. And his head, which had seemed at first glance to be bowed in reverence, was actually lolling forward in a grotesque and lifeless way.

To describe the emotions which this discovery roused in me would be difficult. A dozen fantastic explanations of the man's presence flashed through my mind while I struggled vainly to summon one sensible idea. No doubt I was unduly wrought up, but it seemed to me that there was something peculiarly horrible and mysterious in the sight of that still figure, kneeling in a lifeless imitation of prayer before the silent, shadowy peace of the deserted altar.

At last a measure of sanity broke through my panic, and with it came one clear idea. I must go quietly and notify someone in charge of the Cathedral of the man's strange plight. At once I rose (on knees which, I must confess, were scarcely steady) and turned to make my way toward the door.

But I was too late.

At the very moment when I was about to step into the aisle, there was a subdued sound of voices outside the doors at the rear of the Cathedral, and I turned abruptly to see three men hurrying down the center aisle. It so happened that I stood in the shadow of one of the great pillars, with the result that I was fairly well obscured from the sight of the men. Also it was evident that they were intent upon the unconscious man, for they moved down the aisle, with scarcely a glance to left or right, until they reached the pew where the mysterious figure knelt.

"There he is, Father," I heard one of them say, "right where I saw him before."

The man addressed was a priest, and the one who spoke was evidently an attendant of some sort, judging from the black vestments which he wore. The third man was a police officer.

"Who discovered this?" It was the policeman who spoke.

"I did," the attendant answered.

"How long ago?"

"It must have been about ten minutes, I guess, maybe a little more."

"Was there anyone else in the church when you found him?" the policeman asked sharply.

"No one."

"You're sure of that?"

"Well—no one I saw. I looked around—"

"What did you do when you found this man?"

"I stepped up to look closer. I thought at first he might have gone to sleep—they do sometimes. But when I saw—I—" the man faltered, apparently unable to say anything further, and pointed toward the kneeling figure. Even from where I stood, I could see his finger tremble.

The policeman bent down. I saw him lift the lolling head for a moment, then he straightened abruptly.

"Dead," said the policeman, and the word echoed with a strange hollowness in the empty Cathedral.

The priest, who had remained somewhat behind the other two men, came forward at once.

"Dead?" he echoed.

The officer nodded.

"Sorry, Father, but it's pretty bad. His throat's been cut."

Quickly the priest crossed himself, then murmured a few sentences while the other two stood with heads respectfully bowed. When the brief prayer was ended, the policeman spoke again.

"Now then, Father," he spoke briskly, "you take it easy. This don't look so very good—but you just leave it to me. The first thing to do—" His voice dropped suddenly, so that I could no longer hear the words of his murmured instructions, but from observing his gestures I guessed that he was directing an immediate search of the building.

I knew then that I was trapped. In my position behind the big column, I had not yet been observed by the men— but I realized that it would be impossible for me to leave the Cathedral without being seen. I judged furthermore that it would scarcely be advisable, under the circumstances, to run the risk of being discovered in my hiding place. Obviously I would have to explain my presence—faint and all. (For I had gathered that it was during the time that I lay stretched unconscious upon the pew that the attendant had entered and made his discovery of the kneeling man.) And the sooner I began such a difficult explanation, the better for me.

Accordingly I stepped forth from behind the pillar. The three men, still in a close conference, had their backs toward me. I gathered courage and cleared my throat.

"Excuse me," I began, "but . . ."

I never finished the sentence.

The words were choked in my throat by a murderous blow on the back of my head. I felt the violent snap with which my teeth clicked together, I saw a swirl of bright stars in the blackness. And that was all.

I learned much later that I fell forward against a cushioned pew, but I had no memory of it. I had no memory of anything further until ten o'clock that night—nearly four hours after the blow was struck.

3

I WAKE UP—TWICE

At first the women's voices seemed to come from very far away. Indeed, I was scarcely aware of myself or my condition as I listened, yet the words registered themselves with a peculiar clarity upon my detached spirit.

"Hello, Carter," said the first voice. "How's every little thing?"

"Oh, hello, Gibbs. Fine, thanks. Isn't it hot though?"

"I'll say! Adams told me you were up here, so I thought I'd peek in. I'm in Surgical downstairs. Tonsil case. What's yours?"

"Adams said it was a slight concussion, but I don't know much about it yet. I only came on an hour ago."

"Well, there's something funny about it, isn't there?"

"Funny about what?"

"About your patient. Pete told me she was brought in at the same time as a man with his throat cut, and right afterwards a lot of cops came trailing in."

"Oh," the other voice sounded indifferent. "I don't think that had anything to do with my patient. Anyway, there haven't been any cops around here. It's probably just another of Pete's stories."

"Well, maybe so. But there's certainly something queer going on somewhere. The lobby was full of reporters when I came in—and Adams is in an awful stew."

There was a brief silence, then an exasperated sigh.

"I can see, Carter," the voice was resigned, "that you're having one of your fits of discretion. And since there's no chance of getting any dirt from you—I'll be running along."

"I'm sorry, Gibbs," the other spoke good-naturedly, "but I don't know a thing. Honestly I don't. You know Adams would never tell me as much as her right name— and where else would I find out?"

"O.K., lady, O.K.," the answer was cheerful. "*I* don't care if there's a murder case in the hospital—I only work here."

"So long, then. I'll see you at supper."

"Fine. Save a place for me if you get there first."

"I will—as far from Adams as I can get."

Not until the conversation had ended did the meaning of what I had so clearly heard begin to dawn upon me. Then gradually I became aware of myself in relation to what they had said. They, of course, were nurses, and I was the patient with "a slight concussion—" the result of the mysteriously vicious blow I had suffered in the Cathedral. But how I had been brought to this hospital room, or by whom, I had not as yet the remotest idea.

A moment later I opened my eyes. A heavily shaded lamp lighted the walls and ceiling of a narrow white room which looked precisely like every other hospital room I had ever wakened to see. A nurse, who was young and blond as I imagined she would be, sat in a low rocker near the open window and looked out into the warm darkness of the June night. While I watched her, the nurse turned and saw that my eyes were open. She smiled—an amazingly wide and dimpled smile—and rose to come near the bed.

"Well," she said cheerfully, "are we feeling better now?"

"I don't know," I answered with an effort, "but I'll find out."

Experimentally, I moved a bit, and was aware of a terrific pain in my head and shoulders.

"There," the nurse observed, "that's just fine."

"No," I said firmly, "I'm sorry, but it's not just fine." This time I found it easier to speak.

The smile was in no way diminished by my answer.

"Does it hurt us a little?" The nurse sounded pleasantly sympathetic. "Well, that's just a shame. But we mustn't worry. We don't have to do a thing now but lie still and not try to move around anymore."

"We'll be glad enough to do that." I sighed and closed my eyes. But in another moment, I looked up again.

"Are we," I inquired, "badly hurt?"

"No indeedy we're not." The smile grew even wider. "We're getting along just fine!"

"And did 'they,'" I asked, "find out who it was that hit me?"

Instantly the nurse's hand was on my forehead.

"Now, Mrs. Morse," she said soothingly, "you just forget all about that. Nobody hit us at all, you know."

For a moment it seemed that I simply could not summon the energy to explain what had actually happened. Still, I saw that I must make an effort.

"You've made a mistake," I said carefully. "Two mistakes, in fact. First I'm not Mrs. Morse—and second I was struck by someone in St. Ives Cathedral this afternoon."

The nurse still smiled at me, but when she spoke again her voice was curiously firm.

"I'm awfully sorry, Mrs. Morse," she said, "but I'm afraid we've had a bad dream. You had a little tumble this afternoon, and now you're here in the University Hospital to rest for a while."

I looked up reflectively at the nurse for a moment, but from her cheerful face I could gather nothing whatever.

"You make it sound," I achieved a faint smile, "like rather a nice accident. I suppose I wasn't even near St. Ives when I took this little tumble?"

"Oh mercy no! We aren't going to worry ourselves about anything like that."

It seemed, on the whole, the easiest thing to let the matter rest. The confusion in my aching head made me weakly willing to accept her simple explanation. Indeed, I could scarcely trust my memory enough to be sure, at that moment, just what *was* the truth.

"At least," I murmured, "your version of what happened is a good deal less complicated than mine."

"There," said the nurse happily. "Now we *do* understand each other, don't we, Mrs. Morse?" And for just a moment the pressure of her cool fingers on my forehead deepened significantly.

"Yes," I spoke dreamily, "I think we do."

"And if Miss Adams comes around," the girl went on, "we're not going to bother her with any bad dreams about being knocked down in any old Cathedrals, are we, Mrs. Morse?"

"No," I agreed again, "we're not. Who is Miss Adams?"

"She's just the Superintendent," the nurse said, "and she likes to poke around and ask a lot of questions. But we won't let that worry us, will we?"

The words brought back to me the strangely clear memory of the conversation I had overheard earlier.

"Let's see," I ventured presently. "Would you be Miss Carter or Miss Gibbs?"

"I'm Miss Carter," the girl looked surprised, "but how did you know?"

"Probably," I said, "I dreamed it—along with everything else."

Miss Carter laughed.

"Well, that's just fine," she beamed approvingly. "Anyone can see we're feeling stronger now."

A sharp rap on the door startled me.

"If that's Miss Adams," I whispered, "I'll *need* my strength."

Miss Carter made no reply, save for a glance over her shoulder. And her pretty smile was twisted into a grimace which plainly indicated her opinion of Miss Adams.

In the moment while Miss Carter remained outside the door I made a desperate effort to think quickly. I had not the slightest desire to be mixed any further with the affair at St. Ives, and it seemed, at least in that moment of hasty reasoning, well worth taking a chance on the possibility that, between us, Miss Carter and I could keep the Superintendent from discovering the actual circumstances of my accident. For I was inclined, in spite of the pain which I felt at the moment, to believe Miss Carter when she said that I was not seriously hurt. Supposing that I were able to leave the hospital next morning—there was surely a chance, however slim, that I might be safely out of the whole mess before Miss Adams or the police could establish any real connection between my accident and the killing at St. Ives.

I heard Miss Carter's cheerful voice: "I've brought Miss Adams in to see how well my patient's getting on. Don't we look just fine, Miss Adams?"

"Mrs. Morse is doing very nicely, I'm sure," said the new and chilly voice.

I looked up at Miss Adams. Hair drawn back, lips drawn down, she seemed a dreadfully stiff creature—not in the least like my blond and amiable Miss Carter. More firmly than ever I determined to let her find out as little as possible about me.

"Now then," Miss Adams' tone became official,

"it will be necessary for me to ask for some information, for our records, of course. I should like your name please. Your—ah—full name, Mrs. Morse."

The edge of sarcasm with which Miss Adams spoke made me hesitate briefly—and in that moment a sudden thought flashed through my mind. My pocketbook, which contained the name and address of Belinda Stebbins, had been with me when I entered the Cathedral.

"Miss Adams," I said, "I really am not able to answer questions tonight. Any information about me you will find in my purse."

Miss Adams looked annoyed.

"We were unable," she said rather fretfully, "to find any purse among your things—or any means of identification whatever."

"But—good heavens—then I must have been robbed!"

"Very likely," said Miss Adams coldly. "Now if I may have the full name please—?"

"The name," I said, "is Mrs. Mary Morse." And I thought I caught just a flutter of Miss Carter's eyelid as her glance met mine.

With a silent breath of relief I saw Miss Adams write down my statement without comment. The rest of her questions I managed easily. In al truth I informed her that my age was fifty-two, sex female, and my residence in Philadelphia. (The fact that Maplewood is in a suburb allowed me this answer with technical accuracy.)

Having disposed of these details, Miss Adams cleared her throat, evidently as a signal that her questions were about to become more personal.

"Mrs. Morse," she began, "I have no wish to alarm you unnecessarily, but you must be aware that you were struck a sharp, deliberate and very dangerous blow by some person who apparently had every intention of wounding you— perhaps even killing you. I may say now that you are not seriously injured, but it is absolutely necessary that you give me any information you may possess concerning this person who struck you, and the reason for the assault!"

I regarded Miss Adams in silence. It seemed obvious that she had been primed to ask that question—and I felt a new presentiment of alarm as I wondered who might be the prompter—and what might be their motive. At least it was evident that some account of the true nature of my accident had

already reached Miss Adams. I looked toward Miss Carter, but she seemed not the least bit dismayed. Indeed, as I watched her, I saw her head move ever so slightly from side to side, while at the same time she stroked my forehead soothingly. Plainly she was doing her best—whatever *her* mysterious motive might be—to encourage me in the business of facing the question out.

"Mrs. Morse," it was Miss Adams' insistent voice again, "can you describe the person who struck you this afternoon?"

I looked at her blankly.

"Miss Adams," I said, "no one struck me at all. I simply had a little tumble, and I bumped my head. Miss Carter," I added innocently, "will tell you that."

Above my head the two nurses exchanged a look. I saw Miss Adams raise her eyebrows sharply. Miss Carter answered with a slight shrug.

"Well, Mrs. Morse," Miss Adams' tone was only slightly stiffer than before, "perhaps you can tell me the name of the gentleman who accompanied you to the hospital. No doubt he will be able to supply more accurate information concerning your accident."

I thought quickly.

"Was the man a priest?"

Miss Adams looked startled.

"Certainly not," she said quickly. "The interns who talked with him when you were brought into the Emergency Receiving Room supposed that the man was a—relative of some sort. It was he who gave the order that you were to have a private room and a special nurse."

"In that case," I said reasonably, "I should think the man must surely have given his name—and mine too, for that matter."

"Unfortunately," said Miss Adams, "Dr. Fell reports that this gentleman left the hospital very abruptly, without supplying any of the necessary information. Now I must really ask you, Mrs. Morse, not to delay any further. I presume that this man was with you at the time you lost consciousness?"

"Miss Adams," I answered, and this time I spoke with complete truthfulness, "I was alone at the time of my accident, and I have not the vaguest notion who that man might have been. I have no relatives or friends in the whole city of Baltimore."

Again I saw the two nurses look at each other.

This time Miss Adams was plainly very much annoyed— and not, certainly, without reason.

"I have no wish," she began icily, "to disturb you any longer than is strictly necessary. But you must realize, Mrs. Morse, that this whole thing is most irregular. Unless you make an effort to answer my questions I shall be forced to—"

A sudden knock on the door spared me the necessity of hearing what Miss Adams would be forced to do. A student nurse, in obvious agitation, summoned the Superintendent out into the hall, and there followed an excited conference.

"It's the patient in Emergency Two," the messenger nurse reported. "He's still unconscious and those detectives want to get a statement from him before anything happens. They want an order for a stimulant and I can't find Dr. Fell—"

The Superintendent's voice cut in sharply.

"Keep your head, Miss Ellis. What patient are you talking about?"

"He was brought into the ward this afternoon, Miss Adams, with a severe fracture. He was knocked down by an automobile, and hasn't regained consciousness. The detectives told me to get you—"

"Nonsense. Detectives have nothing to do with that case. They've had no permission to enter the ward."

"But, Miss Adams," the nurse protested, "it was Dr. Fell who let them in—about an hour ago. They say they're sure this patient has something to do with the other case they brought in this afternoon. The man who was killed, you know—"

"Very well, Miss Ellis, that will do. Get back to your ward, and I'll follow immediately."

"Yes, Miss Adams."

It was with some relief that I heard the quick, light footsteps of the two women as they hurried away from my door. But I did rather wish that Miss Adams had not cut off the nurse's explanations quite so successfully. It was, after all, more than idle curiosity on my part when I wondered whether the patient Miss Ellis had mentioned were not the very man whom I had seen struck by the automobile—and if the "man who was killed" might not be the same one who had knelt in the Cathedral. And if, indeed, I were right in these two inferences, then what would be the meaning of the suggested connection between the two cases?

But a moment later I was agreeing with Miss Carter when she observed that I had had enough excitement for one day. The interview with Miss Adams had tired me more than I realized, and I was more than content to close my eyes and await the effects of the sedative drug which Miss Carter supplied. Gradually the throb of my aching head subsided, and the anxious, endless circles of thought faded and blurred into a light sleep.

I cannot say precisely what sound it was that awakened me, but at the moment when my eyes opened, I was already aware that someone had entered my room. Instinctively I looked toward the door, and one glance was sufficient to tell me that I had made no mistake.

Quite plainly visible in the dim light which came through the transom from the hall outside was the figure of a tall man. And a second later I realized that he was moving stealthily toward my bed.

4

I CONFESS—AND REPENT

"Miss Carter," I called sharply, "Miss Carter, are you there?"

It was the man who answered me.

"Miss Carter isn't here," he spoke quietly, "but please don't be frightened. I only want to speak to you for a minute—and I've got something pretty important to say. Important," he added, "to you."

I considered briefly.

"Of course you know," I said, and my tone was as level as I could make it, "that I can ring this bell by my pillow and bring the floor nurse here at once."

"You can indeed," the man's voice drawled slightly, "but if I were you—I wouldn't."

It didn't sound in the least like a threat, but rather more like good advice—and quite suddenly I decided to take it. I can only explain the remarkable passivity with which I accepted this mysterious midnight caller by supposing that the events of the past eight hours had pretty well exhausted my supply of reactions, or else that the effects of the sedative drug I had taken earlier were still present. At any rate, I simply failed to register a proper degree of either surprise or alarm.

"Very well," I spoke with something very like indifference, "say what you have to say."

"Good."

With two quick steps the man crossed the small room
and stood close by my bed, yet even at such short range I
could make nothing of his appearance save for an impression of broad shoulders and above-average height.

"Perhaps," I suggested mildly, "you wouldn't mind
turning on the light? I'd rather like to see who you are."

"Sorry," he spoke pleasantly, "but I can't. It would bring
the floor nurse trotting. Anyway you wouldn't recognize
me—I can tell you that much."

I sighed. In spite of my docile mood I didn't specially
relish the hocus-pocus of a conversation in the dark with
a strange visitor. And his very next words set me sharply
on my guard.

"First," he said, "I know who you are—Miss Stebbins.
And second, it happens that I saw you in the Cathedral
this afternoon."

Futile as it seemed, I felt obliged to make some effort
at denial.

"I'm afraid," I began, "that you've made a mistake—"

"I know, I know," my visitor interrupted soothingly.
"You're going to deny everything. And quite right you are,
Miss Stebbins. If the little Carter tipped you off the way
I told her to, you've been denying things right and left.
But you see, Miss Stebbins, it won't do with me—because
I *know* you were in the Cathedral, and that's why I came
to warn you—"

Quite suddenly I thought I saw the purpose of the
man's stealthy visit.

"If," I said drily, "you are about to indicate that my
presence at St. Ives was not welcome this afternoon—save

your time and mine. I've already had one hint in that direction, by the not very subtle means of a blackjack, and I can tell you that I don't need any further urging to keep out of the whole affair."

There was a pause—a curious pause, during which we seemed to be staring intently at one another through the darkness. Each, I imagine, was waiting guardedly for the other's reaction, when suddenly the man spoke.

"I'm warning you to keep out," he said. "You're right about that. But it just happens that I'm *not* asking favors for myself. I'm tipping you off for your own good, Miss Stebbins, and you can take it or leave it."

Little as I liked this whole odd business, there was a reasonableness about his tone which somehow inspired confidence. And, after all, it scarcely seemed wise to antagonize anyone who, for whatever motive, had taken an interest in my affairs to the point of prompting Miss Carter's earlier advice to me.

"Very well," I said briefly, "I'll take it. Go on with your warning."

"You know, I suppose, that the man you saw kneeling in the Cathedral this afternoon was murdered within a very few minutes of the time when you entered the building."

I made no answer.

"But you may *not* know," he continued, calmly, "that I was the one who picked you up and lugged you out of the Cathedral."

This time I couldn't keep silent.

"You," I faltered, "you brought me to the hospital?"

"Yes."

"Look here," I said weakly, "I really can't go on with this. I—I'm not well enough tonight to play guessing

games. In heaven's name tell me what it is you want—and
who you are."

"I can't tell you who I am, Miss Stebbins. I'm sorry as
the devil, but I honestly can't."

Even in my agitation I had to admit that he *did* sound
sorry.

"And I've already told you," he went on, "that the
whole point of my butting into your business from the
very beginning was to keep you from getting mixed up in
what's likely to be one of the nastiest murders I ever—
" He checked himself abruptly. "It—it's a pretty serious
affair"—his tone was earnest—"and it's bound to be serious for anyone mixed up in it."

"I realize that," I said feelingly, "but I don't suppose
you care to say how you came to be mixed up in it too?"

"Just the same way you did," he answered promptly.
"By the purest accident. You see, I followed you into the
Cathedral because I thought you might be needing help.
After all"—he hesitated—"that accident we saw wasn't ex-
actly a pretty sight, was it?"

"It was not."

"But once I got inside the church, Miss Stebbins, I saw
that—well, we'd both run into a pretty awful mess. As a
matter of fact, I didn't get around to look after you for
some minutes. I don't know, of course, what you did in the
meantime, or how much you saw—"

"I didn't do anything," I put in quickly, "and I didn't
see anything. I was stretched out on a pew in a dead faint
for at least part of that time—and when I came to, all I
saw was the kneeling man—"

"And from there," the man said, "I know the story. I saw
you standing by the pillar when the three men came into
the Cathedral. I tried to warn you—but it was too late."

I listened in amazement. There remained little doubt in my mind but what he was telling me the truth, but to believe his story only made it more strange.

"Surely," I said, "if you saw me struck—you must have seen who did it."

"You were hit," he said quickly, "from *behind* the pillar."

After all, I had no choice but to accept his statement.

"Then what?" I sighed.

"Then I brought you out of the Cathedral through the side door into the close, without either of us being seen by those three men—and drove you here to the hospital in my car. And the point, Miss Stebbins, of all I've said is simply this: no one except me really *knows* that you were in St. Ives today. I won't tell and you'd better not let anyone else find out."

In the silence that followed, a sudden thought came to me.

"If it's true," I said, "that no one but you knows what really happened to me—why did the Superintendent accuse me of being connected with the murder at St. Ives?"

I more than half expected that the man would resent my skepticism, but the grave tone of his answer surprised me.

"That," he said quietly, "is the only really bad break we've had. You may remember you were wearing a string of beads when you went into St. Ives this afternoon. Sort of unusual stones they were—"

"Moonstones—" I felt automatically for the familiar necklace around my throat. "Did something happen to them?"

"The string broke while you were in the Cathedral—probably when you fainted the first time. Anyway, some of the beads rolled out into the aisle, and the cop—darn his sharp eyes—picked 'em up as clues."

"Still I don't see how that connects me with anything in particular—"

"But that's not all, Miss Stebbins. The rest of the necklace, you see, slid down inside your dress, and when the doctor in Emergency started to look you over, out popped another handful of moonstones and bounced all over the marble floor. Everybody was too busy to stop and pick them up— So when, by a bit of fiendishly bad luck, they brought the man you saw kneeling in St. Ives into the *same* Emergency Room, it didn't take our friend the cop very long to spot the loose beads. One question as to who had just been treated there—and they were hot on your trail."

"Oh, good heavens—if they've got *that* much proof against me, what's the use of trying to lie my way out of this mess? I might just as well call in Miss Adams and admit that I *was* at St. Ives—"

In my agitation, I started up from the pillow—only to sink back before the sharp pain which shot through my head and shoulders.

"Easy, Miss Stebbins, *please*—" With surprising concern the man bent down to pat my arm. "I'm darned sorry to put you through all this hocus-pocus tonight—but it had to be done. In spite of the beads, you've gotten away with your story, and there's no reason in the world why you shouldn't stick to it. I only brought up the matter to explain why I had to run out on you when they started asking questions. The hospital was already infested with police, and I couldn't afford to get balled up in the Cathedral business any more than you. So"—he paused—"I beat it. But I made up my mind to come back here tonight and tell you what was what."

I remembered what Miss Adams had said about the sudden disappearance of the man who had brought me to the hospital.

"And before I left you here," he went on, "I gave your name as Mrs. Morse, and ordered a private room and a nurse for you. Incidentally, I found time for a word with the nurse—I hope she did her duty?"

"Miss Carter," I said warmly, "was excellent."

"Good. She looked like a smart girl." I saw him nod. "And that," he said, "is just about all, except that I took your purse with me—to eliminate evidence, of course—and also your crated cat which I picked up in the Cathedral."

As might be expected, it was the reference to Emma which broke down the last of my reserve. Incredible as it seemed, I had until that very moment completely forgotten her.

"Good heavens," I said, "poor Emma! Where is she now?"

"Emma?"

The cat, I explained. "Her name is Emma."

I was grateful when he didn't laugh. Some people do.

"Oh," he said gravely, "of course. I took Emma home with me, and she seems to like the place. You needn't worry about Emma."

Quite suddenly I was overwhelmed with a wave of gratitude toward this stranger which was almost embarrassingly intense. I reached through the darkness impulsively, groped for his hand, and squeezed it warmly.

"Thank you," I said. "Thank you a lot."

"O. K., Miss Stebbins, O. K." He shook the hand cheerfully. "Now all you have to do is to get out of the hospital first thing tomorrow. And you will, all right, if I trot along and let you get some sleep. Just stick to your story, and the rest will be easy."

"But wait," I said suddenly, "suppose I should need you—I don't even know who you are."

"If you need me," he said, "you needn't worry. *I'll* find *you*. But really you aren't going to need anyone. Just walk out of the hospital, and forget you ever saw St. Ives—except," he added, "when you read the papers and see all the lousy publicity you're missing. So good night."

He made for the door, opened it cautiously, then stepped into the hall. And I was left—presumably to settle back in peace upon my pillow. But evidently peace was not for me that night. For at the very moment when the door of my room closed upon my departing visitor, I saw something which sent my weary brain whirling in fresh confusion—and left me to call myself a gullible fool.

It was something which my newly trusted friend wore beneath his coat—something shiny that caught the light from the hall in the second when he put back his arm to shut the door. What my visitor wore beneath his coat was a police badge.

5

I LEARN THE REASON WHY

It was fortunate for what remained of my shattered nerves, that Miss Carter returned almost immediately. Her cheerful white starchiness was very comforting, and when she had snapped on the light, smoothed my pillow, and laid a cool hand on my addled forehead—the memory of that confusing interview in the dark had slipped into a haze of unreality.

"Well," said Miss Carter, "here we are awake. But we did have a nice little nap earlier, didn't we?"

"Yes," I admitted, "only—" I paused.

"Only what?"

"Something woke me up," I explained, "and now I'm too restless, I'm afraid, to go to sleep again."

"Oh," said Miss Carter, "we'll soon fix *that* up. We'll just have a little hypo that'll send us right off."

I looked on gratefully while she fetched small white tablets and the hypodermic syringe.

"What was it," Miss Carter asked presently, "that woke you up?"

I hesitated.

"If I tell you," I said, "I expect you'll say it was a dream."

Miss Carter laughed.

"Of course that's what it was." She was swabbing a small spot on my upper arm with alcohol. "That's what I told Miss Adams."

"You—you told Miss Adams?"

"Yes." She paused a moment while she jabbed the needle in. "When I came back from supper just now, Miss Adams told me that the floor nurse had heard voices in your room—and I told her you were probably having a little nightmare and talking in your sleep."

"That was very clever of you," I said, "as well as very nice. Do you think Miss Adams believed it?"

"I'm sure I don't know," the girl shrugged cheerfully. "She hardly ever believes anything I say since the time she caught me smoking in the nurses' dormitory. But we're not going to worry ourselves over *that* now. We're going straight off to sleep—and wake up in the morning all well."

I nodded drowsily. Already the small tingle of the needle in my arm was spreading a warm comfort through my weary nerves. Not even the vision of a hundred snoopy Superintendents could keep me awake much longer. And the memory of a shiny police badge was fast blurring as Miss Carter settled me snugly and turned out the light. A moment later one last thought opened my eyes.

"Miss Carter?"

"Yes?"

"You aren't going to leave me alone any more, are you?"

From the chair by the window I heard a small laugh.

"If you're afraid the nightmare might come back," Miss Carter said, "don't worry. I won't," she added unexpectedly, "let him in."

And I was far too sleepy to ask Miss Carter what she meant—a fact of which she doubtless was aware.

Next morning I awoke to a sensation of terrific heat. Evidently the June weather had taken a turn for the worse during the night, for the sun seemed to blaze right through the dark window shade and filled the narrow white room with a hot glare. Yet Miss Carter, in the small rocking chair, looked very blond and cool, and in daylight her smile was even more incredibly cheerful than it had seemed the night before.

"Well now," she said, "we *did* have a good sleep, didn't we?"

"We did."

"And no more bad dreams?" she beamed.

"Not one."

"Well, that's just fine. And how's our head?"

"Our head," I answered truthfully, "is a great deal better. In fact," I hoisted myself on one elbow, "I almost think I can sit up."

"That's just *fine,*" Miss Carter's familiar refrain encouraged me while I raised my shoulders gingerly. "I *told* you we'd be all well this morning."

As a matter of fact, she was quite right. Except for a few warning twinges when I moved my head from side to side, I seemed pretty thoroughly recovered. But even the slight effort of sitting up made me realize how appallingly hot the day was.

"Now then," Miss Carter settled the pillows behind me, "how would you like to see your visitor while I go get your breakfast tray?"

It was with difficulty that I held back an exclamation of dismay. There flashed across my mind the words which the strange man had spoken in the night. "Don't worry," he had said, *"I'll* find *you."* And in that moment when Miss Carter spoke of a visitor it seemed impossible that she could mean anyone else. Who, after all, besides the mysterious man could possibly know where to find me? I thought all this and looked at the nurse in what must have seemed a stricken silence, for she laid her hand anxiously on mine.

"Don't you feel so well, Mrs. Morse?" she asked. "Maybe you'd rather not see her just now."

Desperately I grasped at that pronoun.

"Did you say 'her'?" I demanded.

Miss Carter nodded.

"Well—who is it, then?"

"*I* don't know."

For the first time I found Miss Carter's bland smile a bit too bland.

"Why not?" I asked shortly.

"Because she didn't give her name. She said," Miss Carter beamed delightedly, "she'd rather surprise you."

I set my lips.

"You can tell her," I announced, "that I don't like surprises. I've had enough of them in the last eighteen hours to last me the rest of my life. And none of them has been nice—you can tell her that too! Either she'll give her name," I ignored Miss Carter's efforts to silence me, "or I won't—"

Abruptly I stopped—my mouth still open—as the door was flung open and a young woman stepped into the room.

"Oh, please," her voice was distressed, "*please* don't be angry. I thought you'd *like* to be surprised."

At once my irritation vanished.

"*Joan Pell,*" I exclaimed happily, "I *am* glad to see you!"

She came over to the bed and kissed me, while I returned the greeting with genuine warmth. The girl had been a favorite pupil of mine at Maplewood some few

years past, and since her graduation we had continued the
friendship by means of occasional letters and visits. Of all
the people in the world, I believe there was no one I would
have welcomed more gratefully at that moment than Joan
Pell. Just to look at her pretty, sensible young face seemed
to restore my sense of balance after the vague fears and
uncertainties which had beset me.

"But Joan, my dear," the puzzling question was foremost in my mind, "how ever did you know—?"

Her young voice cut in quickly.

"No questions now," she warned me lightly, "until I ask
you a few. First tell me how you are?"

In one breath Miss Carter and I assured her that I was
practically well.

"It was really nothing," I explained, "but a nasty little
tumble."

"Of course," said Joan, and the quick pressure of her
hand told me that by some miraculous understanding
she had grasped the situation. Perhaps Miss Carter . . . I
glanced curiously toward the nurse, but, quite as usual,
her smile told me nothing whatever.

"I think," Miss Carter said, "I'll get your breakfast tray
now, Mrs. Morse, and leave you two to have a chat." She
beamed at each of us impartially and left.

Joan and I faced each other eagerly.

"Now," I said, "for heaven's sake do tell me—how did
you know I was in Baltimore?"

"Why," she answered simply, "I read it in the newspaper."

"Joan," I sank back upon the pillow and stared at her in
horror, "what *do* you mean?"

"Nothing to be excited about, Miss Belle," she hastened to reassure me, "only your picture was in the paper
last night—about the degree from Granger, you know."

The degree—of course.

"I'm sorry," Joan looked distressed, "if I made you think that something dreadful had happened—"

"It's not your fault," I said quickly, "if my nerves are all on edge. But you see, Joan, the trouble is that something rather dreadful *has* happened—I've gotten myself in an awful mess and I want to tell you all about it. . . ." At an abrupt gesture from Joan I stopped speaking.

"Please, Miss Belle, never mind about that now."

"But, Joan," I said, "I've got to tell you about it, because you'll have to help me. I'm here in the hospital without any money and I simply must get out before anyone finds out about—"

Again a quick motion from Joan interrupted me. This time she leaned forward and put her hand on mine.

"Miss Belle," she said earnestly, "you mustn't talk about it *here.*"

The emphasis was unmistakable.

"You don't mean," I glanced toward the closed door, "that anyone—" I cupped my ear to indicate an eavesdropper.

Joan shrugged.

"Stranger things," she said lightly, "have happened."

"But, Joan—how do you know about all this? Did they talk to you while you were waiting to see me?"

"They did their best," the girl laughed shortly, "but they didn't get very far. I knew your story—and believe me—I stuck to it!"

"You knew—?" I repeated blankly.

"Listen, Miss Belle," Joan leaned forward and spoke in a rapid whisper. "I know all I need to—never mind how. That's why I came here, and why I didn't call you 'Miss Belle' before the nurse, and why I've already paid your bill and arranged to take you home with me. And now," she settled back triumphantly, "will you believe me when I tell you that there's nothing to worry about?"

"Yes," I said slowly, "I believe you, Joan. And if you know the whole story, you probably realize how grateful I am. As for knowing how you found out about it," I sighed, "I suppose I'll simply have to wait for the answer."

"And you don't have very long to wait either," Joan observed cheerfully, "because the doctor said you could go as soon as you had your breakfast and felt well enough to dress."

Presently I beckoned the girl nearer.

"Joan," I murmured cautiously, "the man who was—was murdered at St. Ives yesterday was brought to this hospital, wasn't he?"

She nodded.

"And he died?"

"Yes."

"Joan," I scarcely dared even to whisper the question, "who was he?"

Joan drew back sharply. It was her turn to look startled.

"You—you don't know?" she asked slowly.

"No."

For a brief moment the girl hesitated, then she put her lips close to my ear.

"It was Hamlet Winters," Joan said, and the firm pressure of her hand on my shoulder steadied me. "Easy now," she whispered, anxiously. "Don't make a sound."

Actually, the warning was unnecessary, for I am morally certain that the shock of that moment left me entirely incapable of making any sound whatever. *Hamlet Winters.* At first I could do nothing save echo the name stupidly. Then, like a series of explosions, the many implications of the amazing news burst in upon me. Dr. Hamlet Winters.

Few names had more associations for me than his—and
none could have been less likely as indicating the victim
of a murderer. Tall, white-haired, academic Dr. Winters,
formerly my colleague in the English Department at
Maplewood, then head of the same Department at Granger
College, and now—murdered. Kind, gracious, dignified
Dr. Winters who had proposed me as a candidate for the
Litt. D. from Granger, who had written to tell me of the
honor, who was, himself, to present me for the degree.
A hundred memories crowded through my mind in those
moments while I stared at Joan. With a considerable effort
I forced myself back to the present, and realized that the
girl was still watching anxiously lest I react too violently
to the news.

"I do hope the shock isn't too much, Miss Belle," Joan
said gently. "After all, I didn't want you to hear it from
anyone else."

"Oh, I'm all right," I said slowly. "Only it's like everything else that's happened—I just don't understand it."

"But at least," Joan reminded me, "you must see now
why we've tried so hard to keep you out of the whole business at the Cathedral—and why—" she checked herself
suddenly.

"Well," I prompted, "why what?"

"Oh—nothing really," Joan looked uncomfortable,
"only I think one or two people around the hospital may
have an idea—that you knew Dr. Winters."

I was watching the girl steadily. Something had made
her manner uncertain, but what it could be—? Yet even
the question of Joan's curious behavior, of her strangely
accurate information concerning what had happened at
St. Ives, all of this paled before my new realization of
the actual difficulty of my own situation. To have become

involved in the violent death of a stranger was something
to avoid as unpleasant and possibly dangerous—but the
discovery that I had blundered into the murder of a close
friend, both personal and professional, put a new and genuinely serious significance upon the unhappy incident.
Nor did my reflections on this score make me any less
anxious to get out of the hospital. Indeed, it was all I
could do to put off preparations for my departure while I
choked down a portion of the breakfast which Miss Carter
presently brought.

Joan, who evidently shared my anxiety to leave, had
laid out my clothes for me—and, breakfast being at length
disposed of, she and Miss Carter helped me to dress. As
the three of us worked with silent concentration, I found
myself beset by a new fear. How was I actually to leave the
hospital? Would it not involve certain formalities which,
if the authorities suspected me of some connection with
the death of Hamlet Winters, might be made extremely
unpleasant and difficult for me? But I was reckoning without the ever-resourceful Miss Carter.

At the very moment when I gingerly adjusted the angle
of my hat upon my bruised head, Miss Carter glanced out
into the hall and then came to take my arm.

"There's a service elevator," she said, "right opposite
this door. If you don't mind—I think it's the quickest way
for you to leave. You see," she smiled happily, "it opens
right into the street downstairs."

Joan and I hesitated not at all. We paused only to ex-
change one look of relief, then followed Miss Carter across
the hall and stepped into the waiting elevator. Hastily I
grasped the nurse's hand.

"Good-bye, Miss Carter, and thank you very, very
much."

"Oh, that's all right," she patted my hand, "I just thought it would be nice for us to surprise Miss Adams—and the others."

The elevator door clanged shut upon what I supposed would be my last view of Miss Carter's incredible smile, and I turned to Joan.

"That nurse," I observed, as we were trundled downward in the noisy car, "is a remarkable young woman. I'd trust her with my life."

Joan nodded solemnly.

Another moment and the elevator door was opened, leaving me to step out upon the street—free of the hospital and Miss Adams, and, so I believed, of the whole nightmarish sequence of events which had begun the afternoon before in the Cathedral of St. Ives.

6
JOAN'S YOUNG MAN

By the time we had reached Joan's small and attractive apartment, (via a taxi) I had learned a great deal. First that Joan, who had for several years held a government position in Washington, had been transferred to Baltimore; second, that she had, very recently, become engaged to a young man whom she described in vague but glowing terms; third, that she was morally determined that I should then and there become her guest—for the double purpose of inspecting the new apartment and the new young man (who, it appeared, was temporarily in Baltimore on business). Having, at the moment, a very small degree of will-power, I was glad enough to let Joan order me about. And once inside her tiny, chintz living-room, I curled myself contentedly upon the couch and quite forgot the heat of the day while Joan turned the electric fan toward me and went to fetch a pitcher of ice.

When she returned, I opened my eyes and sat up with sudden resolve.

"Joan," I began firmly, "there's one thing you haven't told me yet—and really I must know. How did you know that I was at the hospital—and where did you learn about what happened at St. Ives yesterday?"

Once more I was surprised to observe a certain reluctance in the girl's manner. After a moment, however, she faced me squarely.

"I might as well tell you now, Miss Belle," she said, "that it was Timothy."

"Timothy?"

"Yes. Timothy Fowler—my young man, you know."

The explanation shed very little light upon the puzzle.

"You see, Miss Belle," Joan spoke with evident nervousness, "Timothy happened to be in the Cathedral yesterday afternoon, and when you were—

were hurt, he took you to the hospital—" She paused to glance uncertainly at me. "Then later, when you were conscious again—he—"

"Joan," I broke in sharply as the meaning of her faltered words became suddenly and amazingly dear, "did he come back to see me last night?"

The girl nodded.

"But only to help you, Miss Belle. You see—"

"Is it possible, Joan," I demanded, "that this man is—is some sort of a detective?"

Joan nodded—still watching me anxiously.

"Oh, please, Miss Belle," her tone was pleading, "please don't be upset until you've talked to Timothy."

But her words only increased my growing resolution.

"Joan dear," I spoke as gently as I could, "I don't want to make you unhappy about all this— I'm sure it's not your fault in any way. But I can't possibly stay here after what you've told me. And under no circumstances," I finished with decision, "will I have any further conferences with your Timothy—or any other detective."

Joan accepted my declaration with such meekness that I instantly regretted it. But even for the sake of comforting the girl I was unwilling to risk a further interview with

my mysterious midnight visitor to whom I had already
admitted far too much. Regretfully—but firmly—I rose
from the couch and prepared to depart. It was Joan's
face—a sudden study in conflicting emotions—which first
warned me that something had happened. I turned to follow her look and saw the tall young man just as he walked
into the living-room.

He smiled at Joan and then at me, and if he saw the
awkwardness of our situation he certainly gave no sign of it.

"I've brought your things, Miss Stebbins," he said.

Somehow Joan rallied herself to make an introduction.

"Miss Belle," she said, "I'm terribly sorry, but—this is
Timothy."

"Oh, that's all right, Joan," his cheerful tone still
ignored our obvious dismay, "Miss Stebbins and I don't
need to be introduced."

"No," I said a trifle lamely, "we don't."

I was, in point of fact, unable to decide what attitude
to take. Despite my extreme reluctance to become further involved with any representative of the police, still I
was not unaware of owing this particular man considerable
gratitude. Whatever his motive might have been, the fact
remained that he had assisted me at the time when I was
hurt, and had sent Joan to me at the hospital.

Furthermore, I couldn't help liking Timothy's appearance. There was a curious combination of friendliness and
what my pupils would call hard-boiledness about him—a
look of intelligence and humor in his alert brown eyes
which went strangely with his rather careless manner,
and the slight, cynical drawl of his speech. Definitely not
handsome—yet there was something undeniably attractive
about this young man of Joan's, something I had felt un-
consciously during our strange interview the night before,
and which struck me even more forcibly at this moment.

A silence hung between the three of us which grew mo-
mently more awkward. Plainly Timothy could not account
for the change in my manner which had come about since
he left my hospital room, nor for the distress which was
obvious in Joan's pretty face. Slowly his smile faded as he
looked from one to the other of us.

"What's the trouble, Joanie?" he asked finally. "Did I
do something wrong?"

"Oh, Timothy," Joan was almost in tears, "Miss Belle
didn't want to see you because she thinks you—"

"Oh," he was enlightened at once, "because she thinks
I'm a cop—is that it?"

Joan nodded unhappily.

"Well," Timothy shrugged his broad shoulders, "I am,
all right. But I wish you hadn't told her just yet."

"Joan didn't have to tell me," I put in quickly. "I—I
saw your police badge last night when you walked out of
my room."

"You did? Oh, gosh, I'm sorry, Miss Stebbins." The
concern in his voice was unmistakable. "And you've been
thinking all this time that I'd just been pumping you?"

"Perhaps." I made an effort to be noncommittal—"But
if you think I know anything about—well—about anything—"

"But I don't," said Timothy flatly. "And if just happens
that everything I told you last night was true. I did follow
you into the Cathedral, and I blundered into what was
going on there just as you did. I took you to the hospital
and tried to fix things there so you wouldn't get into any
more trouble. I sneaked back last night to tip you off, and
I sent Joan down to you the first thing this morning—and
I did every darn one of those things to help you out of a
spot because I knew you were Joan's friend and—"

"I'm sorry," I said, "but I still don't see how you could possibly have had the vaguest notion who I was when you saw me go into the Cathedral."

"No?" A slow smile spread over Timothy's face. Crossing the small living-room, he paused before the mantel and pointed to a framed photograph. "Do you think, Miss Stebbins, that I could be engaged to Joan Pell for three months and not know who this was?"

I recognized an enlarged snapshot of myself, posed affectionately with Emma on the steps of our Maplewood Memorial Hall.

"Even if I hadn't known you, Miss Stebbins, how could I fail to spot Emma?"

"Well"—I was weakening—"I'd believe you—in fact I *do* believe you, but if only you weren't a detective—"

"Hell's bells, Miss Stebbins," Timothy's patience was growing a bit thin, "that hasn't anything to do with all this. I'm on the New York City force but that *doesn't* make me a cop in Baltimore. I'm just as much an outsider in this business as you are—and more. I couldn't wriggle in with the authorities here even if I tried, and so far, I'm not trying. That's why I didn't give my name at the hospital, and why I snooped in to see you at midnight. I don't want to be messed up in this St. Ives case any more than you do. But I did want to give Joan's friend a break—and that's the end of it." He turned away abruptly and started toward the hall. "Your things are here—and I'll be on my way."

"Oh, no you won't." I scrambled up from the couch as quickly as my shaky knees permitted. "You'll stay right here until I tell you I'm sorry."

"You do believe him now, don't you, Miss Belle?" Joan's arm was linked in mine, and with her other hand she clutched at Timothy.

"I certainly do," I said sincerely.

Another moment and the three of us were standing, hands clasped, in a suddenly friendly triangle.

"Honestly, I'm sorry," I apologized, "but I couldn't help being frightened—"

"Forget it," said Timothy generously, and changed the subject. "Hadn't you better be looking after Emma?"

Emma again. I went to the hall and there, sure enough, was the crate I had carried to St. Ives. I stooped down, and a plaintive meow greeted me.

"Emma," I said joyfully, and opened the door to let her out.

Presently the three of us were on the floor, petting my small grey cat, and offering her comfort after the confusion of her travels. And if I had needed anything further to make me like Timothy, his technique with Emma would have done the trick. (Which is, I am aware, an absurd thing to admit—but to this day I rely on Emma as a barometer of character.)

It was not until a saucer of milk had been produced and Emma was persuaded to partake of it that we returned to more serious matters. Then, somewhat to my surprise, Timothy brought up the subject of St. Ives once more.

"I think, Miss Stebbins," he began, "that we ought to compare notes on what happened yesterday."

"Good heavens, Timothy," Joan put in, "can't we forget about all that now?"

"I hope," he looked at her thoughtfully, "that we can. But just in case— Well, anyway, we might as well find out how much we really know. Do you agree, Miss Stebbins?"

I nodded, though not without a trace of reluctance.

"You see," Timothy went on gravely, "there's that little matter of the moonstone beads I explained to Miss Stebbins last night. The other part of the broken necklace had to be taken care of, and so I took the liberty of—lifting it, so to speak, with the help of the amiable Miss Carter."

"*You* took the rest of my beads?"

"Right."

"And does that mean you're turning them over to the police as evidence?"

"Nope." Timothy did not seem to resent my instinctive suspicion. "It means that they are now reposing in the bottom of the deepest well I could find." He reassured me with a somewhat cryptic grin. "That's why they couldn't really prove anything against you at the hospital, you see."

"I see this much," I said slowly, "that if it weren't for you, I'd probably have been arrested by this time."

"Maybe," Timothy shrugged, "and maybe not. But let's get back to checking our stories. First—you were coming north on Pearl Avenue toward Charles Street when you saw the accident. Am I right?"

"Yes." Briefly I explained my purpose in taking Emma to the Cathedral close.

"And when the young man was struck by the car," he went on, "you ran up the steps and into the Cathedral, while I followed you."

"By the way," I put in, "do you know who the young man was?"

Timothy nodded.

"It was Laurence Dee—the morning papers gave the dope on him. Queerly enough, he was the son of one Fletcher Dee, who is also on the Granger faculty and a pretty close friend of Hamlet Winters."

"Then you don't think his presence in front of St. Ives was—mere coincidence?"

"Judging from the fact that the kid ran *out* of the Cathedral just before he was hit—I should say it was hardly chance, would you, Miss Stebbins? Now, then, when you got inside the building—did you see anyone before you fainted?"

Recalling the large woman in mustard yellow with whom I nearly collided at the inner door, I gave Timothy my rather vague account of the incident.

"That's pretty darn funny," he looked surprised, "because I wasn't more than a few seconds after you, Miss Stebbins, and I'm plenty sure *I* didn't see the mustard yellow lady."

"And yet," I said, "she was in the vestibule of the Cathedral."

"Which means that she did one of two things. Either she went out the side door of the vestibule—that opens, I believe, into the close, or else scampered up the steps into the balcony. And I can be pretty sure," he went on slowly, "that it wasn't the balcony she picked—because I went up there myself." He glanced up to catch my questioning look. "You remember, Miss Stebbins, I said last night that when I got into the Cathedral I was kept so busy for a few minutes that I couldn't get around to look after you?"

"Yes."

"Well, I was up in the balcony during those minutes."

"But why?"

"Because I was fool enough to follow a false trail." Timothy spoke with a sudden grimness.

"A false trail of what?"

"Blood," said Timothy.

"Blood!"

"Spots," he said crossly, "as big as a quarter, and leading right through the vestibule toward the steps of the balcony."

"You—followed them?"

"I did."

"And what did you find?" Joan and I were listening wide-eyed.

"I found," said Timothy bitterly, "what any ham cop might have expected. A planted trail that led exactly no-where."

"But I don't see," still I was bewildered, "what it could mean. Why should it be planted—"

"For the very good reason, Miss Stebbins, that anyone blundering into the Cathedral at that unfortunate moment would be led, as I was, to dash upstairs and plunge around in a dark balcony. And in the meantime Hamlet Winters was being very neatly killed in a pew downstairs."

7
ENTER THE PRESS

I drew a deep breath. Joan leaned forward to pat my hand sympathetically while she glared at Timothy.

"I don't see why," she said, "you have to put Miss Belle through this third-degree business. She had a narrow escape—but it's all over now, so why not forget it?"

Timothy shrugged.

"It was narrow all right," he spoke gravely, "and if I were dead sure it *was* an escape I'd shut up."

"As far as I'm concerned," I put in, "I'm willing to talk the whole thing out—but I do wish, Timothy, that you wouldn't be so sinister."

"Honestly I'm sorry," said the young man earnestly, "to give you all these alarms. But there is just a chance that we may both be dragged into the business—and we might just as well face it."

"Dragged in how?" I demanded, "and by whom? After all, you got me out of the Cathedral safely, and out of the hospital, and if no one saw us yesterday how could they possibly—"

"That's just it, Miss Belle," Timothy interrupted gently. "I'm afraid you *were* seen in the Cathedral—by one person anyway."

"Go on," I said levelly. "What person?"

"Well," Timothy laughed shortly, "here I go with another alarm. If, as I said a moment ago, Hamlet Winters was being killed while I was up in the balcony, then the murderer must have been on hand to do the dirty deed. And at that very moment Miss Belle was stretched out, in a dead faint and in plain sight of anyone who was lurking about the Cathedral. So—figure it out for yourself."

I figured—silently, and none too pleasantly.

"Of course," Timothy went on, "it may very well be that the person would say nothing about it. Most murderers don't talk any more than they have to."

"But even if he did talk," I said suddenly, "he couldn't have known who I was, could he?"

Timothy was silent.

"Well, *could* he?" I insisted.

Even then I got no direct answer.

"Hamlet Winters knew you, didn't he, Miss Belle?" Timothy's drawl was casual.

"Yes, of course, but—"

"And some of his friends knew you, I suppose?"

"Yes, but surely you can't think that one of his *friends*—"

"Murderers and their victims," Timothy assured me solemnly, "are often the very best of friends. But even so we can be darn sure that this particular friend of Dr. Winters' wouldn't mention being in the Cathedral yesterday if he or she can possibly help it—and there's only the slimmest chance that he might mention having seen you."

"Well, you've certainly succeeded," I said grimly, "in preparing me for the worst. And if it should happen—what would my story be?"

"That," said Timothy, "is what we've got to decide. Now suppose you start by telling me how well you knew Winters, and what kind of a gent he was."

Much as I liked Timothy's breezy manner, something in my academic soul revolted at hearing Hamlet Winters called a gent.

"Dr. Winters," I said stiffly, "was a very distinguished man, and he was by way of being a really great scholar. Probably no one in America has made more contributions to Chaucerian study—"

"Hold everything, Miss Belle," the young man interrupted me good-naturedly. "I didn't mean anything by calling him a gent—but I'll take it back. Only never mind lecturing me now about what he contributed—tell me what he was really like."

"Well, as a matter of fact," I was mollified, "he *was* very much a 'gent'—in the best sense. Charming, gracious, very handsome. He had a great many friends, both personal and professional— I honestly think almost everyone who knew him liked Hamlet Winters."

"In other words," Timothy looked thoughtful, "a smooth article."

I nodded.

"That is, I believe, precisely what the girls at Maplewood would call him—wouldn't they, Joan?"

"Absolutely," the girl agreed. "And they'd mean it respectfully too. He was easily the most popular person on the faculty when I was there."

"Obviously then, Hamlet Winters was not the man to have enemies—that you would know of?"

"Heavens, no!" With one accord Joan and I shook our heads. "On the contrary," I explained, "he was one of the few professors I've known who kept absolutely out of the squabbles and jealousies that flourish in most academic groups. Not," I added hastily, "that any of those little quarrels would ever lead to such a thing as murder—but I do think it's significant that Dr. Winters always seemed to be above unpleasantness of any kind."

"Maybe." Timothy sounded unconvinced. He seemed, at the moment, more intent upon balancing his fountain pen on the edge of an ash-tray than on my remarks about Hamlet Winters, but I was to learn later that his mania for balancing strangely assorted objects came over him at the moments when he was thinking hardest. Presently, having poised the pen successfully, Timothy looked up with an air of satisfaction. "And maybe," he concluded lightly, "Winters was only saving himself for bigger and better quarrels. What was his family life, by the way?"

Joan and I exchanged a quick smile.

"You'd have a hard time," I said positively, "finding any trouble *there*. Mrs. Winters is as charming as her husband, and their marriage was quite ideal."

"No difficulties, eh?" Timothy inquired with interest.

"None," I repeated firmly, "that I can possibly think of. From an outsider's point of view, Dr. Winters' personal life was as successful and well-ordered and above reproach as his professional career."

"What about money?"

"Mrs. Winters had plenty."

"Any children?"

"No."

"Then there was nothing," Timothy reached for a cigarette and perched it opposite the balanced pen, "to complicate the life of Hamlet Winters."

Joan and I were silent.

"He was a good type, all right," Timothy murmured.

"A good type for what?" Joan's question was curious.

"Oh"—he frowned at the cigarette—"to be murdered."

"I don't see that," I said, "at all."

"No." His drawl was deliberate. "I don't suppose you would, Miss Belle, unless you'd been in on a few murders. But I've noticed that people who get themselves murdered are usually one of two kinds. Either everyone hates them—and there are a dozen suspects with excellent reasons for having done the dirty deed—or else you find out that the victim was a perfect saint who gave no one a chance even to dislike him. Either way, of course, you have a devil of a time picking the lucky number—which is one thing that makes jobs for cops like me."

"And what," I ventured with interest, "do you usually find to be the motive in the cases of the murdered saints?"

"Well"—Timothy paused to take up the balanced cigarette and light it—"sometimes they get killed just for being saints."

"And by whom, pray?"

"By someone," he grinned at me through a puff of smoke, "who is most un-saintlike himself or"—he added pointedly—"herself."

"Really, Timothy," Joan broke in impatiently, "what is the use of all this subtle detecting? After all, you're not even on this case."

"Quite so, my pet," the young man nodded. "We'll wind up with just two questions—and then forget the whole darn thing. Miss Belle, had you seen Winters lately, or written to him?"

"No, to the first and yes, to the second. I had written—but on the most unmurderous of subjects." I explained that Dr. Winters had written to me of the honorary degree from Granger.

"That's innocent enough," Timothy agreed. "Now for the second question. Did you know Fletcher Dee, of the Granger faculty, whose son was in the accident we saw yesterday afternoon?"

"By reputation only. I've never even seen him."

"What reputation?"

"That of being a good teacher," I said promptly, "in spite of having a most unpleasant personality. His grouches and bad tempers are almost a legend in the profession."

"In other words," Timothy flicked his ashes carefully, "our man Dee would be quite the opposite type from the late and sunny Dr. Winters—am I right?"

"Very likely," I nodded.

"And I wonder," Timothy looked thoughtful, "if they were friends."

"Well, I can tell you this much," Joan said suddenly, "they're next-door neighbors. This morning's paper gave both the Winters' and the Dees' addresses, and I noticed that they were adjoining numbers on Maryland Avenue— not far from the Hopkins campus I'd say."

"So?" Timothy's drawl had an upward inflection of interest. "You were a good girl, Joanie, to pick that up. It makes me feel a *hell* of a lot better!"

"How better?" I was frankly surprised by the emphasis of his remark.

Timothy grinned.

"Better for you, Miss Belle," he said happily, "and better for me, and a whole lot better for the cops on the case. In fact," he rose and shook himself like a huge puppy, "it makes me think we ought to forget this business and concentrate on a dash of beer—if Joan will oblige."

Joan, obviously glad enough to accept his cryptic dismissal of the subject, went at once to fetch the beer, but I was still curious.

"You surely can't mean," I said, "that the mere fact of those two families being neighbors is going to settle this case?"

"I surely can't, Miss Belle," Timothy returned my earnest look, "but I do mean that a clue as sweet as that one will keep the bloodhounds busy with the house next door to Hamlet Winters'—too busy to follow up our trail even if they do find it—unless, of course—the sky should fall."

And with that he departed after Joan and the beer, leaving me content to believe that we would hear no more from the affair at St. Ives—"unless the sky should fall."

But most unfortunately for all of us, the sky did fall—though not for some hours. Not, indeed, until quite late that night. Having spent the stifling June evening in being refrigerated at a local movie, Joan and I had returned to the apartment and were fast asleep in her bedroom when the front door-bell began to ring.

With one accord we groped for the light switch. Joan snapped it on to reveal us, each sitting up in bed, wide-eyed and blinking in the sudden glare.

"I suppose," Joan whispered fearfully, "we'll have to see who it is."

The peals were growing progressively longer and more violent.

"I suppose so," I nodded, not without reluctance. It seemed to me in that confusing moment that unless we got to the door and got there quickly the entire city would be aroused.

Hastily we fumbled for robes and slippers, and made our way, on tiptoe, through the hall. Joan put her head close to the door.

"Who's there?"

The clamor of the bell ceased, and a man's voice answered.

"Does Miss Joan Pell live here?"

Joan looked at me. I nodded.

"Yes," she said.

"A message for you, Miss Pell," the man's voice again.

Another look from Joan, another nod from me.

"All right," she opened the door a crack, and a strong hand pushed it inward sharply.

A man appeared, amazingly followed by more men— and for a moment it seemed to me that a multitude had descended on us, quite filling the tiny hall with cigarette smoke, and slouched hats and irrelevant questions. It turned out that by actual count there were only five reporters, but even when I was clear upon that point I still had no idea why they had forced this visit upon us.

"You're the young lady," one of the men was addressing Joan, "who helped a woman escape from University Hospital this morning?"

"Is this the woman?" A second pointed toward me.

"May I have a picture please, Miss Pell?" another sing-songed cheerfully. He was unfolding an involved black object which, I realized in sudden horror, must be a camera.

The whole nightmarish effect of confusion was heightened by the fact that Joan and I, backed helplessly against the wall, were quite inadequately covered by the thin summer negligees which we clutched about us. And for some moments we seemed, as in a dream, unable to answer or reason with the stream of insistent questions.

"Were you also in St. Ives Cathedral yesterday, Miss Pell?"

"How long had she," indicating me, "known Hamlet Winters?"

"Did you see the person who knocked you out?" This question was asked of me directly.

"What about the man who took you to the hospital?"

"Is he here too?"

"May I have your statement for the *Blade,* Miss Pell?"

"May I have a picture of both the ladies, please?" Again the camera was pointed menacingly.

Joan stepped forward quickly and with admirable firmness.

"No," she said to the photographer, and "No," to each of the four reporters. "I don't know how you got here," she went on, "or what you want—but it's an impossible hour, and we're impossibly dressed, and since neither of us," she took my arm, "has anything to say, I'll ask you please to leave."

The men looked unimpressed.

"Maybe it'll help you out," one of them suggested, "to know that we got the tip to come here from Police headquarters."

"If you haven't got anything to say right now," another young man shifted his hat to the extreme back of his head, "you probably will when the cops get here." His casual tone held not the slightest trace of menace.

"And so," a third observed mildly, "I guess we'll wait."

The look of alarm which passed between Joan and me was, I hoped, not as obvious as it felt. Certainly Joan rallied surprisingly well.

"In that case," she said coolly, "by all means make yourselves quite comfortable." She led the way into the living-room and snapped on the lights.

The men settled themselves upon the couch and chairs in noncommittal silence.

Back in the bedroom, Joan made straight for the telephone. I knew, of course, that she was calling Timothy, and a moment later she was hurriedly explaining the onslaught of the press.

"Hell's bells," I could hear his deep voice buzz through the receiver, "I'll be right over—just hold everything."

When, some minutes later, Joan and I were dressed, Timothy arrived to be welcomed ardently by us. Out in the hall, he whispered comfortingly.

"They can't know *much,*" he indicated our visitors, "because who could have spilled it?"

Yet his brows were wrinkled in a troubled frown as he peered in the living-room. The men sat in a silent and indifferent circle, all leaning back sleepily, all smoking cigarettes and delicately flicking the ashes thereof upon the rugs.

"Gentlemen of the press," Timothy addressed them drily, "may I inquire what you hope to find here?"

They looked up with no visible signs of interest. "You may," one of the men yawned widely and said no more.

"Ask her," a second indicated Joan.

"Look here," Timothy's expression gave me an idea of his capacities for being hard-boiled. But he got no further.

There were heavy footsteps in the hall outside, and once more the door-bell was rung with lengthy determination.

"The police." Joan clutched my arm.

"Oh, no," I shook my head with not much conviction, "it's impossible." Then I stepped back as Timothy swung open the door and we faced two men, one in police uniform, and a woman.

The man in plain clothes eyed Timothy, then Joan and me.

"Well," he turned abruptly to the woman who stood beside him, "step up and tell us which is which."

The woman obeyed. She wore a dark silk coat and a hat pulled low over her eyes, but suddenly I was aware of two things. Beneath the coat was a white nurse's uniform, and beneath the hat-brim was a face all too familiar to me.

"That," she pointed at Timothy, "is the man who brought Miss Stebbins to the hospital, and this girl," indicating Joan, "helped her get away this morning." She spoke with a pleasant briskness.

"And what about Miss Stebbins?" she was prompted.

The woman turned to look straight at me.

"This is Miss Stebbins," she said clearly. "She was my patient last night." And with the very words which turned me over to the police, Miss Carter gave me one of her most radiant smiles—a smile not one bit less innocent and engaging than those I had received so gratefully the night before.

8

A DEAD MAN'S LETTER

The plain-clothes man stared at me with unpleasantly prominent eyes.

"I'm Inspector Barrett," he said abruptly, "in charge of the Winters investigation. Did you give your name at the University Hospital as Mrs. Morse?"

Instinctively I glanced at Timothy, and my heart sank as I saw the slight shrug which accompanied his nod. Plainly he was signaling that our little game of bluff could proceed no longer.

"Yes," I admitted.

"And what *is* your name?"

I drew a breath. "Miss Stebbins," I faced the hostile looks squarely, "Miss Belinda Stebbins."

"You lied, of course," the Inspector's tone was harshly matter of fact, "because you didn't want it known that you were mixed up in the murder of Hamlet Winters?"

My mouth was open to protest when Timothy made an effort to assist me.

"Miss Stebbins was in a confused state when she reached the hospital," he began, and stopped short before a quick gesture from Barrett.

"You keep out of this," said the Inspector eloquently, and turned back to me. "You went to St. Ives Cathedral to meet Hamlet Winters?" Again his question was more like a statement than a query.

"I did not." This time I spoke firmly.

"Then I suppose," Barrett's scornful inflection was unchanged, "you just stopped in the Cathedral to pray?"

It was at that moment that I plunged headlong into the explanation which was later to become famous as my "cat story." Once launched upon a statement of my unfortunate and accidental connection with the affair at St. Ives, I paused for nothing and omitted nothing—despite the warning looks from Timothy, Joan's restraining hand upon my arm, and my own awareness of the fact that the reporters had roused themselves from comfort in the living-room and were busily taking down my every word. For, being a person whose honesty had never been questioned, I was convinced that my account would be accepted, even by this rude Inspector, for precisely what it was: the truth.

Not so.

Barrett listened to my statement with an expression which altered only in becoming more openly skeptical.

"We won't stop for arguments now," he said when I had finished speaking. "You've admitted you were in the Cathedral yesterday when a man you knew was murdered. You lied about your name and ducked out of the hospital without telling what had happened to you and you were hiding out here until I found you, thanks to this young lady. So I'm taking the three of you," the Inspector concluded, "up to the Winters' house with me."

I looked at Timothy questioningly and again my heart sank as I saw him shrug. His jaw was set hard and his head was lowered, but he spoke civilly enough to Barrett.

"Very well," he answered for Joan and me too, "you lead the way—Inspector."

A moment later when I returned from the bedroom with my hat and purse, Emma padded after me—and paused to stretch her small furry self in the front hall.

"Hey there," a whoop from one of the reporters, "is that the cat?"

"Hold it!" Another scooped up startled Emma and thrust her at me. "Look this way—" A click.

"I got it." The photographer looked up from his camera.

Timothy must have seen signs of trouble in my face, for he stepped forward quickly and lifted Emma from my arms.

"We've got to take it, Miss Belle," he murmured between shut teeth. "And whatever happens, for God's sake keep your shirt on." Then he turned to deposit Emma on a chair and we followed Inspector Barrett from the apartment.

Mindful of Timothy's advice, I "kept my shirt on" and offered no comment whatever when the Inspector ordered me into his car next to Miss Carter. The trip up Maryland Avenue to the Winters' house was made in silence—a silence which was not broken when we filed into the big lighted hall and were ushered by a wide-eyed colored butler to the room which had been Hamlet Winters' study.

I glanced about and thought that the long, low-ceilinged library was quite as I should have expected it to be. The book-lined walls, the big mahogany desk, the elegant simplicity and comfort of the room, all spoke so clearly of the man I had known.

Standing before the great carved oak fireplace, surrounded, it seemed, by the personality of Dr. Winters, I was struck by the enormity of what had happened. That such a man, representative of dignity and learning and gracious living, should have been brutally murdered seemed unthinkable. And yet—I remembered with an involuntary shudder that grotesquely kneeling figure in the dim Cathedral. Impossible to imagine what sinister events could have brought the owner of this room to such a death.

I looked up suddenly to meet the Inspector's unpleasantly intent stare.

"Chilly, Miss Stebbins?" His voice rasped upon the quiet room. No doubt he had observed my shudder.

"Now then," Barrett turned to Miss Carter, "get back to your patient and bring her down here right away."

For a confused moment I thought he must refer to me as the patient, but the nurse's answer gave me the clue to her unexplained presence in this household.

"Mrs. Winters," she said, "is very near a collapse, Inspector. I doubt whether it's wise to get her up at this hour—"

"If she's going to collapse," Barrett interrupted rudely, "she'll do it anyway. I might as well get in a few questions first." With a gesture he waved the nurse away.

So, I thought, by a coincidence Miss Carter had been called to care for Mrs. Winters. Or *was* it—chilling possibility—mere chance through which she had become further involved in this affair? At any rate, I wondered if Mrs. Winters had been taken in as I had by that angelic smile.

"The rest of you," Barrett waved at us, "sit down."

We did so.

"I'll start with you." The Inspector planted himself in front of Timothy. "What's your name?"

"Timothy Fowler."

"All right, Mr. Fowler—" Barrett cleared his throat.

"My better friends," Timothy observed thoughtfully, "call me Inspector Fowler."

"What'ya mean?" For the first time Barrett's voice registered something besides official gruffness.

"Only," said Timothy, "that in my own bailiwick of New York, I'm a cop. In the Homicide Division." Having settled himself in a big leather chair he peered up at Barrett with a mildly apologetic air, yet I thought I perceived a certain gleam in his eyes.

"Well"—obviously the other man was considerably affected by this news—"that makes it different." He coughed. "Now suppose you tell me—er—Inspector, just what your connection with this case actually is."

"Chance," said Timothy laconically, "pure chance."

"Yes, but"—Barrett coughed again—"from what Miss Carter said I judged you must be—"

"I wouldn't take that girl too seriously, Inspector," Timothy lowered his voice confidentially. "I did—and it was a mistake."

"Well"—Barrett was reduced to uncertainty—"you— were in the Cathedral yesterday afternoon—and you must have seen Winters just after he was attacked—or even—" The abrupt pause was significant, but Timothy faced him blandly enough.

"I expect I did see him," he admitted.

"Was he alive or dead?"

"Really I don't know." Timothy shrugged. "The man I saw was kneeling—not, after all, an uncommon thing to do in church—so I paid no attention."

"What about Miss Stebbins?" Barrett turned suddenly to me. "Did you see Winters?"

"What does this mean?" a sharp voice cut in before I had a chance to answer, and with one accord we turned toward the door.

It was Hamlet Winters' wife who had spoken. She stood, tall and dignified, regarding Inspector Barrett with an expression of fixed contempt. Miss Carter, at her side, offered a steadying arm, but the older woman brushed it aside. Certainly Mrs. Winters gave not the slightest indication of being near a state of collapse. She was perfectly dressed, her white hair carefully arranged in smooth waves on either side of a face which, far from being pale or tear-stained, was composed and alert.

"What does it mean?" Her question was repeated in a level tone. "These people in my house at such an hour? These questions about my husband—?"

"It means," said Barrett, "that I'm trying to find out who killed Dr. Winters."

A look of something like amusement flickered across the woman's face. It was a curiously sinister effect. Indeed the whole attitude of Mrs. Winters struck me as strange. Her unnatural poise at such a time and her trick of delivering half-irrational remarks with an air of complete reason were wholly at odds with the charming, gentle, rather soft Mary Winters I remembered. At the moment she seemed quite unaware of anyone save Barrett.

"If you want to find out how my husband died," she said slowly, "why do you ask questions?"

"Well, why not?" A mounting irritation was apparent in Barrett's tone.

Mrs. Winters crossed the long room with slow, even steps and seated herself in a high-backed chair near the great carved fireplace. Not until she had composed the folds of her black chiffon gown with deliberate care did she answer the Inspector's question.

"Because," her clear eyes rested thoughtfully on Barrett's flushed face, "questions are not necessary. I can tell why and how my husband met his death."

Barrett was plainly nonplussed and not, certainly, without cause.

"You told me earlier today," he said, "that you didn't know anything about what had happened. What made you change your mind?"

Mary Winters' steady gaze did not falter.

"Simply this." She opened a small handbag which lay in her lap, and extracted a folded paper. "I received today a letter from my husband, mailed within an hour of his death, which explains everything." With steady fingers Mrs. Winters spread out the page of thin, white letter-paper, and raised her eyes once more to Barrett. "Shall I read it?" she inquired softly.

It was, I believe, the strangest scene I had ever witnessed. The woman's almost hypnotic calm had transfixed us all—yet our wondering stares had not the slightest effect upon her manner, as she awaited the order to read the letter from her dead husband.

"Go ahead," the Inspector's voice was gruff. "Let's hear it."

Timothy, perched forward on the edge of his chair, was frankly regarding Mrs. Winters with an expression of clinical curiosity.

"'*My dear Mary,*'" without the slightest hesitation Mrs. Winters began to read in a low, clear voice. "'*In the event that I shall die under violent or questionable circumstances, I leave this letter for you. Lest you should find yourself, in such a case, in a position of confusion or embarrassment, I think it wise that you should have my signed statement to prove that you knew nothing of the unhappy affairs which will, in all probability, bring me to my death.*

"'*In the last twenty years there have been two great purposes and wishes in my life: my work, and my desire to make you happy. I cherish one last hope—that my life's end shall not undo its work. It is for this reason, and not through any*"

*wish to harrow you with morbid words, that I ask of you
these three final things. First, do not try to discover more
about me than you already know. Second, seek no revenge nor
explanation for my death, but only believe me when I tell you
that it will have been just. Third, and most urgent, do not
grieve for me. Your tears and regrets would be, as they have
always been, the greatest of all sorrows to me. Have faith in
me, Mary, as I have in you.*

"*Adieu! adieu! adieu! Remember me. . . .*

"*Hamlet Winters.*'"

The soft voice stopped. There was no sound in the room
save for the slight rustle of the paper as Mrs. Winters folded
it, carefully, and slipped it into her purse. Then she rose.

"I think you see now," she said to Barrett, "why there
can be no questions about my husband's death, and why
you have no place here in this house."

Slowly she turned and walked from the room, and in
the silence that followed we heard her soft, receding footsteps on the stairs.

I sank back in my chair. It seemed to me that I had
scarcely breathed while the letter was read. I had never
thought of Mary Winters as a dramatic person—but the
effect of her voice and manner could scarcely have been
more moving. The reason for her strange behavior, which
had so puzzled me a few minutes past, was now quite clear.
The message from her dead husband, his last appeal to her
for courage and faith, must have induced in Mary Winters
that exalted, trance-like mood. No wonder she failed to
recognize me, and ignored us all save Barrett. We, the two
men, Joan and myself, must have seemed like dimly unreal
intruders upon the dream in which she moved.

Inspector Barrett was the first to break the spell of silence. He drew a breath and let it out in a long, low whistle. It was his expression of the emotion we all felt.

"Hell," he said, and his tone had a note of something like a reverence in it, "that's no kind of a letter to get from a man who's supposed to have been murdered!"

"Why not?" Timothy caught up the question quickly.

Barrett eyed him with considerable surprise.

"I may be cockeyed," he said slowly, "but it looks as plain as any pipe-stem to me. That was a suicide letter."

Timothy rose abruptly and walked the length of the room.

"I don't agree." He halted before Barrett and shook his head. "I don't agree at all. Hamlet Winters was *murdered*—I'll bet a plugged nickel on that—and what's more he *knew* he was going to be killed, and who was going to do it, and why."

"I think so too," Joan spoke up unexpectedly. "I think Timothy's right about it."

"And look here," Timothy was growing more excited, "what about that quotation at the end of the letter?" He turned to me. "Wasn't that from '*Hamlet,*' Miss Belle?"

"It certainly was," his spotting of the line surprised me a little, "it's from the first act scene where the ghost of Hamlet's father returns to tell his son that he was murdered."

"*Swell.*" Timothy snapped his fingers in a gesture of triumph. "And don't think the old bird picked that particular line for nothing. Can't you see the picture?" He looked at Barrett. "Winters knew he was slated to be killed—God knows why—and he leaves this letter to make it look like suicide because he didn't want the dirty business, whatever it was, to come out after he was dead. But he was just the type to tie himself up with something out of Shakespeare—so he couldn't resist that quote at the end. My God—it's almost too good. Even the name was right— *Hamlet Winters.*"

"Sounds too damn much like a detective story to me." Barrett's voice was still skeptical. "Maybe you boys in New York settle murders by reading Shakespeare—but personally I never get the time."

"Rats," said Timothy impolitely. "Just because I spot one line from *Hamlet* you don't have to get on a high horse and ride off a cliff. God knows I'm no highbrow, but if you can't see any sense in tying in Shakespeare when you're working on a case like Hamlet Winters—then you're no cop."

Barrett received the outburst reasonably well.

"I don't give a damn," he said, "if you tie in the Ten Commandments. As long as you're so full of ideas on this case, why don't you stick around? If you can handle a dame like this Mrs. Winters—you're welcome to it!"

"Do you mean that, by any chance?" Timothy demanded.

"Sure." Barrett shrugged. "I'm not proud—and I've got to hand in *something* on this case. You'll have to stay around anyway as long as I suspect you and your two girlfriends so you might as well be making yourself useful. Personally," he yawned, "I'd welcome a little sleep right now."

"O. K.," said Timothy happily. "Why don't you ask the butler if he thinks Mrs. Winters would bunk you for what's left of the night? And while you're at it—you might snag off a room for Joan and Miss Stebbins too."

"Suits me all right." The Inspector nodded wearily. "Hey, Al," his loud voice summoned the policeman who was waiting in the hall outside, "find that butler bozo in the kitchen and tell him to come here."

"Look here," I put in, "I don't feel that we ought to intrude this way in Mrs. Winters' house. Couldn't Joan and I go back to the apartment—?"

Barrett shook his head.

"Not a chance, lady," he said with finality. "Nobody gets to leave this place unless I say so—and that won't be until Sherlock here finds me some new suspects. After all," he yawned again, "I gotta act as if I had *some* ideas about this job."

If I had any doubts concerning the colored butler's willingness to install us as guests under such unusual circumstances, they were soon settled. A single flash of the Inspector's badge was sufficient to reduce him to a state of wide-eyed and respectful obedience.

"Show these ladies upstairs," Barrett directed, "and then find me a place to sleep."

"Yassuh." The butler rolled his great eyes toward Joan and me, and led the way out into the hall.

As we rose, I saw Barrett glance at Timothy with a curious expression.

"What about you, Fowler?" he inquired. "Will you turn in too—or must you have at your Shakespeare right away?"

"Me?" Timothy's restless glance swept the room. "Me, I'll be busy right here." I saw his eyes narrow as he gazed at the low shelf of well-worn books near Hamlet Winters' desk, then at the broad desk itself. "Right here," he repeated. For a moment his forefinger rested gently upon the polished mahogany table where Dr. Winters had worked and studied; where, perhaps, he had written the last strange letter to his wife. I wondered what secrets Timothy believed the desk would presently reveal to him.

Barrett, observing his new assistant, evidently wondered too.

"Hell," he said in slow disgust, "now you've spoiled *my*
sleep."

"How so?" Timothy's question was absentminded.

Barrett shrugged. "If you think," he said, "that I'm going to give you a chance like this to rummage in God
knows what stuff, and tear up any evidence you don't happen to like—you've got another think. Hey, Rastus—" he
called the butler.

"Yassuh." The tone remained courteous.

"Do like I said with the ladies," the Inspector told him,
"but never mind a room for me. I'll snuggle up right here."
With a resigned sigh he stretched out on a leather couch.
"O. K., copper," he waved toward Timothy, "do your stuff.
And when you come to any little clue that you don't like—
toss it my way."

As Joan and I crossed the wide hall and followed the
soft footsteps of the butler on the stairs, I heard Timothy's
answer.

"Believe me," he said, "there isn't a clue in this whole
room that I don't want. And especially in that little shelf
of Hamlet Winters' books."

Joan and I would have preferred to share a room for the
remainder of the night, but it seemed unwise to quibble
with the butler's obliging hospitality. With a murmured
"good night" I left Joan and locked myself into the single room which Tilden indicated for me. It was a comforting sort of room, bright and cheerful, with turquoise
blue walls and soft peach taffeta hangings at the windows.
There was even a suggestion of a cooling breeze which
stirred the air around my face when, a few minutes later, I

opened the casement window and sank gratefully into the luxurious comfort of the bed.

When first I became conscious of the slight rustling sound, I knew that it must be the breeze which stirred the taffeta at the windows. Not until I heard the faintest echo of a knock did I rouse myself sufficiently to realize that the sound came from *outside* the room. Scarcely breathing, I raised myself upon one elbow and craned forward in the darkness to listen. Plainly, I heard the rustling sound again—then a moment's silence, and quick, soft footsteps fading down the hall.

It must have been almost a minute before I reached out and snapped on the bedside light. At first it seemed that there was nothing to be seen, then something white caught my attention and I realized that a folded square of paper had been pushed beneath the doorsill. I fetched the mysterious message, fumbled for my glasses, and spread out the paper beneath the shaded lamp. The note was printed in a neat feminine hand, and bore neither address nor signature.

"Please do not think," I read, *"that I double-crossed you when I told Inspector B. about your being in the Cathedral. After you left the hospital this morning, I talked to Teddy Mears, who was on duty in Emergency, and he said H. Winters wasn't killed at all by having his throat cut, but was actually murdered a long time before that happened. The police know this but are keeping it dark. You see, the best alibi you can have is that you were in the Cathedral if H. W. wasn't killed there, and that's exactly why I told on you. I'm sure you will understand that I just want to help."*

It was, of course, the amazing Miss Carter in action again. Ordinarily, I suppose, I would have taken the note immediately to Timothy, but with Barrett on guard down-stairs, that obviously was impossible. And with consider-able relief I realized that I had better do nothing about the message and its disturbing implications until morning. For I had reached the stage of exhaustion, both physical and mental, where one more inexplicable move on the part of Miss Carter evoked no response from me save a yawn, as I settled down to sleep.

9
MUSTARD YELLOW

I awoke next morning to a glare of sunshine which signified that the heat wave was still with us. I felt, however,
remarkably well rested considering the events of the night
before, and a cool shower restored me quite thoroughly.
The problem which disturbed me most was the question of
my very awkward position as an uninvited guest in Mary
Winters' home. But when presently Tilden appeared with
my breakfast tray, it seemed that my presence in the household had been accepted naturally enough, at least as far as
he was concerned.

Having consumed a reasonable portion of the delicious
breakfast, I hurried downstairs to find Timothy and show
him the strange message from Miss Carter.

The police officer, who had been stationed in the lower
hall the night before, was still at his post. At the library
door I paused, and peeped cautiously into the room, hoping to catch Timothy's eye and not Barrett's.

It was thus that I happened to see the woman in mustard yellow. For a moment I was struck only by a vague
feeling of having seen her somewhere before—then suddenly I recalled the circumstance. It was the same large
woman, in the same unpleasantly bilious colored dress,

who had passed me in the vestibule of St. Ives at the moment when I entered the building on Friday afternoon.
Save for the dress, I probably should not have recognized
her, yet I would have been willing to take an oath on my
identification—so certain was I that no two women in
the city of Baltimore could ever have hit upon quite such
a distinctively repulsive color as that shade of mustard
yellow.

It was quite apparent that the woman was alone in
Hamlet Winters' study and her presence there struck me
as distinctly queer. She was, as nearly as I could judge,
engaged in searching the contents of Dr. Winters' desk—a
process which she carried on with such concentrated zeal
that she never once looked up to see me spying on her.

Having made up my un-sleuthlike mind that this infor-
mal prowling in Dr. Winters' effects was decidedly out of
order, I removed myself, as quietly as possible, from earshot of the library and beckoned to the policeman.

"Where," I demanded in a whisper, "is the Inspector?"

"In there," the officer jerked a finger toward a doorway
opposite the library, "with the other one. Eatin' breakfast."

I found Timothy and the Inspector engrossed in ham
and eggs at the long oak table in the dining-room, and it
struck me, not for the first time, that the Winters household, as represented by Tilden, was extraordinarily hospi-
table. Unfamiliar as I was with the etiquette of entertain-
ing an invasion of police, I was nevertheless certain that
all of us whom Barrett had brought with him to the house
were being unnecessarily well treated.

The two men rose as I approached the table—Timothy
briskly enough, despite the tired lines which showed plainly on his face. Barrett looked as if he had managed to rest

moderately well upon the library couch, but his attitude was nevertheless disgruntled, indicating that whatever Timothy had unearthed in his night's search had neither cheered nor edified him.

"Did you know," I began abruptly, "that there is a woman in the library going through the things on Dr. Winters' desk?"

"Hell, no!" Almost in unison the two men spoke, but with characteristically different inflections. Barrett's scowl only increased, while Timothy's response gave every indication of hopeful interest.

"If you're running this show, Fowler, get in there and grab the woman." Barrett half rose as though to carry out his own suggestion, when Timothy interfered with a sharp gesture.

"Hold everything, Barrett, *please,*" his tone was serious. "If you *will* let me run this, for cat's sake don't pop in on the woman now."

"Why not?"

"Because," said Timothy earnestly, "you'll spoil a swell clue—and practically our only one so far. Never mind who the woman is, or how she got in, or what she's doing. Just let her get whatever it is she wants—and *then* we'll nab her when she comes out, clue and all. Don't you see?"

"I see this much," Barrett flung down his napkin, "that you've been reading more books than Shakespeare. But— I'll take one more chance on your screwy ideas."

"Wait a minute," I put in eagerly. "There's one thing more *I* know about this woman—" Briefly I recounted the incident of colliding with her in the Cathedral.

"Swell," Timothy grinned at me through a bite of toast. "Now we're really getting somewhere. Come on—let's go and wait for our mustard lady to emerge—red-handed, we shall hope." He took a final swallow of coffee, pushed back his chair, and the three of us moved quietly into the hall.

We hadn't long to wait. Not more than a minute passed, I think, before a heavy step was heard within the study and the mustard yellow lady was suddenly standing directly before us. If she was startled or frightened by the curious line-up which awaited her, there was not the slightest indication of it in her stolid features.

"Pardon me," Timothy stepped forward, "but were you looking for something?"

"Yes," the deep voice matched her heavy frame. "I was looking for Mrs. Winters."

"And did you hope to find her," Timothy's drawl remained polite, "in the late Dr. Winters' desk drawer?"

Apparently the woman's composure was equal to anything.

"Naturally," she said, "I don't know what you mean. I am Miss Dee, a neighbor of Mrs. Winters, and I came here to be with her at this embarrassing time."

Certainly, I thought, the woman had selected an odd word to describe the situation.

"Very thoughtful of you, I'm sure," Timothy murmured, "but you must understand that the—the embarrassment you refer to communicates itself to anyone who comes here. In other words," his voice took on a sudden edge, "this house is under police guard, and I must ask you how you got in, and why you searched the desk in Dr. Winters' study?"

"No doubt," she said a trifle irrelevantly. "I came in, as I always do, by the front door—"

We turned to look at the policeman and saw his florid face grow a shade redder.

"That just ain't so, Chief," he shook his head at Barrett. "I've been right here every minute."

"And," the woman continued, apparently quite oblivious of the interruption, "the fact that I was in the library does not mean that I was searching the desk—or any other part of the room." She spoke without any particular emphasis, seeming neither to resent nor be confused by the questions.

"I see," said Timothy noncommittally. "And while you are so willing to supply me with information, will you also tell me why you were at St. Ives on the afternoon when your neighbor and excellent friend, Hamlet Winters, met his death there—and why you left the Cathedral in a hurry?"

Still Miss Dee regarded him unmoved.

"I went to the Cathedral," she said steadily, "to pray. And I left abruptly when I heard a commotion in the street outside. I think your *witness* will tell you," for a fleeting moment her deep-set eyes shifted to me, "that she saw me go out of St. Ives immediately after the accident had occurred in the street."

"Quite so," Timothy nodded. "But unfortunately no witness could tell me why the noise of a comparatively quiet accident in the street should have upset you to the point of interrupting your—prayers." He emphasized the final word with care.

For the first time Miss Dee showed signs of reacting.

"Since you must know already," her heavy voice shook slightly, "that it was my nephew, my brother's son, who was killed in that accident, your remark strikes me as very stupid."

"Still I don't see," said Timothy reasonably enough, "how you could have known that before you left the building.

Unless"—he paused meaningly—"unless you saw your nephew leave St. Ives just ahead of you."

Miss Dee raised her square-set chin defiantly.

"As a matter of fact," she said, "I did."

"Oh." Timothy's look of interest quickened. "Then he had been with you in the Cathedral?"

There was the briefest hesitation.

"Yes," said Miss Dee.

"And he left before you did?"

"Yes."

"And you heard the disturbance of the accident—and thought it might be the boy who was hurt?"

"Yes."

"So you hurried out to see what had happened?"

"Yes."

"Then *why*," Timothy finished his quick barrage in triumph, "did you cross the vestibule and leave by the small side door that opens into the Cathedral close instead of going straight through the front entrance into the street?"

I realized what Timothy was doing. I recalled his surprise at the fact that I had collided with the large yellow lady in the Cathedral vestibule while he, entering almost immediately on my heels, had not seen her at all. That he had guessed right about the side door was evident from the look of dismay which contracted his victim's stolid features.

So evident, in fact, that her feeble denial was almost an admission in itself.

"I didn't," she said weakly, "that I—know of, anyway."

Timothy was not yet done with questions. "Did you see Hamlet Winters in St. Ives?"

Miss Dee's confusion increased.

"Yes . . ." she nodded weakly.

"And when you saw him, was he alive or dead?"

The woman grasped at the obvious straw.

"He was alive," she answered, not quite without conviction.

"Doing what?"

"Kneeling," Miss Dee said. "Praying."

"How do you know then that he was alive?" Timothy snapped the question at her. "He was found, you know, still kneeling—but quite dead."

"I know he was alive," the woman's voice rose sharply to an almost hectic pitch, "because I saw him—I saw him move!"

The certain lie was too much for me. In silence I stepped up to Timothy and handed him the folded note which Miss Carter had slipped beneath my door the night before. He read it quickly and then faced Miss Dee with a slow and most unpleasant smile.

"It won't do." He shook his head. "It just won't do. I'm afraid you'll have to stay right here, Miss Dee, and let Al keep an eye on you for the present."

She made a feeble effort to protest.

"On what authority—" she began, but Timothy cut her short.

"On this authority," he snapped. Reaching out, he twisted back Barrett's coat to show the badge upon the vest beneath. "And if I were you, lady, I wouldn't argue with that little pie-plate. Now you, Barrett," he turned back to the Inspector, "send a man down to the Cathedral close pronto and have him buzz around that yard to see what he can find."

"What's he supposed to find?" Barrett inquired rather unimaginatively.

"Oh—anything that's not supposed to be there," Timothy shrugged. "For instance, a pocket knife—or maybe an old-fashioned razor." As he spoke I saw him watch Miss Dee from the corner of his eye.

The Inspector nodded his somewhat grudging assent and started toward the telephone.

"And tell your gent not to forget," Timothy called after him, "to look in the fountain pool in the middle of the yard." Then a slow smile of satisfaction spread across his face.

Miss Dee had settled herself heavily in one of the tall chairs, and at Timothy's final words she shrank back with an expression of helpless but unmistakable alarm.

10
A SCENE FROM HAMLET

"Come in here a minute, will you, Miss Belle?" Timothy motioned me toward the library. He closed the door behind us, leaving Miss Dee to be balefully watched over by Officer Al, and directed me to an armchair near Dr. Winters' big desk.

"Now where," he asked at once, "did you get that note you handed me?"

I explained.

"Carter again, eh?" Timothy squinted thoughtfully. "Damn that girl"—his tone was admiring rather than angry—"how much *does* she know?"

"And how much," I demanded, "does she invent?"

Timothy shook his head.

"How much, indeed?" he echoed. "Still"—his tone was doubtful—"there *may* be something in what that note said—for all we know."

"You don't really think, do you, that Dr. Winters could have been killed and *then* taken to the Cathedral?"

Timothy's answer was a shrug.

"Surely," I went on earnestly, "to take a—a dead man through the downtown streets in broad daylight is a fantastic idea."

"A little too fantastic," Timothy agreed slowly.

"But you just said—"

"I didn't say just *that,* Miss Belle," he interrupted me quickly. "But I believe there is a possibility that Winters was murdered before he ever entered the Cathedral." He paused to smile at my expression. "A man can be technically dead, you know, and still walk around, Miss Belle."

The explanation was in no way enlightening to me.

"I haven't the dimmest idea what you're driving at," I said frankly.

"And I haven't much of an idea myself," Timothy sighed. "But if there is anything in what Carter said in that note— we'll know it in a few minutes. The Coroner's due at nine, and it's quarter of now."

I nodded with what I hoped was a more intelligent expression. At least I had read enough detective stories to know what a Coroner was expected to do.

"I suppose then," I said, "that he's made the—the usual examination of the body."

"Right," Timothy answered. "They were at it early this morning."

"And yet the note from Miss Carter was given to me last night. Will you tell me how she could know anything about the autopsy before it was even begun?"

"Don't ask me." Timothy shook his head wearily.

"And for that matter," I added, "whose side is she on? First she helps the police—and then she sides with a suspect."

"Like yourself, for instance?"

"Like myself," I answered seriously, "or Mrs. Winters." Timothy was silent.

"I should think," I ventured, "that you could pretty much settle the Carter riddle by asking her some questions."

"Oh, but no, Miss Belle." Timothy shook his head quickly. "You see—I'd so much rather let her work her own way."

"Even if she keeps interfering all the time?"

"Especially if she interferes," said Timothy firmly. "After all, she wouldn't butt into things without some reason—and I can get a whole lot further trying to figure out what her reasons might be, than by asking her questions and watching her smile sweetly and lie like a carpet. I'm always in favor of letting nature take its course when it comes to the behavior of suspects, Miss Belle. That's why, for example, I was careful to give mustard gas a chance to come in for some snooping this morning." He paused.

"Mustard gas?"

"Miss Dee," Timothy enlightened me with a grin. "I'm just the kind of a simple-minded flatfoot that can't make any headway without clues—and in spite of the fact that I spent half the night going through this room, and particularly this desk," he tapped it lightly, "I hadn't found a darned thing to go on but two measly little facts that might or might not mean anything at all. About seven o'clock this morning, Miss Belle, I was all set to pack up my dollies and dishes and go home to New York where we don't have murders without clues—but *just* at the zero hour I happened to look out of the window and caught sight of this overstuffed vision cutting across the lawn from the Dee house next door. Seven in the morning seemed just a trifle early for a social call, so I figured it must be business. It was easy enough," Timothy shrugged, "to leave the front door ajar—and then to sit back and let fate go on happening."

"What did she do?"

"I don't know exactly. Stalled around, I guess, and kept out of sight until the coast was clear in here while Barrett

and I were in the dining-room. I don't need to tell you
that *this* was her objective." Once again he tapped the desk
before him.

"Then you deliberately let Miss Dee come in," I said,
"to find out what she was after?"

"Right."

"And was it worthwhile?"

"I rather think so," Timothy nodded slowly.

"Frankly I don't see how. It's pretty certain that she
didn't take anything out of the library with her—and unless she destroyed some paper or evidence—"

"Oh, no, Miss Belle, she didn't do that," Timothy put
in emphatically.

"But why not? After all, she was alone in here."

"Quite so. But forehanded Timothy saw to it that there
were no matches left in the room, and the waste-basket, as
you see, is empty." He held it up for my inspection. "Now
how else, Miss Belle, could a woman of no imagination
destroy anything?"

"Maybe you're right," I found myself somewhat dis-
trustful of these tricks, "but even so I don't see that you've
accomplished much."

"Come, come, Miss Belle," Timothy grinned at me,
"you mustn't sneeze at the flower of the New York Force
until you've heard the story out. You remember I told you
that after scouring this room half the night I lit on just
two things that might turn out to mean something?"

I nodded.

"Well—I was smart enough to plant those items very
carefully—so carefully that I'd know it right off if they
were disturbed a fraction of an inch while I was away."

"Yes?" I was really interested then.

"It turned out that I was only half right," said Timothy modestly. "Miss Dee left one of the plants right where it was."

"But the other one?"

"Had plainly been disturbed!"

"What *was* it? And *what* did she do with it?"

"It was," said Timothy, "the top sheet of this." He tapped a combination calendar and memorandum pad which lay on the broad desk top. "The page which was dated Friday, June twentieth—the day, of course, when Winters was killed—and on that page were certain notes in Hamlet Winters' writing. As for what Miss Dee did with the page," he shrugged, "she either took it with her— or hid it somewhere."

"And you deliberately let her get away with it?"

"Why not?" said Timothy cheerfully. "The thing that matters most to me is to know that she had some reason for swiping it. As for what was written on the memorandum—I'd already made a copy of that."

"Oh," I leaned back in relief, "of course."

"And here," Timothy extracted a paper from his pocket, "is the copy."

I opened the small slip of paper. At the top Timothy had printed a copy of the calendar heading: FRIDAY, JUNE TWENTIETH. Beneath that were three small entries—no one of which seemed, to my expectant eyes, significant in the least. The first was a single line, near the top of the page:

Laura—lunch—1 o'clock

The second jotting, further down, was a lone telephone number:

Md. 7245

And the third entry, written across the lower corner, was a strange, irrelevant little couplet:

Dr. Hall

Got it all

Try as I would to see the importance of the memorandum, I could make nothing of it. With a sigh I returned the page to Timothy.

"I'm sorry," I said frankly, "but it doesn't mean a thing to me. I can't see why either you or Miss Dee would attach any particular significance to a casual desk memorandum."

Timothy folded the slip, patted it fondly, and returned it to his pocket.

"*I* think," he said with conviction, "that anything a man writes on the last morning of his life is damned significant."

"Oh surely, Timothy, you don't think Dr. Winters *knew* it was his last day?"

"No?" The question was mild. "Then why, Miss Belle, the letter to his wife—mailed within an hour of the time when he was killed? And why this?" Timothy reached for a certain small volume on the bookshelf next to the desk. "The second," he explained, "of my two clues."

Wonderingly, I reached for the book. It was an unpretentious edition of *Hamlet*.

"My chief reason for bringing you in here for this confab was to ask you about this. Hold the book," Timothy directed, "and let it open where it will."

I obeyed, and the pages fell back readily at a certain place. It was the scene between Hamlet and his father's ghost—the scene from which, I recalled, had been taken the single quoted line in Winters' letter to his wife. *"Adieu, adieu, adieu, remember me."* That the play had been read and re-read at that special place was plainly evident. There

were, in fact, numerous lines within the scene which had
been heavily underscored—and a quick glance through the
remainder of the volume showed clean, unmarked pages.
Still I was not overly impressed.

"What can it mean," I asked of Timothy, "except that
Dr. Winters happened to be interested in that scene? He
wouldn't be, after all, the first to admire it."

"Look again, Miss Belle," he urged me, "at just *which*
lines preyed on the old boy's mind. Read 'em out loud."

Obediently I read. It was the scene in which the ghost
of Hamlet's father returns to tell his son that he was murdered—and direct the young prince to avenge the crime. I
skipped through the pages, pronouncing only those words
which the heavy pencil of Hamlet Winters had underscored:

GHOST: . . . . . List, list, O, list!
    If thou didst ever thy dear father love—
HAMLET: O God!
GHOST: Revenge his foul and most unnatural murder.
HAMLET: Murder!
GHOST: Murder most foul, as in the best it is,
    But this most foul, strange and unnatural.
    . . . . . . know, thou noble youth,
    The serpent that did sting thy father's life
    Now wears his crown.
    . . . . . .
    With witchcraft of his wit, with traitorous gifts,—
    . . . . . .
    . . . . . . wretch, whose natural gifts were poor
    To those of mine!
    . . . . . .
    Thus was I, sleeping, by a brother's hand

Of life, of crown . . . at once dispatch'd;

. . . . . .

No reckoning made, but sent to my account
With all my imperfections on my head.
O, horrible! O, horrible! Most horrible!
If thou hast nature in thee, bear it not;

. . . . . .

Adieu, adieu, adieu! remember me.

HAMLET: . . . . . Remember thee!
Ay, thou poor ghost, while memory holds a seat
In this distracted globe. Remember thee!
Yea, from the table of my memory
I'll wipe away all trivial fond records,
All saws of books, all forms, all pressures past,
That youth and observation copied there;
And thy commandment all alone shall live
Within the book and volume of my brain,

. . . . . .

It was the end, apparently, of Hamlet Winters' special interest in the scene. Nothing after that was underlined. I looked up slowly to meet Timothy's sober glance.

"You can't tell me, Miss Belle," he spoke with evident sincerity, "that it doesn't mean *something*."

"Perhaps." I couldn't fail to be impressed by Timothy's conviction, but it seemed to me that he was fumbling hopelessly in some dark corner of what had been Hamlet Winters' mind. With some difficulty, I put my thought in words. "It seems so incredible," I finished lamely, "that there should have been anything secret—anything sinister or desperate in the life of a man like Dr. Winters."

Timothy nodded understandingly. "And yet," his voice was quiet, "there *was,* Miss Belle—and it's up to us to find out what it could have been."

"How can you possibly?" I protested. "Everything in his life was so orderly—so regular—"

"Everything but his death," said Timothy. "You forget that."

"Well"—I drew a deep breath—"what *is* your theory, Timothy? Or—have you got one yet?"

He leaned back.

"I have, Miss Belle. And I'm going to try it on you—right now."

"Why me? I'm no judge of theories."

"Maybe not," said Timothy, "but you knew Hamlet Winters—and his background. That's damned important. Now my theory is simply this: Hamlet Winters had a *Hamlet* complex."

He leaned back to study my expression. Evidently it conveyed my bewilderment.

"Sounds crazy, doesn't it, Miss Belle? But look—suppose Winters found out some way—never mind how—that some person he knew had committed a crime—and suppose he decided to be a gentleman and not squeal on the guilty party. Now then, imagine, Miss Belle, that you are that person. You are a murderer or a thief or a bigamist or a forger—and Winters knows you are and *you know he knows it.* But—and here's my point, Miss Belle—Winters decides to be a little Christian about it, and say nothing. So he goes on treating you as if you were a perfect lady, always polite, always too damn *cricket* for words. Mightn't it get you down some day? Especially if you had a razor handy?" He was watching me with a strangely eager expression. "Do you see it at all, Miss Belle?"

"Perhaps I would see it," I said slowly, "if I knew more about your theory. If you're just basing the idea on some notion of Dr. Winters' personality—then I think it's hopelessly far-fetched. But if you have some real evidence—" I paused.

"It happens, Miss Belle, that I have some evidence." Timothy spoke with an air of suppressed excitement. From his pocket he drew another paper—this one larger. "My best clue," he said triumphantly, and handed it to me.

It was a letter, signed by Hamlet Winters and addressed to Dr. Hughes, the President of Granger College. Before I had read more than a few lines I looked up in astonishment.

"Where *did* this come from?" I demanded of Timothy.

"From headquarters—early this morning. This Dr. Hughes took it down sometime last night and said he'd decided it would better be turned over to the Police."

I read the letter through once—then a second time, and to this day I believe it must be one of the most completely amazing documents ever to have been posted and received within the chaste circle of an academic group!

> *My dear Dr. Hughes:*
> *I am writing to ask of you an unusual favor, and, while it is impossible for me fully here to set forth the reasons for my request, I shall hope that the confidence which you have always been kind enough to express in me will lead you to accept my word that I am acting to the best of my knowledge and conscience, and in the soberness of due reflection.*
>
> *The favor I would ask is this: At the coming meeting of the Board of Trustees, to take place, I believe, on the afternoon of Friday, June twentieth, may I be granted a hearing? It is my earnest wish that my friend and colleague,*

Fletcher Dee, shall also be requested to appear at the meeting and that he shall not be told of the reason for his summons.

In order that you may not think my communication too cryptic, I shall reveal a part of the motives which lie behind it. For the past three years of my otherwise happy and congenial sojourn at Granger College, I have been tortured by the secret knowledge of a terrible crime. More than that bare fact, I do not feel free to commit to writing at the present time; but I have, after great agony of mind, decided upon the only possible course of full confession.

Should you grant me this hearing on next Friday afternoon, it will be my unhappy duty at that time to present an account of this grave and unfortunate affair which concerns two members of the Granger faculty. I shall, of course, tender my resignation at the close of the meeting.

Confident of your absolute discretion, I shall await your answer. Meanwhile, I ask only that you believe in my earnestness and sincerity in this matter.

> *Faithfully yours,*
> *Hamlet Winters.*

LAURA—LUNCH—ONE O'CLOCK

Slowly I raised my eyes.

"Well—?" said Timothy.

I drew a long breath.

"Well"—I said—"it *does* back up your theory, all right."

"You see it as I do?" Timothy leaned forward eagerly. "You think it points to the fact that Winters knew something about Fletcher Dee—something pretty bad—and that he, Winters, kept quiet about it as long as he could, and *then*—" He paused.

"And then," I finished slowly, "he was about to make a full confession of the crime—whatever it was—on the afternoon that he was murdered."

"O.K., Miss Belle, O.K." Timothy beamed approval. "I think that's the right track—and *you* think it is—and if it is right, we'll have this sweet little mess all cleaned up in time for the church bells."

His optimism seemed to me a trifle overdone.

"Even if you've guessed correctly, Timothy," I shook my head, "I still don't see exactly what you can do about it. Where, for instance, will you find a—well, a starting point from which to work back toward this secret of Fletcher Dee's past?"

"Don't let that bother you, Miss Belle." Timothy brushed my question lightly aside. "My starting point, as you call it, will be none other than Fletcher Dee himself—and maybe," he laughed shortly, "my finishing point too."

He rose, stretched himself, leaned over my chair and chucked me under the chin—a thing which had never, in my memory, happened to me before.

"Excuse me for a minute, Miss Belle," he said cheerfully, "while I go rope in as many Dees as I can lay hands on!"

Half way to the door he was confronted by Barrett.

"There's a gent out here," the Inspector motioned toward the hall, "who looks like he's got something to spill. You better come and see what it's all about."

"Who is it?"

"Hughes," said Barrett. "The President of Granger College."

"O.K." Timothy nodded.

In less than ten minutes the door was flung open and Timothy was back—scowling with furious and unexpected intensity. He strode the length of the room and back, hurled himself into a chair and glared straight ahead.

"*Hell*," he said.

"Good heavens," I watched him with growing surprise, "what *has* happened?"

Timothy uttered a short and distinctly unpleasant laugh.

"My theory," he said, "has been blown into little teeny tiny pieces. That's what!"

"But, Timothy, how—in ten minutes?"

"By a present for Fletcher Dee—from this Dr. Hughes."

"What *do* you mean?"

"I mean," said Timothy bitterly, "that Hughes came here to bring Fletcher Dee a lovely little alibi, done up in blue ribbons—and bound in cast-irons! If you *see* what I mean!"

I was beginning to.

"And there," Timothy went on, "goes my pretty theory —blasted by the simple fact that Dee was at the meeting of the Trustees, just as Winters had wanted him to be, all the while that Winters was getting his throat cut in the Cathedral."

A silence—while Timothy put his head back and heaved a long sigh—and I thought rapidly. For once I was rewarded with an idea.

"Timothy," I said, "if Miss Carter was right about Dr. Winters having been murdered some time before he was found at St. Ives—mightn't that *still* leave an opportunity for Dee—?"

"Not a chance, Miss Belle." Timothy shook his head wearily. "Even if Carter was telling the truth—and I'm none too sure of it—Dee's alibi is still rock-bound. It seems he gave an examination that lasted three hours on Friday morning, and Hughes met him when he was leaving the classroom a few minutes after noon. They went to some luncheon pow-wow together, and while they were there, Hughes propositioned Dee about coming to the Trustees' meeting. Well"—Timothy heaved a great sigh—"the up-shot of it was that Dee was never out of Prexy's sight for a minute until that Trustees' meeting broke up shortly before six o'clock. They had waited around, of course, until it was pretty clear that Winters wasn't going to show up— and by that time, as you and I know, Winters was dead as a doornail in a pew at St. Ives."

"But there's still the chance," I ventured another hope, "that some friend of Fletcher Dee's might have tried to save him from what he knew Winters was going to tell."

"Yes," Timothy agreed. "There's still that chance."

I gathered that he was thinking, as was I, of Miss Dee and her unfortunate nephew—both of whom had been present in the Cathedral on Friday afternoon. But it was evident from his expression, as he leaned back—eyes closed—that he viewed the possibility with no particular enthusiasm.

"The stalwart Miss Dee seems to be our one hope for the moment," he murmured presently, "and we've really nothing against her except the fact that she came prowling around here at seven o'clock in the morning when she ought to have enough trouble—what with her nephew being killed—to keep her at home. And the fact that she was ready enough to lie when we tried a few questions—"

"So," I inquired, "you thought she was lying?"

Timothy opened one eye and peered at me.

"Sure. Didn't you?"

"Maybe," I shrugged. "But she didn't strike me as—well, as the imaginative type."

"Or me either," Timothy agreed promptly. "Of all the reasons she could have given for being in the Cathedral at the wrong time—she had to say that she went there to pray. If that's not a lack of talent in lying, then I never saw it."

"Still," I objected, "it might have been the truth. Some people *do* go to church to pray, you know."

"Not that tub," said Timothy rudely, and closed his eyes again. "Did you see her," he added, "break out in stripes when I told Barrett to have his man drag the fountain pool in the Cathedral yard? We've still got clues," he sounded no less dismal than before, "and plenty of 'em—but right now I'll be damned if I know what any of them mean. You're a better cop than I am, Miss Belle. You said there wasn't any starting point in this case—and you were right. There's all the hocus-pocus of Mrs. Winters and her ghost letter—wanting us to lay off investigating the murder. And then there's Carter acting out some little sideshow of her own—God knows why; and the fact that Hamlet Winters seems to have been pretty sure he was going to get a razor in the neck—" Timothy was checking off the oddly assorted items on his fingers. "Even with all those leads I can't get under way."

"And above all the letter to Dr. Hughes," I reminded him. "Even if it doesn't prove your first theory—it must mean *something.*"

My hopeful remark in no way cheered Timothy. If anything, he looked slightly more gloomy as he bent over the desk and made half-hearted attempts to balance a paper-knife on the inkwell rim.

"It means this much," he finally admitted, "that Winters was no slouch at dramatics. Add that letter to the one he left for his wife, and you've got an exit from the scene of life that might have been staged by the bard himself."

"And not forgetting," I put in, "that whoever killed Dr. Winters was pretty dramatic too. Making a dead man kneel in a Cathedral pew, after all . . ."

"I don't forget it, pal, I *don't.*" Timothy rose. "And now to work again. We're sunk for the moment, but I've sent for Fletcher Dee and his wife—and in the meantime I'll take a swing at finding out about this '*Laura*' who lunched at 1 o'clock," he was consulting the copy of Dr. Winters' desk memorandum, "and who belongs to this lonesome telephone number '*Md. 7245.*' Likewise this '*Dr. Hall*' who '*got it all.*'"

"And you told me that the Coroner was on his way, and that he might bring—"

"A ray of light," Timothy finished it with a grin, "in his little black satchel. Maybe he will, at that."

Timothy had scarcely left the room when I looked up to see Tilden usher in a large, bald, resentful-looking man.

"De Coroner, ma'am." Wide-eyed, the butler presented the stranger and departed, to leave us facing each other awkwardly.

In silence the large man regarded me, then settled himself and his satchel with care upon the sofa and produced a toothpick from an inner pocket. Still silent, he polished it with minute attention, then contemplated the result for several moments. Satisfied at last, he opened his mouth and applied his implement with uninhibited diligence.

I watched—first with surprise then with increasing interest—the remarkable progress of that toothpick. At the very moment, however, when the Coroner was really warming to his task, Barrett and Timothy appeared, and operations were, regrettably, suspended.

"Jim."

"Fred."

Barrett and the Coroner greeted each other with marked restraint.

"Well," the Inspector looked at Timothy, "do you want to ask the questions?"

"I do."

"O.K., Sherlock. But"—Barrett cleared his throat— "what about—" With a minimum of subtlety he gestured in my direction.

"For the present," said Timothy, "Miss Stebbins will stay where she is."

I sank back onto the chair from which I had half risen, and tried not to notice the scowl that Barrett turned on me.

"Say—" the Coroner had been listening. "Who is this bird?" He motioned toward Timothy.

"Inspector Fowler, of the New York force," said Barrett, and coughed a trifle uncertainly.

"Well, what's the idea," the Coroner turned to Timothy, "of gettin' me up here on a Sunday morning when I ought to be in church? I got my report ready and it'll be down to headquarters inside of another hour. You could of got the information there. . . ."

"It just happened," said Timothy, "that we couldn't wait an hour. And you can tell me what I want to know in about three minutes,—if you will."

The Coroner grunted.

"What," the question was perfunctory, "killed Hamlet Winters?"

"He was attacked two ways—his throat was sliced, and he was poisoned." The Coroner spoke in a loud, undifferentiated voice.

"Poisoned," said Timothy reflectively.

"Yeah." The toothpick reappeared. "And it wouldn't do for me to say whether the poison was enough to've killed him or not. It was veronal—a good big dose—and it probably had him in a coma for a coupla hours before the knife got him in the throat. That finished him off good and proper but it's likely the poison would have done the trick in' a coupla more hours by itself."

"I see," said Timothy. He looked suddenly as if he saw a great deal. "How long," he asked, "would you say the veronal had been taken before Winters died?"

"I'd say from the looks of things," said the Coroner reminiscently," that it must've been taken a good four hours before death." He paused to wield the toothpick judicially. "Around about lunch-time, I'd put it," he said at last.

There was a silence.

Timothy stared, Barrett looked uneasy, the Coroner yawned. I could think of just one thing—the single line which Hamlet Winters had written on his memorandum pad for Friday the twentieth of June.

"Laura—lunch—1 o'clock."

12
ICED COFFEE

"I see," said Timothy to the Coroner. "Now one last thing—and I'll be much obliged for your trouble. During the two hours or more that elapsed between the time that Winters was given the dose of veronal and the time he lapsed into a coma—am I right in thinking that he was probably conscious and able to move about in a fairly normal manner?"

"Generally speaking I'd say yes. The effects come on pretty slow—and a person's likely to fight sleepiness in the middle of the day as long as he can. But to hold out against a dose that size for *more* than two or three hours wouldn't be the easiest thing in the world unless the person was set on doing something important—and wouldn't give in to his feelings."

"Then you believe that Winters might have taken the veronal between one and two o'clock—and still have been able to get to the Cathedral under his own power as late as four in the afternoon?"

"Speaking of a man who looked to be in as good condition as this party did—the answer is still yes."

"Thank you," said Timothy. "Thank you very much."

"No trouble at all." The large man spoke without conviction. He rose promptly at Timothy's glance of dismissal, polished the toothpick with final care, and returned it to his vest pocket. "Good day." He bowed in my direction with unexpected gallantry, and was ushered out by Barrett.

"Well, there"—Timothy spoke thoughtfully when the door was closed—"is the answer to the Carter riddle anyway. The gal *was* right when she said Winters was 'really killed' before he ever went in St. Ives—but how she ever—"

Barrett's voice from the hall door cut him short.

"The dame's here—" he announced. "Do you want to see her?"

"Which dame?"

"Mrs. Fletcher Dee."

"Sure." Timothy's expression brightened noticeably. "Bring her in." As the Inspector closed the door once more, Timothy squared his shoulders. "Maybe we're not so sunk after all, Miss Belle."

I seized the moment to put in the one question which was foremost in my mind.

"Timothy"—I leaned forward anxiously—"are you going to do anything about *Laura?*"

An emphatic nod reassured me.

"Why else," he asked, "do you think I told Barrett to bring her in?"

There was a pause while I absorbed his meaning.

"Laura"—it dawned on me slowly—"is—is Mrs. Dee?"

"I'm so darn sure of it," said Timothy with conviction, "that I didn't even bother to find out—which would be easy enough."

"And *she* lunched with Hamlet Winters—on the last day."

"Unless Winters broke that date—she did."

A moment later, Barrett opened the door, and I saw the sharply appraising look which Timothy turned on the woman who entered. And instantly his verdict was

registered in the courteous manner with which he addressed her.

"Mrs. Dee?"

"Yes."

"Will you sit down?"

"Thank you."

Mrs. Dee took a place on the sofa and looked up at
Timothy with an air of grave composure. She was slim,
fortyish, and well groomed; her face reflected both intelligence and wisdom, and her manner was pleasantly reserved.

"I'm honestly sorry," Timothy spoke sincerely, "that it
was necessary to bring you here—at this time."

"I quite understand," said Mrs. Dee. Her voice was low
and a trifle husky.

Timothy cleared his throat.

"I shall have to ask you, Mrs. Dee, when you last saw
Dr. Winters?"

"At luncheon," Mrs. Dee answered clearly, "at my
house—on Friday."

I caught Timothy's fleeting glance. So—he had been
right. Mrs. Fletcher Dee *was* "Laura—lunch—1 o'clock."

"Did Dr. Winters come—alone?"

"Yes."

"And were you—ah—" Timothy hesitated.

"I was alone. My husband was unexpectedly asked to
attend an alumni luncheon, my sister-in-law had gone
downtown for the day, and my son Laurence," she spoke
with only the slightest trace of a quiver, "was at his frater-
nity house—on the Hopkins campus."

"Was your lunch with Dr. Winters purely a social engagement?"

No. I asked him deliberately at a time when I knew we
should be alone, so that I might approach him on a matter
of business. Personal business," she added carefully.

"I'm sorry, Mrs. Dee," Timothy's manner was still considerate, but he spoke firmly. "I'll have to ask you to be more explicit."

For the first time she hesitated.

"The business was a favor that I asked of Dr. Winters," she said slowly, "for my husband. It concerned money. It's not pleasant to say this," her deep blue eyes were fixed steadily on Timothy's face, "but it was necessary for me to ask Dr. Winters for a—loan."

"A large loan?"

"Yes," said Mrs. Dee. "I asked him for enough money to enable my husband to have a year abroad—for special research and study."

"Research directly connected with his work?"

"Yes."

Timothy's eyebrows rose.

"I thought," he said, "that sort of thing was taken care of by"—his gesture was slightly vague—"by scholarships or foundations—or something like that."

"In this case," Mrs. Dee explained, "the regular procedure was not possible. My husband had reason to believe that he was on the brink of a really important literary discovery. A discovery so—so sensational that it would have been quite impossible to go about getting a scholarship grant in the usual way. For one thing—my husband hadn't enough concrete evidence to convince any group of academics that there was anything in his idea—and for another, he hesitated to reveal any part of his plan. There are, you see," she smiled faintly, "occasional pirates—even among scholars."

Timothy was watching her closely.

"So," he said, "you appealed to Winters for a personal loan—which, I take it, would allow your husband to follow up this hunch of his and prove his notion one way or the other."

"One year abroad would have settled it," she added.

"And you weren't afraid to tell Dr. Winters what this discovery was?"

"I trusted Hamlet Winters—of course," Mrs. Dee spoke matter-of-factly.

"I see." Still Timothy was watching her intently. It was evident that his mind was working hard—and fast. "How long had your husband had the idea of this discovery?"

"Since our one trip to England, three years ago."

"And you mean to say," once more Timothy's voice rose sharply, "he'd done nothing about it in all that time?"

"It was impossible," said Mrs. Dee levelly, "to—as you put it—do anything about it. My husband's salary is not large—and our obligations have been unusually heavy. That was why I decided at last to appeal to Dr. Winters. It seemed to me very unjust that a man should be kept from investigating such an important scholarly discovery for want of a few thousand dollars."

"And so you explained all this to Dr. Winters at lunch on Friday afternoon?"

"Yes."

A curious silence. In spite of Mrs. Dee's outward composure, there was a tension in her low voice which seemed to affect all of us.

"How did Winters take the proposition?" Timothy's question was abrupt. "Did he seem willing to make the loan?"

Mrs. Dee's eyes were lowered suddenly.

"No," she said.

"He refused?"

Mrs. Dee continued to look downward at her folded hands.

"He told me," she spoke quietly, "that what I asked was impossible."

"Impossible?" Timothy repeated thoughtfully. "Impossible why? Because he couldn't or wouldn't lend you the money—or because he didn't believe in your husband's idea?"

"I don't know." Mrs. Dee raised her eyes. "I didn't question his answer, because I had already put my request as clearly and as—as appealingly as I could. So, of course, I accepted his refusal as final. And besides"—she hesitated briefly—"the whole matter seemed to distress Dr. Winters very much."

"Distressed him how—exactly?"

Mrs. Dee shrugged.

"It's hard to say—exactly," she admitted. "But it was impossible not to see that he was nervous and upset while I talked—"

"He made no suggestions, Mrs. Dee, for any other way your husband might get the necessary loan?"

She shook her head.

"He said nothing at all, until I had finished speaking, and then he answered as I've told you, 'I'm sorry, Laura, but what you ask is impossible.'"

"What happened after that?"

"Nothing important. We talked of other things for a short while—and then Dr. Winters left. It was the last time," she caught her breath, "that I saw him."

"Do you remember what time it was when he left your house?"

"Not precisely," said Mrs. Dee, "but it was somewhere between two o'clock and three. I remember that we got up from lunch at just about two."

"By any chance, Mrs. Dee, do you know where Winters went after leaving you?"

"I'm afraid not."

"He didn't mention any particular engagement for the afternoon?"

"Why yes," the woman recalled, "he did say something about an appointment later—four o'clock I believe he said it was."

"Did he speak of it in any special way?" Timothy leaned forward eagerly. "I mean to indicate that it was a matter of unusual importance?"

"Not that I remember," she said. "I think he mentioned it quite casually during lunch. But of course, my mind was rather thoroughly occupied—"

"Of course." Timothy rose abruptly and fetched a cigarette from the table. Not until he had lighted it and gone back to his chair did he proceed with another question.

"Can you tell me, Mrs. Dee," he squinted at her through the smoke, "what you had for lunch Friday?"

"Why—yes." Her look plainly indicated surprise but she answered readily enough. "We had cold consommé, then a soufflé and asparagus, and melon for dessert."

"No coffee?" Timothy's tone was casual—a little too casual, I thought.

"Oh, yes," said Mrs. Dee without the slightest hesitation. "Iced coffee."

"Did you prepare the lunch yourself?"

She nodded.

"And did you eat everything that Dr. Winters did?"

"Well—yes." This time she looked more puzzled than ever. "All except the coffee. I never drink coffee."

"I see," said Timothy.

"I suppose," Mrs. Dee added with every indication of innocence, "that's why I forgot to mention the iced coffee a moment ago."

"I—ah—suppose so." Timothy shot a quick glance in her direction, and then studied the tip of his cigarette intently. "Can you tell me, please, when that coffee was made?"

For the first time Mrs. Dee questioned the curious direction of the inquiry.

"I—I don't understand," her candid face was turned toward Timothy, "why you ask me these things. It—isn't possible, is it," there was a note of fear in the husky voice, "that there was anything—that you think anything could have been—" She faltered miserably and stopped.

Timothy cleared his throat.

"For the moment," he said not unkindly, "I can't explain my reasons. But I'll be much obliged if you will answer the questions—anyway."

"Of course," Mrs. Dee murmured after only the briefest hesitation. "I made the coffee," her tone was steady, "at breakfast time Friday morning—and left enough to ice for lunch."

"Thank you," said Timothy. He flicked his ash carefully in the tray at his elbow. "Thank you very much. Now then," his tone was more brisk, "two questions more—and we're through. First—had Dr. Winters known anything about your husband's plan, or his need of money for the trip abroad, before he came to your house on Friday?"

"Not that I know of." Mrs. Dee shook her head. "In fact, I could say quite definitely that he hadn't."

"And yet your husband and Winters were good friends, weren't they?"

"The very best."

"Isn't it possible then, that your husband might have confided his plan at some time?"

Mrs. Dee considered.

"It's possible, of course—but not likely. If Dr. Winters had already known of Fletcher's idea, I am certain he would have told me. There was no reason, after all, to conceal it. And of course my husband is far too proud ever to have mentioned a need of money."

"My second question," Timothy went on, "is in two parts. Part one: did anyone in your family know that Winters was coming to lunch with you that day?"

"Only my husband knew," said Mrs. Dee. "He happened to be in the room when I telephoned Mrs. Winters to ask if she and Dr. Winters could come to lunch—as otherwise I expected to be alone."

"So," Timothy observed, "Mrs. Winters was invited too?"

"Yes—but," apparently Laura Dee was incurably honest, "as a matter of fact I knew she would refuse. She has a regular club luncheon on Fridays, so Dr. Winters accepted for himself—and that was as I had planned it should be."

Timothy made no comment on her surprisingly direct answer.

"Part two of my question," he said, "is to ask you whether any person in your household knew *why* you particularly wanted to have lunch alone with Hamlet Winters?"

At Timothy's words Mrs. Dee's color heightened perceptibly, but she continued to look straight at him.

"Of course not," she said quietly. "I shouldn't have dreamed of telling my—" Again I observed the slight hesitation which seemed to accompany any reference to Fletcher Dee. "I didn't mention my plan," she concluded simply, "to anyone—either before or after I talked to Dr. Winters."

Timothy accepted her answer in silence, but he was frowning slightly as he crushed out his cigarette. His face cleared, however, when he turned toward Laura Dee with a look of genuine friendliness.

"I won't keep you any longer," he said, "and I appreciate your frankness very much indeed."

It was a nice speech, sincerely delivered, and Mrs. Dee answered with a smile—her first since she had come into the room. It lighted her pale, serious face with an unexpected charm, and when Mrs. Dee had gone Timothy remained for a moment, staring after her.

"There," he murmured, "goes an honest witness—for a change. And I have a very certain feeling," he added with sudden conviction, "that a man named Fletcher Dee is going to turn out to be one elegant specimen of a horse's neck!"

For once I felt that the less polished portions of Timothy's vocabulary could be, at times, both refreshing and accurate.

13
ICED TEA

When Barrett returned he was mopping his red face vigorously.

"My God but it's hot," he shook his head, "and getting worse all the time. I guess we're due for a storm before long."

"I guess we are," Timothy murmured, "in more ways than one." He stood in the center of the room—hands thrust deep in his pockets, feet planted far apart, his eyebrows gathered in a concentrated frown.

"About that telephone number," Barrett said, "I got a report on it."

"So?" Timothy looked up with interest.

"It belongs to a gent named William Flagstaff, and it's his office 'phone."

"What kind of an office?"

"Printing."

"Printing, eh?" Timothy's frown deepened.

"Some kind of a special whoozis," Barrett explained, "called the Flagstaff Press."

"Where is this business?"

"Pearl Avenue and Charles Street. On the southwest corner." The Inspector seemed unaware of any special significance of the location—but Timothy jumped at the words.

"*So?*" with a rising inflection. "Well—I think"—Timothy moved slowly toward the desk telephone—"I'll just have me a little talk with the Flagstaff Press."

"Not on Sunday morning, you won't," the Inspector pointed out with logic.

"Damn." Timothy turned impatiently. "What about the gent's home number?"

"Hasn't got any."

"Well—his address then?"

Barrett consulted a memorandum.

"24 Hall Street. But I don't see—"

"I want that man," Timothy said.

"What for?"

"I don't know—that's why I want him."

The Inspector muttered something.

"So here goes." Timothy was headed for the door.

"Not so fast there." Barrett heaved himself up. "*I'll* get your man."

"But I can just as well—"

"Don't mention it." The tone was sourly polite. "I've got to stop in at headquarters anyway. And besides—I might have an idea of my own."

"What about?"

"I don't know"—Barrett mimicked Timothy's earlier remark—"that's why I'm going." Without leaving time for a reply, he banged the door behind him.

"Timothy," I turned indignantly, "why do you stand for it?"

"Stand for what?"

"The way Barrett acts. After all, you're doing his work for him—and he does absolutely nothing but make

himself unpleasant. He hasn't a single idea of his own—
and I should think you'd just walk out—"

"Hold everything, Miss Belle," Timothy's mild drawl
interrupted me. "You're going too fast. For one thing, I
can't walk out—any more than you can."

"Timothy—you don't think Barrett still suspects us?"

"Of course I do. He's not such a bad cop as all that."

"Well—why doesn't he *do* something then?"

Timothy laughed.

"He's doing plenty, Miss Belle. What do you think
he's going to headquarters for? And what do you think he
meant by having an idea of his own? And why do you think
he wouldn't let me go after this printer bird?"

I had no answer for any of the questions.

"He's gone to headquarters," Timothy explained, "to
find out about you and me. He's had them checking on us
since we first got here last night—and the reason I go on
doing Barrett's work for him, as you put it, is not that I'm
so stuck on detecting that I have to do it on my vacation
too. I'm working like a yellow pup, Miss Belle, to save
your hide and mine."

He paused to fetch a cigarette.

"Barrett's a good enough flatfoot," Timothy continued
thoughtfully, "but he's single-tracked—and he got started
on our track. Not that I blame him either. *But*"—he waved
a match at me—"the one way we can get ourselves counted
out, Miss Belle, is to find another goat. *The* goat."

"And do you think"—I was impressed by his evident
seriousness—"that you *can* find the goat?"

"Oh, I guess so," said Timothy mildly.

It was not in the least like a boast, but something in
the quiet tone seemed definitely reassuring. I gave him a
grateful smile.

"Thanks for the vote of confidence, Miss Belle." Timothy answered my expression with an encouraging grin as he rose from his chair. "And now stick around while I haul in Fletcher Dee as first candidate for goat."

When he returned, after a brief interval, he was alone.

"What did I tell you, Miss Belle?" He looked half angry, half amused. "Dee's not here, of course, although he was supposed to come over when his wife did—"

"Why didn't he then?"

"Oh—he wasn't awake yet or some damn reason like that," Timothy gestured impatiently, "but the important thing is that muscle-man Al at the front door wouldn't let me go over and rout out Dee myself. In other words, my little hunch that Barrett is still working on us was right. He left orders to keep me in this house."

"But, Timothy, if Barrett really suspects you—why does he let you work on the case?"

"He gives me lots and lots of rope to play with," the answer was prompt, "in the pious hope that I'll wind an end of it around my own Adam's apple. It's a bit of technique I'm strong on myself. That's why," he grinned, "I think Barrett's not such a bad cop."

"While actually"—I watched him curiously—"you plan to slip the rope around the—the goat's neck?"

"Right."

"Fletcher Dee's for instance?"

"Maybe." Timothy would not commit himself. "At least I sent one of the boys after him—with orders to pry Dee out of bed and dress him if it's necessary."

"Which," I laughed, "is no small order—if all I've heard of his disposition is true."

"Meanwhile," Timothy said, "I'm going to quiz the large-eyed Tilden a bit." Someone knocked. "There he is now."

"I need your help, Tilden," Timothy began with a deliberately casual tone.

"Yassuh?"

"You've worked here some time, haven't you?"

"Six years, suh."

"Like the job?"

"Yassuh," promptly.

"I suppose then," Timothy waxed diplomatic, "you're willing to help—in any way you can—to find out what happened to Dr. Winters?"

"Yassuh." There was rather less conviction in the tone. "But I don't think I knows anything, suh."

"Perhaps not—but you do know a good deal about certain people in the house—and that's why I want your advice."

A slightly more favorable reaction from Tilden.

"About this nurse, for instance," Timothy was proceeding with care. "I—frankly don't know how much to trust her. A stranger in the house at such a time, you know—"

"You talkin' about Miss Carter?"

Timothy nodded.

"Well, you-all don't need to worry about Miss Carter. She ain't a stranger."

"Well"—Timothy's imitation of surprised relief was excellent—"so Miss Carter has been here before?"

"Yassuh." Tilden was warming noticeably. "She took care of Madam last winter when Madam was sick. You-all don't need to worry about her bein' here—'cause Madam thinks the world of Miss Carter."

"It's a great help to know that, Tilden," Timothy nodded solemnly. "I suppose she's more like a family friend then—"

"Yassuh. Miss Carter comes here right often when nobody's sick even."

"You mean she did last winter?"

"I mean all the time."

"Even—ah—lately?"

"Oh, yassuh. She was here just a couple of days ago."

"Indeed?" said Timothy—rather as if he doubted it.

"Thursday afternoon it was." Tilden nodded. "She come to see Madam."

"And I suppose she saw Dr. Winters too?"

A doubtful moment. It seemed to me I could almost see Timothy holding his breath while the butler deliberated.

"No suh." Tilden finally shook his head. "He wasn't here, suh."

"She and Madam were alone then?"

"Yassuh—" A pause. "Well—no suh."

"Which was it, Tilden?"

"They wasn't exactly alone, suh. Miss Bertha was here too."

"Miss Bertha?"

"That's Miss Bertha Dee—the fat one settin' in the hall right now."

"Of course," said Timothy hastily, "Miss Bertha. I wanted to ask you about her too. She"—the tone was lowered confidentially—"she's waiting here to see Mrs. Winters—but we weren't quite sure whether it would be wise?"

A puzzled silence on the part of Tilden.

"You see," Timothy cleared his throat, "I don't want anything to upset Mrs. Winters."

"No suh."

"But if Miss Dee is a very good friend—"

"Well, ef I was you, suh"—with decision—"I'd leave Miss Bertha see her. I got orders from Madam just lately to *always* have Miss Bertha come straight up to Madam's room—no matter when she comes here. And she been comin' a lot the last weeks."

"Always especially to see Mrs. Winters?"

A nod.

"Maybe then Miss Bertha wasn't quite so friendly with Dr. Winters?"

"Dr. Winters," Tilden explained, "was always glad to see *anybody*—but it seemed more like Miss Bertha didn't want to see so much of him. Anyways she always asks me is Madam in."

"And Madam liked to see her?"

"I reckon so."

"Thank you, Tilden. Thank you very much. Now—another matter. On Friday, Dr. Winters was out for lunch, wasn't he?"

"Yassuh."

"Do you know where he went?"

"Yassuh," promptly. "Madam told me when she went out that he was havin' lunch at Mrs. Dee's house."

Timothy registered convincing surprise.

"You're *sure*, Tilden, Mrs. Winters told you that?"

"Yas*suh*," with decision. "She told me special not to forget it."

"Why special?" As Tilden hesitated, Timothy bent forward quickly. "Did she leave some message for Dr. Winters?"

"Come to think"—the butler's reply was deliberate—"Madam did say something about"—a breathless pause—"about a paper."

"What paper?"

"She say have Dr. Winters be sure to look at it."

"Where was it?"

"Upstairs, she say, in his room."

"You don't know what the paper was?"

"No suh."

"But you gave Dr. Winters the message?"

"Yassuh—when he come in."

"And he went upstairs?"

"Yassuh."

"Then what?"

Tilden frowned uncertainly.

"I reckon he come down again."

"But you didn't see him?"

"Not till he ring for me."

"Where was he then?"

"In here—at his desk."

"How long was that—after you had seen him go upstairs?"

"'Bout twenty minutes, I reckon."

"Why did he ring for you?"

"He asked me to bring him tea, suh."

"*Tea?*" This time I felt certain that Timothy's surprise was genuine.

"Yassuh, iced tea."

"When he'd just come back from lunch?"

"Yassuh—but he say he'd be out all afternoon, and Madam made a special pitcher for him. It was a right hot day, Friday."

"So it was." Timothy nodded quickly. "You brought him the pitcher then?"

"Yassuh."

"What next?"

"He tell me to set it down."

"Did Dr. Winters seem worried—or nervous?"

"I reckon not exactly."

"Did he seem—different in *any* way?"

"Only like—like he was right hurried."

"I see. Then you gave him the tea and left the room?"

"Yassuh."

"And did you see him again?"

Slowly Tilden shook his head.

"I heard him go on out 'bout fifteen minutes later, suh—and that was all."

"That must have been around three-thirty?"

"I reckon it was."

"What time did Mrs. Winters come in?"

"'Bout four, suh."

"Do you think she knew then that Dr. Winters had been—that anything had happened to him?"

"No, suh. She ask me right away was Dr. Winters upstairs asleep?"

"And you told her—"

"That he'd gone out."

"What did she say?"

"She ask me did he drink his tea."

"You told her yes?"

A nod.

"What did she say then?"

"Nothin'. She turn around and went right out again."

"And stayed how long?"

"Till long about half-past four, I reckon. Then she came back with Mr. Laurence."

"Do you mean young Dee?"

"Yassuh."

"Do you know why Mrs. Winters brought the boy back here with her?"

"Not exceptin' I hear Madam say somethin' about lookin' for Dr. Winters."

"They seemed worried?"

"I reckon they did, suh, Mr. Laurence specially."

"Do you think he was afraid something had happened to Dr. Winters?"

"Most likely, suh. Mr. Laurence and he was mighty friendly always."

"The boy was often in the house then?"

"Yassuh," emphatically. "Mr. Laurence was all the time comin' here to see Dr. Winters when things wasn't goin' right at home."

"How do you mean—not going right at home?"

"I mean with Mr. Dee, suh. I reckon Mr. Laurence never did get along so good with his father."

"So"—Timothy drew a long breath—"Mrs. Winters and the boy were looking for Dr. Winters—and they were anxious." He considered briefly. "How long did they stay in the house, Tilden?"

"Just a few minutes. Then they went along out together."

"You don't know, I suppose, what they did during those minutes?"

"No, suh—only they was in this room."

"And after they left the house—did anything else happen?"

"No, suh."

"Nobody came here?"

"No, suh—not till Madam came back 'round seven o'clock."

"As late as that?"

"Yassuh. We was waitin' dinner—but she didn't eat none after all."

"Had she already heard about Dr. Winters then, when she came in?"

A solemn nod.

"Did she say anything to you about it?"

"Madam tell me to call Miss Carter right away—then she went on upstairs."

"Did you get Miss Carter?"

"No suh. They tell me she was busy at the hospital."

For just a moment Timothy's eye caught mine.

"Two more questions." He faced Tilden briskly. "First—did Dr. Winters use an old-fashioned open razor?"

"Yassuh."

"And second—have you any reason to think that Mrs. Winters and Miss Bertha might have quarreled—since Friday afternoon?"

"No *suh,*" a violent shake, "Madam and she is too good friends ever to fight over nothin'. They's about the best friends I ever—"

Of the touching revelation we were to hear no more.

From the hall outside came a sudden noise of confusion—and then a woman's imperious voice demanded clearly:

"*Why is Bertha Dee in my house?*"

More sounds of commotion followed the question—and over the hubbub Miss Dee's heavy protesting accents were audible.

"*Ask her to leave at once.*" The sharp words cut through with unmistakable authority. "*Please tell Miss Dee that after what has happened I never wish to speak to her again.*"

There was no doubt in my mind as to who had given the command. Even from our side of the closed door there could be no mistaking the voice of Mary Winters, ordering her friend and neighbor out of her house forever.

14
TEA OR COFFEE?

At the first signals of disturbance, Timothy had started for the door. I followed close behind him, and a moment later we were faced with a scene fully as dramatic as it had sounded.

Mary Winters, draped not in widow's black—but in pure white, stood like a Duse in the center of the hall, her face as pale as the chiffon scarf which framed it, her long arm outstretched to point the exit for Miss Dee.

And Bertha Dee, presenting in every respect a precise opposite of Mrs. Winters' tall, dignified white anger, remained huddled in the big chair. The mustard yellow dress was bunched awkwardly about her ample figure, and her deep-set eyes stared in beady resentment from a face flushed with anger and confusion.

While Timothy and I stood there, neither woman moved. It might have been a carefully rehearsed tableau for a second act curtain.

Then slowly Mary Winters' arm was lowered to her side, and she turned to move toward the stairs. Half way around, her glance met mine and to my infinite surprise she registered instant recognition.

"Why, Miss Stebbins." For the first time her voice was shaken from its frozen clearness into something like her natural gentleness. "How kind of you to come here." She laid her slim hand in mine—and I was startled by the icy touch of her fingers, despite the day's terrific heat.

"I—I can't tell you how shocked and distressed I am by what has happened—" I fumbled awkwardly for some conventionality which would bridge the moment.

"Yes." There was an odd vagueness in her faint smile which answered me. "Yes, I'm sure you are, my dear." The cold fingers patted my hand. "But we mustn't feel that— really—" Mary Winters' voice trailed off uncertainly. As in her interview the night before, she completely ignored the presence of everyone except the person whom she addressed. "Why don't you come upstairs with me, Miss Stebbins?" she said. "We must have a great deal to say to one another."

Personally I felt that, in such a situation, we would have nothing whatever to say to each other. It would have been, indeed, difficult to imagine anything more trying than to talk with this strangely distraught woman. But, instinctively, I glanced at Timothy—and a small but emphatic signal from him told me that I was by all means to accept the suggestion.

Obediently I followed Mary Winters as she led me up the stairs and down the long corridor to her own luxurious sitting-room.

Actually the interview was neither as painful nor as awkward as I had feared it would be. For all her vagueness, Mary Winters was definite enough on one point— she would *not* discuss the subject of her husband's death. Even the matter of my own curious position in the affair, which I did my best to explain, aroused only but the most casual response from her.

Not until, in an effort to break through the woman's amazing reserve, I told her flatly that I had been brought to her house by the police, and was being held there as a suspect, was Mrs. Winters at last willing to touch on the situation.

"No harm will come to you, Miss Stebbins," she said gently. "We must simply allow these men—these—police"—it seemed difficult for her to pronounce the word—"to go through their formalities. They don't understand, you see, that they can never know the answer to death."

It was plain from the way she spoke that Mary Winters expected *me* to understand what the police were too benighted to see. Actually I felt incapable of any comprehension whatever—either of the cryptic observation or the state of mind which prompted it. I attempted, however, a look of general sympathy, in the hope of encouraging further revelations.

"It's quite useless to try to stop these men," Mrs. Winters continued presently, "since they are proceeding according to the law—so I have told Tilden that he must do everything for them that they wish. Fortunately"—she leaned toward me with a confidential air—"they can discover nothing—because there is nothing there. Hamlet left only one record of his death—and that was for me." She tapped a small purse that lay beside her and which, I supposed, contained the letter she had read to us the night before. "The death of Hamlet Winters," his widow said with strange conviction, "was just. You and I who knew him must believe that—and the men will discover it someday—if they are clever enough."

Mary Winters leaned back and regarded me with an exalted look in her clear eyes—as if she had pronounced some divine truth. It was difficult, with those eyes upon me, to attempt a rational argument—but I did what I could.

"It's never just," I said earnestly, "to take a man's life—whatever the circumstances. Surely you must want them to find out who killed your husband so that the person may be brought to account—" I stopped abruptly as Mary Winters uttered a small sound that came perilously near to being a laugh.

"There can be no question, Miss Stebbins"—once more there was the half-fanatical light in her eye—"of calling anyone into account. I hold no more malice against anyone in the world than Hamlet himself does at this moment."

"Then why," I plunged in boldly, "did you just order Miss Dee out of your house and say that 'after what had happened' you never wished to speak to her again?"

For a moment, a very long moment, there was no answer. Then, when it came, it seemed strangely irrelevant.

"Bertha Dee," she said, "was in love with Hamlet, and because he was always kind and courteous to her—she once was stupid enough to believe that he loved her. You know," she appealed to me, "how—how he was."

I knew. I could, indeed, imagine that the natural graciousness of Dr. Winters might have misled a woman like Bertha Dee—but how that fact in any way explained the scene we had witnessed in the hall—I could *not* see.

"When Bertha realized her mistake," Mrs. Winters went on, "she turned against Hamlet—and she tried to turn me too—with lies."

"What sort of lies?"

"She told me that he had done something dreadful—and that some awful punishment was hanging over him."

"And you believed her?"

"No," said Mary Winters steadily. "Thank God I never believed her—but I did listen to her talk. And now—after what has happened—I can never forgive myself, nor Bertha Dee."

"You mean," I ventured, "you can't forgive yourself for not having warned your husband of this—this punishment—whatever it was?"

The clear grey eyes of Mary Winters stared blankly into mine.

"Why—no," she said at last. "I mean that I should never have listened to such lies."

"But really, Mrs. Winters"—her innocence in the face of so obvious a situation was too much for even my ample credulity—"you must see that Miss Dee's warning came true. Your husband was punished—and if either you or Bertha Dee know why it was done—or by whom and how"—my coherence was succumbing to the general state of tension, but I plunged on—"it's your duty," I said, "to report it at once—"

"Miss Stebbins—please." Mary Winters rose and looked down upon me coldly. "You simply do not understand," she said. The quiet words were spoken with finality.

I realized, with a feeling of helpless anger, that I was dismissed. But I did not go without one parting shot.

"It is you, Mrs. Winters"—I spoke with all the dignity I could muster—"who either cannot or will not understand that your husband was murdered—that a police investigation of the murder is now under way in this house—and that the attitude you are taking about the whole thing is liable to lead you into serious difficulties."

And with that partial expression of my mind, I marched from the room—only to stop stock-still in the hall outside at the sound of a voice behind the closed door of the room I had just left.

It was not the voice of Mary Winters. It was a young voice—full of enthusiasm, and the effect of the cheerful words, which were spoken on the very heels of our tense interview, was electrifying.

"Atta girl, Mrs. Winters!" said the voice of Miss Carter in a tone of hearty congratulation.

Perhaps two minutes later, I found Timothy in the library with Joan, who had just come downstairs. Without delay, I reported the story of my strange interview—and the still stranger words which Miss Carter had spoken after the door of Mrs. Winters' room had closed behind me.

Timothy received my account in silence. When I had finished speaking, he rose with a determined expression on his weary face, and started for the door.

"Right now," he said grimly, "I'm going to find out once and for all whether the Widow Winters is staging this act of hers—or whether she's just plain lost her mind."

When he returned, some minutes later, Timothy answered the questioning looks from Joan and me with a snort of disgust.

"Wild goose chase," he said, "with emphasis on the goose. And what's more," he crossed the room, "the goose is a whole lot smarter than she has any business to be. I can't even get a squawk out of her!"

"Oh, Timothy"—Joan scanned his tired face anxiously—"didn't you find out *anything* upstairs?"

"Well—I wasn't a complete flop, if that's what you mean." He gave the girl a brief smile. "I still don't know what the act is all about—but I *did* make sure that Mrs. Winters' trance is faked and that the Carter wench is coaching the performance."

"How did you get them to admit that?"

"I didn't." Timothy shook his head. "I simply stood outside the bedroom door and listened—which is practically the last resort of a thick-headed cop—and in a couple of minutes I had them cold! Carter was right in the middle of telling the old lady how to act. 'You haven't got a thing in the world to worry about, Mrs. Winters,' I heard her say, 'even if the police *do* keep after you. Just give 'em that vague stare—and if they happen to ask something that really bothers you—then, you know, you can always cry.' And it went on like that"—Timothy gestured wearily—"with a lot of hooey thrown in about keeping faith with her dead husband."

"And how," I put in curiously, "did Mary Winters answer all this?"

"I'm coming to that," said Timothy. "It's the only thing that makes any sense about the whole business. She didn't say a thing, you see, until Carter got all through with her spiel, and then she sighed—it was a sigh, don't forget, that I could hear right through a shut door—and she said: 'You're wonderful to help me, Miss Carter, but I can't go through with it. I'm too frightened.' Of course that was my chance. Right through the door I popped, and looking her straight in the eye, I asked: 'Frightened of what, Mrs. Winters?'"

"What *did* she do?" With one accord Joan and I breathed the question.

"Do? She didn't do a damn thing—then or any other time."

"Surely you can't mean that they *dared* to face you out after what you had heard?"

"As it happens," said Timothy, "that's just exactly what I mean. I talked, I threatened, I was as nasty and as nice as I knew how to be—and all the time the Widow Winters just looked at me like the Great Stone Face, and Carter went on smiling. My God," he shook his head wearily, "how that gal can smile."

"But, Timothy," Joan was indignant, "why didn't you arrest them or something when they lied like that?"

"Me arrest anybody in this man's city?" Timothy's eyebrows rose in a comical expression. "Do you want me to give Barrett an attack of beri-beri? You forget, Joanie, that I'm just a cop without a country on this case—no real authority at all, and I wouldn't even have had a look-in if Barrett had been of normal mentality. But, as a matter of fact," he went on soberly, "I wouldn't have cuffed the two dames even if I could. They can't do any harm running around for a while—and there's always the hope that one of them might stub her toe and go into a tail-spin, figuratively speaking, of course."

"You know, Timothy," I was very much in earnest, "I can't possibly tell you how amazing it is that Mary Winters would deliberately *act* at a time like this. It's absolutely incredible."

"Yes," said Timothy slowly, "I suppose it is—and I expect it will go right on being incredible until we get at her motive. Then, maybe, we'll see some light."

"But, Timothy, what *could* her motive be? Unless"—I was remembering Tilden's words—"unless you think that the pitcher of iced tea she left for Dr. Winters was—" I hesitated.

"Was poisoned?" Timothy finished my thought in a matter-of-fact tone.

I nodded.

"Or—do you think it was the coffee at Mrs. Dee's luncheon?"

"Tea or coffee?" Timothy murmured thoughtfully. "That *is* the question. And the answer"—he sighed—"is the answer to every riddle in this case so far."

"What is it then?"

"The motive," said Timothy bitterly, "the motive— the motive—the motive. Until we find that everything is equally possible—and equally impossible. Mrs. Dee could have put veronal in the iced coffee—but why should she? Fletcher Dee or his dead son or Miss Bertha might have done it—but *why?* Mrs. Winters or Miss Carter or Tilden could have planned the poisoned tea—but again— Oh, well," he broke off with a quick shrug. "What's the use of harping on that? If I can't locate the motive and then work forward—which, I've read, is the proper technique of detecting—I'll take what I *have* got and work backward. So here goes," he rose and shook himself, "for the great offensive—Fowler's last gasp in two installments. The first step"—he squinted thoughtfully at Joan and me—"is simple. A trip to the local drugstore—and a few small questions about the recent sales of veronal. The second"—he paused—"not so simple. To get the three members of the Dee family into one room together—to scare 'em—and then to watch 'em!"

15

WE RESCUE EMMA

"Well—that's my program," Timothy said. "It'll take maybe an hour or more to get it under way—meantime you girls better have a nap or something." He glanced at the clock. "And if you want to be in at the death—be back here at noon."

I watched Timothy as he moved slowly toward the door. In the past few minutes, there had come over him a sort of desperate seriousness which surprised and impressed me. Whether his extreme concern over the outcome of this mystery were personal or professional I could not know, but it was obvious that he was bending every ounce of wits and energy toward his final twofold effort to solve the riddle of Hamlet Winters' murder.

"Timothy"—I spoke with more than a little reluctance—"I *do* hate to bother you just at this moment, but you remember we left Emma shut up in Joan's apartment last night—and *do* you suppose I could go over sometime before noon to look after her?"

Timothy turned to look at me with an expression so blank that for a moment I wondered whether my request had even registered. Then, quite suddenly, his face relaxed in a good-natured grin.

"Hell's bells—I'd forgotten Emma. Of course you can go, Miss Belle, only"—he hesitated—"I don't want to get in Dutch with Barrett just at this point, so—I'm afraid I'll have to send a cop along—if you don't mind."

"Of course Miss Belle doesn't mind." Joan took my arm. "I'll come too, if she wants me."

Timothy went to fetch a suitable escort and to explain the urgency of our errand.

He returned with an officer, whose only name appeared to be Spike, and who accepted his orders with an admirably uncritical air.

"Sure," he agreed reasonably. "The cat's gotta be fed, but the only thing is this—what car am I gonna use—or do the ladies mind riding in the wagon?"

"The ladies would love to ride in the wagon," Joan answered promptly.

So, with considerable gallantry, Spike presently assisted Joan and me into the dark and stuffy interior of the police patrol car, and there we clung to the narrow leather seats as—with speed if not style—we were whirled through the quiet Sunday morning streets to the rescue of my poor languishing Emma.

Spike took his mission as an escort seriously, and accompanied us upstairs to the apartment. It was he, in fact, who discovered the telegram, addressed to me, which had been slipped under the door.

It was a message from the president of Maplewood College.

DEEPLY REGRET YOUR BEING IN-
VOLVED IN SHOCKING DEATH OF OUR
FORMER COLLEAGUE BUT CANNOT
UNDERSTAND YOUR SENSATIONAL

STATEMENTS TO THE PRESS STOP
PUBLICITY EXTREMELY UNFORTUNATE
FOR YOURSELF AND MAPLEWOOD
AND MUST ASK YOU DROP ACTIVITIES
IN CASE AT ONCE STOP HAVE COM-
MUNICATED LONG DISTANCE WITH
CHIEF OF BALTIMORE POLICE AND
EXPLAINED CIRCUMSTANCES YOUR
CHARACTER AND POSITION ASKING
YOU BE RELEASED AT ONCE IN ORDER
PREVENT SERIOUS CONSEQUENCES OF
SHOCK STOP SUGGEST YOU CONTACT
CHIEF IMMEDIATELY FOR PERMISSION
RETURN MAPLEWOOD STOP IF I CAN
ASSIST WIRE OR TELEPHONE STOP
UNDER NO CIRCUMSTANCES ALLOW
PRESS SUBJECT YOU FURTHER DETRI-
MENTAL PUBLICITY.

HUDSON PRENTISS.

Not until I had read the telegram a second time did I
begin to resent the idea of being thus summoned home to
safe Maplewood. There was, it seemed to me, an implication in the message that Belinda Stebbins, spinster, 52,
was not able to conduct herself through anything as complicated as the investigation of a murder—an implication
which, three days before, I should not have resented in the
least. No doubt it was a rationalization of simple feminine
curiosity, of my desire not to miss the end of the show,
but at that moment I inwardly declared a noble indepen-
dence from Dr. Prentiss and his precious institution to
which I had brought "extremely unfavorable publicity." In
other words, having tasted the pleasures of excitement and

suspense—and having taken a good deal of grief in the tasting—I had not the slightest intention of running home to Maplewood just because Hudson Prentiss had convinced the Baltimore police chief that I was too entirely harmless to play any part whatever in the murder of Hamlet Winters or the investigation thereof.

In silence I handed the telegram to Joan. She looked up from it with an odd expression.

"I guess that lets you out, Miss Belle," she spoke slowly, "if you want to go."

"But—I don't." I set my lips.

The girl's surprise was somewhat less marked than I had expected.

"It's evident," I went on, "that what really bothers Dr. Prentiss is not what might happen to me, but what I might do to disgrace dear old Maplewood. And personally, I think it would be definitely a case of locking the barn after the horse is stolen to go running home now."

"And besides, Miss Belle, if you stay you'll be able to help Timothy ever so much."

This was sweet of Joan, but even in my moment of self-justification, I found myself quite unable to believe her.

"Be that as it may I *shall* stay. Even," I added grandly, "if it should lose me my job."

"Well, if it does, Miss Belle, you can always write a book about the case."

"A book?"

"Of course. If this murder only has a good solution it ought to make a lovely detective story—and you know all about it right from the start."

Presently, Spike looked up. He had cheerfully assisted with the preparation of Emma's dejeuner and then put in a fascinated ten minutes watching her consume it.

"She's a real nice little cat," he said sociably. "Much better looking than the picture made her out to be."

I was, as always, gratified by a compliment for Emma—but for the moment I failed to catch the reference.

"Her picture?" I repeated.

"The one in the paper," Spike explained, "with you holding her."

Of course. In a flash of mingled dismay and amusement I remembered the midnight scene in the apartment hall—the reporter who had thrust Emma into my arms.

"Joan," I said, "is there a morning paper here?"

"There ought to be—at the back door." She went to look for it, and returned with a copy of the *Ledger*. "Please, Miss Belle, don't mind too much." With an anxious frown Joan put the paper into my outstretched hand.

I did not mind too much. Embarrassing as it certainly was to see myself reproduced in a startled and undignified pose, clutching Emma—smack in the middle of the front page—still it was impossible not to smile at the thought of the consternation that photograph must be causing in Maplewood. Particularly satisfying was the vision of Dr. Prentiss—least cat-minded of men—faced with the picture and its howling caption: BELINDA STEBBINS, MYSTERY WOMAN IN WINTERS CASE, PHOTOGRAPHED WITH THE CAT ON WHICH HER ALIBI DEPENDS; not to mention the even more painfully explicit remarks in the news column beginning: "The little gray-haired professor from Maplewood College, who was discovered last night in her hide-out at the home of Miss Joan Pell, a former pupil, had but one explanation to offer for the riddle of her presence in St. Ives Cathedral at the time when Dr. Hamlet Winters, friend and former colleague of the mystery woman, met his death at the hands of a fiendish murderer. 'Actually,' averred Miss Stebbins, with signs of emotion in her trembling voice, 'I was only looking for a place to exercise Emma, my pet cat.'"

I could not but be consoled for the whole maudlin account by the malicious thought that Dr. Prentiss must also have read it. I wondered if, in his rage, he might not perhaps recall a certain unfortunate occasion when, in the midst of a formal tea at my house, he had inadvertently lowered his presidential bulk onto a chair already occupied by Emma—and had received her resentful claws in a gesture of protest.

But enough of my irrelevant reflections. I record them only to indicate the completeness with which the reserve and propriety of my life previous to June twentieth had disintegrated in the course of three short days.

When Emma had been sufficiently fed and exercised, Joan and I were once more assisted into our equipage—which had by that time attracted a circle of enchanted bystanders—and returned to the Winters' home.

Inside the house again, my frivolous mood vanished before the atmosphere of deadly seriousness which seemed to pervade the place. Murder had been done, and a murderer was being hunted—and for one panicky moment I was tempted to change my mind and escape from whatever unknown dangers might be revealed in the unravelling of this puzzling and sinister affair. Joan's hand on my arm reassured me, however, and together we advanced into the silent hall.

Officer Al, at the door, greeted Spike in a subdued voice.

"Barrett's not back yet," he said, "but Connell brought this in a couple of minutes ago. Said he fished it out of a fountain in the Cathedral yard." And whatever my qualms

of a moment before—they were not sufficient to keep
me from craning curiously for a glimpse of the object,
wrapped in a handkerchief, which Al extended. Nor was
I more than mildly surprised to hear Spike's exclamation.

"Gosh," he said. "A razor."

"Yeah," Al nodded. "And it's got the guy's own name
on it too."

"Whad'ya mean?" Spike peered.

"Right on the handle here—see?"

"Well, what do you know about that?" Spike's tone was
marveling. "So old Doc Winters got his throat sliced with
his own monogrammed razor!"

16

TWO PRESCRIPTIONS

The four of us, Spike, Al, Joan and myself, were still grouped before the door, staring at the open razor when Timothy swooped down the stairs to join us. Officer Al presented his exhibit, handkerchief and all, explaining briefly that it had been found, quite as Timothy had anticipated, at the bottom of the pool in the Cathedral close.

Timothy noted the engraved letters of Hamlet Winters' own name upon the handle without undue astonishment. He merely nodded twice and then returned the razor to Al.

"Show it to Barrett," Timothy directed, "when he comes in. You two," he indicated Joan and me, "come in here a minute." He led us into the study.

"Timothy"—I could not resist a question when we were alone—"why weren't you more surprised to find that it was Hamlet Winters' own razor that was probably used to—attack him?"

"Because," he answered me promptly, "it fits my theory."

"Your theory of what?"

"My theory of the murderer," said Timothy. "I've been figuring that he—or she—must be a pretty logical bird—and to use a man's own razor to cut his throat strikes me as excellent logic."

"I'm sorry"—I was groping helplessly to see the sense of it—"but I *don't* follow."

"Any smart murderer knows," he explained patiently, "that a weapon—any weapon—is both hard to get rid of and easy to identify. So wasn't it the logical thing for our smart murderer to choose a razor plainly belonging to the victim himself—making the identification of it meaningless and, of course, eliminating the necessity of trying to hide the weapon at all."

"But Timothy—the razor *was* hidden in the fountain. You practically accused Miss Bertha Dee of putting it there—and she practically admitted the accusation."

"Quite so, Miss Belle," he nodded, "but Miss Bertha is *not* very smart—nor, I think, is she the murderer. So my theory still stands—for a while anyway."

"Was she in league with the murderer then?"

"If I knew that," Timothy shrugged, "I'd know a lot more than I do."

"Well *I* know *one* thing," Joan spoke up suddenly, "and that is that you must have found out something while Miss Belle and I were gone, Timothy. Because when we left, you were about as cheerful as an open grave—and now," she turned to me, "doesn't he look like the cat that's swallowed a brace of canaries, Miss Belle?"

Timothy laughed.

"I haven't swallowed them yet, Joanie," he said. "In fact I haven't even located the canaries—but things are looking up."

"How?"

"Like this," said Timothy. "I put the first half of my two-part plan to work by propositioning the neighborhood drugstore for information on recent customers for veronal—and I found—" He drew a deep breath.

"Which one *was* it?" Joan demanded.

"Not so fast, my girl," Timothy soothed her. "It wasn't *one*—but *two* who bought veronal."

"For heaven's sake, Timothy—*which two?*"

"On Thursday evening"—the answer was deliberate—"Miss Bertha Dee led off by bringing an old veronal prescription to the local druggist and asking to have it filled. Not twenty minutes after she had left the store—in toddles Mrs. Winters with a prescription for sleeping tablets—"

"Not the *same* prescription?" Joan demanded.

"No—this one was made out for Hamlet Winters, and it was a new one that had never been filled before. The druggist looked the order over carefully and it was regular enough—but he did notice that it wasn't signed by Winters' usual doctor—"

"How would he know that?" I put in.

"Easy enough. It's the only drugstore in the neighborhood, and all the Dees' and Winters' medicines have come from there for the past five years. But—even though it began to look like a run on the veronal market—there was no reason for the druggist not to fill the prescription."

"Which he did?"

Timothy nodded.

"But not," he said, "without remarking that he hoped Dr. Winters wasn't ill. To which, of course, Mrs. Winters replied no indeed—not exactly ill—but the truth of it was he hadn't been sleeping well. The druggist then came forth with a neat quip about there being the same difficulty in the Dee family—and he hoped it didn't mean the neighborhood was getting so noisy that no one could sleep."

"And how did Mrs. Winters take *that?*"

"Just the way you'd expect her to." Timothy shook his head. "She looked the druggist straight in the suspicious eye, said indeed she hoped not, and departed—veronal in hand."

"Is that *all*, Timothy?" Joan sounded disappointed.

"That's all," he nodded cheerfully, "of part one."

"And what do you think it means? How can it help you to know that two people were after veronal—and that both of them got it?"

"It means," said Timothy seriously, "that those two people did *not* intend to kill Hamlet Winters by an overdose of veronal—and to know that helps me a hell of a lot."

"But I still don't see—" Joan looked thoroughly bewildered.

"Come, come, Joanie," Timothy reproved her amiably, "if you intend to poison a man, do you go to the neighborhood store—where you and your victim are well known—to buy the drug?"

"Well, I suppose not—but why else would both the women want veronal? And Dr. Winters *was* given an overdose by someone—"

"Not necessarily, Joan."

The girl stared.

"But the Coroner *said*—" she insisted.

A quick gesture from Timothy cut her short.

"The Coroner said that there was a dose of veronal in Hamlet Winters' stomach which might have killed him—if his throat hadn't been cut before the drug had time to work. But the Coroner did *not* say that any person administered that dose."

"Oh"—Joan's big eyes widened even more—"then you really think that Dr. Winters took the veronal himself?"

"No," said Timothy patiently, "I don't. I simply mean that two and two make four." And, as Joan continued to look blank, he added: "If you still don't see it—stick around for part two of my plan"—there was a knock at the door—"which is probably about to start right now."

It was Officer Al who announced, when Timothy opened the door, that the three members of the Dee family were waiting.

"Send them in here."

Al vanished, and a moment later Mrs. Dee entered, looking calm and serious as before. She was followed by Miss Bertha, who seemed as subdued as her bulk would allow her to be—and then—all our eyes were on the door as Fletcher Dee appeared. He was an enormous man, tall and broad like his sister, and with a pouchy, sagging build which was emphasized by careless dress and a stooping posture. Slowly, insolently, he walked into the room, selected the most comfortable armchair, and settled himself in it without so much as a glance for any of us who watched.

It is difficult to describe the effect of deliberate offensiveness conveyed by Fletcher Dee's appearance and manner. I saw Timothy's jaw set in a hard line as he observed the expression of sneering contempt which seemed to rest naturally on Dee's heavy features.

Both Mrs. Dee and Miss Bertha were watching Fletcher Dee intently, but I felt certain that there was more than a superficial difference between the covertly anxious glance of his wife and the hostile stare which his sister Bertha fixed on him. Not, of course, that Dee himself paid the slightest attention to either of the women—nor did he so much as look up when, after a moment, Timothy approached him.

"Mr. Dee, why didn't you come over here when you were first sent for this morning?" Timothy himself, I observed with satisfaction, was no novice at making his manner unpleasant.

Fletcher Dee raised his eyes at the question, stared for a moment at Timothy's face, then glanced away with an odd laugh which was more than half a sneer.

"Answer my question, please. Why didn't you come when you were sent for?"

"Because," said Dee, "I wasn't at home when your messenger came."

"Where were you then?"

"Where is any self-respecting citizen at half-past ten on a Sunday morning, Inspector? In church, of course."

Once more I find it impossible to convey on paper the degree of mocking insolence which Fletcher Dee managed to impart to his words.

"Why did you go to church this particular morning, Mr. Dee?"

"A very stupid question, Inspector. Even *you* must know that any Christian goes to church for simple fear of hell-fire."

"A very stupid joke, Mr. Dee," Timothy's quick retort snapped out unexpectedly. "And even *you* must know better than to make stupid jokes when you are summoned by the police for an investigation of murder."

"I beg your pardon, Inspector"—Dee's apology was elaborately ironical—"from the nature of your remarks I had no idea why we were here."

I saw Timothy's lips silently frame what I judged to be a fairly emphatic oath.

"Since you now understand the situation, Mr. Dee, you will please answer my questions."

"With pleasure."

"We'll begin," Timothy said, "with the fact that you were summoned to a meeting of the Trustees of Granger College on the afternoon when Hamlet Winters was killed."

"Quite right."

"And it was President Hughes of the college who asked you to appear at the meeting?"

"It was."

"For what purpose, Mr. Dee?"

"To satisfy some damn theatrical notion of Hamlet Winters'." Once more Dee uttered his sneering laugh.

Timothy raised one eyebrow inquiringly.

"You find that idea amusing, Mr. Dee?"

"I found everything about Hamlet Winters amusing."

"Even his death?" Timothy rapped out the question with a suddenness which made me jump, but Dee never flinched.

"Particularly his death," he said deliberately. "To be found—kneeling in St. Ives Cathedral, with his throat cut! It's almost too perfect a finish for a romantic like Winters. There are so few ways left in this machine age, Inspector, for a romantic to die appropriately. Hospitals are no good for dramatics, you know, and even the average murder is commonplace enough. But this one"—he paused to laugh silently—"was marvelous. I'd almost say Hamlet Winters staged it himself."

"I had thought," Timothy spoke quietly, "Hamlet Winters was your friend."

"So he was." Dee nodded complacently.

"And yet—you find his death only amusing?"

"I find most people only amusing, Inspector, either in life or death."

"You realize, of course, that you are talking very dangerously?"

"Well, after all," Fletcher Dee's half-closed eyes met Timothy's sharp glance, "isn't that what you brought me here for, Inspector?"

A long moment—then Timothy's answer came forth with unprofessional feeling.

"No," he said, "but I wish it were. I'd just as soon pin a murder on you as on any man I ever saw—but, unfortunately—you didn't kill Hamlet Winters."

Without a trace of emotion, Dee bowed slightly.

"*Unfortunately*, as you put it, Inspector, you are correct. I didn't kill Hamlet Winters."

"Nevertheless," Timothy went on, "he was killed to save your extremely ungrateful skin."

"Please explain yourself, Inspector." Dee's tone was level, but the shot had not been without effect. For the first time his heavy face registered something apart from its habitual expression of contempt.

"I mean," said Timothy slowly, "that the request for your presence at the Trustees' meeting on Friday afternoon came, as you correctly stated, from Dr. Winters. But it was not a mere theatrical gesture on his part. He was going to make a confession at that meeting—a confession which involved you. If Hamlet Winters had not been prevented from reaching the meeting"—I could see that Timothy was choosing his words with care as he skated perilously near the limits of his certain knowledge—"if he had not been prevented," he repeated, "by someone who wished to protect *you,* Hamlet Winters would have confessed a crime. To make that confession, and clear his conscience, he was prepared to sacrifice his position here—to blast his own reputation—to risk the very attack which ended his life. Even you, Mr. Dee, must admit that this is not a thing to be dismissed as merely amusing. Hamlet Winters did set the stage for his confession—but believe me it was no idle gesture. He did it as seriously—as desperately—as the original Hamlet who prepared a stage from which to accuse"—Timothy paused to draw a long breath—"to accuse a man"—he pointed a finger straight at Fletcher Dee—"of—"

"Of murder!" It was Miss Bertha Dee's hysterical cry which rang out.

With one accord we whirled to stare at the woman as she sat, in her hideous mustard yellow dress, staring with wide-stretched eyes from a face which worked convulsively.

"It was murder," she repeated wildly, "murder that Hamlet knew about—and he was going to tell it all—"

"Bertha," the slightly husky voice of Mrs. Dee cut through, "Bertha—*be quiet!"*

"You can't stop me." Miss Dee turned savagely upon her. "You've protected Fletcher Dee long enough—and now *I'll* tell what *I* know—and no one can stop me. It was murder I tell you"—her shrill words were directed at each of us in turn—"and they won't keep me from telling—"

"Stop it!" With two quick strides Timothy crossed to Miss Bertha's chair and seized her heavy shoulders in a businesslike grip. *"Stop it!"* He shook her until Miss Bertha's teeth clicked shut upon her hysterically babbling words. "Now then"—as she sank back in silence, Timothy stood over the hunched figure—"tell me exactly what you are trying to say."

17
FOUR AND TEN

The silence which hung over the room while we waited for Miss Dee to speak was charged with an almost electric tension. Laura Dee, her face as chalk-white as her dress, sat forward on the edge of the couch—still as a statue except for the slow twisting and untwisting of her long, clenched fingers. Once I saw her glance swiftly from Miss Bertha's flushed face to her husband, but Fletcher Dee, slouched heavily back in the big chair, looked neither at his wife nor his sister. His downward gaze remained fixed on some imaginary spot upon the floor, and whatever suspense or fear he may have suffered was betrayed only by the sound of his rapid breathing.

"Now then"—once more Timothy bent over Bertha Dee, as her hysterical sobbing subsided to a quiet whimpering breath—"what murder are you talking about?"

In a quivering echo of her usual voice Miss Bertha answered him.

"The murder that Hamlet Winters was going to confess."

"I understand that," said Timothy quietly, "but *what* murder? Who was killed?"

"I—don't know."

"Who was the murderer then?"

"I don't know that."

"Suppose you tell us what you *do* know."

"Only that"—Miss Dee gulped—"Hamlet said he had discovered a crime and he was going to confess it at the Trustees' meeting Friday afternoon even though he said that it meant—death for him."

"Winters actually *said* that?"

"Yes." The word was uttered in a long, quivering sigh.

"To you, Miss Dee?"

"No"—bitterly—"to—Mary."

"How did you know of it then?"

"She told me."

"When?"

"On Thursday afternoon. The day before Hamlet was— before he died."

"Tell me exactly what she said to you."

With an obvious effort Miss Dee rallied herself to speak coherently.

"That afternoon," she began, "Mary telephoned for me to come here. When I arrived Tilden sent me upstairs, and I found Mary terribly upset. She told me that in the morn- ing she had found in Hamlet's desk—quite by accident—a letter, addressed to herself, saying that he might die under peculiar or violent circumstances—and she, Mary, was not to be blamed for anything that might happen. She was horribly frightened, of course, and didn't know what to do at first. But after lunch she told Hamlet that she had seen the letter and asked him what it meant."

"What did he say?" Timothy was bending eagerly for- ward to catch every syllable of the low, toneless voice.

"Nothing at first—"

"But was he upset?"

"Very much, Mary said. Finally he told her that if she loved him she must have faith—and believe that what he was about to do would be the finest act of his life. He said that he had happened on a discovery of a certain fact—and that his honor depended upon his revealing that fact, even though the confession would mean death for him. She asked him, of course, *begged* him to tell her what the discovery was—and finally he said just one word: *'Murder.'* More than that he would not tell—but he did say twice that *'after Friday'* she would know the truth."

"Was that all?"

Slowly Miss Dee nodded.

"That was all he would say—and Mary promised him that she would have faith in whatever he did."

"It was after this conversation that Mrs. Winters sent for you?"

"Yes—but there was more. When Hamlet had left the house, he was giving an examination Thursday afternoon, Mary went over and over in her mind what he had told her—and she kept remembering his saying that 'after Friday' she would know the truth. While she was thinking—almost frantic with worry—President Hughes telephoned and wanted to speak to Hamlet. When Mary said that he wasn't at home, Dr. Hughes asked her to tell him that the Trustees' meeting was scheduled for four o'clock on the next afternoon, *Friday* afternoon. Mary knew, of course, that it wasn't the usual thing to have any faculty members appear at those meetings—and she asked why Hamlet was to be there. Dr. Hughes simply said that Hamlet would understand why—and hung up. Naturally Mary put two and two together, and it seemed to her likely that if Hamlet were going to make some public confession of this mysterious 'discovery' on Friday afternoon—he probably planned to do it at the meeting. So after she had thought everything over, she decided to go to Dr. Hughes' office and beg him to tell her what, if anything, he knew about the matter."

"And would he tell?"

"He didn't have to. When Mary reached the office, Dr. Hughes was not there, but the secretary said he was expected back at once. Mary asked if she might wait in his private office, and as soon as the secretary left her alone there, she began to search Dr. Hughes' desk. You understand"—for the first time Miss Dee lifted her eyes to Timothy's face—"Mary was desperate—and she thought she might find some letter or memorandum about *why* Hamlet was to be at the meeting the next day—"

"I understand." Timothy nodded hastily. "And—*did* she find the letter from Winters?"

"Yes." Miss Dee showed no surprise at Timothy's knowledge of the letter. "It said that he, Hamlet, had something he must confess at this meeting—and it asked that the President have my brother Fletcher there also—without letting Fletcher know why he was summoned."

Miss Bertha did not look toward Fletcher Dee as she spoke, but the rest of us turned to see how he had received the revelation. He remained, eyes downcast, apparently unmoved. Only a slight curl of his lips—half smirk, half sneer—disturbed the stolid set of his features to show that he was even aware of the dangerous direction of his sister's testimony.

"It was after Mary had seen that letter," Miss Dee's low, toneless voice proceeded with the story, "that she came back to the house—without waiting to see Dr. Hughes— and telephoned for me. When I arrived she told me everything that had happened—and asked me to help her."

"In what way, Miss Dee?"

"She wanted me to keep my brother Fletcher from appearing at the meeting Friday afternoon—by giving him a heavy dose of veronal at lunch time."

"So—?" Timothy's voice rose sharply. "How did Mrs. Winters believe that would help matters?"

"She planned to keep Hamlet away from the meeting also, by—by the same means. You see," once more Miss Bertha's eyes were raised appealingly to Timothy, "she was so afraid that Hamlet was about to do something terribly foolish—she couldn't believe that he actually had anything so dreadful to confess—and yet"—the woman spread her hands in a helpless gesture—"at the same time she was terrified."

"I quite understand, Miss Dee," Timothy reassured her patiently, "but what, exactly, was Mrs. Winters' plan?"

"Simply to keep Hamlet and Fletcher away from the meeting the next day. Mary believed that if she could only postpone this confession, for even a short time, she might be able to learn what lay behind it all—"

"And so she asked you to give your brother sufficient veronal to prevent his going?"

"Yes."

"May I ask why Mrs. Winters appealed particularly to you, Miss Dee?"

There was a moment's silence. When Bertha Dee answered, her voice, pitched even lower than before, betrayed the first emotion which had crept into her long recital.

"Mary chose me," she said very slowly, "for two reasons. Because she knew that I hated my brother—and because she knew that I—loved Hamlet Winters, and that I would have done anything in the world to help him."

For all her unattractive appearance there was a certain dignity about Miss Dee in that moment. It was evident that she spoke in all sincerity when she disclosed these two facts—perhaps the two most powerful and fundamental emotions of her life—hatred for her brother, and love for the dead Hamlet Winters.

Once more, in the silence which followed Miss Bertha's words, I glanced at Fletcher Dee—and still he gave no sign of having heard his sister's words.

"You agreed, then, to help Mrs. Winters by giving veronal to your brother?"

Timothy's quiet words seemed to restore Miss Dee to the former unemotional level of her story.

"I did."

"And did she give you explicit directions—how many tablets to give him, and so on?"

"Yes."

"She gave you those directions *herself?*" Timothy's question was insistent.

"She and a nurse—Miss Carter."

"Oh." I saw the quick lift of Timothy's shoulders. "Then Miss Carter was here—on Thursday afternoon?"

Miss Bertha nodded dully.

"And did Mrs. Winters tell her all this story that she told you?"

Another nod.

"Was it Miss Carter who suggested the veronal plan?"

"Yes. She got a prescription for it, made out in Hamlet's name, from some doctor she knew—and she told Mary to have it filled, and to give me four tablets for Fletcher and keep four for Hamlet. She said that dose would make them sleep all afternoon—until the meeting was safely over—if they took it at lunch-time."

"You agreed to that exact plan, Miss Dee?"

"Yes."

"And yet—Thursday evening you took a veronal prescription of your own to the local druggist and asked him to fill it?"

Again Miss Dee showed no surprise at Timothy's unexpected information.

"I did," she admitted.

"*Why*, Miss Dee—when Mrs. Winters was to give you as much of the drug as was necessary? *Why?*" Timothy leaned over her.

"Can't you guess?" Her deep-set eyes narrowed cunningly as she stared up at him. "You heard me say that I—I hated Fletcher Dee."

"So—you planned to increase the dose Miss Carter had prescribed?"

Miss Bertha nodded, her eyes still fixed on his face.

"You planned to make the dose large enough to kill your brother?"

"*Yes.*" Clearly, with a hissing emphasis, she gave her answer.

"You must have known that you were running a very great risk—that you were almost certain to have been discovered."

"Of course I knew it," Miss Bertha's voice rose impatiently—but this time there was no trace of hysteria in her shrill words. "But I didn't care. Do you understand that? *I didn't care.* I only wanted to make sure of one thing—that Hamlet Winters would be safe. From what Mary had told me, you see, I was sure that whatever this trouble was—the crime that Hamlet felt he must confess—was somehow Fletcher's fault. I knew that Hamlet could never have done anything wrong—that it must be Fletcher who had done it—whatever it was. And I was willing—I was eager, I tell you,—to risk my life ten times over to save Hamlet from suffering for something that my brother had done. That was why I got my own veronal prescription filled. Miss Carter had said that four tablets would only put a man to sleep—I planned to give Fletcher ten of them—" For the first time since she had started to speak, Miss Bertha turned to look squarely at her brother. "Do you hear that, Fletcher Dee?" Her tone was deadly. "I was giving you ten tablets—one for every wretched year I've lived under your roof."

Fletcher Dee did not raise his eyes.

"Why don't you answer me?" her voice rasped sharply.

"Because," at last Dee looked into his sister's face, "you have already been answered. I am here, before your loving and grateful eyes—and *Hamlet Winters is dead!* There's your answer, my dear sister."

"Wh-what do you mean—?" Slowly a look of terror crept over Miss Bertha's flushed countenance. "What does he mean?" Frantically, she appealed to Timothy, to Laura Dee, to each of us. *"What does he mean?"*

"He means," Timothy answered her at last, "that Dr. Winters was given an overdose of veronal at lunch on Friday—a dose which probably would have killed him if his throat had not been cut with a razor before the drug had taken its full effect. And he means, Miss Dee, that it was you who prepared that potentially fatal dose. For Hamlet Winters took your brother's place at lunch that day—and he drank the coffee which you had drugged for Fletcher Dee."

18
DR. HALL—GOT IT ALL

The moments which followed Timothy's explanation to Miss Dee were too hectic to be adequately described. It took every bit of Timothy's firm and cool-headed control to drag some kind of coherence out of the confusion and chaos of the hysterically pitched scene. Gradually, painfully, the tangled emotions, the crossed motives, the strange mixture of intentional and accidental circumstances resolved themselves into a clear picture of what had actually befallen Hamlet Winters on Friday afternoon.

Miss Bertha had, on the morning of that day, prepared the would-be fatal dose of veronal for her brother by dissolving ten tablets in the coffee which Laura Dee had set aside to serve iced for lunch. That only her brother would take the coffee was assured, since she, Bertha, and young Laurence Dee were to be out for lunch—and Laura Dee never drank coffee. It was after Miss Bertha had left the house that Fletcher had been summoned to preside at the alumni luncheon, and Mrs. Dee—taking advantage of the opportunity to see Hamlet Winters alone and present her plea for money—had bidden her guest to lunch and served to him, in all innocence, the coffee intended for Fletcher. The dose of veronal had not, of course, taken effect

381

immediately—and Winters was able to leave the Dee house at something after two o'clock, return to his own home, attend to some business, drink the glass of iced tea which his wife had prepared for him, and then start upon the mission—whatever it was—that led him eventually to the St. Ives Cathedral.

That much of the story we knew when Timothy had pieced it together, bit by bit, from the mutual recriminations and confessions of the three members of the Dee family. Many riddles remained as yet unsolved: much of the story remained to be uncovered—but from this beginning of established truth Timothy set himself to reconstruct the rest of Hamlet Winters' fate.

"At least we're beginning at the right end this time." His brow furrowed with furious concentration, Timothy surveyed the three witnesses—now subdued and silent before him. He moved swiftly to the door, and gave an order to Al. "The next thing," he returned to us, "is to get Mrs. Winters and the Carter wench straightened out."

Considering all the trouble and confusion which the two women had brought to the case so far, the truth came from them with surprising ease when Timothy confronted them with the part of the story we already knew. It did not take an eye more experienced than my own to observe the look of open relief which passed between Mary Winters and Miss Carter when Timothy informed them of the accidental circumstance through which Dr. Winters had been drugged with the veronal intended for Fletcher Dee.

"Now," Timothy's sharp eye fixed them sternly, "for the last time will you two stop acting out Macbeth and tell me the truth?"

It was then that Mary Winters looked at Miss Carter—and drew one long, heartfelt breath of relief that ended in a sob.

"Oh, my God yes—I can tell you now." Her head went down into her hands and for the first time Hamlet Winters' wife wept—not hysterically, but in silence.

Miss Carter stepped forward.

"I'll explain," she said quietly.

Timothy permitted himself one glare at the girl—in payment for all the riddles and confusion with which she had complicated the case.

"You'd better explain," he said grimly, "and make it fast."

"I know I've caused you a lot of trouble"—she accepted his rebuke humbly—"by trying to help Mrs. Winters. But I had to do it—because it was all my fault that she got into this dreadful thing. It's true, as Miss Dee told you, that I suggested the doses of veronal to keep Dr. Winters and Dr. Dee away from the meeting on Friday afternoon—and that I got a prescription for the drug from a friend of mine. It was wrong of me to do it—but I was honestly devoted to both Dr. and Mrs. Winters, and they had done so much for me. Mrs. Winters begged me for some way to keep her husband from making this desperately serious confession until she could find out what it was all about, and I had absolutely no idea of plotting anything more serious than a few hours of unexpected sleep which might keep Dr. Winters from doing some dreadful thing. Frankly, from what Mrs. Winters had told me, I thought Dr. Winters must be suffering from some sort of a delusion. Knowing him as I did, and knowing the quiet, respectable life he lived, I simply could not believe that there was anything really serious behind his talk of this dreadful thing which he said he had discovered. And, of course, it never entered my mind that either Mrs. Winters or Miss Dee would dare to increase the dose I instructed them to give." The girl paused to look at Timothy. "After all the lies I've told—I suppose I can scarcely expect you to believe me, but I swear I'm telling you the absolute truth now."

"Keep talking," Timothy said.

Miss Carter sighed.

"Very well," she went on quietly. "I left Mrs. Winters, as I have said, believing that I had helped her—and never dreaming that my suggestion for help would be used to harm anyone. But the next afternoon, Friday, I was at the hospital, in the Emergency Room—"

"On duty?"

"No, I'd had no case for two days. I just stopped in to talk to the interne on duty, and I was still in the Emergency Room when they brought in Dr. Winters. I—I guess I don't need to tell you," the girl spoke earnestly, "that it was a pretty stiff shock when I saw what had happened. I didn't know, of course, why he had been killed—and I still found it hard to believe that Dr. Winters could have been mixed up in anything that would lead to murder—but there he was—dead—with his throat cut. My first thought was Mrs. Winters. *I* had advised her to drug her husband—and it didn't take much imagination to realize what a position she would be in if the police discovered that she had bought veronal the day before the murder and had given Dr. Winters a stiff dose of it sometime before he was killed.

"That much"—Miss Carter shook her head—"was bad enough. But a minute later I heard the interne say something about drug poisoning. From an examination of his eyes, and from the way the wound had bled, it seemed pretty certain that Dr. Winters had been pretty close to death from an overdose of drugs before his throat was cut. That much the interne said—and no more. The man was already dead and it was the hospital's business to turn the body over to the Coroner. My one idea then was to get in touch with Mrs. Winters and to try to discover what had happened. I never believed for a moment that she had intentionally increased the veronal to an overdose—but I had to warn her of what had happened—and try to help. I was on my way to the telephone when Miss Adams, the Superintendent, saw me—and asked me to take a case that had just come into the Emergency Room. That patient was Miss Stebbins. I had no excuse to give Miss Adams for not taking the case—so I did—and you know the rest of that story. It didn't take many of your hints," she gave Timothy a shadow of her smile, "to tell me that my patient, Miss Stebbins, was somehow mixed up in the murder of Dr. Winters—and that you wanted to keep her out of the mess if possible. Well—I did my best for both you and Miss Stebbins, because I was just as anxious as you were to hush up the case until there was a chance to see how things were going to break. You know, of course, that I helped Miss Stebbins get away from the hospital the next morning."

"But what I *don't* know," said Timothy, "is why you dragged us all back into the case last night by leading the Barrett bloodhound to Joan's apartment."

"That," said Miss Carter simply, "was because everything looked so terribly bad for Mrs. Winters. I came straight here to her after Miss Stebbins left the hospital yesterday morning—and I told her what I had heard the interne say about the overdose of veronal. Mrs. Winters told me—and I believed her—that she had done exactly what I told her to about the veronal. She had put four tablets, and four only, in some iced tea for her husband—and had left him a message telling him to be sure to drink the tea before he went out. Beyond that, Mrs. Winters knew absolutely nothing about what had happened. I don't need to tell you that we were both terribly frightened. Up to ten o'clock last night, Inspector Barrett hadn't got hold of the veronal idea—but I knew that the Coroner's report would be coming in soon—and that he would report the overdose of drugs. It would be simple enough for the police to trace Mrs. Winters' purchase of the tablets at the local drugstore—on a prescription that was not from Dr. Winters' own physician. So—when Inspector Barrett called me in last night for a grilling, and I saw that he was already hot on Mrs. Winters' trail, I hit on the desperate idea of dragging you three"—a quick look at Timothy, Joan and me—"back into the case. Not that I thought for a moment that any of you had anything to do with the actual murder—but there *was* a rather good circumstantial case against Miss Stebbins, and I put it to Barrett as strongly as I could—hoping it would take his attention from Mrs. Winters for a while at least."

"Your hope," said Timothy drily, "was certainly realized. Barrett got on our track—and nothing has derailed him yet."

"Meanwhile," Miss Carter continued, "I've stayed here with Mrs. Winters and encouraged her all I could. It was my idea that if she acted as if she were in sort of a trance and both of us were as mysterious as we could be—we might be able to lead the investigation off the track—"

"Once more," Timothy murmured, "you didn't hope in vain."

"Until the truth about the veronal poisoning should be discovered—making it safe for Mrs. Winters to admit her perfectly innocent part in the story—as I have done for her just now."

"That's all, Miss Carter?"

"That's all Mrs. Winters knows of what happened, and all I know." The girl spoke with convincing simplicity.

"I see." Timothy nodded very slowly. "I see, for one thing, that there's an awful lot that we *don't* know—yet. Why, for instance, did Dr. Winters go to St. Ives? Who followed him there and cut his throat? Who was even more anxious than Mrs. Winters to keep him from attending that meeting—to silence forever the 'confession' which Winters was apparently determined to make? *Who*—and *why?*" As he spoke Timothy's eyes rested in turn upon each of the persons before him. Mrs. Dee, Miss Bertha, Mary Winters, Miss Carter, Fletcher Dee, Joan and myself. So far as could be observed, his glance was impartial—remaining no longer on one face than another. "To get on," his tone was suddenly brisk, "we've traced Winters to the point where he returned to his home after the luncheon, was given the iced tea prepared for him by Mrs. Winters, and immediately after that—according to Tilden—he left the house. One point there must be cleared up. Where was Dr. Winters between the time he left here and the time he wound up in St. Ives Cathedral? Can you, Mrs. Winters, suggest an answer for that question?"

Her quiet tears ended some minutes past, Mary Winters looked up at Timothy clear-eyed and calm.

"No," her voice came low but distinctly, "I cannot."

"It must have been," Timothy said thoughtfully, "a darned important errand. With a stiff dose of veronal at lunch-time, plus the smaller amount in the tea, Winters was probably pretty groggy by the time he started out— and I think it's safe to say that he wouldn't have gone at all unless there were some excellent reason for that errand. You were surprised, weren't you"—again Timothy addressed Mrs. Winters—"to find your husband out of the house when you returned shortly before four o'clock?"

"Yes."

"You had expected to find him here—asleep?

"Yes."

"What did you think, Mrs. Winters, when you found him gone?"

"I—I didn't know what to think."

"You left the house yourself then?"

"Yes."

"In search of your husband?"

"No. I went next door—to speak to Bertha—but she wasn't in."

"Did you find anyone at home?"

"Yes—Laurence Dee was there"—she glanced at Mrs. Dee—"the—the boy, you know. He told me he was alone in the house. I knew then that our plan, Bertha's and mine, for keeping the two men away from the meeting had somehow gone wrong. And I was badly puzzled and frightened—"

"So what did you do?"

"I asked Laurence Dee to help me find my husband."

"How much did you tell him of what had happened—and what you feared?"

"Everything," said Mary Winters, "that I knew. As quickly and clearly as I could."

"And was the boy willing to help you?"

"Oh—yes."

"Wholly willing?" Timothy's question was insistent.

Mrs. Winters drew in her breath sharply.

"Why do you ask that?" For the first time her clear glance wavered.

"Because," said Timothy, "if you told young Dee everything—he must have gathered that his father was somehow involved in all this mystery. You asked him to help Dr. Winters, but I should think it would have been a more likely impulse on the boy's part to consider his father first—"

"Not before Hamlet," Mary Winters said quietly. "The boy adored him."

"Enough so that if he had to choose between Dr. Winters and his own father—?" Timothy allowed the question to remain unfinished. There was not the slightest hesitation in Mary Winters' answer.

"He would have chosen Hamlet," she said. "Laurence was not—not very loyal to his father." Mary Winters sent a look of mute appeal to Mrs. Dee. "We all knew that. He was a strange boy—sensitive and impetuous—and I believe Hamlet understood him as none of the rest of us ever did."

For one long moment Timothy was silent, then he resumed his questioning.

"The boy was willing to help you," he said. "What then?"

"We had no notion where to start looking for Hamlet. But Laurence suggested that we come back here first. He hoped to find something, you see, that would give us a clue. So we returned to the house—"

"And what did you find?"

"Nothing at first—then Laurence saw a memorandum on Hamlet's desk—a telephone number. On a last chance, he called the number—and discovered that it was the office of a Mr. Flagstaff, some sort of a printer he seemed to be, and Laurence asked whether Hamlet were there—or whether he were expected sometime in the afternoon. At first this Mr. Flagstaff said no—then he hesitated when

Laurence insisted on the importance of his question, and
finally admitted that he had had an appointment earlier
with a man who *might* be Dr. Winters, but he was unable
to say for certain. That was all of their conversation. To
me it seemed a very vague clue—but Laurence, for some
reason which he would not explain, was determined go to
this printer's office in person. A few minutes later we both
left the house—he to go downtown, and I to the college
building where the Trustees were meeting—in the hope of
stopping Hamlet if he should appear there."

"Just a moment, Mrs. Winters. A couple of questions
come in here. First, did Laurence notice any other item on
Dr. Winters' desk memorandum?"

"Yes, but"—the woman hesitated, frowning—"I—have
no idea what it meant. There was a little verse—scratched
across the corner of the pad—and I remember Laurence
read it aloud. It said '*Dr. Hall—got it all.*'"

"So—the boy noticed that? Did he make any comment
on it?"

"One sentence only—and he refused to explain it to
me. He simply said, 'I knew it.'"

"Right!" said Timothy with emphasis. "Now then, before you left the house, did Laurence go upstairs?"

"Yes."

"To Dr. Winters' room?"

"Yes. He insisted that Hamlet might have left a message
there and that he would better look to make sure."

"Right again!" Timothy snapped his fingers.

He made a quick dash for the hall and a moment later
he returned with a folded handkerchief in his hand. I knew
at once that it was the razor he had fetched. "This," he unfolded the linen square before the reluctant eyes of Mary
Winters, "was your husband's razor, wasn't it?"

She nodded—one hand pressed tightly against her mouth.

"And it was kept until Friday afternoon—in the bath adjoining Dr. Winters' bedroom?"

Another nod.

"Then"—Timothy spoke quickly—"that's that. Laurence Dee went upstairs before he left the house—not to look for a message but to take this razor. And"—he straightened abruptly and once more his glance travelled around the circle of faces—faces now strained with an almost unbearable tension—"the office of Mr. Flagstaff—to which Laurence went, with the razor in his pocket—happens to be on the corner of Pearl Avenue and Charles Street—the corner directly opposite St. Ives Cathedral."

19
HOW MANY WERE GOING TO ST. IVES?

"I expect"—Timothy's sharp glance settled on Miss Bertha—"you knew that."

"I—knew what?" Her counter-question was almost a whisper.

"That the office of the Flagstaff Press was in the building opposite St. Ives. You knew that, Miss Dee, because you saw your nephew leave that building and cross Pearl Avenue to enter the Cathedral—didn't you?"

This time Miss Bertha's answer was inaudible—but we saw her nod.

"And you followed the boy—into the Cathedral?"

"Yes, but not then—not right away—not until—" The heavy voice faltered and broke miserably.

"Not until"—Timothy bent forward with his question—"not until *after* the murder was done? Is that it, Miss Dee?"

The room was deadly silent as we waited for the answer. A long moment passed, and Miss Dee did not speak. Then, like a flash, Timothy seized her shoulders in an iron grip—and was literally shaking her into speech as earlier he had silenced the too ready flow of her hysterical words.

"*No—no—*" All at once the shrill denial came from between her chattering teeth. "I went in sooner—*I saw Laurence do it!*"

"Thank God for that." As Timothy released his hold, he breathed the words with a fervent relief. In the moment of stunned quiet which followed, he drew a handkerchief from his pocket and mopped his forehead. "For a minute"—his voice was solemn—"I thought I was cornered. I thought we might never know—for sure—that a dead boy killed Hamlet Winters." With an effort he went on. "But you saw it, Miss Dee—thank God, you saw it. Now then"—he steadied the woman's heaving shoulder—"there's not much more. Just tell me what you saw."

"When Laurence crossed the street and went in the Cathedral," the words came slowly from Miss Bertha's trembling lips, "I was standing on the corner—waiting for a bus to take me home. I called to the boy—he must have heard me—but he didn't stop. He was running wildly—across in front of two cars—and I knew something must have happened. I couldn't imagine *what*—but I knew something was terribly wrong. After a few minutes Laurence hadn't come out of the Cathedral—and I followed him inside."

"You passed no one in the vestibule?"

Miss Dee shook her head.

"It was dark in the church—and I couldn't see very well at first—but I stood still, and presently I could make out the figure of a man who seemed to be kneeling in a pew quite far up front. Another figure was leaning over him—and I recognized Laurence. I was about to speak—to call the boy—when I saw him make the most horrible gesture—he jerked the man's head to one side and something flashed—it must have been the—the razor as Laurence threw it aside. I didn't know then what he had done—but the boy turned and ran straight past me—out of the Cathedral—and I saw his face—" the shuddering voice collapsed in a wild sob.

"*Go on.*" Timothy's command, sharp as an electric shock, seemed to restore Miss Bertha's failing power of speech.

"I saw his face"—the gulping words continued painfully—"I called to him—I must have screamed his name—but he ran on. Then I—I didn't know what to do. Whether to follow him, or try to help the man who was still kneeling up there in front. I must have hesitated—I don't know how long—it seemed forever—and then I followed Laurence. The vestibule was empty, so I went out onto the steps. The boy was not in sight—I couldn't imagine where he had gone, but as I came back into the vestibule I saw something on the floor—a sort of trail—*of blood*—leading up a side staircase. I followed it—up into the balcony, and there I saw Laurence crouching. I spoke to him, and at first he didn't answer—then there was a sudden flare that lit up his face—and I realized that he was burning something—"

"*Burning something?*"

"Yes."

"Did you see what it was?"

"Only vaguely. It seemed to be a large sheet of very thin paper, perhaps a very old paper—for it flared up so suddenly, and then nothing was left. Laurence stood up, and I saw him rub the light ashes into the floor with his foot. He turned toward me and he looked quite calm—not wild or frightened as he had been when he ran past me downstairs. I—I spoke to him, of course—I asked him what he had done—and he walked over and looked straight into my face when he answered me—"

"Can you remember exactly what that answer was, Miss Dee?"

"Do you think"—the woman looked up gravely—"that I would be likely to forget? Laurence answered my question with just one sentence: *'I've saved one life,'* he said, *'and ruined another.'* Then before I could speak, he turned to go—and at the door he looked back for just a moment. 'I've done it all,' he said, 'but just one thing. You get the memorandum from the desk in Dr. Winters' study—*and burn it*—then Dr. Hall can rest in peace forever.' And with that he was gone—"

"Just a minute." Timothy broke in excitedly. *"Did Laurence say Dr. Hall?"*

Miss Bertha nodded, obviously startled by the intensity of his question.

"Then my God—that's it!" With an expression of triumph Timothy turned to face us. "Don't you see—it all fits! The crime that Winters was determined to confess—the mysterious murder he hinted at—the words he wrote: 'Dr. Hall—got it all'—Laurence Dee's statement. It all means that Dr. Hall was the murderer! Now all that remains is to find out who—" He checked himself suddenly. "Mr. Dee," Timothy pointed a finger which very nearly touched the man's nose. "Mr. Dee—*you* know who Dr. Hall is."

There was a blank moment—then Fletcher Dee slowly nodded. The contemptuous sneer which had so long twisted his features was at last gone. Until this moment it seemed that nothing could pierce the man's shell. Through the revelation of his friend's murder, of the plot against his own life, of his own son turned murderer—through

all the terrible past hour—Fletcher Dee had remained unmoved. But now—faced by Timothy's words *"You know
who Dr. Hall is"*—the man seemed stricken by some emotion almost too great to bear—emotion which contorted
his heavy features as he strove to speak.

"Yes"—the broken words were scarcely heard—"I—I
know—who Dr. Hall is."

"He murdered someone?" Timothy's excitement was
growing.

"Yes—" Another faltering nod.

"And Hamlet Winters discovered that fact!"

"No." Instantly Fletcher Dee was on his feet. *"I* discovered it. It was *my* discovery that Hamlet Winters stole.
I—"

"Fletcher—stop!" The frozen control of Laura Dee was
shattered suddenly. She sprang up to face her husband.
"You can't say it—you must not—"

With a single gesture Timothy brushed the woman
aside.

"Say it—" he commanded Dee curtly. "Say what it was
this Dr. Hall did—and he'll be brought to justice—"

For an instant they stood quite still—the three of
them—facing each other, taut and silent. Then the tension broke. Fletcher Dee threw back his head and began to
laugh. A moment later he had collapsed into a chair and
was trying to speak—his words strangled by choking gasps
of merriment.

"Brought to justice—*Dr. Hall*—my God but it's funny."

"What's funny about it?" Timothy demanded furiously.

"You—you *fool!"* Dee rocked with renewed peals of
laughing. "Dr. Hall—has been dead—*three hundred years!"*

Timothy had not time to move or speak before the door
was flung open and Inspector Barrett entered the room.

"I've got him," said Barrett.

"Got—who?" Slowly Timothy turned his dazed look toward the Inspector.

"Got *who?*" Barrett echoed the question harshly. "Why—Flagstaff—this printer bird you sent me after. And here he is." A tall, blondish man stepped uncertainly into the room and stared with evident apprehension at the circle of strained, frightened faces before him.

"Yes." Timothy collected himself with difficulty. "Oh—yes." He glanced for a moment at Fletcher Dee, still rocked with helpless laughter, and then turned back to the strange man. "Mr. Flagstaff," he said, "I have only one question for you, but I warn you to answer it truthfully. One Friday afternoon did you give a certain paper—a very *old* paper—to someone who came to your office?"

The man's pale eyes blinked fearfully.

"Yes," said Mr. Flagstaff, "I—I did."

"And did that paper contain evidence of a murder?"

The man hesitated only for an instant—but that delay was too much for Timothy's taut nerves.

"Answer me!" he commanded savagely.

"Y-yes," said Mr. Flagstaff once more.

"Speak up then—*who was murdered—and where?*"

This time the man dared not hesitate.

"William Shakespeare," he said, "in Stratford-on-Avon."

20
THE ANSWER

For a moment I thought that hard-boiled Timothy Fowler, pride of the New York Homicide Squad, was going to faint. It was a miracle, indeed, that all of us did not succumb to the unbelievable shock of that statement. But somehow we survived the moment and Timothy was able to finish piecing together the strange truth of Hamlet Winters' death.

It was not an easy task to draw out the tangled threads of motives and circumstances—to draw them out and then re-weave the proper pattern of events. But at length it was done, and we had before us the whole story of a man who stole another man's discovery—and was murdered by the wronged man's son, *in order that justice should not be done.*

First of all, Timothy returned to Miss Bertha—and from her he drew the final testimony of what had happened in the Cathedral. It appeared that after the scene in the church balcony, when Laurence Dee had destroyed the evidence of the priceless scholarly discovery, she had followed him downstairs, negotiating the dark steps with difficulty, but when she emerged into the vestibule, the boy was nowhere to be seen. Not knowing whether he had left the building, she looked first in the church proper. Once through the big door, Miss Dee saw that there was no one

within save the still figure kneeling in the pew far front.
It was then, when her eyes were more accustomed to the
dim light, that Miss Bertha recognized, for the first time,
the line of Hamlet Winters' head and shoulders, slumped
forward in the grotesque position which I remembered so
well.

She ran to him—and in one dreadful moment saw what
had happened. The razor which Laurence Dee had cast
aside lay near the pew, and as the realization swept over
her that her beloved Hamlet Winters had been murdered
by her beloved nephew—Miss Dee snatched up the razor
with some confused thought of saving the situation by hiding that bloody evidence. Hurrying back through the vestibule, Miss Bertha collided with me—and, quite as Timothy had earlier suspected, she left the building through
the side door into the Cathedral close—and dropped the
razor into the fountain pool.

Meanwhile Laurence Dee, whom she was seeking blind-
ly, instinctively, to protect, had run straight out of the
Cathedral and stepped—whether intentionally or not, we
shall never know—directly into the path of an oncoming
automobile.

Thus Timothy had come into the Cathedral proper to
find no one there save me, still prone upon the pew, and
Hamlet Winters kneeling—dead. While he pondered how
best to help me, the Cathedral attendant entered, discovered the condition of Winters—and hurried out to give
the alarm. Timothy realized then that both he and I were
trapped in an extremely awkward situation—but since neither of us had so far been observed, he decided to try to
hide it out. He waited, hidden from view behind the pillar near me, until I regained full consciousness. By that

time the attendant had returned, bringing the priest and
policeman with him, and I—still unobserved—started forward to confess my presence. It was then that I was struck,
from behind the pillar, by the butt-end of a revolver. And
it was not the murderer who delivered the blow, nor anyone concerned with the death of Hamlet Winters.

It was Timothy Fowler who struck me.

He did it in order to prevent my revealing my presence
in the Cathedral, and when I dropped—fortunately without a sound,—he carried me quickly up the shadowy side
aisle, through the deserted vestibule, out the side door
into the close, and finally through the gate into the street.
By this time the crowd outside was very large, and in the
general confusion his exit attracted no particular attention. To one or two curious bystanders Timothy simply
explained that I had fainted in the crowd, and without
further delay he loaded me into his car. And then—before driving me to the hospital, Timothy paused to execute
what I shall always regard as an act of supreme heroism.
He returned to the Cathedral and rescued Emma—crate
and all. How he escaped being seen by the three men I
shall never know—and must simply set it down to the fact
that, as he himself says, a detective has got to be wise in
the ways of not being detected.

And that was the story of what took place in St. Ives
Cathedral on the afternoon of Friday the twentieth of
June.

As for the amazing motive which lay behind the murder
of Hamlet Winters—the key to which was so dramatically
supplied by Mr. Flagstaff—it was a tale of rivalry which
reached back three years into the lives of Hamlet Winters
and Fletcher Dee. A rivalry that had remained secret and

unspoken—even unknown to Dee himself until the revelations of that investigation in the study. And the explanation of it all lay in Laurence Dee's words to his aunt: "I've saved one life and ruined another." By murdering Hamlet Winters—who had stolen his father's rightful scholarly discovery—the boy had saved Winters from the confession which would have blasted his bright career—and by the same gesture had deprived Fletcher Dee forever of the honor which should have been his.

For the paper which Bertha Dee had watched her nephew destroy was the *original* and *only* evidence of a priceless scholarly and historical discovery. It was one single page of a diary three hundred years old—a diary kept by one John Ward, vicar of Stratford. And on that page was recorded a death-bed confession, made to the vicar, by Dr. Hall—son-in-law, heir and physician of William Shakespeare. In this confession Hall admitted that he, when attending Shakespeare in his last illness, had deliberately let him die. As sole motive for his terrible crime he gave the fact that under his father-in-law's recently revised will, he, Dr. Hall, together with his wife Susanna (Shakespeare's own daughter) would inherit and administer all of the poet's very considerable estate. The vicar Ward had further recorded Dr. Hall's admission that it was his effort to prevent possible discovery of the crime which led to Shakespeare's curious burial. I quote a standard authority on this subject:

> ". . . the grave (Shakespeare's) was made seventeen feet deep, and was never to be opened, even to receive his wife and daughters, although . . . they expressed a desire to be buried in it."[1]

It was Dr. Hall who gave these orders, supposedly issued by the dying Shakespeare himself, and Dr. Hall also who composed the famous lines for the poet's grave:

> "Goodfriend, for Jesus' sake forebeare
> To dig the dust enclosed heare;
> Bleste be the man that spares these stones,
> And curst be he that moves my bones."

I need hardly dwell upon the importance of such a discovery as this of John Ward's diary. Suffice to say that any new fact, however small, concerning the events of Shakespeare's life, is now a scholarly find of major proportions, bringing fame and praise to the discoverer not only within academic circles, but from the world at large. The rewards of a find like this—*the death-bed confession of the murderer of William Shakespeare*—are almost past contemplation, particularly when one considers that the actual cause and circumstances of Shakespeare's death have, despite the best efforts of scholars, remained shrouded in a haze of mystery. I quote again: *"The cause of Shakespeare's death is undetermined."*[2]

The only theory commonly advanced as to the cause of the "fever" in which he died, is the story of a drinking party in which Shakespeare was joined by his friends Ben Jonson and Michael Drayton. According to an earlier and well-known entry in this same John Ward's diary: (the three men) *"had a merry meeting, but Shakespeare, it seems, drank too hard, for he died of a feavour there contracted."*[3] It has likewise long been known that Dr. Hall was the only physician attending the poet's last illness—and now to have discovered that Dr. Hall deliberately allowed his patient to die! Small wonder that it was a discovery important enough to lead to a contemporary murder!

It was Fletcher Dee who, in the course of his only trip to Stratford three years past, found certain clues indicating the existence of that secret portion of John Ward's diary. It was, of course, the discovery to which his wife had referred in her interview with Timothy. Having discovered these clues, Fletcher Dee was confident that somewhere among the privately owned and uncatalogued records, papers, or books, to be found in or near Stratford, he could unearth and obtain possession of the original document that would prove his amazing suspicion. He had even worked out plausible devices by which the true significance of his find could be successfully concealed—until the precious document should be safely in Dee's possession. But such a search, as Mrs. Dee had said, would require at least a year—perhaps more—of the most intensive work. And that was something which Fletcher Dee could not afford. Nor, as his wife had stated, would it be likely that any scholarly grant of funds would be given for a piece of scholarship so improbable, so sensational, as this discovery which Dee believed he could establish—even had he been willing to risk a possible pirating of his idea by divulging it in his appeal for a scholarship. What Mrs. Dee did not tell us, because she had not known it, was that Fletcher Dee *had* confided his great idea and all his plans for its realization to Hamlet Winters—asking his counsel on how to proceed.

And Hamlet Winters had advised his friend to sit tight and say nothing. Meanwhile he, Winters, through what temptations of ambition and curiosity no one will ever know, had basely taken advantage of another man's discovery. With his ample income it was a simple thing for him to take the required year abroad, and thus he had, after months of patient research, found himself in possession

of the one original, authentic page of John Ward's diary—
and, having found it, must have suffered heaven knows
what tortures of indecision. To publish his find in the face
of Fletcher Dee was impossible. Yet to keep secret such a
discovery, the publication of which would bring world-
wide prominence and distinction to its author—to keep
secret this supreme achievement of a scholar's lifetime
must have been maddening. At last, apparently, Hamlet
Winters had come to his decision. He determined to have
the document and his record of its finding printed—and
then—with a final *beau geste* typical of his dramatic personality, he planned to confess what he had done—and
turn over the discovery to Fletcher Dee, its rightful author. Thus, when he had. spoken to Mary Winters of his
confession which would mean "death" to him, Dr. Winters
was referring to the death of his honorable and distinguished career—the death of even greater honor and distinction which he had rashly dreamed of attaining.

Up to this point Timothy had drawn the story chiefly
from the reluctant lips of Fletcher Dee. It was he who had
been able to tell, in detail, what that priceless document—
destroyed forever by Laurence—must have contained. But
it was the printer Flagstaff who supplied the final chapter
of evidence.

To him Dr. Winters had come on the Thursday morning
before his death, bringing the manuscript which described
his discovery, and the actual page of the vicar's diary.
He had ordered the printer to strike off several copies of
his account of the finding, and to have made photostat-
ic copies of the document itself. On that same morning
Hamlet Winters had also dispatched the letter to Dr.
Hughes, and composed the message to his wife which
she had found upon his desk. (It was, Timothy believed,

Winters' intention to kill himself after making his confession—hence the reference to his possible "violent death.")

But on the next day, Friday, Dr. Winters made a sudden and typically dramatic decision. He would present, at the time of his hearing before the Trustees, the actual page of the diary as proof of his crime. He had therefore telephoned Flagstaff and said that he would call for the document that afternoon—even though the photostats had not yet been made. Thus it was that when Laurence Dee burned the original page of John Ward's diary, there remained no photographic evidence of its existence—and Fletcher Dee's brilliant discovery of the murder of William Shakespeare could never in this world be proved.

Immediately after keeping his appointment with the printer Flagstaff came the first slip in Hamlet Winters' plan. For when he left the office, after collecting the precious evidence for his confession, the heavy dose of veronal had already taken serious effect. And he was never able to reach the meeting where he was to disclose the secret which would have ruined his career and made Fletcher Dee famous forever.

Mr. Flagstaff described Winters' curiously uncertain manner in their brief interview. And a few minutes later the printer had watched, from his office window, Winters' staggering steps as he emerged into the street below and headed—after a moment's hesitation—for the Cathedral entrance across the avenue. No doubt Winters, unaware of the cause of his dizziness and weakness—which must by that time have been nearly overpowering—intended only to rest in the Cathedral until the spell of illness should pass. And, once inside, he lapsed into a coma from which he never wakened.

At something after four o'clock, about an hour after he had seen Winters disappear into the Cathedral, Mr. Flagstaff was startled by the telephone call from Laurence Dee which Mrs. Winters had already described. Since he, Flagstaff, knew Dr. Winters only by an assumed name, he first denied any knowledge of such a person. But when Laurence persisted, the printer relented enough to say that he had had business with a man who *might* be the missing Dr. Winters. Almost immediately after that call, young Dee appeared in the office and demanded that Flagstaff tell him what he knew of Hamlet Winters. And Flagstaff, mild, pale-eyed, gullible man that he was, had been unable to hold out against the boy's insistence, and had divulged the fact that Winters had taken his priceless document and then disappeared into St. Ives Cathedral.

Laurence, the one person besides his parents and Hamlet Winters who knew the secret of Fletcher Dee's discovery, had made his last long guess at what his beloved Dr. Winters had done. And in a wild, desperate spurt of action he had dashed across the street—heedless of his aunt's restraining call—and entered the Cathedral. There he must have taken the precious paper from Hamlet Winters' unconscious possession—the paper which proved the boy's suspicion correct. And to prevent his father from coming into his rightful reward (a reward, one must remember, to be gained only at the price of Hamlet Winters' confession and disgrace) Laurence Dee had murdered Hamlet Winters whom he loved, and then destroyed forever the priceless evidence of that three-hundred-year-old document.

Such was the revenge of a hot-headed boy. Such must have been the hate which Fletcher Dee inspired in his son.

There was, after all, no arrest to be made. Laurence Dee, the murderer, was already dead. Hamlet Winters, the unfaithful friend, was likewise dead. And the rest of us, shattered in nerves and emotions, were free to go our way when Timothy had finished the long story.

Not until that evening, when Timothy, Joan and I were reunited with Emma in the safe haven of the quiet apartment, did I remember to tell Timothy of the telegram I had received from Dr. Prentiss—and of my rash disregard of his instructions to come home before the case was settled.

A slow smile spread over Timothy's tired face.

"Are you sorry you stuck it out, Miss Belle?" he asked.

"No," I said resolutely, "I'm not. But it probably *will* lose me my job."

"I should think you'd want to lose it," Timothy's eyes closed wearily, "after what we saw of academic life this morning."

"I suggested," Joan put in, "that Miss Belle should write a book about the case."

"Well—if you do, Miss Belle"—Timothy reached out a lazy hand to tickle Emma's ear—"don't forget to blame your part in it and mine on this darn pussy-cat."

"I won't," I promised, "and what's more—I'll have it ready in time to give you two a copy for a wedding present."

"Swell," said Joan and Timothy in unison.

And I've kept my word. The very first copy of *Going to St. Ives* will grace the library of Inspector Timothy Fowler and his wife, Joan, and now it remains only to be seen whether a detective story—and a true one at that— will be as profitable a source of livelihood as teaching English to the young ladies of Maplewood College.

Notes

[1] Lee, Sidney: *A Life of William Shakespeare*, N.Y., 1916 (revised edition), p. 485.

[2] Lee, Sidney: *A Life of William Shakespeare*, N.Y., 1916 (revised edition), p. 481.

[3] Lee, Sidney: *A Life of William Shakespeare*, N.Y., 1916 (revised edition), p. 480.

COACHWHIP PUBLICATIONS
CoachwhipBooks.com

THE HOUSE THAT
JACK BUILT

with, **MURDER IN AMBER**

COLVER HARRIS

COACHWHIP PUBLICATIONS
CoachwhipBooks.com

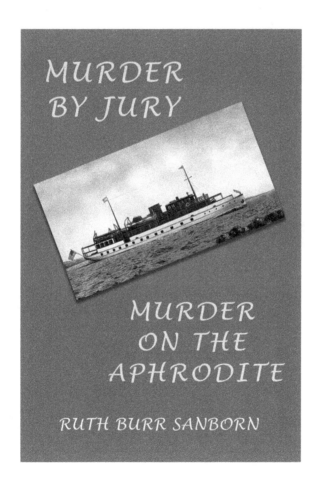

MURDER
BY JURY

MURDER
ON THE
APHRODITE

RUTH BURR SANBORN

COACHWHIP PUBLICATIONS
CoachwhipBooks.com

DEAD
WEIGHT
ADDISON
SIMMONS

COACHWHIP PUBLICATIONS
CoachwhipBooks.com

ANONYMOUS FOOTSTEPS | JOHN. M. O'CONNOR

COACHWHIP PUBLICATIONS
CoachwhipBooks.com

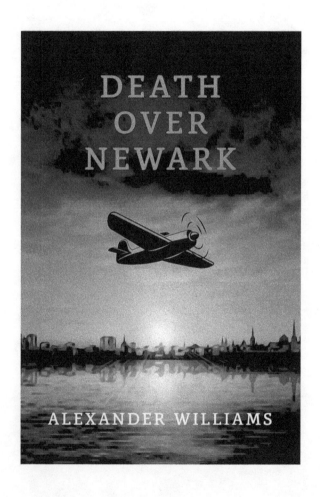

DEATH
OVER
NEWARK

ALEXANDER WILLIAMS

COACHWHIP PUBLICATIONS
CoachwhipBooks.com

VIRGINIA RATH

DEATH AT
DAYTON'S FOLLY

COACHWHIP PUBLICATIONS
COACHWHIPBOOKS.COM

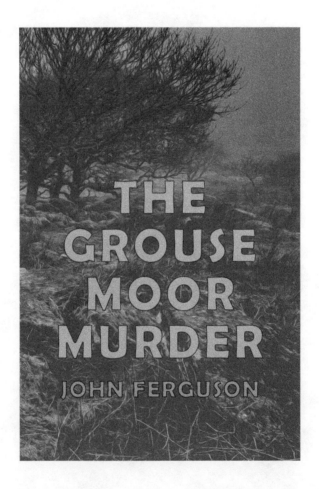

COACHWHIP PUBLICATIONS
COACHWHIPBOOKS.COM

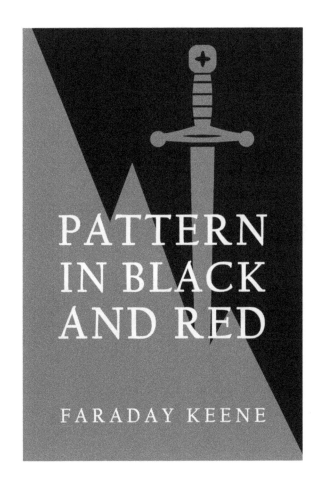

PATTERN
IN BLACK
AND RED

FARADAY KEENE

COACHWHIP PUBLICATIONS
CoachwhipBooks.com

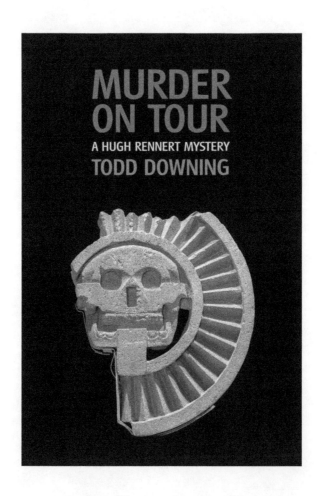

MURDER
ON TOUR
A HUGH RENNERT MYSTERY
TODD DOWNING

COACHWHIP PUBLICATIONS
CoachwhipBooks.com

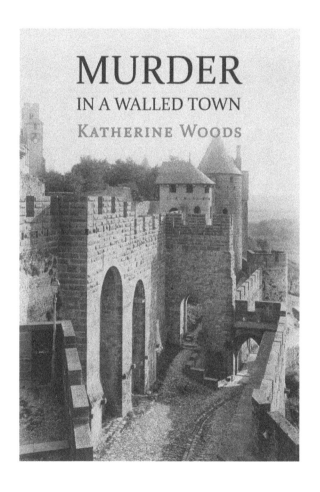

MURDER
IN A WALLED TOWN
KATHERINE WOODS

CPSIA information can be obtained
at www.ICGtesting.com
Printed in the USA
BVHW071408070621
608939BV00001B/28